What the critics are saying...

"Enter the Dragon was a superbly written and collated anthology with stories that engrossed and kept me captivated from beginning to end." ~ *Sheryl eCataRomance Reviews*

"This anthology contains three wondrous stories involving dragons. Each story has its own take, ranging from contemporary to futuristic to fantasy, and each will draw you into the world where the characters exist." ~ *Cindy Warner Coffee Time Romance*

"*Enter the Dragon* is a brilliantly written book. Each storyline is unique and well written. The characters will charm and delight you. This book is so engrossing that before I knew it I had finished it in one sitting and was sorry to see it end." ~ *Luisa Cupid's Library Reviews*

D1316911

Enter the Dragon

Tielle St. Clare
Madison Hayes
Mlyn Hurn

ELLORA'S CAVE
ROMANTICA PUBLISHING

An Ellora's Cave Romantica Publication

www.ellorascave.com

Enter the Dragon

ISBN # 1419952714
ALL RIGHTS RESERVED.
By Daylight Come Copyright © 2005 Tielle St. Clare
Hyde! Copyright © 2005 Madison Hayes
Tale of the Dragon Copyright © 2005 Mlyn Hurn
Edited by: Briana St. James, Mary Moran, Linda Carroll-Bradd
Cover art by: Syneca

Electronic book Publication: April, 2005
Trade paperback Publication: October, 2005

Excerpt from *Close Quarters* Copyright © Tielle St. Clare, 2004

Warning:

The following material contains graphic sexual content meant for mature readers. *Enter the Dragon* has been rated *E-rotic* by a minimum of three independent reviewers.

Ellora's Cave Publishing offers three levels of Romantica™ reading entertainment: S (S-ensuous), E (E-rotic), and X (X-treme).

S-*ensuous* love scenes are explicit and leave nothing to the imagination.

E-*rotic* love scenes are explicit, leave nothing to the imagination, and are high in volume per the overall word count. In addition, some E-rated titles might contain fantasy material that some readers find objectionable, such as bondage, submission, same sex encounters, forced seductions, etc. E-rated titles are the most graphic titles we carry; it is common, for instance, for an author to use words such as "fucking", "cock", "pussy", etc., within their work of literature.

X-*treme* titles differ from E-rated titles only in plot premise and storyline execution. Unlike E-rated titles, stories designated with the letter X tend to contain controversial subject matter not for the faint of heart.

Contents

By Daylight Come

Trademarks Acknowledgement

The author acknowledges the trademarked status and trademark owners of the following wordmarks mentioned in this work of fiction:

X-Files: Twentieth Century Fox Film Corporation
Etch A Sketch: Ohio Art Company

Chapter One

Tina listened to her nieces giggling as she walked up the stairs to the attic. It was almost time for their parents to come get them after their evening with "Aunt-T". About once a month, Tina took the girls for the evening so her sister and her husband could be alone. She usually tried to do it on the weekends but a Thursday night worked as well. Only one more day of work before the weekend.

"Hey guys, it's almost time to go."

"Wait. Aunt-T, you've got to see this."

Katrina, the oldest, lifted a heavy leather-bound book from her lap. Tina had never seen it before but the attic held treasures from generations past and no one really knew what was up here.

"What did you find, sweetie?"

"It's a book of magic," Elena announced, her eyes wide and filled with wonder.

"Magic? I didn't know there were any magic books up here."

Her crazy great-aunt Hilda had owned the cabin/house in the woods for thirty years. Upon her death, she'd willed it to Tina and her sister. Tina loved the isolation, even if it did mean an hour-long commute to work. The forest and the silence were worth it. She'd bought her sister's half of the cabin a year ago but still hadn't gone through her aunt's cluttered attic.

"It's dragon magic," Katrina said. She traced her fingertips across the elaborate dragon embossed on the cover. "Isn't it beautiful?" The awe that filled the child's voice aroused Tina's curiosity and she sat down beside her niece and looked over her shoulder.

"It's a lovely book. I've just never seen it before. I didn't know it was up here."

Katrina pushed it into her lap. "You should say a spell."

"Me?" Tina tried to push the book back.

"Yes," Katrina said. "There's a spell in here to call your true love. You should say it."

Tina shook her head. "I don't think so."

"But Mom says you need a man," Elena piped up.

Tina tried not to glare at her six-year-old niece for the words her mother had put in her mouth. Especially since it was true.

"Come on, Auntie. It will be fun."

Elena jumped up and down. "I wanna see a dragon."

"A dragon. Right." Tina looked into the hopeful faces of her nieces and sighed. She was a sucker for cute. "Fine, let's see this book." She flipped open the pages. Dragons illuminated every page along with words written in elaborate script. Spells to vanquish your enemies, create a storm and…Tina stopped on the page. *Call Your True Loves.*

"That's the one. Come on. Read it."

Tina ran her finger down the page. It seemed innocuous enough. Entertainment for the girls. Elena jumped up and down until Katrina — older and wiser at age nine — pulled her down beside her.

"Don't distract her. It's magic. She has to concentrate."

It was all Tina could do not to roll her eyes. Concentrate? To read a "magic spell". Yeah, right.

"Okay, here goes…

"By Dragon's Light and Dragon's Fire

Bring me now my heart's desire

Warrior, Maiden, Protector, Three

By daylight come my Loves to me."

She finished the words and waited. And waited. The girls sat silent, listening intently to every creak the old house made. A heavy weight clogged the air around them.

The doorbell rang, shattering their anticipation.

All three gasped.

"He's here," Katrina breathed, her eyes popping open wide. Elena jumped up and started to scream. Waving for her niece to be quiet, Tina leaned over and peeked out the window that looked down on the driveway.

"Sorry to disappoint you. It's your parents. Come to take you home."

"But where is he?" Elena asked as Tina gathered the book and followed them down the stairs.

"Maybe it doesn't work immediately. Maybe you have to wait," Katrina said, obviously still hopeful.

Tina smiled. "Well, then I'll keep waiting." *Yeah, right. I'm done waiting for Mister Right. I'm looking for Mister Well-Hung. But my nine year-old niece doesn't need to hear that.*

She set the book on the couch and nagged her nieces to gather their stuff before opening the door and greeting her sister. Pam looked remarkably satisfied and a little rumpled and Tina couldn't resist saying so. Pam smiled.

"It's amazing what having the house to yourself for five straight hours will do for you." Her husband, Mike, stepped out of the car and waved. He also had an air of relaxation about him.

"Glad somebody's gettin' some," Tina said with a smile.

Pam laughed. "You could be, too. You just need to get out there."

"I've been 'out there'. I didn't care for it. And what's this business about telling your girls I need a man?"

"You do. It's got to be lonely living all the way out here by yourself and wouldn't it be nice to have a man to cuddle up next to on cold nights when your heating goes out."

"The only man I need when my heating goes out is the plumber."

Pam shook her head. "You're missing out. I think you should reconsider some of the men in town. Dane watches you like you're ice cream on a hot day."

Tina felt the center of her stomach fall away at the mere mention of his name. Dane Sheridan, sheriff, stud and…ex-husband to one of her best friends. Despite the intense attraction between them, that alone kept her from following through. Still, there had been that one time when they'd almost…

The girls came to the door, their backpacks slung over their shoulders. Tina ignored the brief, erotic memory and with hugs and kisses, sent them on their way.

The house was quiet when she walked back inside. She missed the girls when they left but also enjoyed the silence of her own space. Strolling into the living room, she stopped at the couch and traced her fingers across the cover of the book. The luminous eyes of the dragon seemed to stare at her—wise, solemn eyes with pale purple sparkles.

"Right," she said aloud. "I'm looking for a purple-eyed dragon to save me."

* * * * *

Tina stood in front of her class. They all had their heads down, focused intently on their tests. With only a few minutes left in class and no one having completed the test, she considered the fact that she might have made it too long. Even her best students were struggling—chewing on pencil erasers like they were candy. Yuck.

Deciding how she would curve the test, Tina wandered to the bank of windows at the back of the room. Sunlight glittered on the grassy alcove down below. She let her eyes wander to the sky. It was a nice spring day and the beginning of a three-day weekend. She would go home after school and spend the long weekend planting—

A speck appeared over the spires of the administration building. She wouldn't have noticed it but while it looked a like a bird — a huge bird — it didn't fly quite like a bird. Its wings beat an irregular rhythm. As the speck grew larger, so did her eyes. The thing was flying directly toward campus and was soon close enough for Tina to recognize the shape. That was no bird. It looked like a flying dinosaur.

Or a dragon.

Air exited her lungs in a rush and got caught in her throat, making her choke on her own breath.

"Ms. Branson, are you okay?"

She glanced down at the student seated next to her. "Of course. I got…a bug caught in my throat."

"Ewww, gross."

She drew herself to her full five-foot-six height and did her best impression of a schoolmarm. "Just go back to your tests."

As soon as all the heads were lowered, she spun back to the window. It wasn't possible. It just wasn't possible. It couldn't actually be a dragon. Not one day after she'd said a dragon spell. It just wasn't possible.

The creature drew closer and Tina felt her eyes widen. This creature wasn't anything anyone in this world had ever seen before. As it flew by, she caught a clear vision of it. Huge white teeth and rows of greenish-bluish scales. And lavender — like the light in the dragon's eyes. Lavender flowed from what appeared to be wounds in its side.

Her side ached in sympathy as the dragon flapped its massive wings and flew on, bypassing the school and heading into the forest.

Heading toward her cabin.

She whipped around and stared at the clock. It was almost three. In just seconds class would be over and she could go home and see if there really was a dragon waiting for her at her cabin…or if she needed to investigate some serious therapy.

Maybe both, she decided as the bell rang.

"Turn the tests in now," she announced.

"But I'm not done."

"Just a few more minutes."

"No!" Her voice was harsher than she'd meant so she smiled, something she didn't often do in her classroom. "I'll be sure to grade on a curve and take into account that there wasn't enough time to finish." None of her students moved. "I'll give you all ten extra credit points if you'll just write your names on your tests and turn them in. Now."

They moved as a unit, scribbling and jumping up to place the papers on her desk. She stood at the door, anxiously hurrying the last student out of her classroom, then grabbing her purse and bolting for the door.

"Hey Tina." Jessie, the teacher from across the hall stopped her escape. "There's an emergency staff meeting called for after school."

Tina shook her head. "I can't make it. Doctor's appointment. Very important. Can you take notes?" she asked, hearing her voice squeak as she pleaded. The other teacher nodded, her eyes wide. *Great, now she's going to think I'm terminally ill, instead of the truth…that I think I have a dragon waiting for me on my front porch.*

What else could it be? she thought as she hurried to her car. Not that this was possible. It wasn't, but that had definitely been a dragon she'd seen flying by her window.

She'd said the spell last night and then this afternoon— poof, dragon airborne and heading to her remote home. There was nothing else that direction. She lived on the edge of a state park, for goodness sake.

Breaking any number of traffic laws, Tina practically flew home herself. She flicked on her radio, needing the noise to distract her from worrying about what she would find when she arrived home. The news came on. She listened through the latest political snafu and a local fire—she'd have to send some food the rescue shelter—then the newscaster ended with a story about…a flying dinosaur.

"A what?" the cocky afternoon drive announcer asked when the newsman had finished.

"Really. Dozens of people have reported a huge creature flying through the air. They say it looks like flying dinosaur, but alas, people, it's nothing so exciting. We hunted down the truth and it's actually an experimental plane. It seems the crews that work on it were playing a joke and painted it to look like a dinosaur."

Tina stared at her radio, then looked up in time to swerve her car back on the road.

That was no plane.

She floored the gas pedal. She had to get home. Now.

Thirty minutes later, she pulled up the long, winding dirt road that formed her driveway. Relief spiked through her system as she stared at her house. There was no dragon on the porch or on the roof or even on the large lawn. Nothing seemed out of place. Heart pounding and keys clutched firmly in her fist, she gingerly walked across the lawn.

Maybe she'd been mistaken. Maybe it had been a plane.

She stopped. Pale purple streaks formed a dotted line across her grass. It was the same lavender she'd seen pouring from the dragon's wounds. Purple blood? Wishing she had a weapon—though what kind of weapon would be useful against a dragon she had no idea—she followed the scattered trail into the forest.

Several walking trails broke off from the main path heading in various directions deeper into the woods. The plot of land her aunt had willed her was huge, with the back boundary designated by a slow-moving river. Tina picked the path closest to the purple trail and began a slow jog, feeling an urgency building as she progressed. She had to find this dragon. Or find nothing and prove to herself that she was insane. Trickles of purple—clinging to leaves and pine needles, continued to guide her.

The path went deeper into the woods until she could hear the ripple of water. A clearing opened before her, smooth rocks and boulders lined the river's bank, and beside the rolling water, lay...a dragon.

As if it had stepped out of the dragon magic book, it was here. Blue and green scales shimmered in the sunlight with each labored breath of the creature. Lavender blood flowed from deep wounds on its side, pouring onto the mossy forest floor. Black tinged the end of one wing. He'd been shot. He'd been coming to her—coming because she'd called him—and now he was wounded, probably dying. Her chest ached as she stared at the wounded creature. *What have I done?* It was just a silly spell but now this beautiful animal was hurt, possibly dying. Guilt crushed the traces of fear that struggled to escape. She had to help him.

She stepped forward. The creature was huge. Its head alone was bigger than she was and its body would stretch halfway around her house. But this wasn't the time for caution. When a fairy-tale creature appeared after you wished for it, Tina decided, you had to trust it not to hurt you.

Not knowing if he would understand her if she spoke, Tina knelt down beside his head. His eyes fluttered open and she felt his pain. The purple eyes—just like those of the dragon on the book's cover—were hazy and fading.

"I'm so sorry. Is there anything I can do?"

Maiden? I found you.

The beast seemed to mentally project the greeting to her. Tina instinctively answered.

"You're hurt. I need to get you some help." But who was she going to call? She couldn't exactly call the local vet to help a dying dragon.

No. You can help me. You called me.

"Yes, but I didn't mean to. Not really." She looked at the huge body. Even assuming she could save the creature, what was she going to do with it? *I really don't have room for a pet.*

Its massive head lifted inches off the ground. She could tell the movements strained the animal's strength. A long tongue slipped out of its mouth and touched the back of her hand. The delicate caress sent a flurry of hot shivers down her spine.

Do you accept me? he asked.

"Uh, yes, of course," she answered, not wanting to upset the creature.

His body seemed to slump and for a moment it appeared that the animal had passed out. He began to shimmer and change. His body shrunk and changed, twisted and bent until the beautiful blue-green cast was decidedly pink and his dragon body had collapsed into a human form.

Human? Her mind tried to process that information when it got another jolt. A naked human.

He lay on the ground, flat his stomach. Long blond hair that reached well past his shoulder blades covered his face and arms. Tina took a moment to observe him. The body he'd turned into was well made. Long, muscular legs with just a scattering of pale hair on them led to a nicely rounded backside that made her fingers twitch with the prospect of giving it a squeeze. His back was sleek and powerful.

A low tremor started between her legs and spread warmth into the core of her body. The sensual ache had been distinctly absent from her life for a long time. Something about this man called to her. *Well, it could be the fact that he's naked and I haven't seen nearly enough naked men in the past two years.*

No, it's something else. Something about him.

She'd said the spell and he'd appeared. Now he was hurt. Purple fluid still flowed from the wounds on his back and side.

"Uh, dragon?"

He pushed himself up on his arms and weakly brushed his hair out of his face. His eyes were glassy and pain-filled—and purple. The lavender streaks that seemed to match his blood captivated her, drawing her closer. She'd never seen a more beautiful color.

"Maiden, I have come to you."

Feeling like she was in a trance, she placed her hand on his. What was she supposed to say? The words appeared in her mind as if they'd been there forever. "I welcome you, my Protector."

Her answer seemed to soothe him. He half-smiled but even that seemed to pain him. The action snapped her out of the purple haze that had captured her.

"Who are you? Uh, what's your name?"

"I'm called Raython."

"Raython, I'm Tina."

"Maiden."

"Uh, right." She stood. "Can I ask what happened? How did you get these wounds?"

He shook his head. The motion seemed foreign and stiff. "I do not know. I entered through the void following your call and soon creatures with high-powered arrows were shooting at me. I barely managed to out fly them."

High-powered arrows? Bullets, she thought. Or missiles. Well, it was clear that someone had seen him.

"Either way, you've been hurt and you're bleeding." At least she thought that purple liquid was blood. "We need to get you to a hospital." Lavender dripped from a cut in his side. "Okay, maybe not a hospital but at least we need to get you to my house. Can you walk?"

He nodded and slowly pushed himself upright. When he came to his full height, he was easily six inches taller than Tina's five-foot-six frame. Her arm fit comfortably around his back. Despite the fact that as a dragon he'd been huge, as a human, he was tall and thin. Muscular but not bulky. Like a swimmer.

Long, strong muscles. She groaned softly thinking of how he would feel against her, over her. Driving into her.

She shook her head and tried to concentrate on taking care of him but the etched lines of his muscles distracted her as she helped him toward the path.

His smooth chest blended easily into six-pack abs. Her gaze kept on its downward path. She caught a mere glimpse of his cock before she snapped her head back up. The man-dragon had just arrived and she was ogling him.

Maybe her sister was right and she needed a man.

Of course, that's what had gotten her into this mess in the first place. A wicked thought entered her head. If he'd come because she called him, did that mean she could use him before sending him home? She didn't know the cosmic rules on this sort of thing. She couldn't keep him, she knew that much, but maybe once he'd healed, before he turned back into a dragon, she could…

She mentally slapped herself. What was she thinking? The man—and she had to think of him as a man—was injured and she was already planning to have sex with him. *You've gone too long without, girl.*

Raython swayed in her arms. "Oh boy, I've got you." She tightened her arm around his back and pulled him against her, encouraging him to use her body as a stabilizer. She could only hope that he could make it to her house because there was no way she could carry him if he passed out.

With struggling steps, she managed to help him down the path to her house and in the front door. The climb up the stairs to her bedroom left them both breathing heavy.

"We need to take care of those wounds," she said through gasping breaths.

"If you have a bathing chamber, I can cleanse myself. That will be enough."

Somehow she didn't think cleaning those wounds was going to be enough but he knew his body better than she did.

It was convenient that he was naked because she could guide him directly into the shower. Still weak, she stayed with him, supposedly to make sure he didn't fall over but the truth was she couldn't bring herself to walk away. This was dragon. She'd seen it with her own eyes and she'd never been prone to hallucinations. With the bulk of blood washed away, he looked at her with blatant question in his eyes. It took her a moment to understand but then she jumped forward. She grabbed the softest washcloth she could find and began to stroke his skin.

"You have delicious hands, Maiden." His voice was stronger and more seductive alerting latent emotions in Tina. Still, the man was injured. She focused on helping him, ignoring the sex that dripped from his words and focused on what he'd said.

"Why do you call me that?" She wasn't exactly "maiden" material.

"You are the Maiden. I am your Protector. With our Warrior, we will defend you." He tilted his head to the side, letting his long blond hair fall over his shoulder. "Is this not the way of your people?"

"Uh, no. I don't think so."

"But you called to me. You read the spell."

"Yes, but that was just a game…for my nieces. I never wanted—"

The light faded from his lavender eyes and she saw the faintest stirrings of panic. *Upsetting the dragon is probably a bad idea.* She spread her lips into a wide smile. "Let's talk about it later. First, let's get you into bed. You need to rest." She looked at the wounds. They were no longer bleeding. In fact, many of them were closed and scarred like newly healed marks. Fascinated, she stroked her fingers across one of the scars. When she pulled her hand away, the mark was gone—as if he'd never been wounded.

"How is that possible?"

"I am dragon. It is how we heal."

The concept pressed down on her already overwhelmed brain allowing her to focus only on the practical. Get him dried off, get him some clothes and then they had to talk.

Tina shut off the water and handed Raython a towel. When he stared at it as if it was a foreign tool, she took it back in her hands and began to wipe him down. He turned to face her, baring his body to her. A fat water drop trickled down his chest, across the tight abs like a child riding a roller coaster and it was all she could do not to lean forward and capture the drop before it escaped into the tuft of blond hair springing around his growing cock. Tina swallowed—*growing cock*? The dragon was getting aroused? Her body responded, heating and melting. Her center felt heavy and empty. The towel fell from her hand and she began to brush away the water with her palms, loving the cool warmth of his skin.

It seemed so natural to touch him. She smoothed her hands across his shoulders, down his hands, swishing away the droplets that clung to him. *The heat coming from my body alone should dry him*, she thought with a slow smile. A vague worry nagged her mind that she was caressing a stranger but it didn't seem to matter. All that mattered was touching him. Having him inside her.

The thought sent off more warning bells—louder this time but not quite enough to convince her to draw back. He moved with her, sliding into her touch. She skimmed her hands down his chest and stomach, retracing the first water drop's path—across the tight ridges and down.

"Mistress, where is our Warrior?" Raython's husky voice interrupted her sensual trance.

Warrior? She didn't know any warriors—except maybe one. "You mean Dane?"

"He is our Warrior?"

Tina thought about it. Yes, Dane was a warrior—strong, powerful, defender of the weak.

"Yes," she sighed. Her mind quickly created the image of Dane, sword drawn, advancing on a horde of evil attackers. The picture changed—Dane, fresh from battle, naked, above her, his cock filling her. Her knees weakened and she leaned against the bathroom counter. *Hard and thick he drove into her, using her body as comfort from the memories of destruction. She wrapped her arms around his back and clutched him, feeling her nails dig into his tight skin, knowing he loved to feel the prick of her claws.*

Raython groaned as if he could see the image in her head and shook his hair back. "Oh Maiden, he is an excellent choice. Where is he?"

"He's not here."

"The triad joining will take place when he arrives. We should wait but I'm afraid I need the healing power of your cunt."

"What?!"

"If we fuck, I will heal faster."

She squinted her eyes in disbelief. More at herself than his words because…she was actually considering it. She should be taking him to a hospital or a lab run by someone from the X-Files, instead, she was thinking about crawling into her bed and letting that long, thick cock ride between her thighs.

"But you've healed already." It was a minor protest but she felt the need to offer a token resistance.

"That is the surface. Deep inside the wounds still fester. If we fuck, my body will produce the material needed to heal me." He pulled her into his arms. "Will our Warrior permit it?"

Tina's mouth bobbed open like a fish while she tried to find the answer to that question. Finally she nodded. Dane would "permit it" because he would never know.

She looked down Raython's body, taking in the full package. He was truly magnificent. Strong, sleek muscles. Tall and thinner than Dane—not quite so broad across his chest—but still buff and tight. Her fingers fluttered, eager to return to touching him. She continued her perusal, anxious to see the final stages of his aroused cock.

"Oh, boy." It was long and hard, curving upward, reaching for her.

"Do you not find my shaft pleasing? It is the one aspect of my human form I can control. I can make it smaller." She shook her head. "Or bigger if you desire."

"Lord, no."

"Perhaps thicker?"

"It's fine. Just the way it is." The center of her tummy felt warm and liquid. "It's perfect."

"Oh Maiden, I'm glad you find it so." He gripped the edge of the sink as if he too was having trouble staying upright. "I have seen many in the act of Joining but I've never done it."

The dragon was a virgin?

"But my staff is so hard now, I feel as if I will explode if I'm not allowed inside your passage."

"Yes," she said, throwing caution to the wind and blocking out those damned warning voices in her head. She wanted this. Her body was calling out to feel him inside her.

Guided by an instinct she didn't understand, she took Raython's hand and led him into her bedroom. The high four-poster bed dominated the space. She hesitated, not sure where to go from here. She'd initiated sex before but once the idea was planted in her lover's mind, it was an easy ride to let him lead. Raython looked at her with anticipation. Now, she was the one with the experience.

A powerful, feminine energy poured into her body. She felt slightly wicked. An older woman leading the young man astray.

A smile curled her lips as he stared at her with bright purple eyes. It was time to take the dragon to bed.

Chapter Two

Tina stopped beside the bed and stared up at her would-be lover. Her eyes didn't linger long on his face. She let her gaze drift down, over the sleek lines of his chest and the ribbing of his stomach muscles to the hard rise of his cock, stretching up to meet her.

He waited, open and bare before her. She reached forward and placed the pads of her fingers on his shaft. Tension whipped through his body as he straightened—but he didn't pull back. Keeping her touch light, she petted his cock, savoring the heat and power beneath his skin.

"May I also touch you, Mistress?" he asked, his voice strung tight.

She nodded and slowly released her prize. Not knowing if a creature from another world would understand the intricacies of pantyhose, she unbuttoned her skirt and let it fall to the floor. Raython watched as if he'd never seen anything so fascinating as her legs. She grabbed the waistband of her nylons and dragged them down, taking her panties along. There was no reason to be coy. She was going to fuck Raython. She might as well get naked as quickly as possible.

The flaps of her shirt fluttered against her bare skin and sent a cool shiver through her body. She was really going to do it. She was going to have sex with a man she didn't know at all—and for some reason it seemed right. Maybe because she knew he wasn't really a man, or because she had called him. She didn't understand it but despite the voices shouting concerns in her head, this felt natural—in her heart and in her body it felt right. It was only the logical side of her that was balking.

"May I assist you in removing your garb?" he asked even as he reached for her blouse. His fingers were awkward as he opened the first button but he discovered the motion after one attempt and quickly undid the clasps.

He opened her blouse and dragged it down her arms. Tina shivered under the intensity of his stare. If she hadn't figured it out before, she knew it then—this would be like nothing she'd ever experienced before.

His fingers brushed the sides of her breasts. "Oh, Maiden, why are you bound in this contraption?" Quick intuitive fingers found the front clasp and released her bra, allowing her breasts to spill into his hands. Her sigh joined his groan. "They are most wonderful, Mistress. Why do you bind them so? Does our Warrior demand this torment of you?" As he asked the question, he massaged the firm mounds with slow circular pressure, easing the day's aches away. The simple motion rejuvenated her, sending energy into her core. "Hmm, yes, I can see why our Warrior would bind you in such a manner." It was a challenge to follow his conversation. The sweet grip of his fingers seemed to know just the right amount of pressure to apply, the exact location of the invisible tension she hadn't known she'd been carrying.

"Not only does it protect you from the eyes of others but it must give him delicious pleasure to ease your pain at the end of each day."

Tina couldn't speak—too much noise rattled through her head. The picture of Dane's hands on her skin, rubbing her breasts, soothing her aches, captured the energy that Raython had released and sent her nipples into full peak. He seemed to notice the tightening as it occurred.

"Yes, Mistress, most lovely." His wickedly sensual fingers stroked down, fluttering across her nipples. She'd never thought of her breasts as being particularly sensitive but beneath Raython's touch, they felt heavy and full and so alive. "May I taste them? I have seen many men take comfort from their women in this manner and it seems most enjoyable to both parties."

Her voice still locked somewhere south of her stomach, she nodded. It was unusual to have a man request permission for each action. And to hear him speak so directly...her pussy fluttered at the possibilities.

Raython dropped to his knees, staring at her breasts like they were objects of art. With reverent fingers, he stroked the full mounds, exploring her skin with the fascination of a supplicant. Tina held herself still and let him touch. His hands were warm and so gentle. She felt herself sinking into a sensual daze. Anticipation faded and she savored in the luxurious caresses.

Her eyes drifted shut and she was filled with images of her and Raython and Dane, twisting and sliding across cool, cotton sheets, of both men filling her body and riding her with long, slow strokes.

"Yes, Mistress, as soon as our Warrior arrives, we will Join." His breath teased her skin and heightened the tempting fantasy her mind was concocting. She licked her lips—the visceral sensation of Dane's hands holding her hips as he fucked her, driving hard into her, flowed into her sex.

The heat of Raython's mouth closing over her nipple snapped her free of the wicked dream and pulled her back to the immediate sensations. He groaned as he laved his tongue across the tightened peak.

"Most delicious. I understand why men are so fascinated with this activity." Before she could respond, he'd opened his lips and begun to suck, gently but with a steady force, drawing her breast into his mouth. She groaned as the sweet pressure reached into her core, every motion creating new aches inside her pussy. She needed more, needed his cock filling her.

Breath was in short supply. The vibrations flitting through her body terrified and thrilled her but if she wanted more, she would need to take charge.

She took Raython's free hand and slid it down. With gentle pressure, she pressed his fingers against her mound, silently commanding his touch. After a few seconds, he seemed to understand her wishes and pushed his hand between her legs, one long finger sliding into her slit.

Air caught in her throat. He swirled his tongue around her nipple with a firm stroke before lifting his head.

"Mistress, you are so wet and hot. And such a warm, luscious scent is rising from you." His eyes on her, he let his fingers explore her sex, dipping gently between her folds, circling the hot opening. Tina held herself still, fighting the urge to grab his hand and jam three fingers into her pussy. An accidental flutter of his fingers across her clit made her gasp. He stopped and his eyes widened. "Have I done something wrong?"

"No," she said shaking her head. "That was good."

He seemed to relax and there was a hint of arrogance in the slow upturn of his lips.

"Was it here?" He continued his exploration, watching her closely to see her reactions. He slowly circled down, teasing her entrance with the tip of his finger. "You like that, yes? But it was not what made you squeak."

Squeak? Tina blinked. *I squeaked? How embarrassing, how—oh, he found it.* She must have made another sound—though she didn't recognize it as one—because Raython's eyes began to twinkle.

"This is where you find pleasure? I shall continue to stroke you here." It was difficult for her to find breath enough to speak so she nodded. His touch was gentle as he circled her clit. He stared at her intently as if gauging her reactions to each touch until he found the stroke that made her hips roll in slow response.

The arrogance of her dragon seemed to reappear as he smiled and leaned forward, returning his mouth to her breast. With a short learning curve, he figured out how to stroke her clit and suck her nipple in sweet counterpoint until her body was throbbing.

Pressure exploded inside her sex and spread through her torso. She slapped her hand against the wall to keep herself stable. The guy was a fast learner. She pumped her hips against his fingers, needing more than the light caress on her clit. She needed to be fucked—needed to feel him inside her.

As if he heard her thoughts, he lifted his head again.

"Mistress, your plump nipples are delicious but I find my rod is painfully full. Is it perhaps time that I may put it inside you?"

"God, yes." She spun around and climbed onto bed. She'd never felt so needy, so desperate, or so bold. "Come here," she commanded, sliding backwards and giving him room on the mattress. He followed like a man in a trance, his eyes focused on the apex of her thighs, settling beside her. The urgency racing just beneath her skin wouldn't let her slow down. She grabbed his shoulders and pulled him over her, spreading her legs and creating a place for him.

With the intensity of a man focused on doing something exactly right, he situated himself between her thighs, cuddling his knees beneath her raised legs. He gripped his cock in one hand and gently spread her pussy open with the other. Tina scraped her fingernails across the sheets, her body strung tight with the furious need. He placed the tip of his cock against her opening. He looked up, his eyes silently seeking permission.

"Maiden, may I enter you?" His request sounded formal and weighty but Tina couldn't concentrate on that. She needed him. Now.

"Yes."

He pushed the first few inches into her. Tina tensed. Despite the hunger raging, it had been a long time since she'd had sex and what if she didn't please him? All the latent feminine concerns suddenly rose to the surface. She stared up at him. The grim determination on his face soothed her fears. He was completely intent on pleasing her. He wanted *her*. They were somehow cosmically connected. He pushed another inch inside her and she moaned, loving the sensation of being filled.

"Oh Raython," she said, smoothing her hands up his shoulders. "That feels so good."

"I'm glad you find it so, Mistress," he said through clenched teeth. "I had no idea it would be this tight. Should I make my rod smaller? I have no wish to hurt you."

The hesitation in his voice melted away any self-consciousness. This would just be about them.

"No, it's wonderful. You feel amazing inside me." Light seemed to flare in his eyes. She rolled her hips upward, easing him deeper. "See, you'll fit. We'll fit together."

His jaw muscles twitched and she knew he was fighting the urge to drive into her. Feeling sensuous and powerful, she curled her leg around his back and nudged him forward with her heel. The pressure seemed to trigger something inside him and he thrust forward, driving fully into her. She gasped. He was long and pressed deep inside her.

"Have I hurt you?"

She shook her head while she recaptured her breath. "It feels good."

"It is most wondrous, Maiden," he agreed. "I am honored to have been called by one such as you. Our Warrior must be most pleased with the tightness of your cunt." Tina shivered at the bold words and the thought that Dane might be pleased. Strange how the mental reminder of another man didn't crush her desire at all.

Raython had made several other references to the Warrior having made love to her and she felt no need to correct him. Not now. Not when he was balls-deep inside her. All she wanted to think about was him fucking her. He held himself still as if savoring the sensation of being inside her.

After long moments when she thought she'd scream, he spoke. "Mistress, may I move?"

"God, yes."

He rolled his hips forward as if wanting to go deeper before he slowly withdrew. The pleasure reflected on his face made Tina's heart beat faster and her insides melt a little more. He didn't rush—just kept a steady wave of long, slow thrusts in and out. The whole experience was new to him and strangely it felt new to her...as if she'd never taken a man inside her body before. Certainly she'd never had a man like this before.

She gripped his shoulders and planted her feet on the mattress. Slow and sweet was wonderful but the delicate strokes weren't enough to allow her to come. As he sank into her again, she thrust up, driving him deep and hard. His head snapped up, his eyes wide. He froze for a moment then again started his slow withdrawal but this time, he punched his hips forward plunging into her with strength.

"Yes," she groaned, holding onto him and countering the hard thrusts. His hips drove faster and faster, massaging her clit with each penetration. It seemed to be an instinctual movement—as if the dragon knew precisely where to stroke her body.

The wicked pressure moments before an orgasm drove her onward, making her crave more and more of him. Their bodies slapped together. Raython's hair hung down around his face, forming a curtain around them. The silky strands caressed her skin like thousands of fingers.

She drove upward, loving the hard slide of his cock drilling into her. She was close. The sweet release was just out of reach. She cried out, the desperate need to come binding her body with tension. But the release hovered just beyond her reach.

"Mistress, how may I serve you?" he asked, panting as he rode her.

"Touch my clit," she whispered.

He immediately freed his tight hold on her hip and slipped his hand between their bodies. With an experienced lover's touch, he honed in on the right place, lightly rubbing the outer edge. It was enough. Sparklers went off inside her body. Tina screamed and arched up, intensifying the climax with another hard drive of Raython's cock.

His groan melded with hers. As the sharp spike of her orgasm departed, it left behind a sweet rush of pleasure. Each stroke sent another teeny ripple into her pussy. Raython kept on—as if he knew she was still experiencing minor orgasms.

"Mistress! I feel my release coming." Raython's breathless words verged on panic. "May I take my climax?"

He was asking permission to come? Though she loved the feel of him, she couldn't be selfish.

"Yes," she moaned.

He tossed his head back and she saw the strain on his face, the torture in his clenched jaw. He pumped into her hard and fast. Seconds later a roar filled her bedroom and hot semen splashed into her womb.

Raython froze for a moment, trapped in the sensations of his first orgasm and then collapsed down, landing on her with an inelegant thud.

The breath broke from her chest with a grunt. Raython lifted his head. His eyes were hazy. "I'm sorry, Mistress. I was not expecting the sensation of coming inside you to be so powerful."

His words triggered a momentary panic in her. "Oh my God. Can I get pregnant from this?" She started counting days. She didn't think it was near to her fertile time of the month but to be honest, she didn't monitor it that closely. It wasn't like she had to worry about missing a period. She hadn't had sex in so long it wasn't an issue...until now. Unprotected sex with a dragon. *Oh my gosh, what would the children be like?*

"Surely not, Maiden. Only the Warrior may get you with child." As he said the slightly slurred words, he dropped his head down to her chest. After a few long moments, she realized he'd fallen asleep. On top of her. His cock had slipped out but the rest of him was curled around her.

His hair formed a white waterfall over his shoulder. He looked so sweet. She stroked her hand down his back. When he woke up, they would have to do some serious talking about the situation. Like how long he was staying and how some silly spell book had actually called him from another world.

Yes, when he woke up, they would talk.

But when Raython woke up, he had other ideas.

* * * * *

Tina stared down at the man—uh, dragon—asleep in her bed. His body golden in the pale light of the room. The sun had set while he'd slept through his first afterglow. When she'd finally become too stiff to lay beneath him any longer, she'd attempted to roll him off her. The process had succeeding in waking him.

She planned to talk to him, to find out what was happening in the "bigger picture" but then he'd sweetly begged for another "healing fuck" from her and with those beautiful eyes and that hard cock staring at her, Tina hadn't had the will to refuse him. He'd loved her hard and fast, shooting her to a bright orgasm before he once again came inside her. And then he'd fallen asleep again.

But this time he'd collapsed beside her so she could escape to the bathroom. After cleaning up she'd paced the tiny space trying to figure out what to do. She'd just had sex with a creature out of a fantasy novel and it had been great. Her stomach dropped away as desire plunged into her again. With whimper, she repressed the sensation. She needed answers, not more sex.

What she needed was help. *Dane.*

His name popped into her head but she pushed it aside. Explaining this to Dane would be impossible. No, she needed feminine help.

Her sister.

Tina opened the bathroom door and peeked out. Raython was spread out taking up three-fourths of her mattress. She tiptoed toward the robe as he rolled over.

"Maiden, you've returned."

Before she could think about what to say, he grabbed her arm and tumbled her onto the bed. His mouth latched onto her nipple. Like a fiery string connected to her pussy, her sex began to throb with each pull of his mouth. He reached between her legs and plunged his fingers into her wet slit.

Tina whimpered and punched her hips upward, driving him deeper.

Raython lifted his head and looked down at her. "Our Warrior must well appreciate the heated passion that flows through your body."

Tina sighed, pumping against his fingers. "He wouldn't know because he's never made love to me."

Raython's fingers stopped moving and tension invaded his body. Tina opened her eyes and stared at the man above her.

"You've not Joined with the Warrior?" Panic lurked at the edge of his voice.

"Joined? You mean had sex with? Uh, no. We've never had sex."

"Oh no." He rolled out of bed, his naked body glowing in the low light of the room. "How is this possible? I saw your thoughts. You had such clear images of him. You know what it feels like for him to fuck you."

Tina remembered her fantasy of Dane coming to her. It had been pretty explicit and specific. But how had Raython seen it? Well, he was dragon, obviously he had some kind of psychic power as well. She'd have to remember to keep her sexual fantasies to herself.

"I've thought about it a lot," she said with a little shrug, pulling the sheet up and over her body. It was fine for him to stand around naked. He had to body of a Greek god in his early twenties. She had the body of a woman in her mid-thirties who should probably exercise more. "I have a very vivid imagination. What does it matter?" Exasperation was fast on the heels of confusion. She'd had two pretty spectacular climaxes and from the rise of his cock, there was potential for more tonight but not if he didn't climb back into bed.

Raython paced the small space between Tina's bed and the door. "The Warrior has every right to kill me." He came about, his long blond hair snapping around his head. "Will he? You know him best. Will he kill me? If I apologize?"

"You want to know if Dane will kill you if you apologize for having sex with me?"

"No, if I apologize, will he forgive me and not kill me?"

"Why would he kill you in the first place?" Tina said, sitting up, realizing her hopes of any more orgasms tonight were fading fast. Probably for the best. Her body was starting to ache from the unusual activity. Still, there were other ways besides a hard fuck. She snagged her lower lip between her teeth and considered the possibilities. Raython, licking her. Her returning the favor. It definitely had potential. She just had to lure Raython back to bed.

"The Warrior has the first right to make love to the Maiden. You belong to him. I am the Protector—sent to bind and guide the love between you. It was not my place to come inside you before he had done so."

"I'm sure Dane won't mind." Well, he might mind a little, she thought. The heat between them was pretty strong and Dane didn't like to share.

"I will apologize when we first meet," he said earnestly. "Then perhaps he will not kill me before the Hunters attack."

"Okay, that's it." Tina threw off the sheet and climbed out of bed. She walked to her dresser, pulled out a nightshirt and jerked it on before she spun around and faced him. "You have a lot of explaining to do. I ignored some of it because I was...well, I was horny and you seemed willing but if you're not going to oblige my hormones any longer, we're going to talk."

She handed him a thick terrycloth robe and stalked out of the bedroom. She padded down the stairs to her living room and plunked herself down on her couch. Seconds later she heard the tap-tap-tap of Raython's feet. He walked in, naked.

"Where's the robe?"

He looked around. "That thing you handed to me? What did you wish me to do with it?"

"Wear it. Don't they have clothes where you come from?"

He drew back and she could tell she'd offended him with her sarcasm. "Of course. I've simply never worn them before. This is my first time in human form."

"I'm sorry. Don't worry about it. Just have a seat." She indicated the other end of the couch. "And use a pillow to cover that thing."

She wasn't going to be able to have a serious discussion with his cock waving at her.

"Yes, Maiden." He sat down and pulled a pillow onto his lap.

"Now, talk. Act like I don't know anything about this—spells, Maidens, Warriors. And what was this about someone attacking?"

"The Hunters. They will come for me. They awakened also when you said the spell."

"I said the spell which was supposed to draw my true love to me…not a dragon. No offense."

"No, the spell calls both of your loves. Your Warrior and your Protector." He shifted forward. "A true love is made up of three. The Warrior, the Protector and the Maiden."

"But I thought love triangles always end badly. At least they do in the movies. Someone ends up hurt."

Raython drew back. "No, the triangle is the most stable form. The three points create the plane of love and allow the three to exist on that plane. If all are open to it, no one is harmed and all are loved."

And he thought Dane was her Warrior. Somehow she couldn't see Dane in a three-way.

Not that she had convinced Dane into a two-person relationship. Not yet. They'd skirted the issue—even ending up in a lip-lock on one occasion—but neither had made the move that would push them beyond that point.

"So, this plane is created—and the three lovers are together and happy, right?" Raython nodded. "Where does the *attacking* come in?"

"The Hunters. They are demons, created by the evil wizards in my world to hunt down dragons. They cannot see us until we are freed by our Maiden's spell. Then they seek us."

"And what happens if they find you?" she asked, leaning forward.

"We will fight. The Warrior and I. And if we are triumphant, the Hunters will be killed and none shall bother us."

"And what if you aren't triumphant?" She didn't like the idea of relying on Dane for this. He was a tough guy but involving him would mean explaining Raython's presence and she wasn't sure she could do that.

"Then the Hunters will succeed in capturing you and me. We will experience the torments of Hell before ultimately dying."

"Oh, goody. I'm involved in this as well?"

"Yes, the Hunters seek dragons for their blood and their Maidens for the pleasure the woman can give them." He stared at her with purple and serious eyes. "It is not a pleasure for the Maiden."

"No, I expect not."

"Do not fear, Maiden. If the Protector and the Warrior work together, it is almost impossible for the Hunters to succeed."

There was too much going through her head. She dropped back on the couch and stared up at the rugged wood ceiling. She loved this place. It was comforting. Even when the world was not. But nothing could calm the raging torrents in her head.

"How will the Hunters find you?" she asked to the sky.

"They will track me. They are slow and not too bright but they will come and we must be ready. We must call your Warrior."

Great. She just had to get Dane out to her cabin and convince him to defeat creatures from another world.

"Will they arrive before morning?" She cracked an eye open to Raython.

"I do not believe so. I was most careful in masking my travel and as I said, they are not bright. Still they will come."

"I'm going to bed. It's late. I'll call Dane in the morning and give him a heads-up." *He's never going to believe this.* She barely believed it and she'd seen the dragon and the instantly healing wounds…and the purple blood. *If I call him tonight, he'll think I'm drunk. At least in the morning, he'll think I'm sober. Crazy but sober.* "Any possibility of changing my Warrior?"

Raython drew back as if she'd waved a dead mouse in front of his face. His nose crinkled, his eyes tightened and his upper lip arched up. "But he is the chosen one. How can you think about Joining with another once you've Joined with him?"

Tina peeled back the afghan she'd dragged over her legs and stood up. "I haven't actually 'joined' with him if you'll remember. And I had sex with you which you didn't seem to mind."

"But it is acceptable, even desirable, for the Maiden to join with the Protector, under the Warrior's permission of course. Do you think he'll kill me for having you first?"

For a moment, he looked young and worried. Tina sighed. "Dane won't kill you. He might not be too thrilled with either of us, but he won't actually hurt you. Now, I'm going up to bed. Are you coming?" He stood up, his cock was still hard and strong. She smiled. "Maybe you are," she teased with a wink.

She'd be willing to go another round or two with him and that thick shaft before morning.

He shook his head and took a single step back. "Not until our Warrior gives me permission. At that time, I will fuck you as often as you wish. Let us go upstairs and I will cuddle you while you sleep."

Tina glowered at the dragon but she couldn't *make* him have sex with her. Still, it irritated her a little that he could be so obviously aroused and still refuse to fuck her. She turned away and started toward the stairs, adding a little more swing to her hips, enough to draw his attention. She wanted him to see what he'd be missing.

"Tomorrow we will contact our Warrior and we will gain his permission," Raython announced. The tension in his voice soothed her ruffled ego.

She smiled over her shoulder. He hadn't moved from his position in the living room. His eyes were connected to her backside.

"Early tomorrow."

Raython nodded, not raising his gaze. "Very early."

Chapter Three

The irritating "bing-bong" of her doorbell jerked her from a pleasant dream that involved Dane, Raython and a can of whipped cream. Her eyes snapped open and she glared at the clock. It was nine in the morning.

Tina twisted out of Raython's binding embrace, grousing softly as she stumbled from her bed. She peeked out the upstairs window and yelped. Four cars and two vans filled her driveway and the road leading toward her house. And there were men. Lots of men. Pouring out of the vans and cars, dressed in camouflage and carrying rifles of some sort.

"What the hell?"

The doorbell rang again. She glanced down and saw a familiar form. Dane. And another man she didn't recognize. With a quick glance toward Raython, she dragged on her robe and left the room, leaving the door open enough so the click didn't wake the sleeping dragon.

She hurried downstairs, scraping her fingers through her hair as she moved. Raython's hands had made a mess of her long brown strands but with the insistent ring of the doorbell a third time, she knew she didn't have time to stop and brush.

Streaks of apprehension raced down her spine. There was only one reason strangers would be on her front porch at nine on a Saturday morning. And that reason was lying naked in her bed.

Trying to act confused but not too panicked, Tina opened the door. A little flutter went through her stomach as she smiled up at the local sheriff. It had nothing to do with fear and everything to do with lust. *You'd think after last night, I'd have every bit of arousal out of my system.* But Dane's serious face still made her ache.

Beside him stood another man — dressed in a black suit and with a face dominated by grim eyes and lips. Two others, dressed in the same dark suits, climbed the three steps up to her porch and stood behind Dane.

Dane, wearing a dark green long-sleeved shirt and khaki pants, looked more casual than the others.

"Dane? What's going on?" she asked, deciding to attack directly.

"Mornin', Tina, sorry to bother you so early."

The deep, gravelly sound of his voice sent another tingle into her sex. She pressed her lips together to stifle a moan that threatened. What was wrong with her? She'd been around Dane a lot in the past four years and while she'd been tempted to jump him any number of times, it had never been this acute.

"Can we come inside, ma'am?" The man in the dark suit beside Dane moved forward.

Tina didn't open the door any farther, waiting for a nod from Dane. *Him* she trusted. She didn't know these other men.

"What's going on?" she asked, hopefully with enough innocence. "Who are these guys?" She lifted her chin toward the cars behind Dane's shoulder.

He grimaced. She didn't know if it was real or faked for the purpose of putting her at ease.

"Can we come in?"

She hesitated for a moment longer then opened the door, trying to focus on being a helpful, curious citizen. Not someone who knew that the creature they were seeking was currently naked in her bed.

Dane and the others stepped into her living room. She backed up just enough to let them in but didn't walk down the three steps into the seating area. She didn't want these men here — except for Dane. She definitely wanted him there.

Actually she wanted him upstairs in her bed but that was currently occupied by a creature from another world.

Stifling the bubble of hysterical laughter that threatened, she gathered the edge of her robe and tried to look serene.

"What's this all about?" she asked, her nerves snapping.

"Did you watch the news yesterday or this morning? All those reports about a flying dinosaur?" Dane asked. She nodded. Her heart moved into her throat and she was glad she didn't have to speak. "Well, this is Special Agent Frank Donavon with the FBI. They are investigating that incident."

Donavon stepped forward as if he was trying to capture some of the room space that Dane's presence held. "Ma'am, we are sorry to bother you this morning. In reality, what everyone saw yesterday was a test plane. A glider really. The crew thought it would be funny to paint a dinosaur head on it before it made its first flight."

Tina didn't respond. She wasn't sure if she could lie to the FBI. Then again, he was lying to her.

And he did so with friendly smile.

"They think it crashed on your property, Tina," Dane interjected. "They'd like to search your lot."

It was a lot of land and they wouldn't find anything.

"Well, I think that…" She stopped speaking when the four men in front of her stopped listening. One by one she watched their eyes leave her and turn to the stairs. Bracing herself for what she knew was behind her, hoping that Raython had put on the shorts she'd left lying at the end of the bed, she slowly turned.

Nope. He was naked. Gorgeous, sensual, and definitely naked. Raython stood halfway down the stairs, his hair brushed back over his shoulders baring his body to everyone in the room. Even more revealing was the look on his face. He had that aura about him that said he was satisfied. Even Tina could see it. He gave off the attitude of having fucked the night away.

Which he could have, she thought with a silent groan, except he'd made his little *discovery* and refused to touch her except to hold her while she slept. It had been sweet and loving but her body craved more. The telltale ache in the pit of her stomach rumbled again.

He strolled down the stairs and snapped her out of her arousal. Unaware or uncaring that the four men stared at him, Raython walked directly toward Dane. Raython stopped in front of him and with a blatant inspection, he scanned down Dane's body. Pausing at his chest and his crotch, and finally reaching his feet. Tina held her breath.

"Excellent choice, Maiden. He will make a fine Warrior and bear you strong sons."

"What the f—"

"Uh, sorry." She grabbed Raython's arm and pulled him backwards until he stood beside and a little behind her. "This is Rayth—uh, Ray. He's my brother…" She saw another widening of the eyes from the FBI agents. "In-law. *Ex*-brother-in-law."

The three FBI men nodded wisely. She wasn't doing a good job of lying about this, but none of them seemed to mind. They just thought she was trying to cover up an illicit love affair. Dane wasn't so easy. He folded his arms across his chest and glared at Raython. Raython stared back, not cowed at all by Dane's stare.

"Don't you have some clothes to put on?" Dane asked.

Raython tilted his head to the side then looked down at his body. After a long moment of self-inspection he looked back up to Dane. "Why? Am I not pleasing? Do you find my form offensive?"

A hint of red marked the base of Dane's neck. "No, but there is a lady present."

Raython shook his head, causing his hair to drape forward over his chest. "Tina does not mind. She finds my shape and size most enjoyable."

A strangled sound erupted from her throat and mixed with the quiet chuckles of the FBI agents. Dane wasn't laughing. The heat in his eyes warned her to stop this before it went any farther. "Why don't you go upstairs and put on some clothes," she suggested to Raython. "I'll talk to these men and then you and I will talk. Go." The last words were spoken through clenched teeth. It was a good thing she trusted Dane not to gossip or the fact that she'd had a naked man in her house would be all over town by evening.

"But we must Join with our Warrior," Raython protested as she nudged him away.

"We'll talk about it later. Now go." She pushed his back, directing him upstairs. With a final glance at Dane, Raython walked away. If her living room hadn't been filled with FBI agents and a would-be lover, she would have turned around and watched him as he climbed the stairs. She knew from last night that he had an incredible ass.

She waited until she heard the upstairs door open then flashed a half-smile, half-grimace at her visitors. "Sorry about that. He's a little strange."

"Obviously." Dane's voice had retained his grim, mocking tone.

She glared at Dane then offered a tight smile to the FBI agents. "You say you want to search my property."

Agent Donavon smiled but the emotion didn't reach his eyes. "We tracked the glider this direction and we think it crashed somewhere in the woods behind your house. If you'll just give us permission, we'll clear this up. Funny how one plane makes people start seeing flying dinosaurs."

"Dragon," Tina felt compelled to say.

"What?" All three of the agents, in the process of turning away, stopped and looked back.

"Well—" She gave a shrug and a tinkling laugh. "The reports I heard were that it looked like a dragon. Not a dinosaur."

"Ahh." Suspicion she hadn't wanted to inspire wavered in Donavon's eyes and Tina wanted to kick herself.

"It's fine. Search away." There was little evidence of Raython's landing, except for some purple blood. "How long will it take?"

"Probably just a couple of hours." He looked to Dane. "It will take us a few minutes to get organized and then we'll head out."

Dane nodded. "I'll be right out."

The three agents nodded politely to Tina then left, leaving the front door open. Half-turned away from her, Dane stared out, watching the soldiers checking their gear.

"I'm going to stay with them just to make sure they —"

He paused.

"To watch out for me?" she offered.

He nodded but still didn't look at her. "I didn't know you were seeing anyone," he said casually.

"I'm not." But that didn't explain the naked man in her house or the fact that she'd spent most of last night having sex with that man. "I mean I wasn't." She stopped. "I'm not really sure that I am," she said, not caring if Dane was confused. She was confused.

He nodded and turned back to face her. His eyes grew hard and the line of his mouth flattened out. Tina looked over her shoulder. Raython had come back downstairs, silently watching them.

"Maiden, we must tell him."

"Tina, what's this all about?" Dane looked at her with those direct, "no-nonsense-so-don't-bullshit-me" eyes.

She pushed the door almost shut and took a bracing breath.

"Does this have something to do with the FBI knocking on my door this morning?" Dane demanded.

She nodded. It did no good to lie to him. He would know the truth soon enough. "It's a little unbelievable so I want you to keep an open mind."

Dane shrugged a little but didn't speak.

"No, I mean a *really* open mind."

"It's open, now tell me what's happening?"

"They aren't looking for a plane. Or a glider, or whatever they're calling it. They're looking for a dragon." She blurted out the words in a rush.

Disgust and confusion zipped through Dane's eyes. "What?"

"A dragon. A flesh and blood, not of this world, only exists in fairy tales dragon."

His lips curled into an exasperated grimace but Tina didn't let him speak.

"You said you would keep an open mind and I warned you it was unbelievable." To give Dane some credit, he nodded and let her talk. "It started Thursday night. I made wish…" She quickly ran through the spell, seeing the dragon fly by the school, and finding it in the wood behind her house. "And while I was standing there, it changed." She pointed to Raython. "Into him."

Crushing silence fell on the room. And stayed there for long seconds until Dane's explosive "What?" shattered the quiet.

"Raython is the dragon," Tina said patiently. "*He* is what they are looking for."

Dane's body tensed and for a moment she thought he was going to pace but he stayed still—ready to pounce but frozen. "You're telling me that this guy—" He slashed his hand toward Raython. "—is really a flying dinosaur who just happened to land in your backyard."

"My name is Raython and do not be absurd," Raython announced with a strange combination of arrogance and defensiveness. "It was no *mistake* that I flew to these forests. I was summoned. When Mistress Tina read the spell, she freed me from my prison and called me to her side. Now, we must complete the triangle and bring her true loves into union."

Dane felt his mouth sag open as he stared at the blond man. The blond *naked* man. Didn't he own any clothes? Obviously Tina didn't mind that her houseguest was naked. Not that it was any of his business, Dane acknowledged through mentally gritted teeth. Tina could see anyone she wanted. Sleep with anyone she wanted.

He'd just sort of hoped that she wanted to sleep with him. Instead she'd picked a stud some fifteen years younger than both of them. And this guy had somehow drawn her into whatever twisted world he lived in.

"Tina, honey, you can't seriously believe all this?" he asked, deciding to ignore the naked intruder. He took her hands in his and stared into her eyes, trying to reassure himself that she was the sane, reasonable woman he'd always known her to be.

She winced but nodded. "I wish I didn't, but it's true. I saw it with my own eyes. When I walked up, the dragon was laying there, bleeding from a half a dozen wounds. I knelt beside it and it turned into him."

He glared at the man he now saw as the rival to get into Tina's bed. Being as the man was naked, it was obvious he hadn't sustained any injuries. All Dane could see was smooth bare flesh.

"There's not a mark on him."

"He healed. Overnight."

"Tina—" Dane sighed and shook his head.

"Yes," Raython interrupted. "Mistress Tina was most accommodating to give me access to her cunt and by releasing my seed, I was able to create the energy to heal myself."

Dane stepped away and didn't bother to hide the mockery in his words. "Oh, that's a novel approach. Fuck me and I'll feel better. What game are you playing?" He directed the last comment to Raython.

"It is no game, Warrior." Raython sounded deadly serious.

All of Dane's instincts went on alert. Even if the man was crazy, he believed this to be true and that made it worse. It made him much more dangerous than some schmuck who was trying to con a beautiful woman into bed.

"I came here because I was called by our Maiden," he announced. Dane opened his mouth to protest but the other man held up his hand in an arrogant command of silence. Shock made Dane's mouth fall shut. "Have you a dagger?"

"A what?"

"A dagger. A knife. Do you have one?"

The commanding tone of the man's voice made Dane raise his eyebrows and move slowly as he unclipped the little holster at his hip and pulled out his knife. He flipped open the blade and handed the weapon to Raython.

Stepping closer to Tina, in case Raython decided to attack, Dane watched as the man drew the knife toward his arm.

Tina tried to step forward. Dane reached out and held her back.

"Raython, you're just healed. Is this a good idea?"

"Our Warrior needs proof and we have little time." With that announcement, he slashed the blade across his forearm.

Pale purple blood flowed from the wound.

If Dane hadn't known that it was his blade that had cut the man, he would have mocked it as a prop. But that was a real wound with real lavender blood flowing from it.

He stared for a long time then shook his head, hoping that as he did, the image would disappear like an etch-a-sketch. The picture remained.

A man—tall, blond, physically perfect from what Dane could tell and bleeding lavender blood.

"Oh my God." The words finally found release.

"Exactly." Tina placed her hand on his arm, drawing his attention. Slowly, he pulled his eyes away and looked down at her. "Ready for another surprise?"

He shook his head then nodded. He could handle it, he told himself. He was a cop after all. He'd seen worse than some man who bled in purple. His eyes flicked back to the wound which Raython was allowing to bleed.

"It seems that in Raython's world, every woman has two...love...rs."

He could tell that wasn't the word she wanted to use but the delicate blush in her cheeks warned him not to ask.

"And?" he prompted when she didn't continue.

"Well, it appears that...that I and—" She indicated Raython, who was still dripping purple onto her floor. "Raython and uh, well..."

She whipped her head around and stared intently at the other man. Raython blinked and then as if he understood her silent question, he said, "In my world—the loving relationships are based on three points. The three points form the plane of loving. Maiden, Protector, Warrior. Tina is the Maiden, I am the Protector, and you are the chosen Warrior."

Dane knew his mouth had to be hanging open but he couldn't contain his shock. His day had been hellish from the start. No day started out right when the FBI was waiting on your front porch at dawn but to find this asshole was fucking Tina had sent the day sliding into Hell. And now, this guy wanted him to believe he was the third rung of a mystic ménage à trois.

"Raython, that's enough. Let him just deal with this. He's got enough on his mind."

"We do not have time," Raython protested. "The Hunters came awake the moment you read the spell. Our passion will act as a guide." He bowed his head, looking remarkably contrite for one who'd seemed so cocky. "I apologize, Warrior, for fucking our Maiden without your knowledge. I thought you had already penetrated her else I never would have presumed to do so." He glanced at Tina. "She had such a clear image in her mind of how it felt when you fucked her that I assumed it had already happened."

The red that had been lingering in Tina's cheeks blossomed again. So, she'd imagined fucking him, had she? Well, that was the first good news he'd heard all day.

"But now that you are here, we must Join. Before the Hunters find us."

"Join how? What hunters?" His mind captured the words, instantly banishing the image of being inside Tina to the far corner of his mind.

"Join as is normal. As is expected," Raython responded, as if the answer was obvious.

Dane looked at Tina, hoping she could explain.

"I think he means by sex. We 'join' by having sex."

"You and me?" He'd been hoping for that for more than a year. If this instigated getting into Tina's bed, he could accept it.

"All three of us must Join," Raython answered.

Dane thought his heart would stop. He knew it missed a few pertinent beats and when it started again, it was racing as if to catch up. He'd opened his mouth to ask what in the hell the dragon-boy was thinking. He wasn't having sex with another man. No way. But before he could speak, Agent Donavon tapped on the not-quite-closed door and it swung open.

"We're ready, Sheriff, if you'd like to join us."

"Right. I'm there." He backed toward the door, not knowing where to look. For the first time in his twenty years as a cop, he was flabbergasted. Gobsmacked as his Australian buddy would say. Sex with Tina. He could handle that. Sex with Ray or Raython or whatever the hell the man called himself. No way. Never in his wildest imaginings was he letting another man touch him like that.

But damn it, he didn't want to leave Tina alone like this. He didn't trust this guy or the insane story about dragons and purple blood.

"I'll come back. When they've finished their search."

Tina nodded.

"We'll talk then."

He stepped onto the porch and pulled the door shut behind him. Donavon waited at the bottom of the steps. "Problem?"

"No," Dane said, shaking his head.

"So that guy was her ex-brother-in-law?"

It was clear that the FBI agent didn't believe a word of it.

Dane shrugged. "They always were a close family."

* * * * *

Tina peeked out the kitchen window, watching Dane as he spoke with Agent Donavon and then followed as the groups of men began trekking into the forest behind her cabin.

She wanted Dane. Her body hummed with a low-level need. It was as if last night had merely primed her for more. She wanted to feel him, fucking her, between her legs, making her scream as he pushed inside her.

"Yes, Maiden, that's it. That will bring our Warrior back to us."

"What?" Tina turned around and stared at the all too close Raython. "What are you talking about?"

"Your desire will bring our Warrior to you. You must spend the day focusing it, drawing it into your body."

She smiled and shook her head, trying to ignore the flutter of need in her pussy. Why was it that both Dane and Raython could make her hornier than hell with a look or a few words?

"I think I'll get some work done," she announced with a false attempt at putting the situation behind her. "I've got papers to grade and...why are you shaking your head?"

"We have much to do before our Warrior returns."

"Yes, I was thinking about that. Doesn't Dane have to agree to this whole Warrior/Maiden/Protector thing?"

"Yes."

"What if he doesn't?" Dane was a good guy but he was immensely practical. Telling him there was a mystical connection between them had probably sent him running for the woods. He might not ever come back.

"Then he is not your chosen one but I have a good feeling about him," Raython announced. "He is handsome, strong. He will get many fine sons on you."

Since Tina knew for a fact that Dane had had a vasectomy while married to Beth, she knew that wasn't going to happen. But it would be nice to have him act as her Warrior for a short while—just long enough to defeat the demon warlords who were chasing Raython and her.

Tina shook her head, stunned by her own thoughts. Somehow her life had turned into a fantasy novel. She looked at Raython. An erotic fantasy at that.

"Anyway, I really do need to get some work done."

"But we must prepare you."

"Prepare me for what?"

"For our Warrior's return."

Tina let herself be led back upstairs. How was she supposed to prepare for Dane's return?

* * * * *

Seven hours later, when he knocked on the door, she had her answer.

She'd never been so ready to fuck someone in all her life.

Raython had begun the "preparations" with a warm bath, followed by a full body massage. When he'd finished massaging the larger expanses of skin, he turned his attention on smaller, select parts—primarily her nipples, her clit and her pussy. Each touch brought her arousal to a new level, bringing her excruciatingly close to climax before easing her away, until she whimpered with each caress, her voice weak from begging.

Raython's response was always the same. "Our Warrior will satisfy you."

He'd damn well better, she thought as she opened the door.

Just seeing him, grim and handsome, his lips curled into an irritated frown, made her pussy clench with unfulfilled need. She took a deep breath. Every sense in her body seemed to focus on his scent. He smelled clean—of soap, a light aftershave, and male.

"Dane." His name came out as a sigh. Almost a moan. Her body—tormented and teased—felt full and sensual. Heavy with desire. God, she needed him. It was all she could do not to jump him right there in the doorway but she knew she couldn't. He hadn't accepted anything that Raython had told him this morning. He was back so they could discuss it—not so that he could fuck her until she couldn't walk.

The thought made her whimper.

"Tina? Are you all right?" Dane stepped inside, coming close and cupping one hand around her upper arm and placing the other on her hip.

Her knees weakened and she sagged forward. Dane caught her and pulling her hard against him. It was too much. A distant voice reminded her that he was there to talk but her body wouldn't be denied any longer. She rubbed against him, pressing her breasts to his chest, feeling her nipples poke at him. It felt so good. She couldn't stop herself from repeating the motion. Her nipples tingled and sent bright stars into her sex. She grabbed her lower lip with her teeth, trying to contain the groan but still a sound slipped out.

She needed him. Now.

He was her Warrior. Destined to be her lover.

But until he agreed, nothing could happen. Using all her strength, she pushed against his chest and stood upright.

"Sorry about that." She looked at his mouth and licked her own lips. God, she needed to taste him. Raython had enhanced his caresses with images, whispered fantasies of Dane inside her, kissing her, touching her. Always leading her back to him fucking her.

Dane cupped his hand under her chin and lifted so that she looked into his eyes. "Are you all right? You look flushed. Almost feverish. Are you hot?"

The mere touch of his hand set off new tremors of need inside her pussy.

She swallowed and stepped back. She had to get away from him. She couldn't stay near and not have him naked. Damn Raython and his preparations.

"I'm fine," she assured him, scraping her hands through her hair. "What did you find?" she asked, hoping to sound normal.

"Not much. Some tracks…and purple blood. They took samples."

Tina watched his mouth but barely heard the words. All she could think about was his lips on her skin—his tongue sliding into her pussy. A whimper echoed from the back of her throat. Dane looked around, searching with his penetrating eyes.

Raython stood at the bottom of the stairs, dressed in a pair of old sweats Tina had cut off just above the knees. They were stretched tight across his crotch, revealing the thick line of his erection. The teasing he'd tormented her with for the past seven hours had obviously had an effect on him as well but that didn't ease Tina at all.

Dane glowered at Raython.

"What's wrong with her?" he demanded.

She opened her mouth but couldn't find the ability to put into words what she needed.

"I have prepared her for you." Raython left the stairs and walked to her side. "Since you left, I have caressed and stroked her body, arousing her for your pleasure when you returned. You are here and she is ready." Raython stroked his hand over Tina's hair. Her head followed the movement, tilting backwards.

She groaned softly. "As promised, I have not penetrated her without your permission."

Dane stared at Raython and then at Tina. She had the look of woman completely trapped in passion. "You've kept her on the verge of coming for almost seven hours?"

Raython winced and the regret soothed Dane's snapping nerves.

"I had expected you to return before now else I would not have begun preparations so early. But her body needed to be ready to accept yours. We must Join. We must come together. The three of us. Her climax must occur with us inside her body."

Dane shook his head, trying to assimilate all the information "Ray" was throwing at him, all while fighting the urge to flip Tina around and cram his cock inside her pussy. She would welcome it, he knew. At this point, she'd accept any relief.

He stopped. That's what he could give her—relief. Glaring at Raython to let him know he wasn't happy with the situation, Dane bent down, slipped his arm behind her legs and picked Tina up. She curled into him, wrapping her arms around his neck and placing her mouth against his skin. The hungry nip of her teeth sent a shaft of need down into his cock. Damn, he wanted to fuck her.

The idea of making love to Tina—of finally being in her bed and inside her—had kept his cock semi-erect all day. Now, his erection fought against the constraints of his jeans. He needed to be inside her. And from the looks of her, she needed it as well.

Ignoring all the concerns—that another man had aroused her, that this man claimed to be a dragon—he carried her into her living room. None of that mattered as he placed her on the couch. Her legs instantly separated. Her white robe hid her secrets but the sweet action of her spreading thighs made him crazy. For almost a year he'd been moving toward getting Tina into bed. He'd only resisted because of her friendship with his ex, but now, none of that mattered. She was here, hungry, desperate for sex.

His cock leapt in his jeans.

He was finally going to have the woman he'd fantasized about.

Chapter Four

"Let me help you, baby." Dane pushed her shoulders until she leaned against the back of the couch. Her hands reluctantly released him. He reached down and lifted the edges of her robe, baring her body. More hands joined his, separating the top and revealing her naked breasts.

"Her nipples are quite sensitive, Warrior. I have spent a long time arousing them."

Dane stared at her breasts—the tips were pink and puffy. Full and stretching forward. He couldn't resist. He placed his fingers over one of the tight peaks and pulled gently. Tina groaned and arched up, matching his touch. Her legs shifted and he knew she felt the need in her pussy.

He sat back on his heels. "Spread your legs, baby, let me see your pretty cunt."

"Dane, please." The hunger her beneath her words called to a need deep inside him. He couldn't let her ache like this. She widened her legs, completely baring herself to him. The seductive perfume of her arousal rose from her heat and Dane groaned softly. He bent down, moving toward the center of her need, his own desire building with each passing moment.

"But, Warrior—" Raython placed his hand on Dane's shoulder. "She must come with you inside her."

Dane slipped his fingers up the inside of her thighs. She was wet—before he could even get near her pussy he encountered her moisture. The tip of his index finger brushed the lower lips of her cunt.

"Does it have to be the *first* climax?" he asked, his voice soft, his eyes focused on the deep pink flesh open to him.

"No. Just that she climax while you are inside of her."

Dane bent down and laved his tongue up the inside of her thigh. Her feminine moisture coated his tongue. He wanted to growl at the warmth that exploded in his mouth. "She'll come more than once tonight," he vowed. First he would satisfy the vicious arousal that controlled her body then he would take her. He would give her his cock and fill her with his juice. Vague warnings went off in his head—that he was too accepting of Raython's presence—but it no longer seemed to matter that another man was joined in their love play, as long as he was the one to plunge into her hot, wet cunt.

Dane growled and pressed his mouth against her pussy. Liquid fire poured from her sex. He gathered it into his tongue then pushed inside her, needing more, needing her flavor.

Tina arched into his hands, her ragged cry alerting him she was close. Too close. He wanted to enjoy her, linger over her flesh, but her need was so strong that he relented, circling her clit with his tongue and slurping it between his lips. With one gentle suck, shudders racked her body and she screamed. Her knees clamped around his head, holding him in place as he continued to lick her, bringing her back down to earth.

Her taste was incredible and he wanted more—wanted to make her come with his mouth, his cock. Feel her wrapped around him.

"Warrior, we must Join."

For a moment he'd forgotten the other man was in the room. Dane lifted his head, staring first at Tina then at Raython. Raython knelt beside the couch stroking Tina's breasts. He was naked once again, his cock hard and thick.

Dane shook his head. He couldn't believe he was considering this. None of it made sense—it probably wasn't even real. It was just some con Ray had created to make unsuspecting women sleep with him. But that didn't explain the purple blood…and it didn't ease the desire in Dane. This was his chance to have Tina. To finally be inside her.

Despite the concerns racing through his head, his body was driving him one direction — Tina.

"How? What's involved?"

"We must Join. The two of us loving our Maiden." Raython lifted her hand and sucked her middle finger into his mouth. Tina groaned. "She is capable of much pleasure. We can give her that pleasure."

Dane looked at the other man's lips on Tina's skin and felt his own crotch tighten. The sensual web that Ray had bound Tina in was stretching out its tendrils to include Dane. He could feel himself being drawn in but there was no will to resist.

Her body was still tight and twitching with need. Dane had no trouble imagining her twisting beneath their hands, screaming as they each fucked her.

He looked into her eyes. The haze of desire blurred the green depths. He pushed his finger into her cunt and felt the sweet grip as she clung to him.

"Is this what you want?" he asked. "Both of us, fucking you."

She hesitated but Dane could see the answer in her eyes — along with her hesitation and fear. She wanted both of them but was afraid to say it.

"If it's what you want, baby, I'll give it to you," he said meeting her sensual gaze…and realizing as he spoke the words, it was the truth. "We'll both fuck you — if that's what you want."

"Yes."

Her breathless response and the slow roll of her hips sent more pressure into his cock. It was time. He would have her…and then he would have to let Raython have her. He still didn't know if he could handle that but he'd promised Tina.

"Come on, baby, let's get upstairs and get comfortable."

Both men helped her to standing. Her knees were wobbly and still weak from the hours Raython had spent touching her and the killer orgasm Dane had given her. It had been sharp and clear — a bright climax that had zinged through her body. But now, the need had returned. She needed to be fucked. Needed a cock inside her.

She turned slightly. Her body was practically vibrating. She opened her mouth and Dane was there, conquering and consuming. His tongue thrust between her lips and she tasted the dark musky flavor of her own sex. She leaned into him and exalted in the power of his kiss. The bright new sensation filled her. She entwined her tongue around Dane's drawing him inside, needing him.

Another hot mouth covered the nape of her neck — and the true possibilities of two lovers filled her.

After all her fantasies, she would finally have Dane…and Raython. Her knees weakened further and she clutched her would-be lovers, holding herself upright.

"May I assist you, Maiden?" Raython asked. Before she answered, he lifted her up, pulling her from Dane's grip. She glanced over Raython's shoulder. Dane hesitated and she knew he was considering bolting from the room. He watched them until Raython was halfway up the stairs. Then Dane followed. A slight brush of sympathy flooded her chest. It was a lot to spring on a man but she needed him.

It was imperative that she have these two men — that she be able to claim them for her own.

Raython shouldered open the bedroom door and placed her in the center of the bed. He stared down at her body then carefully curled his hands around her thighs, pulling them apart until her sex was open and bared. He stepped away and looked at her critically, as if he were arranging flowers. Seemingly satisfied with what he saw, he turned as Dane entered the room.

"For your pleasure, Warrior," he announced. Dane walked to the end of the bed and she could see the edge of his mouth kick up.

Words of defiance flared inside her head but she controlled them. Her feminist sensibilities could be soothed tomorrow. The passion flaring in Dane's gaze told her all she needed to know. He wanted her.

She lay on the bed, watching the two men who would be her lovers. Heat spread through her body.

"Perhaps you'd like to undress, Warrior," Raython said, stepping forward. "I could assist you, if you'd like."

Dane's lips curled down. Tina wondered if that was too much for a man like Dane to accept. She tensed, waiting to see if he would leave but he just shook his head warning the other man away. Raython took a step back but continued to watch with clinical interest. She didn't have any idea how far Raython expected to take this "Joining" but she was pretty sure she knew Dane's limits.

Flat on her back Tina watched as Dane slowly unbuttoned his shirt. Raython's hours of sensual "preparation" swamped her with renewed force at the mere sight of Dane's bare chest. Broad and muscled. She knew he worked out but she'd never seen him naked before. The sharp lines of his chest rolled into the sweet curves of his shoulders and tight biceps. She sighed as she watched, wanting to trace the individual lines with her fingers and her tongue. She pushed herself up and crawled to the end of the bed.

Dane stepped forward to meet her. Her body silently whimpered with relief as she stroked her fingertips down the tight muscles of his stomach. She continued the downward caress, scraping her nails across the thick bulge of his erection.

"Open the metal bindings containing his shaft." Raython's words slipped into her already swirling consciousness and guided her hands. She eased the metal tab of Dane's zipper down and pulled the clinging material of his boxers and jeans with it. The hard line of his cock sprung forward, hard and long. Thick.

Feminine distress mixed with the anticipation in her pussy. Soon, she would feel his cock inside her.

Foreplay, seduction, temptation. The words circled through her head but none of them mattered. She needed to be fucked. She wrapped her hand around his erection and held it. The warmth flowed into her palm promising sweet release. A dribble of pre-cum pearled at the tip. She leaned forward and swiped her tongue across the head of his cock, collecting the drop.

Masculine groans reached her from two directions. Her tongue peeking out from between her lips, she looked up at Dane. His hands were curled into tight fists at his side. The tight line of his jaw made her teeth ache in sympathy. Watching his face, she smoothed her palm up and down his hard shaft. Desire exploded from his eyes.

"Keep that up, baby, and we'll never make it to this 'Joining' you and your boyfriend think we have to do."

The words were low but not harsh. More of a sensual threat than anything else.

With a slow, gentle stroke, she slipped her hand away from his cock and rolled onto her back. Raython moved to stand beside Dane.

The heat from one pair of eyes was devastating—with both men watching her, she was amazed that she didn't burst into flames.

She moaned softly, her body desperate for something to fill her.

She spread her legs and pushed her fingers into her pussy. The wet warmth of her sex heightened the wicked need inside her. She stared at both men as she pumped her fingers in and out of her pussy.

The two cocks pointed at her seemed to rise even more. Dane reached down and stroked his erection as he watched her finger-fuck herself.

"Maiden, you must let the Warrior have you." Raython's voice was filled with concern. "We must come inside you to complete the Joining."

We? Raython's choice of pronouns made her tremble. She knew both men would fuck her but it seemed deliciously wicked to have both of them coming inside her.

Dane pushed his jeans down, letting them crumple to the floor.

She looked at the two naked men standing side by side. They were different in so many ways—Dane was broader, more muscular. Raython was long and sleek. Dane's cock was thick and hint shorter than Raython's. Both were impressive. Hard and ready.

God, she wanted them.

She opened her mouth to beg them to fuck her, but the words that slipped from her lips were foreign. They came from a place deep inside her that she'd never recognized.

"Warrior, Protector, will you Join with me?"

They moved as one. Dane climbing on the bed and kneeling between her spread thighs. Raython moving to her left side. She was surrounded and overwhelmed by the masculine strength around her.

Dane reached between her legs and pulled her hand away. He carried her fingers to his mouth and slowly licked her juices from her skin. Each stroke of his tongue tingled through her clit. She glanced at Raython and saw him watching Dane as well. His mouth hung slightly open as he observed the sensual banquet Dane made of her fingers.

"You're delicious, Tina." Dane swiped his tongue across the pads of her fingers. "I'm going to eat your sweet pussy, and next time, I won't be rushed."

She nodded, hungry for that sensation.

"But now, I need to fuck you."

"Yes." The moan erupted from her throat.

"Ray, you said you liked playing with her tits." He lifted his chin toward her breasts. "I think Tina would like you to suck on her nipples while I fuck this pretty cunt here." He followed the words with a slow thrust of his fingers into her pussy. "Oh, baby, you are wet. Like you really need to be fucked bad."

"Dane, please." He was teasing her, damn it.

He stared at her with hard, hot eyes. "We'll do this in my time." A shiver raced down her spine and settled in her sex. "Ray, her breasts."

"Yes, Warrior." Raython immediately bent over and covered her nipple with his mouth. She arched up, pushed her breast into his mouth.

"That's it, baby. Feel us both." Dane pumped his fingers inside her. "Oh baby, you're going to hold me so tight."

She squeezed her lips together to hold back the groan that was threatening. Her nipples were stretched to their limit. Raython's relentless tonguing and licking had made them sensitive to the mere brush of air. Dane's fingers inside her kept on the verge of coming.

"I think she's ready for some cock." Dane covered her free breast with his hand giving the mound a gentle squeeze. "Do you want my cock, baby?"

"Yes!"

He pulled his fingers from inside her and stroked his shaft, smearing her cunt juices on his cock.

"Warrior, your rod is so thick," Raython said. "Will it not hurt our Maiden? Perhaps you should make it smaller."

"Noooo," Tina cried. She wanted him, just as he was—now. The edge of Dane's mouth curled up but her heart was racing so fast with the anticipation of finally fucking Dane, that she let the arrogance pass.

"It's all yours," Dane said softly fitting the rounded head to her opening. He pushed the first inch inside and Tina held her breath. Raython was long but Dane's width would stretch her aching flesh. He pushed in deeper—giving her just a little more—then he drew back. He pulsed his hips within her, shallow and slow, massaging her entrance.

Raython's mouth trailed between her breasts, his tongue leaving tendrils of heat in its wake.

Dane pulled back until he almost slipped free. Raython lifted his head and looked at Dane. Some signal seemed to pass between them. Raython covered one straining nipple and sucked hard as Dane plunged inside her.

Her cry filled the air. She snapped her teeth together and endured the sweet pain of having him inside her. After so many dreams, he was finally fucking her.

Dane held himself deep inside her for a moment, then began a long, slow retreat followed by a fast, hard penetration. Each stroke into her seemed to go deeper, filling her more every time.

"Excellent, Warrior. She finds much pleasure on your cock. I can feel the need rising in her."

She planted her heels on the mattress and thrust up, countering each heavy drive into her. He rode her hard as if he'd been aching to feel her as well. She wrapped her hand around Raython's shoulder and reached out to clutch Dane's arm as they loved her body.

Pleasure rose fast and strong—the steady thrusts of Dane's cock and the pulls of Raython's mouth pushed her higher.

In the corner of her hazy thoughts, she remembered something Raython had said. That they had to come together. And she didn't think he meant just Joining. They had to *come* together.

"I'm close," she whispered. Raython's head snapped up and he knelt beside her. The sudden movement seemed to startle Dane and he drove into her one more time and froze. Tina groaned and tried to roll her hips. One more touch, the lightest graze against her clit and she could come, she knew she could. Dane's hands gripped her waist and held her still.

"We must Join but I did not have the time to properly prepare her for a second penetration, Warrior." Raython bowed his head as if apologizing. He dropped his hands to his side and waited, his long cock reached high, stretching toward his stomach.

Dane took a few shallow breaths. "You need to come inside her to complete this joining thing?"

"Yes, Warrior."

"Will fucking her mouth count?"

"Yes."

Dane reached up and scraped the sweaty hair back away from her forehead. "Can he do that, baby? Will you take him into your mouth?"

He made it sound as if sucking Raython off would be doing Dane a favor.

"Yes," she whispered, eager to have her mouth filled. The light taste of Dane's cock had left her craving more.

Dane drew her hips high up his thighs, keeping the connection between their bodies. He ground his crotch into hers and was rewarded by the delicate tightening of her cunt as he watched the other man direct his cock toward Tina's mouth. Raython leaned forward, wrapping his hand around his cock and offering it to Tina. She turned her head and opened her lips. Dane couldn't suppress the groan that clawed at the inside of his throat. He never would have thought it was sexy to watch his woman suck another man but seeing her take Raython's penis between those pink lips while Dane penetrated her cunt was amazing.

As Raython's cock slid into her mouth, Dane returned to fucking her. Her body was still tense but the break had given them all a moment to pull back. He slowed his thrusts and allowed himself to enjoy the sweet push and retreat into her pussy.

She groaned. The sound seemed to squeeze his cock. He watched Ray's eyes drift shut as she sucked, as he pumped his shaft between her lips.

"That's it, baby. Take him. Swallow him whole," Dane whispered, encouraging her and subtly reminding her that he was the one fucking her. "Do you like having him in your mouth?" he asked knowing she couldn't speak with her mouth full of cock. "He likes it. Don't you, Ray."

"Yes, Warrior," Ray said through gritted teeth. "Her mouth is truly as wondrous as her cunt."

Dane drove in—hard and deep—and reveled in the sound of her moan.

"Then it must be something wonderful indeed because this tight little pussy is something very special." He knew Tina was listening to every word. Her eyes flickered toward him, glazed with lust and hunger. "That's it. Take us both. Let us fill you."

Let us fill you with our seed.

The strangely formal words entered his mind but he held them back.

There would be no "seed-planting" between them. For the first time in years, he regretted his decision to have a vasectomy. The image of Tina pregnant with his child exploded into his head. He knew it was impossible, but his body wanted to fulfill it. He began to pump inside her, the need to pour himself into her now desperate. Each stroke brought him closer. He had to come—had to come *inside her.*

Her hips met his with each thrust. It wasn't necessary to hear her muffled groans to know she was with him. Her body was still creaming, still clutching his. She was close to orgasm. He was vaguely aware of Ray's growls of pleasure as the other man rocked into Tina's mouth.

The thought pushed him to the edge but he fought it. Something deep inside him held him back. He needed them. With him.

He reached down and grabbed Tina's right hand with his left. Their fingers twined together as he thrust inside her. There was no way he could stop. His body was driven on some instinctual path. He had to come. She had to come.

He felt another hand and looked down. Ray had taken Dane's right hand in his. Dane looked up. Ray held Tina's free hand.

They'd formed a triangle.

Energy exploded around them. Dane felt his palms heat, turning to fire, burning until he wanted to pull away but couldn't. It was as if electricity shot from his body and flowed into Tina's and Ray's through the connection of their hands. Even as he sent the power into them, in came back to him — different and distinct. Masculine and feminine.

He thrust forward one more time — his body no longer able to hold back. His semen erupted from his cock, flooding her womb. The tiny contractions through her cunt fluttered along his cock. He felt the gentle massage of her pussy on his cock but also inside — as if his body was creating the sensation.

Ray shouted his release and Dane's cock twitched and poured more cum into Tina.

Tina's hunger, her pleasure at Ray coming in her mouth, seeped into Dane's body.

He felt it all. His pleasure, her pleasure and Ray's.

After a long, seemingly endless climax, Dane opened his eyes. The world seemed to have stopped spinning around them and the strange electricity that had reverberated between them was gone. His breath struggled to fill his lungs. Dane looked down at Tina.

Her eyes were filled with the same stunned surprise that he was feeling.

What the hell had just happened?

He pushed up on his arms and started to withdraw, knowing he'd been inside her long enough to make her sore. Her gasp was seconds behind a jolt of pleasure into his cock. He stopped. It wasn't possible but he had to check. He reached between their still connected bodies and gently massaged her swollen clit.

She groaned and his cock hardened, like someone had stroked a hand down his penis. Ray moaned.

Dane snapped his head up. *He'd* felt it to. It was if they'd all shared the same orgasm.

It was too much for Dane to handle. The whole fucking day was too much for him to handle, he decided as he pulled out of Tina. Dragons, purple blood, Joinings. And now community orgasms?

Voices screamed in his head, all shouting advice. The loudest of which was he needed to get the hell out of there. To think. Something wasn't right. He still didn't quite believe Tina's dragon story. Not that he disbelieved it exactly, but a dragon? It was crazy.

He rolled away, planning his escape. He glanced at Tina. She was still on her back, his cum dripping from between her legs. Raython was hunched over her, licking her nipple. His mouth encircled the one closest to him and he began to suck.

Dane felt his own nipples tense in response. He licked his lips. He wanted to taste her. Without consciously directing his movements, he crawled up the other side of her and latched his mouth onto the peak of her free breast. She arched up and groaned. Soft sighs and whispers had been replaced by deep throaty pleas. He felt each sound deep in his chest. Dane swirled his tongue over the tight nipple, keeping his touch light but persistent, drawing the peak higher and scraping his flat tongue across the tight surface.

Her fingers slipped behind his head, holding him there.

Tina stared up at the ceiling trying to capture the remnants of her soul — they were scattered in the atmosphere. She'd never felt anything so wildly sensuous as having these two men caress and touch her. Her body was a wicked contradiction of exhaustion and desire. As contradictory as their styles. Raython sucked her as if he wanted to swallow her whole — a desperate kind of need. Dane swirled his tongue slowly around her nipple as if he was calling it out to play and when it arrived he teased it and taunted it.

Raython lifted his head, flipping his long hair back over his shoulder in one smooth, flowing move.

"Warrior, may I penetrate our Maiden?"

Tina tensed—and she couldn't decide if it was because *she* hadn't been asked, or if it was the anticipation of Dane's answer. For all his appearance of a modern man, he was a Neanderthal at heart and he'd just been asked to allow another man to fuck his woman.

She didn't know if Dane had truly claimed her but she felt claimed. She felt bound to him. Joined.

Just as Raython had said.

Dane allowed one last swipe of his tongue across her taut nipple then lifted his head and stared at the other man. "You want to fuck her?"

"Yes, Warrior." Raython kept his head bowed, strangely submissive for one who had somehow gotten all three of them in bed together.

Tina couldn't help but look at the long, heavy shaft that rose between Raython's legs. She knew precisely how long. Not only had she taken it inside her vagina, she'd sucked him and been unable to swallow more than half.

Dane pushed his hand between her legs. He slipped one long finger into her pussy and pumped as if testing her. Her hips punched upward to meet his touch. Dane tickled the inside of her pussy and let his fingers fall free.

"She's wet and still hungry."

The scent of her sex combined with his cum filled her head, making her feel drunk with need.

"You may have her," Dane agreed.

Raython raised his eyes—lavender fire glittered in their depths as he smiled.

"For our pleasure, Warrior."

Dane's hand cupped the breast Raython had been sucking, flicking the nipple with his thumb while Dane casually—occasionally—licked the peak before him. Tina and Dane watched Raython as he positioned himself between her legs.

He held his cock in his hands, poised at her entrance, but didn't move forward.

"You may enter her," Dane announced.

Raython plunged inside, driving deep. Tina screamed. She couldn't hold the sound back.

"Stop!"

Dane's command froze the room. He traced his fingers along her cheek and stared into her eyes. "Are you all right?" She nodded. "I won't let him hurt you. I won't let anyone hurt you."

His final words settled into her chest and she knew his vow was now part of her.

"I was just surprised," she whispered.

"Do you want him to continue?"

She nodded, then realized what it would look like. She wanted *Dane*. She'd been lusting after *Dane* for four years—long before her friend had divorced him.

And here she was telling him she wanted another man to fuck her.

"But only if you agree," she said.

Dane drew back. His eyes wandered down her body to the point where Raython's penis filled her.

Her body was hungry for Raython's cock—for his style of fucking—but she couldn't, wouldn't lose Dane over this. Not so soon after she'd found him. She would do almost anything to hold him.

"I will let him have you."

She groaned with relief though a secret corner of her mind was amazed that she'd so willingly given up control of her body. He turned to the Raython. "Make her come," he commanded.

"Yes, Warrior."

Raython pulled out, his long, lovely cock taking ages to withdraw from her body before he drove back in. As he worked in her pussy, Dane lavished his attention on the rest of her body. The inside edge of her elbow, her breasts, the sweet curve of her neck. So many forces worked on her body that Tina couldn't keep track of them. She clutched at whichever body was nearest, not knowing if it was Raython or Dane she grabbed. It didn't matter. They blended into one being. Fucking her and loving her until her body exploded in another orgasm. She heard Raython's shout.

And Dane's growl. Seconds later he was back between her legs, driving deep, driving toward his own climax. Tina tried to help, but her body was quickly losing strength. He thrust in deep — fast and hard — and she felt him flood her once again.

Chapter Five

Tina drifted into a quiet doze—her body replete and warm. Her lovers surrounding her. She cuddled into the broad chest in front of her, feeling the other man behind her. Two cocks, not fully hard but not soft either, pressed against her.

"It appears we've exhausted our Maiden."

She recognized Raython's voice and smiled because he still referred to her as their "Maiden". She was pretty sure the term implied "virgin" and if she hadn't been disqualified before—which she had—she certainly was now.

"Yes," Dane agreed.

The cock in front of her—from the thickness she recognized it as Dane's even without opening her eyes—began to harden.

"She'll be sore and uncomfortable if we leave her in this state," Raython said. "With your permission, Warrior, I will bathe our lady and return her to your side."

If she'd had the strength, she would have protested. Not because she didn't desperately want the attention Raython was going to give her, but she feared that Dane would leave. That while they were away, he would think about what had just happened and run.

The warmth behind her disappeared and strong arms lifted her from the bed. Even with her eyes closed, she knew it was Raython who carried her. The soft brush of his hair tickled her cheek as he took her into bathroom. He placed her gently on her feet and Tina knew it was time to open eyes and face the world...face Dane.

Raython bent forward to turn on the faucets. Steam built inside the small shower stall. Tina looked over her shoulder.

Dane stood in the bedroom, naked and watching. The turbulence in his eyes reached her from across the divide. She started to speak but Raython's touch stopped her. He wrapped his arm around he waist and lifted her slowly into the shower. Her knees trembled as her feet hit the floor.

"Don't worry, Maiden. Our Warrior is strong and will abide with us."

Raython's voice was low and she knew it was meant for her alone. Before she had a chance to respond, he followed her into the shower. He spun her around so her back was to the nozzle. When she lifted her gaze, she looked directly out the door. Dane was still watching.

Water splashed down her back. Raython dropped to his knees before her. The quick movement drew her eyes away from Dane. She watched the blond head as he lathered up a washcloth. Slowly, he began to stroke her skin, starting with her ankles and moving upward. She placed her hand on the shower wall to stay steady. Exhaustion threatened to drag her to the tub floor and she gave the wall more of her weight. The mental pressure of uncertainty added to her exhaustion.

She was afraid to look up, to see if Dane was still watching them, waiting for them.

The bubbles teased her already sensitive skin. Raython's touch turned slow and sensuous as he moved to her torso. He placed the rag to the side and covered her breasts with soapy hands. Her body still vibrated with the violence of the orgasms she'd received so the firm massage of her breasts sent renewed waves of need into her pussy.

"Raython—" she sighed his name and sagged against the wall, her knees trembling. He slipped his fingers along her breasts tugging on her nipples, drawing the peaks even tighter.

He knelt before her and silently nudged her legs apart. There was a momentary rush of cool air followed by heat as Raython's hands slipped between her thighs and began to wash her. He lathered up her pussy and slid his fingers into her slit.

As he washed her, he stroked her, circling her clit in seemingly random patterns.

It seemed like the dragon wasn't done with her yet. She let her eyes drift shut—afraid to look at Dane.

Raython stood up and spun her around, facing her into the spray. He lifted her left leg to the side of the tub and let the water sluice down her breasts and rinse the bubbles from between her legs. His hands followed, aiding the water and heating her skin with his touch. He reached her sex and pushed two fingers into her passage, driving deep. The pretense of bathing disappeared—it was a straightforward finger-fuck. He pumped into her, each stroke a wicked temptation for more. Without her command, her hips swung forward, countering his thrusts.

"That's enough, dragon." Dane's growl shattered the sensual haze that surrounded her but the hunger that lingered beneath his words triggered a new desire. "Bring her back to bed," he commanded. There was no doubt he expected to be obeyed. Raython bowed his head in silent acknowledgement of Dane's dominance.

As if prodded along, Raython snapped the water shut and quickly dried her with a towel. He didn't let her help but there was none of the sensuality of the bath.

Again, it seemed as if he could hear her thoughts. "The Warrior wishes you to return to his side." There was a hint of triumph in the dragon's eyes. "We should not keep a lustful man waiting."

Nodding her agreement because she couldn't really think of another response, she followed him out of the room. It was odd walking into a room—even her own bedroom—naked. Particularly when two equally naked men waited for her. Her fingers twitched at her side—anxious with the need to cover herself from their intense scrutiny. She raised one hand but the tightening of Dane's jaw stopped her.

"She is most beautiful, is she not, Warrior?"

"Yes, she is."

The low rumble of Dane's words sank into her sex—another layer of sensation in her overly wired body.

Raython stepped forward and led her to the bed, once again positioning her in the middle. He nodded to Dane then took up a place on her left side, stretched out beside her, his hands skimming across her breasts and stomach.

Tina tried to stay still but the need was too great. She twisted, sliding her feet across the soft sheets, seeking some relief to the growing need.

"Spread your legs for me, baby." She heard Dane's order as a visceral command and there was no way she could ignore it. Dane crawled up on the bed, settling himself between her open thighs. "I was rushed earlier," he said, whispering against her skin. "I won't be this time."

Dane licked the inside of her thigh, teasing her skin with his fingers and tongue, warming her cooled flesh. It was impossible to contain the soft, needy sigh she heard slip from her lips.

He took his time, making a slow approach to her sex, wandering fingers and tongue across her thighs, drifting down to tease the backs of her knees. Raython's hands tightened on her breasts. She looked up at the young man but his gaze was on Dane, watching the other man lavish attention on her skin, drifting ever closer to sex.

"Please," she begged softly, needing more. Dane raised his eyes and stared at her. The hunger in his gaze melted her very insides.

"I won't be rushed," he said, reminding her. He pushed her legs open farther adding to her feeling of vulnerability. Raython leaned over to look at her spread pussy. Dane let him stare for a moment then placed his mouth against her outer lips. The whisper kiss he placed on her skin sent a warm shiver up her spine. He traced the inside of her folds, licking and tasting every inch, drawing close but never quite touching her clit.

Hours of sensual torture had given her the confidence to know what she wanted. She scraped her fingers into Dane's spiky hair and held his head, holding him against her as she pressed up. He took her silent command and slipped his tongue into her pussy, sliding just inside and fluttering the tip.

"Ah!" She squeezed his head as the tension shot into her cunt.

Still slow, but with more deliberation, he swirled his tongue around her clit, lapping at it before gently sucking it between his lips. Raython's fingers tightened on her breast as she twisted beneath Dane's slow assault—his wickedly clever mouth leading her higher and closer to another orgasm.

The mattress dipped beside her drawing Tina's attention away from Dane's wickedly clever lips. Raython knelt at her hips. He hovered beside Dane, watching curiously.

Finally, Dane seemed to sense Raython's inspection and lifted his head. Tina watched her lovers. The tension hanging between the two men was foreign and seductive. Raython stroked his hand down her stomach, through her curly hair.

"You've done this before—put your mouth on her cunt," Raython said, tilting his head and giving her the impression of a confused puppy. "Our Maiden seems to find great pleasure in this."

Dane used his thumbs and spread her pussy wide. Then with Raython and Tina watching he licked the long line of her slit. She cried out, arching her back as he fluttered his tongue across her clit.

"Have you never eaten a pussy before?"

Raython shook his head. "I was forbidden to take human form until my Maiden called to me."

Dane leaned away, his thumbs still holding her open.

"Taste her. She's delicious."

Raython didn't hesitate. He bent down and dipped his tongue into her sex, following the path Dane had traveled. Tina gasped at the delicate roughness of his tongue.

Raython's eyes were wide as he looked at Dane. "She is delicious. May I taste more of her?"

Dane considered the request for a long moment then nodded. He placed a final kiss on her clit, leaving her with a flash of his tongue and a promise of more. Raython whirled around and took Dane's place between her legs. He dragged his tongue along her damp flesh. It was the most amazing sensation. Different from the slow loving Dane had given her. It was untutored and quick but the desire was there.

Dane rolled out of the way. The surreal feeling of the whole situation struck her as Dane whispered instructions on how to eat pussy. "Slow down, kid. Let her feel it. She'll let you know when she wants more. There. That's it. Suck on those sweet lips." Raython learned quickly under Dane's tutelage. He sampled her with delicate flicks of his tongue and then delved deeper, seeming to enjoy pushing his tongue into her passage.

Dane watched the sensual tension flow through Tina's body. He'd brought her so close to climax and then given access to her cunt to another man. And all he felt was desire—his and hers. She pressed her shoulders into the mattress and rolled her hips up, smashing her mound against Raython's face. The dragon seemed eager to please and it looked like he'd taken her silent direction and begun to suck on her clit.

Her eyes were heavily clouded with passion.

A growl rumbled in the back of his throat. *This was his woman.* He'd brought her this far and now another would make her come.

He felt his hand move, like he was going to physically pull Ray out of the way. Tina's warm fingers stopped him. She grabbed his arm, digging her nails into his skin—holding onto him as if he was her anchor. He looked at her body—flushed and pink, so ready to be fucked. Her eyes fluttered open and she stared at him. She was beautiful—her body consumed by the experience. He'd never seen anything so arousing.

He had to taste her again, feel her skin against him.

Dane curled over her and covered her mouth with his, driving his tongue into her warmth, instinctively matching the rhythm that Ray was setting between her legs. It didn't make sense—hell, none of this made sense. He sank into the kiss, losing himself in her taste and the desperate hunger of her lips. Every subtle stroke of her tongue called a response from inside him, as if he knew what she needed. Her fingers circled his cock and Dane moaned, feeding the sound into her mouth. The slow stroke of her fingers—and the hot licks of Raython's mouth on her—drove Dane to the edge.

He ripped his mouth away and gasped for air. They were stealing everything from him. His ability to think, breathe, his existence was wrapped up in the two of them.

It had to stop. He still wasn't sure she believed Tina, or Raython, about the other man being a dragon, but something had happened when they'd fucked the first time. His body was still pulsed with the energy.

His chest rising and falling in long, ragged breaths, he stared down at Tina. She looked back. Beyond the arousal there was concern, maybe even fear. She was as unsure of this as he was but he couldn't stop now. He turned and looked at Raython, lapping at Tina's sex with true abandon, and from the tension in Tina's thighs, some newly learned skills. He had his face buried in her pussy.

Tina groaned and arched her back, pumping her hips up. Raython lifted his mouth but he didn't turn to Tina. He looked to Dane and as if the dragon had spoken, Dane knew the question. *How do I make her come?*

Dane reached down and separated her pussy lips with his fingers. "Suck her clit. Swirl your tongue around it then suck lightly."

The dragon eagerly fell on this new treat and Tina's groans reached a fevered pitch. She clutched at Dane's arms, pulling him over her, back to her mouth.

"Let him make you come. You want to come, don't you?" he whispered, pressing his lips to her ear. "Then I'll fuck you. I'll drive my cock so deep you'll never forget what it's like to feel me inside you."

He leaned away and watched her, watched her body writhe beneath Raython's newly trained tongue. Passion flowed out of her and it was all he could do not to push the dragon out of the way and fuck her now. Instead, he let her enjoy the pleasure's being fed to her...knowing that more awaited.

The rise of her orgasm swirled around Dane, weaving itself into his body, into the space between his pores until he was consumed with her need. She was close, but Raython had withdrawn, gone back to his delicate licks. Dane didn't understand how he knew this but damn it, she needed to come.

"Finish her off," he commanded, his body responding to the need vibrating through her cunt.

Raython lifted his head and a smirk curved his mouth. "If it pleases you, Warrior."

Raython returned to her clit. Dane could almost feel every stroke of the dragon's tongue, as if it was moving around his cock. Phantom strokes licked the head of his shaft and then as if a warm, moist mouth encompassed him, he began to pump his hips. Tina's hand tightened around his shaft and he fucked himself against her fingers.

Her body bowed back as she struggled to have more.

"Damn it. Make her come," Dane said again, feeling the rising need in his cock.

"Yes, Warrior."

Raython circled his tongue around the tight bundle of nerves and Dane thought he'd go through the roof. He leaned over, taking Tina's breast in his hand, and capturing her mouth with his, needing something, needing the connection. She attacked his lips, slipping her tongue into his mouth, demanding more sensation. He gave her what he could, all while feeling the steady rise of her orgasm.

She pulled back, gasping for air…and shouted his name.

"Dane!"

The climax ripped through her body and Dane felt it echo through his own. He had to have her, had to fuck her.

Raython lifted his head and rolled away, opening the space between her thighs.

"Fuck her, Warrior," he said. "Fill her."

"Dane, please."

The hunger surging through him sent him to his knees. Raython reached out, slipped his hand between Dane's legs, and cupped his balls, gently fingering them as Tina's hand pumped his cock. The double caress stole the breath from his body. Not even the foreign sensation of a masculine hand touching him could wilt his hard-on.

"Fuck her, Warrior. She's yours."

Dane snapped at the dragon's urging. He grabbed Tina's legs and spun her around until her open sex was spread before him.

Tina held her breath as he placed the thick head of his cock against her opening and began to push inside her. Her body was sensitized—primed for any touch, for any caress. He drove into her—hard, sinking into her pussy until he filled her completely.

"Yes," she whispered. Her tiny cry seemed to trigger something inside him. Dane pulled back and plunged in deep, filling her, stretching her.

Her hands gripped convulsively, grabbing whatever was near her. The depth of her soul knew that Raython held one hand and Dane held the other.

Dane's cock filled her cunt. She opened her mouth and screamed, the pleasure-pain too much to hold inside. He didn't stop. He drew back, always holding her hand, and plunged inside her.

Voices swirled through her head—Dane and Raython's—urging her higher, faster, making it impossible to resist. Long, steady thrusts, filling her pussy time and again until she couldn't contain the sensation.

"Come for me!" Dane shouted. And her body responded. The orgasm erupted from her cunt and spread through her body. As if she was truly connected to him, she felt the jolt vibrate through her pussy into Dane. His cum filled her vagina, hot and pulsing.

A tight grip formed around her left hand. Raython pressed up on his knees, holding her hand and Dane's. Raython tilted his head back and his cum shot forward splattering in trails across her stomach.

* * * * *

Tina woke up slowly, her mind waking with the slow sure knowledge that her body had been fucked beyond all recognition.

She cracked open her eyes as the reality came flooding into her head. Every memory of every touch reverberated through her body. She shifted and winced. The ache between her legs reminded her that the three of them hadn't stopped until early morning. They'd collapsed into a pile and fell into a heavy sleep.

She raised her head. Raython lay beside her. The covers were thrown away. His naked body bared to world.

But she knew something was missing.

Dane was no longer beside her.

He'd left her. A wail joined the frantic beat of her heart.

The rush of the downstairs toilet flushing sent her flying from the bed. She had to see him. Had to explain.

Except how did she explain everything that had happened? She didn't understand most of it herself.

Snagging her robe off the floor, she threw it on as she hurried down the stairs.

Her pride was slightly eased when she saw Dane hadn't fled for the door. He'd stopped to have a cup of coffee — started by her automatic timer. She crept into the kitchen, unsure of her reception.

Dane drank from his cup then paused as if he sensed her behind him. Slowly he turned.

Heat flowed through her body as she looked at him, melting her sex, and drawing moisture from deep inside.

His eyes were cool, distant, as he nodded her direction. She braced herself for his rejection, trying to slow her racing heart. But even as she stood there, she recognized that not all of this warmth was hers. Some of what she was feeling came from Dane. The strange ability to sense the other's emotions had lingered with the sunrise.

"You're leaving," she said.

"I need to get to work."

It was Sunday and she didn't think even the sheriff worked on Sunday, unless it was strictly necessary. He was trying to escape.

"About last night—"

He shook his head, stopping her words.

"I don't know what happened last night. Or what's going on." He took a long drink of hot coffee. "I just need to go."

Tina nodded.

A self-mocking smile curved Dane's lips. "You seem so accepting of this. Doesn't it bother you?" He waved his hand in the general direction of the bedroom upstairs. "We both fucked you last night. And you let it happen. Hell, *I* let it happen. I don't know how you can accept all this."

Tina shrugged and walked forward. She needed to touch him. Needed to connect with him in some way. "I saw it happen. I know what he's saying is the truth." She smiled, trying to lighten the mood. "And I got two incredible lovers out of the deal."

Dane nodded. But when she reached out to touch him—he pulled away. It was subtle and gentle but she knew he'd avoided her touch.

"I need to think about this, Tina. I need to think about everything."

He put his mug on the counter and walked away. She heard the front door slam shut seconds later. Unexpected tears welled up in her eyes and tripped over the edge. She stood there, listening to the sound of her own breath, feeling her cheeks grow wet.

"Please do not cry, Maiden." Raython's warm body pressed against her back. She relaxed into him, needing the comfort. "He will return. He is the one."

She shook her head. "You didn't see his eyes."

"He is our Warrior. He will fight for us."

She didn't answer. She couldn't. She didn't have Raython's confidence that Dane would return to her. To them.

And the thought of losing him made her chest ache. As if her heart would never beat the same without him.

Dane rubbed the center of his chest trying to ease the ache. It didn't feel like a heart attack but if ever a day deserved one, it would be this one. The pain had begun when he'd left Tina that morning. And hadn't stopped all day.

What made it worse was—he thought it was emotion that caused it. Damned if he could tell if it was his or hers. Ever since they'd—he stopped. He didn't really know what to call it. Had sex? Fucked? Made love?

Whatever it was, when the three of them had touched hands and climaxed together, something had happened. He'd thought about it all day, trying to figure out if it had been his imagination or some kind of electrical shock. He had no answers but something had changed. He was able to sense their emotions. Tina's were strongest, but Ray's were present as well.

Dane decided *that* was the foreign sense of anger he felt. Ray was pissed that Dane had left them. But damn it, he had a job to do and he needed to think—something he couldn't do around Tina.

"What are you doing here on a Sunday?"

Dane looked up. Agent Donavon, looking as formal as he had the previous day, stood in the doorway. Dane had been so lost in his thoughts he hadn't heard the other man walk in.

"Just catching up. Come in." He nodded to one of the two chairs in his office. "I'm assuming you're looking for me or you wouldn't be hanging around an empty office. Things are pretty quiet on a Sunday in this town." That was one of the reasons Dane liked it. He'd had his share of high-crime areas and explosive murder rates when he'd lived in Chicago. When he'd married Beth, they'd moved back here to get away. By the time they'd divorced, Dane had gotten himself elected Sheriff and felt like this was his town. And he was ready for the FBI to leave it.

Whatever was happening between him and Tina and Raython, it wasn't something that the government needed to become involved in.

"I was just checking to see if you'd heard anything else?" Donavon said, finally lowering himself into the chair.

"About what?"

"About that plane. I know how small towns are. The folks are more likely to talk to you than someone like me. Wanted to see if you'd heard any strange rumors floating around." Donavon gave a shrug which wasn't nearly as casual as he probably meant it to be. "Things like that sometimes lead us in the right direction. No matter how wild they sound at the time."

Dane shook his head. "I haven't even spoken with anyone except you...and Tina."

"And did she say anything? She seemed a little nervous when we were there yesterday."

Dane scratched his neck. "I think she was embarrassed at being caught with a younger, naked man in her house. Things like that get out, it could ruin a woman's reputation." He added a touch of warning to his voice. "She teaches at the fancy boarding school down the road. She can't afford to have her morals questioned."

The answer seemed to satisfy Donavon. He pursed his lips together and nodded. And waited. It was a technique interrogators used to get people to talk. Leave a heavy silence and someone will feel compelled to fill it. Typically, Dane would have waited him out but he was curious how much the FBI knew.

"What about that purple stuff you guys found? What was that?" Dane had been stunned when they'd found puddles of the purple liquid by the river on Tina's land. It had matched Ray's blood.

"It's a new kind of fuel. Very hush-hush, you understand."

"Ahh." Dane tried to look suitably impressed but wasn't sure he succeeded. Donavon was lying to him and doing a pretty good job of it but Dane knew the truth. The source of that purple liquid was currently hiding in Tina's house.

"Well, I guess that's it." Donavon stood and walked to the door. "You'll let me know if you hear anything." It wasn't a question so Dane didn't answer. "I'll be around for a few more days, keeping an eye on things."

The implied threat wasn't missed by Dane. He nodded and watched as the FBI agent left.

He would have to warn Tina.

Donavon wasn't going to give up.

By late afternoon, Dane had made deep inroads into his piles of backed-up paperwork. He could probably spend another few hours working but what was the point? He was stalling because he didn't know where he was going to go when he left the office. Home? Back to Tina's?

The work he'd done had been fairly mindless giving him plenty of opportunity to think but time hadn't helped. He was no closer to an answer than he'd been when he'd run from Tina's cabin this morning. He wanted her. He'd been dancing around her for almost a year trying to figure out how to approach a friend of his ex-wife's without the town exploding in scandal.

Like this wouldn't cause a scandal. He massaged his forehead with all ten fingers. *Dane, Tina, and a dragon.* That would get people talking.

It should have been simple to walk away but it wasn't. There was something about Tina that drew him. It had felt right last night when he'd fucked her for the first time. Even with another man there, it had felt right. The memories of seeing Raython with his mouth between Tina's legs, licking her sweet pussy. The amazed look of the other man as he'd learned the thrill of making a woman come with his mouth. Damn it, even *that* made his cock hard.

A strange restlessness pushed him to his feet. An urgency to move throbbed in his chest. He paced around the front of his desk, clenched and unclenching his right hand. Strange. It felt empty. It *was* empty—but it felt like there should be something in his grip. After circling his desk three times, he decided he wasn't going to get anything else done.

But he still hadn't decided where he was going when he left.

He knew what he'd find if he returned to Tina's cabin and he knew what would happen. He'd end up in bed with her and Raython. And he still had no idea how he felt about that. And that first time together. He'd never experienced anything like that before. It was like his orgasm had been magnified by three—like he was feeling Tina's and Ray's inside his own body.

His cock hardened as he walked to his car. Well, it hardened further. He'd spent much of the day fighting off a hard-on.

He started his car and pulled onto the main road. It took him a few minutes to realize he'd turned right, heading out of town toward Tina's house, not left toward his own. As he acknowledged the decision that he was going back to her place, a line of tension that had pulled on his shoulders all afternoon seemed to disappear.

But a new sensation began—like fire in his stomach. He gripped the steering wheel, pulling on it. He needed to go…needed to be somewhere. There was danger. Fear.

The cell phone buzz shattered his thoughts.

"Sheridan," he answered.

"Dane, we need help."

"Tina? What's wrong?" Her panic welled up in *his* gut and he floored the gas pedal. The need to get to her wiped out all the concerns from the afternoon.

"The Hunters. They've come for Raython. He ran out of here a few minutes ago and flew away."

"As in turned into a dragon and flew away?"

"Yes."

"Where did he go?"

"I don't know. I think toward Flattop. He was trying to lure the Hunters away from me. We can't let anything happen to him."

"I'll find him." He snapped the phone shut and looked out the window, toward the tall peak Tina had mentioned. Something circled the mountaintop. It looked like a bird but there was no way he should be able to see a bird from that distance. It had to be Raython. Four other dots filled the sky near the dragon.

Dane slammed on the brakes and spun around the tight corner. Dust filled the air as he hauled ass up the dirt road. It was early spring. Few tourists or locals would be on the trails. He kept his foot to the floor. They were attacking Raython.

Fury filled him and the need to howl clawed at the inside of his throat. Dane stretched his neck up, trying to break the tension. After a long moment, he realized it wasn't his own rage that filled him — it was Raython's.

Dane was connected to the dragon in the same mystical way he felt Tina's pain.

As if he could hear Raython's thoughts, one thing kept repeating through his head — protect his Maiden.

Chapter Six

Dane reached the parking lot of the popular trailhead and was glad to see it was empty. Grabbing his gun, he took off at a full run, up the trail. The first plateau wasn't far up the hill and that's where he found them.

A blue-green dragon crouched low. Pale purple flowed from wounds at his side as the dragon growled and snapped at three men. A fourth lay on the ground. Green blood poured from a gaping hole in his chest. Raython's teeth had obviously connected at least once. The other three men attacked him from three sides.

The fantastic reality of the picture before him had only a moment to sink in before he reacted like a cop.

"Drop your weapons." Dane sighted his gun on the middle attacker.

"It's the Warrior. Kill him," one of them commanded.

The nearest Hunter spun around and ran, full speed and sword drawn at Dane. Dane turned his gun and fired. The Hunter bounced backwards as the bullet struck him. He landed on his back. For an instant he froze, then kicked his legs out and was back on his feet. No visible wound.

Dane looked at the gun and the man stalking him.

"Human weapons won't kill us, Warrior. Surely you have some other way to defend your Maiden," the Hunter taunted as he strode forward. The threat against Tina sent fury exploding through Dane's chest and into his limbs. The Hunter casually spun his sword in his hand. Dane aimed and fired seven straight shots in the Hunter's chest. Even if it didn't kill him, the impact knocked him backwards. Dane scanned the area for a weapon. The sword of the fallen Hunter flashed in the sunlight. Dane fired again and ran, picking up the sword and spinning to face his attacker.

Beyond wooden sticks as a child, Dane had never experimented with any weapon bigger than a knife, but as his hand molded to the hilt, knowledge seemed to flow into his body. It wasn't a clear thought or specific direction—his body simply knew.

He lifted the sword and blocked the Hunter's downward stroke. Dane kicked the man in the chest, knocking him backwards. The fury turned to rage inside his head, inside his heart and he let it flow into his muscles. These men had threatened his Maiden. The Hunter flew with the force of Dane's thrust and landed hard on the ground. Dane followed, raising the sword and plunging it deep into the chest of his attacker.

A voice in his head whispered that he'd just casually killed a man but the concern disappeared as the body around the sword crumpled to dust, leaving behind only tiny puddles of green blood.

Raython's scream snapped Dane back to the fight. He whipped around in time to see a Hunter twist a sword in Raython's side. The dragon howled again.

"Back away," Dane commanded. He walked forward, the sword comfortable in his palm. The Hunter jerked the sword from Raython's side and faced Dane. He was vaguely aware of Raython's attention on the remaining Hunter. Raython would handle him. Dane swung the sword with all his strength. *This* Hunter didn't assume that Dane was inexperienced. They fought, metal crashing against metal, each stroke vibrating Dane's arms but instead of weakening, his rage carried him on— making him stronger. The world collapsed around him until all he could see was his attacker. All he knew was he must kill him.

Dane beat him back, stalking him and weakening the Hunter with hard, furious blows. The man's eyes widened as he realized Dane was winning. He stumbled, tripping over a rock and landing on his back. Battle strategy allowed no room for thought or consideration. Dane knocked the sword from the

Hunter's hand and drove the point of his weapon into the man's chest.

Again, he evaporated into a puddle of blood.

Dane stared at the remains, his heart pounding loud in his ears, his breath harsh and shallow as he regained control of his body. And his mind. He looked over. The final Hunter was in a crumpled pile, wounds dripping with green blood. Raython stood over the body. He opened his mouth and fire exploded from his throat, incinerating the Hunter and leaving a pile of dust behind. The flames stopped. He turned to the remaining body and repeated the same treatment. All that was left of the four Hunters was dust and blood.

"Will there be more coming—"

Fear. Pain. Rage. The triple emotions assaulted him— binding his stomach into knots. Raython cried out.

Dane clenched his teeth and fought the urge to double over.

"What is that?"

He looked up as Raython raised his head.

"Tina." *Our Maiden*, they said in unison.

More Hunters. After her.

Her fear built and the anger grew with it. She was strong but she needed help.

Dane ran toward the dragon. "Get us there. Now." Dane moved through instinct. Just as when he'd picked up the sword his body knew how to use it, he knew that Raython was his companion, his partner.

Raython lowered his head and presented a space on his neck.

Dane climbed on—the Hunter's sword still gripped in his hand—and wrapped his arms around as much of Raython's throat as he could.

Muscles contracted beneath him as Raython leapt into the air. Cold rushed past him as the dragon flew. The steady flaps of his wings rocked Dane back and forth. He climbed high and then plunged down screaming a warning as he dropped. Tina's emotions continued to bombard him. They combined with the rage burning inside his chest. Raython screamed and Dane echoed the sound.

The dragon hit the ground hard and Dane leapt from his back. The world was strangely clear—focused to the point of pain. Without thought he catalogued the situation. One Hunter lay on the ground, a dribble of bright green flowing from his forehead. Seven others backed Tina against the wall of the cabin. She gripped an iron frying pan between both hands, a sturdy weapon against her attackers. They circled, not able to get close before she would swing for their heads.

A corner of Dane's mind admired Tina's strength and ingenuity but the violence in him barely recognized it. He grasped the Hunter sword in his fist and strode forward. The Hunters immediately forgot Tina and turned to face Dane and Raython.

One raised his sword challenging Dane. A second dared Raython. The third crumpled to the ground. Tina stood over him, her cast iron skillet marked with green blood. Dane grunted his approval then turned his focus on the creatures that dared come near his Maiden. A battle cry, ripped from deep inside his soul, shattered the near silence of the forest and Dane plunged into the crowd. He lost focus on anything beyond the men attacking him. His sword was in constant motion, tearing through Hunter flesh, his body exulting as each died shuddering under the weight of his blade. Vague awareness of heat and flames told him that Raython was fighting the demons as well.

Dane didn't stop. He moved forward, cutting down anything that dared challenge him.

Two Hunters lunged into his path. Hatred and fear illuminated their eyes but Dane didn't care. He raised his sword and swung. The slow, steady thunk of his blade shattering their bodies barely penetrated his thoughts.

He was the Warrior and he would defend his Maiden.

* * * * *

Dane swung around—looking for more. Where were they? He would tear the flesh from their bones. The sword fit his hand to perfection, a part of him. He scanned the battlefield, barely noticing the green bloodstains or the burning patches of grass. Or the blood dripping from his own wounds.

Kill. He must kill those who dared touch his Maiden. He could smell them, their vile stench lingering in the air even as their bodies were incinerated by Raython's fire.

The field around him was empty. They were gone. The threat was gone, but his body didn't relax. Adrenaline, fear and fury still flowed through his veins.

The soft press of a footstep in the grass spun him around, his sword raised and in motion. He swung around and down. His mind cleared an instant before he struck, realizing it was Tina. He jerked his momentum, pulling back and away, narrowly missing her.

She froze as the blade flashed inches from her body.

"Oh my God, Tina, baby." He drove the point into the ground and reached for her, silently thanking God she hadn't moved. "Are you okay? Did I hurt you?"

She shook her head and he could feel her heart pounding. She'd been terrified but she was safe. He wrapped his arms around her and pulled her against his chest. Seconds later, she was struggling. It took another few moments for Dane to realize he was crushing her.

He released her and stepped back. Red blood dripped from the cut on his arm and mixed with the green on his hands. With all the energy pouring through his body, he should have been shaking but his grip was rock solid. And strong. He could break her with one hand.

"Dane—" She reached out.

He backed away. "Don't touch me." Concern filled her eyes. "Not now. I don't want to hurt you."

"You would never hurt me," she said with such assurance that Dane wanted to howl. How could she trust him so much? She didn't know the hatred running through his body. The need to kill. Destroy those who dared approach her.

"The Hunters are gone," Raython announced as he walked up beside Tina. He'd returned to his human form at some point.

"Will more come after her?"

"No. They followed the energy of our first Joining. Now that that is done, there will be no way for future Hunters to find us."

Dane nodded, his body barely containing the fury still riding his veins.

"Why don't we all get cleaned up?" Tina suggested with a hesitant smile. Damn, he'd frightened her. He shook his head. "Dane, you're hurting and you're covered in green muck. You need to—"

"I think our Warrior needs a moment to gather himself," Raython said, placing his hand on Tina's shoulder. "Perhaps you would care to go upstairs and bathe."

Dane's mind—so clear and sharp moments ago—was fuzzy and confused. He nodded and turned to go. He only knew he had to get away from Tina before he hurt her.

Tina watched Dane's back as he trudged into the cabin. It was as if the life had disappeared from him and all that was left was a shell.

"Do not worry. I have heard of this when a man is not trained to be a Warrior. He was not prepared for the power and energy that gave him the strength to defend you."

"But I can't leave him like that." She turned and looked up at the dragon. Her own fears faded into insignificance. The devastation on Dane's face had wiped them clean. "He's hurt."

"He will heal as I have." He held up his arms. Dried purple marked his skin but there were no cuts. "We are Joined. His body will take on the healing properties of mine."

Tina nodded. The physical wounds she could have possibly healed, but the pain in his gaze—she didn't know.

"I don't think he should be alone."

"And he will not be. Give him a few moments to quiet himself and then you will go show him that he is the Warrior and the man for you."

She felt her eyes widen. "How am I supposed to do that?"

"By giving and speaking your love for him."

Tell Dane she loved him? Could she really do that?

She did love him, after all. It seemed so simple standing there. She'd *been* in love with him. Raython's presence had merely triggered that love and drawn it to the forefront. She rolled back her shoulders and stared at the upstairs window. She'd given him enough time.

He'd protected her—now it was time for Tina to take care of her Warrior.

She quickly washed up in the downstairs bathroom, her fingers shaking slightly as she watched green blood swirl down her drain. Raython appeared with one of her robes and held the edges open. She slipped her arms inside. He closed the soft material around her and held her back against him.

"Remember that he is our Warrior. You do not have to be frightened of him or of the emotions inside you." He was reading her mind, again. The sensation was strange but not intrusive. It seemed natural for him to know her thoughts.

She nodded and went upstairs. The bathroom door was partially open so she pressed her hand to the panel and stepped inside. Dane's massive presence filled her shower. She stood in the doorway and stared at his naked form, water cascading over the grooves and curves of his muscles. *He is truly beautiful.* Rugged and masculine and pure, powerful animal.

He didn't look up at she entered. He dropped his head against the shower wall, concealing his face.

"Tina, you shouldn't be here."

"Here is where I need to be."

"I don't want to hurt you." His words were slow and harsh, as if he was speaking through clenched teeth.

"Dane—"

He lifted his head, finally turning to look at her. The weight of the last two days hung on his shoulders.

"Did you see what I did to those men? I killed them and if there had been more, I would have killed them too."

"You were defending me and Raython. And they weren't men. They were demons." She placed her hand on his shoulder. Dane wanted to draw away but couldn't find the strength. Her touch was warm and some of the pain inside him began to melt away. "You became the Warrior when you were needed, but you won't stay like that forever."

She continued to stroke him, rubbing her hand down his back, refilling the well of his humanity with each touch. The pure comfort and companionship that flowed from her presence soothed the mental wounds he'd caused his psyche. He lifted his head and turned to look at her. It struck him that while he'd fucked her last night, he'd spent very little time loving her.

He leaned down and placed a whispered kiss across her mouth, breathing in her taste. Her lips chased his, opening in a feminine welcome he wasn't strong enough to resist. The Warrior screamed inside him to grab her and take her but Dane brutally crushed the urge. He looked into Tina's eyes—love pouring out of her gaze—and a humbleness filled him that silenced the Warrior's cries.

Last night there had been desperation, need.

Tonight there would be love and tenderness.

He shut off the water and climbed out of the shower. Tina was there with a towel and quickly dried him. The fluffy towel sensitized his skin as she stroked every inch of him. He stood, letting her minister to him, knowing she needed this as much as he did. When he was dry, he straightened and faced her—bare and open. Letting her see the man that she was binding herself too, because he knew after tonight, there would be no way he could let her go.

She shrugged her robe off her shoulders and took one step away, as if she too was giving him a chance to see her. All of her.

"You're beautiful, Tina."

A hint of red bloomed in her cheeks and Dane told himself he would tell her of her beauty every day of their lives together.

"Come with me, Dane."

She said his name distinctly and he understood the significance. They were the Maiden and the Warrior but they were also Dane and Tina. And that is who they would be tonight.

She led him into the bedroom and with a sensuality he didn't think she even understood, she crawled onto the bed and opened her arms to him. He followed, laying down beside her, their bodies touching, their eyes matched and peaceful.

He made love to her, being as gentle as he could, drawing on the silence in his mind to soothe her fears. Her body was so sensitive—reacting to every caress. He licked and kissed her breasts, tasting the firm flesh but never applying his teeth. He didn't want her memories of him to be the creatures covered in green blood. He would be a man worthy of loving her. She twisted on the sheets, moaned sweetly as he smoothed his hand over her stomach down her legs. He followed the path with his lips, learning the crease where her legs met her body, dipping into the hot warmth of her pussy.

Now it was just the two of them and there was no rush, no urgency. This was about loving and touching. He pushed his tongue into her slit and moaned at the warm rush of liquid that greeted him. He took his time, savoring her flavor and the delicate moans that were breaking from the back of her throat.

"So sweet," he whispered.

"Please, Dane, I need you." Her climax was rising but she didn't want to come without him inside her.

He raised his head and she could feel the conflicting emotions rattling through him. He wanted to keep licking her, loving her gently. The fear that he might return to the violence of the Warrior tore at him.

Now she understood how Raython seemed to comprehend her worries before she did. "I love you," she whispered. "And I trust you." As she spoke she wrapped her hands around his upper arms and pulled, encouraging him to come over her. "You won't hurt me, Dane." He held himself above her, his hard cock pressing against her pussy, close but not entering her. "Come inside me."

Tension zinged through his body and she knew he was fighting himself. She smoothed her hands up his shoulders and waited, giving him the time he needed. He looked up and stared into her eyes.

"I love you." The low whisper of his voice wrapped around her heart. He took a deep breath, placed the head of his cock at her entrance, and slowly pushed in.

They came together in slow, luxurious strokes, voices blending together, their bodies matching perfectly as they made the long ride to climax.

* * * * *

Dane pulled her back against his chest and insinuated his hand between her legs, cupping the pussy he now considered his. He slipped his middle finger into her warmth, tickling her clit. She sighed contentedly and even without seeing her face, he could tell she was smiling. She would accept more. If he chose to roll her over and push himself into her, she would welcome him.

She'd accepted his darkness. After coming down from his battle berserk, he'd realized what he'd done. He didn't regret killing the Hunters. There would have been no other way to stop them. But the way he'd reveled in the fight—his body almost exulting in the power to destroy. That was what frightened him most.

Tina's acceptance had smoothed that over. It still lurked beneath the surface and probably would for a long time. And if someone dared threaten his Maiden again, he knew the Warrior would rise inside him. He would be there to fight for her. Just as Raython would be there to protect her.

The mental reminder of the other man cleared out the last of Dane's post-orgasmic daze. Raython was still here and it was clear he was staying around. Raython was as bound to Tina as Dane was. And he'd defended her just as strongly.

But if Raython stayed, he would do more than protect her—he would continue to be her lover.

Dane stared up at the ceiling. Could he accept that? He couldn't let Tina go. He loved her. She was a part of him. So was Raython.

"Where is Raython?" he asked, knowing Tina wasn't asleep.

"Downstairs, I think." She looked over her shoulder. "He sent me to you. Saying you would need my comfort."

Damn. The dragon was right again.

Dane shifted, pressing his growing cock against her butt and resetting his hand between her legs, giving him better access to her opening. She was getting wet.

"Would you like me to summon him?" Dane asked, once again finding himself falling into the formal language of Raython's world. "Shall I call him up here to fuck you?"

Her pussy fluttered at the thought but Tina hesitated. And that eased Dane's heart. She wanted the dragon to join them but she was concerned about Dane's reaction.

"You enjoy him, I know."

Tina took a deep breath and considered her answer. She couldn't lie. She wouldn't. The triad joining had bound them all but she knew that Dane could just as easily pull away. She didn't know what she would do if that happened.

"I do," she said speaking from her heart. "But I also enjoy just being with you." She turned in his arms and smoothed her hand down his chest. "I don't know what I'm supposed to say or feel anymore. It seems so strange to want two men."

Dane nodded but didn't speak.

"I mean, I love having you inside me. And tonight has been wonderful." She shrugged. "Last night was wonderful as well—with both of you." She looked into his eyes. "I guess I need to know how you feel about it. How you feel about Raython?"

Dane rolled to his back, drawing Tina with him. She pushed up on her arm so she could see his eyes.

"I don't know," he finally admitted. "I've been trying to deal with it all day. At times, it pisses me off to think of another man touching you. But last night, watching Ray with his mouth between your legs." He brushed the hair away from her face. "It was hot. And I wanted you to have it. I wanted you to have all the pleasure you could." He smiled and shook his head. "And I knew that soon it would be my turn to make you scream."

She let the silence build for a moment before asking the question she knew hung between them. "So, what happens now?"

Dane paused. She felt it in his body. Then he smiled. "Now, we summon the dragon and the Warrior and Protector make love to the Maiden." Tina opened her mouth but Dane shook his head. "We'll deal with tomorrow then."

She licked her lips, not knowing precisely what she should do. Dane took the responsibility from her.

"Raython," he called softly. "Our Maiden has need of you." Even as he spoke, Dane pulled Tina over him. He lifted her up and spread her legs until she straddled him, then wasted no time in sliding into her pussy. Tina felt her sex relax around him, welcoming him back inside where he belonged. She gripped his shoulders as she savored the deep penetration.

When he was fully seated inside her, Dane stroked his fingers down her sides, over her hips until his warm hands covered her ass cheeks. He cupped her and pressed her against him, rubbing their bodies together. Tina's eyes drooped closed. It was so good, feeling every inch of him.

His fingertips brushed the sensitive crack between her cheeks, tickling her dark opening. She gasped and snapped her head back, staring at her lover. Was he really suggesting what she thought he was suggesting?

Dane looked over her shoulder and she realized Raython had entered the room. "Is she not beautiful, Protector?" Dane separated her ass cheeks just slightly baring her to Raython's view.

"Yes, Warrior, she looks most enticing while mounted on your cock."

Tina felt his hunger—not only in his words, but inside him. She could sense his desire to fuck her ass. The image sent wild flutters through her sex. She'd only ever imagined it, never dreamed anyone would. Raython's hungers heightened her own. As she was sorting through the emotions and sensations running through her body, she stared down at Dane.

"Will you accept him?" Dane asked. He reached up and brushed her hair back away from her face. "You want him. I can feel it." He stroked his fingers against her anus. "You want both of us, filling you, coming inside you."

His voice was the final level of seduction and Tina could resist any longer. "Yes."

"Do not worry, Maiden," Raython said softly as his hands joined Dane's on her skin. "I will be well oiled and I have made my rod slightly smaller to not cause you any pain."

Tina remembered he'd told her could control the size of his cock. She tensed as she felt his fingers grow slippery and begin to slide across her skin, dipping into her opening, massaging gently.

"Relax, baby, I won't let him hurt you."

Tina nodded and tried to focus on something besides what was happening to her. She wanted this but still, it was frightening.

"Kiss me, honey." She followed Dane's whispered command, reaching up to his mouth, feeling the shift of his cock inside her. Their mouths met and opened, each seemingly desperate for the taste of the other.

Pressure built against her ass as Raython began the slow, tight penetration. Tina instantly recognized that he had indeed changed the size of his cock. There as no way this was the same shaft that had filled her pussy. It felt thick but nothing compared to when he'd fucked her.

Dane held her steady while Raython pushed into her. When she tensed, he soothed her, kissing her, squeezing her breasts, whispering to her. The words filled her as surely as their cocks.

"That's it, honey. Feel him. Feel me. Do you like it? Having both of us inside you?"

She nodded, unable to speak. Raython continued to press, the sensation growing tighter and more painful. Every inch that slipped into her was new. It was impossible to keep her mind focused on the pain when so much pleasure was overwhelming her body.

"Enough," Dane commanded. "Only pleasure tonight."

"Yes, Warrior."

"Now, we fuck her. Slowly."

Tina shivered at Dane's command and the slow withdrawal of his cock. She whimpered at the loss but sighed as he slid back into her. As if on cue, Raython pulled out. The lube he'd used allowed him to slip easily inside her. Slowly, he penetrated her again, pushing a little deeper.

She gasped.

"You like that?" Dane asked. The full weight of his cock inside her was more than enough but the added entrance of Raython's cock into her ass was too powerful for her to combat. She nodded and reached for his mouth with hers. The delicate twining of his tongue distracted her as Raython pushed the last few inches into her.

"Let us make her come hard, Warrior. I love to hear her scream when she finds her pleasure."

Fire exploded in Dane's eyes at Raython's words and Tina felt them resonate in her pussy. "Yes," he agreed, his eyes holding hers captive. "Let's make her scream with pleasure."

Both men moved in time, withdrawing and penetrating in a delicious rhythm that left no part of her body free from their touch. She bit her lower lip to keep from screaming and dropped her head on Dane's chest as Raython took control and began to thrust into her ass. The pain was sweet and the gentle slides built into pleasure as Dane rocked slowly against her. Raython continued the slow, steady pulses, never driving too deep, just illuminating the sensitive nerves with each pass.

"That's it. He's close, can you feel it?"

Again Tina nodded. On the edges of her own pleasures lingered Raython's and Dane's, combining and increasing her own. "Feel him come inside you." Dane's voice moved inside her head like a caress. She arched her back and pushed back against Raython's thrust. She moaned, feeling him slide deeper. "That's it. Take him. Let him fill you."

She felt Dane's words inside her head—encouraging her, driving her on—like he was a part of her, already inside her.

She braced herself against Dane, holding her hands on his shoulders and rocked in time with Raython. Dane gripped her hips, moving with her to keep his cock inside her. Raython's pace picked up but he was still gentle. The steady press of his shaft rubbed her hard against Dane's cock.

"Come inside her," Dane commanded. He gripped Raython's hand where it was pressed against Tina's hip. The dragon raised his head and stared into Dane's eyes. Ray reached out slowly and placed his hand on Tina's. His stare bore into Dane and without word, Dane knew what to do. He covered Tina's free hand with his, completing the triangle.

Raython tipped his head back and groaned as he thrust into Tina's tight passage. Dane felt it as if it was his own orgasm. The sound and fury seemed to set off her climax and she shivered in Dane's arms. The warm contractions of her pussy along his cock were enough to trigger his orgasm and he poured himself into Tina's welcoming sex.

They held themselves still all three bodies trapped and entwined together.

Raython's voice whispered across the silence. "Three points to complete the plane of love."

Chapter Seven

Dane dragged himself out of bed at the sound of a car engine coming up the driveway. It was barely seven in the morning. Who the hell would be visiting Tina at this hour? He padded over to the window and looked out.

Donavon. The FBI agent got out of his car and looked around. Before walking to the door, he strolled through the lawn, stopping at the burned patches. Splatters of bright green Hunter blood were scattered across the grass. Donavon knelt down and stuck his finger into the viscous liquid. He rubbed it between his thumb and forefinger.

Dane pulled on his jeans anticipating the ring of the doorbell. When it sounded, Tina rolled over and looked up at him. Love and lust combined together in his heart as his watched her. Raython lay behind her—the doorbell hadn't woken him but Tina's movements seemed to disturb his sleep. He grumbled and pulled her back against his chest.

"Who is it?" Tina asked. Her voice was husky and soft. And sent a shaft of need into his cock. It was all so new but still that seemed like a powerful reaction to a simple question. He momentarily wondered how long this intense connection between them would last, then decided he didn't care. Tina was his and Raython belonged to both of them.

"It's Donavon."

Fear erupted in her eyes and she placed a protective hand on Raython's arm. Dane waited for the jealousy to hit him but it wasn't there. He knew how Tina felt about Raython and about him—he had her love, her desire. He could feel it pounding through his body even as it did through hers.

"Don't worry. I'll handle it."

He walked to the bed, leaned over and kissed her. The hot, wild taste of her mouth almost tempted him to stay but the doorbell rang again. Donavon wouldn't go away.

"I'll be back," he said.

As he walked down the stairs, he felt every inch the Warrior Raython claimed him to be. His Maiden and Protector were up in his bed. Now, he just had to get rid of the interloper before his castle was secure.

He opened the door.

"Good morning," Dane greeted, leaning against the doorframe, not letting the man see beyond him. Raython was more than likely to walk down the stairs naked again.

Donavon's only reaction was a slight tightening around his eyes but beyond that there was no indication he found it strange that Dane was filling Tina's doorway.

"Morning. Sorry to bother you so early but there was another incident yesterday."

"Another plane?" Dane asked with as much innocence as he could muster.

"Uh, yes. Very similar to the first one." The clever light in Donavon's eyes warned Dane not to underestimate the man. "You wouldn't know anything about these new reports, would you?"

"Me?" Dane drew on his years of training and years of watching criminals lie and kept his eyes on the other man. "No. I have no idea what's going on."

Donavon stepped away, walking to the edge of the porch and looking over the side. Dane had no choice but to follow him. He should have cleaned up the Hunters' blood, he realized, but there had been other, more important things on his mind at the time. Like fucking Tina. Feeling her tight cunt wrapped around his cock. And Raython joining them—binding them. He'd needed that. Needed the two of them to keep him sane. The battle rage still lurked in his chest, ready to break free at the first sign of attack.

"Would you mind telling me what that green substance is on the lawn?"

Dane shrugged. "I have no idea."

"It seems remarkably similar to the purple liquid we found in the woods."

"I thought you said that was a new kind of fuel."

"I lied." Donavon turned and faced him, his stance aggressive, the light in his eyes daring Dane. "We don't know what that stuff is. We shot at something and this stuff leaked from it. Our labs can't identify it. I think something strange is going on and I think you and the woman who lives here know more than you're letting on."

The Warrior responded to the implied threat. His hand curled into a fist, ready to defeat any who might harm his Maiden. Dane's chest rose and fell in short heavy breaths, filling his body with energy, strength, power…then it hit him. Sharp in his groin—tension and need.

Tina's. And Raython's. They were making love. He could feel it. Feel the rise of arousal that flowed between them, the love created by their three connecting points. His cock hardened, pressing against his jeans. He needed to return to his woman. Needed to give her the pleasure.

"Sheriff, are you listening to me?"

Dane blinked and looked up, refocusing on Donavon.

"Actually, no."

"I think you'd better tell me what you know about these spots on the grass. Whatever it is, it isn't natural. It could be dangerous."

Tina's need was building. Raython had pushed her hard and fast, close to orgasm but not giving her the release. Dane knew Raython was waiting for him to return to give their Maiden the first climax of the morning.

"I honestly can't tell you anything about those spots on the grass. If you want to call your crew out and test them, you're welcome to." Dane was pleased he sounded so professional considering his mind was back in the house, mentally driving his cock into his woman.

"And you're sure you didn't see anything?"

The front door opened quietly. Dane and Donavon turned at the sound. Tina stepped onto the porch wearing nothing but Dane's shirt, buttoned in two places—one across her breasts, one at the bottom to keep the tails closed and her pussy private. She sagged against the wall, looking exhausted and aroused. He thought she would speak—to plead with him to come to her—but Raython walked out. He'd pulled on shorts but there was no hiding his erection pressing against the material. He wrapped his arm around Tina's waist, sliding his hand inside the shirt and pulling her back against him.

Along with the pulsing in his cock, Dane felt his lips try to pull up in a smile. *In for a penny, in for a pound.* No doubt this would spread around town.

Dane watched his lovers for a moment then turned back to the FBI agent.

"I've been a little busy," he said with a slow, seductive smile. And he could have sworn there was hint of red along Donavon's collar.

"Yes, well, I'll let you get back to your…friends." He walked the length of the porch nodding to Tina and Raython. Tina didn't notice. Her eyes were closed and her head tipped back against the wall. Raython's hand stroked softly across her belly. Dane could almost feel the caresses on his own skin.

As Donavon walked by, Raython leaned forward and placed a hot, openmouthed kiss on Tina's throat. She moaned. And there was a quiet hitch in the back of Donavon's throat. He stopped and stared at the seductive tableau before him. Raython trailed his tongue up the side of Tina's neck, then looked at Donavon. "Delicious."

Donavon swallowed and spun around, stomping down the steps.

"I'm going to take a sample of this green substance," Donavon announced. He paused and once again dared Dane with his eyes. "And I'll be keeping an eye on this area."

Dane nodded and strolled down the porch to Tina and Raython. "Good day, Agent Donavon," he said.

Tina opened her eyes as he drew near and reached up, wrapping her hand around his neck and pulling him down, demanding his kiss. He quickly forgot the FBI agent's existence, knowing he had to ease the pulsing need in Tina's cunt. She moved forward, pressed against him by Raython, who continued to kiss and lick her neck, lifting her hair to reach the back.

Dane cuddled his cock between her thighs and was rewarded as Tina rubbed against him. Her whimper warned him she was close but damn if he was going to let her come without his cock inside her. He hitched one leg up, widening the space between her legs for his hips and giving him direct contact with her clit.

"Soon, baby, soon I'll be inside you," he whispered against her lips.

The clatter of metal against glass jerked Dane from his sensual fog. He ripped his mouth away and spun around, putting Tina behind him.

Agent Donavon stood on the lawn, a glass jar and spatula in his hand—his eyes locked on the three people on the porch. This time the blush crept past his collar up his cheeks. Dane looked down. The man's trousers were tenting.

"I'll just be leaving now." Steeling his jaw, he strode quickly to his car.

Dane smiled. If there was a Mrs. Agent Donavon, she was going to enjoy her husband's homecoming.

"Dane, please, I need you."

With a nod to Raython, they moved as one, stumbling into the house, away from any more prying eyes. Dane didn't doubt that Donavon was serious when he said he would be keeping an eye on them for a while. But that concern was for later. Now, he needed to satisfy his woman.

As soon as the door closed, Tina groaned and pulled herself up. Raython helped, lifting her hips so her open pussy was directly matched to Dane's cock.

"Please, Dane, come inside me."

While Raython held her, Dane opened his fly, his cock springing forward, reaching for the cunt that belonged to him. He slipped his cock inside, slowly penetrating her, filling her inch by inch in a way he knew would drive her insane. She wanted it hard and fast but he wanted to enjoy sliding into her. Feeling her tight passage cling to him.

When he was balls-deep, and could go no further, he felt Raython shift, giving the majority of Tina's weight to Dane. He knew he was lubing up, ready to slide into her ass.

Tina rocked on Dane's cock, trying to get him to move but Dane held her still, keeping her in place for the second penetration. The thought made Dane's heart try to burst from his chest. She wrapped her arms around his neck burying her face against his shoulder. Her whimper told him when Raython started to enter her. Dane whispered softly to her, helping her relax and let herself be filled. He tickled her clit, making her cunt tighten around his shaft.

The pressure to thrust was incredible, but he held back, needing to have her completely filled. The dragon pushed in slowly, still gentle. Dane held her, holding her ass cheeks wide until Raython was full-hilt inside her as well. By silent agreement, neither male moved, letting her adjust.

Tina lifted her head and glared at Dane.

"Damn it, both of you. Fuck me."

She watched the arrogant smile that Dane flashed over her shoulder and knew Raython had one to match. She was going to be well challenged keeping these two men in line. But she was up to it.

Then they started to move and all thoughts but the drive to satisfaction left her head. Dane leaned back against the door, pumping his hips up, driving deep and hard while Raython held her still, keeping her in place for Dane's thrusts and slowly pulling his cock out of her ass. The heavy pounding in her pussy, countered by the almost delicate fucking of her ass, sent all her nerves into overdrive. Dane's hands cupped her breasts, pinching and teasing the tight peaks.

She knew she was lost, totally in their control, her pleasure was theirs and theirs belonged to her. She relaxed and let them take her. She dropped her head back. Dane's mouth opened on her pulse. The delicious heat flooded her body. The bodies around her grew tight, ready to explode. She felt Dane's rise to orgasm and it pushed her higher.

"That's it, Maiden, feel the pleasure we share." She felt more than heard Raython's voice in her head. It infiltrated her being until she accepted him as a part of her—and Dane as well.

The energy ricocheted between them until she could no longer tell who was coming and who was on the verge. Her body shook, her arms clutched Dane but beyond that, she knew nothing except the long wave of pleasure.

She opened her eyes and stared at the tangled mass of limbs. They'd somehow ended up on the floor and from their position—halfway down the three steps into the living room. It hadn't been a graceful slump.

"Is everyone okay?" she asked, lifting her head and surveying the damage.

The two men grunted. She looked at her lovers. Their eyes were closed and their bodies wrung out in exhaustion. There was still a lot to work out. Real life was going intrude on their sensual world but for now, she was just going to enjoy being with these two men. A spear of sunlight broke through the window casting a long shadow across their bodies.

She smiled and remembered the words of the spell.

"By daylight come my loves to me."

Epilogue

Dane ground his back teeth together and slapped his hand on top of his desk. The sound jolted his secretary. Her head snapped up then she smiled sympathetically.

"Should I get your wife on the phone?"

Barely able to speak, Dane nodded. He knew he should be embarrassed by the fact that Jennie seemed to understand what was happening but he couldn't. His body couldn't handle the emotion of embarrassment when fucking was on the line. It had been going on all morning and his cock was ready to explode.

Dane and Tina had married four months ago—about six months after Raython had landed in the forest behind her house. The three of them lived in Tina's cabin. There was plenty of speculation about the relationship and Tina's weird "cousin" but few said anything out loud. Dane had become used to the sly looks and "nudge-nudge" comments. It was just something he had to live with. Ray was a part of their lives.

But it was moments like this that Dane wanted to strangle the dragon.

"Tina's on line one."

Dane nodded and sighed with relief as Jennie closed his office door. He grabbed the handset.

"Baby, what are you doing to me?"

Tina panted in his ear. "I'm sorry. It's not me." The soft little groan that she gave moments before she was going to come slipped through the phone line. Dane felt it curl around his cock a like hand, rubbing him, squeezing him. "It's Raython. He's been on me all morning."

Dane felt everything. "I know, baby. Tell him to knock it off. I can't concentrate."

"I've tried. He just keeps...oh God...licking me." She screamed and Dane almost came in his pants.

"Hand the phone to Raython," he said, knowing she was useless for long moments after she'd come.

"Hello, my Warrior."

Though he tried to resist it, Raython's voice sent another strike to his groin. When Ray was loving Tina, his voice became pure sex and Dane couldn't fight its pull. It brought to mind the full impact of Raython's mouth. Dane had learned its power five weeks ago.

"What are you doing, Raython?" he sighed, trying to sound irritated and not aroused.

"Tongue-fucking our Maiden. She is most delicious."

Dane closed his eyes and ground his teeth together. "I know, but could you—"

"You should come home and fuck your wife. She needs you."

Dane glanced at the clock. It was only one o'clock. "I'll be home at six," he said firmly.

"Now."

"I have work to do."

There was a silence on the other end of the phone. Then Raython said, "My tongue is quite strong. I can continue licking her pussy until you get home. I will prepare her. Arouse her but not let her come so she will be most hungry for your touch."

Dane felt a punch in his gut. He couldn't last another five hours of this. He'd be insane and Tina would be desperate for some cock.

"I'll be home as soon as I can," he growled. He slammed the phone down and quickly straightened his desk. The tension in his crotch wasn't fading. Raython obviously was not taking any chances. He was going to keep on Tina until Dane walked through the door.

He grabbed his coat, thankful that it was long enough to hide the erection that was obvious against the button fly of his jeans. He walked into the reception area.

"Jennie, I've got to head home."

She nodded. "Will you be back this afternoon?"

Dane remembered the need in Tina's voice. Raython had been licking her all morning. It was going to take both him and Dane hours to satisfy her. "Probably not. Uhm, frozen pipe." *Mine.*

He made it to the cabin in record time—Raython had increased the pressure. Even before Dane walked in, he knew that Ray had kept Tina on the verge of coming since he'd left the office.

It was a beautiful sight that greeted him. Tina lay naked on the couch. One hand massaged her breasts and the other was buried in Raython's hair, holding him in place. Her hair was wild, stretched out across the pillows as if she'd ripped it from the tight bun she wore while she was working.

Raython was also naked, kneeling on the floor with his face buried between her legs. Tina's eyes fluttered open and she saw him. Reaching for him, she whimpered.

"Oh, thank God, you're home."

Raython lifted his head and turned to face him. Her sexual fluids glittered around his mouth.

"I have prepared her for your rod, Warrior."

As Dane walked forward, he began undoing the button fly, jerking his jeans down until his cock was free. The atmosphere was strange, like he was taking part of some momentous occasion. Dane knelt down, moving into the space between her legs that Raython had vacated.

The dragon leaned forward, swiping his tongue across her slit. Tina shivered, her body primed. Then Raython lifted his head and turned to Dane. He moved toward Ray, accepting the other man's mouth on his, his tongue twining around his. He could taste the warm flavor of Tina's sex. The blatant sexuality of the kiss struck him. Dane drew back, more than a little surprised that he'd just allowed another man to kiss him, but the concern faded into insignificance as he stared at Tina, open and waiting for him.

"You are most ready to fuck our Maiden, Warrior."

Raython crawled up to lay beside Tina. He fingered her breasts, plucking at her nipples, drawing them high and tight as if to present them to Dane.

He looked at Tina to stabilize himself. She stared back at him with clear eyes and whispered, "Come inside me, Dane."

His heart exploded with love and need. He pushed forward. The familiar grip of her cunt made him groan. It was exciting and familiar and felt like coming home. He drove fully into her, seating himself to the hilt. Tina's back arched and she came. The contractions that massaged his cock lured him to follow her but he stopped, wanting to watch her. She was so beautiful when she came—her breasts flushed a pale red, her eyes sparkled.

As she sank back on the couch, Dane looked up. Raython was watching him. He nodded. "Very nice, Warrior. Give her more." With that, the dragon bent down and began to kiss on her breasts, sucking long and deep on her nipples. The sight of his mouth on her skin and Tina's tiny moan made Dane grow impossibly harder. It was like Raython was half of himself. There was no jealousy. Only pleasure.

Dane leaned forward, moving over her, pounding harder and harder into her sex, losing all ability to control his actions, only knowing he needed to be inside her, deeper, needing to join with her. Exhausted from his fucking and Raython's oral attention, Tina could barely respond, moaning with each penetration. Dane reached out, taking her right hand in his left, binding them together as he rode her. Raython captured Dane's other hand, linking their fingers together as well. It seemed natural and right. At the edge of his vision, he noticed that Raython had closed the triangle by taking Tina's free hand. Dane knew Raython only did this when something big was going to happen but the desperation in his cock wouldn't let him stop or focus on anything but Tina—fucking Tina.

The pressure built—for him and for Tina. He could feel her on the verge of coming again and knew her orgasm would send him over. He worked harder, needing her release for his own. Then the subtle flutter in her cunt pressed against his cock and he let go, flooding her with his seed. He gripped the two hands in his, feeling the power flow through them, building and echoing between their three bodies.

Another climax jolted through his cock and Tina screamed as she came again. Raython followed seconds later.

Five hours later, amid a tangle of sweaty, exhausted but very well-sated male bodies, Tina lifted her head and stared at her two lovers. They'd taken their positions against her—Raython on the left, Dane on the right—but something was different. Where usually Dane was very careful to not touch Raython, their wrists crossed each other as they each reached around Tina and neither pulled away. She was pretty sure it had something to do with that very sexy kiss they'd shared.

When the three of them loved together, Dane kept both males' attention on Tina but she could feel it shifting, feel Raython pressing Dane for more intimate touches. Her mouth kicked up in a small smile. She needed to prepare herself for a time when Dane and Raython would become lovers without her between them. The thought sent a teasing shiver into her sex. She held herself still despite the urge to move. If she shifted too much, one of her lovers might see it as an invitation for more and she wasn't sure her well-loved body could handle it.

Instead, she snuggled between her men. They were all awake but silent, listening to the room and feeling the energy that still hung in the air and moved through their bodies. It hadn't been this intense since the first time they'd made love together. When they'd first bonded with each other.

"Raython, why did you drag Dane home so early in the day?" she asked softly over her shoulder. There had to be a reason. He'd specifically set out to arouse her to the point of forcing Dane to come home.

"You were fertile and it was the prime window for impregnation."

Tina and Dane sat up, twisting around to stare at the dragon.

"What?" they asked in unison.

"You wanted a child, did you not? Now, you will have one." He smiled.

"Uh, Raython, I can't father children," Dane pointed out. Tina could hear the hint of disappointment in his voice.

Raython scoffed—a talent he'd learned in the ten months in this world. "Human mechanics cannot counter destiny. You will have a child together, and I will have someone else to protect."

With that announcement, he rolled out of the bed and left the room, closing the door behind him. He did that when he wanted to give Dane and Tina time together.

She looked up at her husband. "We're going to have a baby?" The stunned joy in her voice matched the look on his face.

"He hasn't steered us wrong yet," Dane admitted with a self-mocking smile.

"What do you mean?" she asked, curious. Dane had adapted to having Raython in the relationship, but he was definitely the Alpha male around the house. He tended to keep Raython out of their discussions.

Dane rolled over, insinuating himself between her almost constantly spread thighs. His cock slipped into her pussy, filling her with that delicious sense of fullness that never seemed to go away.

"Well, he was right about the Hunters attacking us."

"Yes," she smiled.

"And about me wanting to be with you for the rest of my life."

This time she blushed and said, "Yes."

He pumped his hips, giving her a sweet taste of the fuck to come. "And didn't he say something about you finding your true love?"

"I believe he did," she said, teasingly.

Dane turned serious. "Well, no one loves you more than I do."

About the author

Tielle (pronounced "teal") St. Clare has had life-long love of romance novels. She began reading romances in the 7th grade when she discovered Victoria Holt novels and began writing romances at the age of 16 (during Trigonometry, if the truth be told). During her senior year in high school, the class dressed up as what they would be in twenty years—Tielle dressed as a romance writer. When not writing romances, Tielle has worked in public relations and video production for the past 20 years. She moved to Alaska when she was seven years old in 1972 when her father was transferred with the military. Tielle believes romances should be hot and sexy with a great story and fun characters.

Tielle welcomes mail from readers. You can write to her c/o Ellora's Cave Publishing at 1056 Home Ave. Akron, Oh. 44310-3502.

Also by Tielle St. Clare

Close Quarters

Dragon's Fire

Dragon's Kiss

Dragon's Rise

Ellora's Cavemen: Legendary Tails II anthology

Irish Enchantment anthology

Just One Night

Simon's Bliss

Hyde!

Chapter One

The Baron Jay Kel stretched lazily, drifting in his bed. When his feet came up against the limits of the reduced gravity field, the action moved him back smoothly in the opposite direction within the confines of the bed's limits. Like a boat adrift, he bumped up against something warm and smooth.

His head came around with a jerk.

"Shit!" he cursed then gave the system order to dampen the bed's gravity field. "C-BedOff."

Sinking to a gradual landing on the flexible surface, Jay shrank from the body sharing his bed. Rolling quickly to the bed's edge, he stood to stare down at the golden form sprawled facedown on the smooth, black surface. Warily, Jay traveled to the other side of the bed in order to better observe the turned face.

The bedroom floor was littered with the clothes he'd worn yesterday and he cursed as he stooped to fish up a pair of white short pants. Glaring at the grubby knees, he pulled them up his legs then swept his boots from the floor, shoving his feet into the soft, supple footwear.

Returning his attention to the person on the bed, he frowned at the thick brush of yellow hair sheered brutally short, in a style suggestive of military school. Either a beautiful man or a handsome woman, he decided, still not certain which was the case. He flinched—his action one of distaste—as his eyes traveled down the slim, naked back and over the bare, bloody buttocks. Reaching out a cautious hand, he took the intruder's shoulder and turned the being onto its back.

A woman then, but only barely so. The baron's head tilted back on his corded neck as he observed the almost flat, muscular chest rise to take in several shallow breaths.

Damn! Hyde had gone too far this time—bringing home this shit and leaving it in his bed for him to find. For several moments, he glared at the long, golden woman in his bed. When the body stirred, he drew an automatic step backward, preferring not to be identified when the girl opened her eyes.

"C-Broadcast." Jay ripped out the order, which was immediately picked up by his System Network as his message was broadcast throughout his villa. "Huvisdank, come to my bedroom."

Retrieving his frilled shirt from the floor, Jay pulled it on, tucking the shirt ends into the top edge of his pants. With his eyes on the girl, he backed his way across the room, until he came up against a heavy antique sideboard where two robust nymphs stood carved out of cherry wood. Wonderfully naked, their arms stretched over their heads, supporting a slab of black marble that was the sideboard's countertop. Turning enough to pick up bottle and glass, he splashed out a short drink while waiting for his manservant.

A battle cruiser of a man stepped through the opaque doorshield and continued into the room, his head only just clearing the doorframe. "My Lord?"

Picking up the drink with his right hand, Jay nodded at the bed as he threw the dark red liquor down his throat. He licked his lower lip. "Get her out of h—"

"My Lord?"

Grasping the marble edge of the ancient sideboard with white-knuckled fingers, Jay sagged suddenly at the knees. "Wait, Huvisdank. Wait!" he cried with a curse.

The large man hadn't moved. "My Lord is having one of his spells?" Huvisdank suggested with utter disinterest.

Jay glared at his manservant. "Yes, 'My Lord is having one of his spells'," he gritted. He stared at the floor with fierce intensity, as though waging some inner war within himself, then muttered, "Put her in one of the spare rooms." Again, his knees buckled. "The big room on the main floor. Start a bath for her." He stared up at his manservant from beneath his brows, eyes dark and shadowed. "A real bath...with water."

Jay watched Huvisdank approach the bed. "The young woman is injured," his servant stated. "Shall I flash for a medoc?"

"No!" he answered swiftly. "It's just a few bumps and scrapes."

Huvisdank turned to put doubtful eyes on his master.

"We'll doctor the girl ourselves," he told the clone, picking up his fine brocade jacket and shaking it out with an air of annoyance.

Nodding, the servant scooped the girl from the bed as Jay followed the man out of the room and down the hall to the large, sunny room his guest was to occupy. Glancing around the walls, lined with the very finest of his antique furniture, the baron made a face of regret. It wasn't the room he'd have chosen for some girl off the street. The most elite members of Virtzue's ruling class had slept in this room! More than a little disgusted, he slung his jacket on the fabulous twenty-third century bed.

After filling the white enamel tub, the manservant left his master to administer to the girl. Rolling up his sleeves and sinking to his knees, the aristocrat grumbled obscenities as he lowered the girl into the warm water. Absently, his hand slid beneath the curves of her bottom, between the woman's warm flesh and the tub's cool antique enamel. Having overcome their preliminary inertia, the baron's hands continued up over her thighs to smooth down her legs.

She looked as though she'd been dragged through Roughside at the back of a jet bike. And it didn't take a medical scan to see that her left leg was broken below the knee. Several shallow abrasions marred her legs and hips as well as her buttocks, and a dark purple bruise was mapped out as large as a continent on her right shoulder.

She must have hit her knees hard, he thought, his eyes narrowing on the scraped and crusted flesh capping her knees. Turning one of her hands to gaze into her palm, he found both hands just as badly abused. His eyes drifted down over her belly, where he stared at a dark, thumb-sized bruise just inside her pelvic wing.

Hyde, he thought coldly. Apparently, the brute had raped the girl and brought her home for more.

"C-Access. Case right tibia. Create mirror image and apply to left leg." The baron watched as the invisible casing program moved the bone into place and the purple protrusion on her shin diminished beneath his fingers. With the casing program holding her broken bone in place, he reached behind him for a palm-sized regenafix and pushed the button as he drew it along the shin of her left leg. When the girl moaned uncomfortably, Jay slapped a narcodot on her arm. Immediately, she slumped, quiet and unconscious in the bath.

While she was still, he spread a thin film of cauterizing cream over her open wounds, submerging the wounds when the first smoky threads from her seared flesh reached his nose. A few passes with the medimagnet over her bruises, and the deep, harsh color of those injuries faded to faint yellowish stains.

Kneeling beside the tub, he continued washing the girl, his hands lingering on the firmly stretched muscles of her arms and legs, paying them the respectful homage he couldn't quite scrape up for her unremarkable breasts.

Several times, his hands returned to her stroke her buttocks, pleased with the firm, resilient flesh, the muscles of her bottom almost as hard as his own. Eventually moved to male curiosity, his middle finger tracked into the crease between her cheeks, over the tight crimp of her ass and almost missed the tiny pussy opening. Interested, he nudged his finger at her opening. His eyes stretched in surprise. That had to be the tiniest little slit he'd ever snagged his finger in! Slipping his smallest finger in an inch, he smiled as her vagina closed to hug his narrow digit.

Blood began to pound its way into his cock and he moved his knees apart so its growth could continue unhindered. Slowly, languidly, he drew his fingers through the folds tucked between her lips and out the top of her cleft…then frowned an instant. Hesitantly, he returned his questing fingers between her lips and sucked in a breath. Lifting one long limb, he put her knee over the edge of the tub and pulled her legs open. With his fingers spreading the girl's labia, he cocked his head to view the most prominent clit he'd ever seen in his lifetime. Even in its quiet state, it protruded beyond the full lips of her pussy. Jay's breathing roughened as he considered how much he'd like to see it excited.

With new regard, he lifted the girl from the bath and, almost gently, laid her out on the antique guest bed. She looked good on it, he decided. Her slim golden form displayed like erotic jewelry on the royal blue satin beneath her. Her long, neat body nearly filled out the length of the bed. That left her several inches shorter than he, but tall for a woman. Gold eyelashes rested on high cheekbones that curved down into the sort of strong, rounded chin most closely associated with Greek sculpture.

The baron was a man accustomed to luxury as well as elegance, and he particularly enjoyed beauty in bed. If the woman was art, it was after the minimalist fashion—simple, handsome and streamlined. Hyde's interest in the girl hadn't been completely off-center, he concluded.

For a long time Jay stood there, considering the long sensuous line of her wide mouth as though trying to make up his mind. When she opened her eyes, he came to a decision. His eyes narrowed on her stunning green gaze, an eye color incredibly rare on the planet Virtzue. Virtually all blondes had brown eyes, like his.

Those green eyes were enough to tip the scales in her favor.

He was going to have the girl, regardless of Hyde.

One way or another.

One way *and* another.

With that thought, Jay rummaged through his first aid kit and found a steriledot to press against her thigh. A man in his position couldn't afford to father an accidental child with an unstationed woman, regardless of how interesting he found her.

Chapter Two

Teller woke to a thick head stuffed with shattered dreams and shards of fractured nightmares…and the most handsome man she'd ever seen in her life.

Almost immediately, she recognized she was on drugs—narcodot of some sort—and wondered what had happened to her that she required medical attention. The drug worked to enhance her visual input, everything in the room was brilliantly defined, edged sharp and clear and bursting with vivid color.

The beautiful man standing at the end of the bed was outlined in hard edges—his broad shoulders a wide horizontal line above a triangle of chest that narrowed down to his hips. Below that, the two long, straight lines of his legs stretched to the floor.

Picking her eyes up off the floor, Teller returned them to his face. Above his broad shoulders, she found an angular face that looked as though it had been carved out of stone to create perfectly chiseled features. Golden brown eyes watched her from a sun-bronzed face. His blond hair wasn't overly long, only long enough to be smoothed away from his face, caught up and snapped into a thick curl at the nape of his neck. The long lines that bracketed his hard mouth spoke of strength and determination…and didn't mention compromise. He looked like a man who was used to getting what he wanted—a man who got *everything* he wanted, by whatever means necessary.

His clothing, though rumpled, represented the height of court fashion. His longcoat, a luxurious shade of deep wine, scraped at her eyes. Painfully white shortpants were tucked into gnad-skin boots that winked and sparked with each small movement. The color rebounded against her eyes and she blinked back the tears that smeared her vision.

"What happened to me?" she asked thickly, her mouth full of tongue.

"You were attacked," he answered in the sophisticated accent of the cultured elite. "I found you injured on the street and brought you here."

"Attacked?"

"You don't remember anything?"

Teller shook her head minutely. "I was with my...friends."

His eyes narrowed. "When I found you, you were alone."

"My...clothes?" It had just occurred to her she was lying before him entirely naked, every inch of her body revealed for his open study. Self-consciously, she picked at the satin bedspread, trying to get enough into her hand to drag up over her hips. The shining stuff slipped through her fingers as a small smile from her host revealed his reluctance to aid her in this matter.

"You had none."

"What...what's the damage report?" she queried, narrowing her own gaze to sift out some of the blinding color and light produced as a result of the drug coursing through her system.

"I had to regenerate the bone in your leg." With his right hand, he indicated her left leg.

Alarmed, Teller dropped her eyes to her shin.

"You'll be up and running again in four days," he assured her. "If not sooner. But your right shoulder was a mess. Looked as though you got hit by the mean end of a sonic earthmover. I've treated the bruise. Other than that, you had some pretty deep abrasions. Your hands and knees in particular." He stared at a deep purple bruise just inside her pelvic wing. He'd missed treating that one.

Hyde, he thought again.

She raised one palm to stare at the faint network of white scars. "Hands and knees?"

He nodded. "I think you might have been raped."

An involuntary shudder gripped her body. "I don't feel anything," she offered hopefully.

"That's the narcodot. You won't feel anything for days."

"That's hardly a comforting thought," she muttered to herself. "Have you flashed for a medoc?"

"I'd rather not do that."

Teller frowned at the handsome man.

"I'd like to keep this whole episode out of the Gossip-Cs."

She shook her head slightly to indicate she didn't understand.

"It's probably the drugs," he explained, "but I should look at least a little familiar to you — unless you're from offworld. I'm the Baron Jay Kel."

"My Lord," she gasped when his words had finally threaded their way through her flotsam-filled skull.

"Yes," he drawled, his tone sardonic. "My Lord, indeed."

Teller rasped a dry tongue over cracked lips as her eyes slid to a bottle on the table across the room. She squinted at the flash of cut glass on a background of deep burgundy.

"I'm sorry. You're probably thirsty." The baron glanced at the time on the palm of his left hand where a tiny implant projected the hour on his skin in glowing blue characters. "C-Broadcast. Huvisdank, bring a measure of water to the main guest room."

Automatically, her eyes lifted to the C-Link crescent set in his ear. Eyes fixed on the earpiece, Teller tried not to stare at the expensive piece of work. Like most people, including herself, the flat flange of the baron's ear had been removed at birth so he could easily carry his C-Link as well as his I.D. emitter on his person at all times. The C-Link allowed him full access to his

System Network, along with both his in-house and outgoing communication system. The baron's earpiece was fashioned out of a fabulous piece of translucent plastic almost impossible to find in this day and age. The C-Link was a deep, luscious shade of strawberry that amplified the gold in the smooth, neat strands of his tawny hair. Self-consciously, she fingered her own simple earpiece molded from flesh-colored Biowick.

He backed up to sit, leaning on the table behind him. "Please feel free to access my C if you want to flash your friends and family—let them know you're all right—but I'm afraid you're probably stuck here for a few days until you mend. During that time, it would be nice to know your name."

"Teller," she told him. "Teller O'Four."

"Teller," he smiled. "I'll have you scanned for measurements and order some clothes formulated for you. Would you like to view a catalogue?"

She raised one shoulder in an expression of disinterest.

"You could design your own fashions if you prefer."

She shrugged again. "I'm not particular. Anything standard will suit me fine."

He raised his eyebrows. "Well, if you're not particular, I'll put a few things together for you."

"My Lord! Please don't put yourself to any trouble!"

He gave her a lazy smile. "It will be my pleasure to dress you," he said.

Teller's eyes swung around to watch the baron's servant shoulder through the doorshield. A visitray followed him into the room.

Teller regarded the man with curiosity. The baron's manservant had a good four inches on his master, and the baron wasn't a small man. His clothing was romantically archaic, Teller recognized. Gleaming black leather cased his muscular legs, the leggings held together by a line of silverlike fastenings that trailed down the side seam of his pants. From each shining, round decoration hung a short pair of leather strings. His loose white shirt hung open to the waist, exposing a wide chest furred with dark hair. A steel snaplock gleamed at the bottom of the long black braid that hung over one shoulder and the man stared out at her from cold, colorless eyes.

"A clone?"

The baron nodded. "Engineered clone. Fully reasoning, high-end model. Takes orders like a dream. No free will whatsoever—his DNA has been scrubbed clean of any emotions. More brute strength than a blast-missile." The baron pointed at his manservant. "You can order that thing to do anything and he'll either deliver or die trying." With his right hand, he motioned toward his guest and the clone nudged the tray toward Teller.

Carefully, she shifted herself back into a sitting position, pulling some of the satin bedspread into her lap as she reached for the packet of water. "Can I order a hard-on?"

The baron choked in the middle of his account. "Everything but! Without any emotions or sex drive, that would be impossible. At any rate, he answers only to my commands."

"Shame," she said, eyeing the servant thoughtfully. "He's beautiful."

Jay laughed. "You're an ambitious little chit. Huvisdank has a three-inch diameter at his root. He'd bust you wide open." The girl's eyes widened and he nodded in return. "Would you like to see it?"

With her expression, she told him she would. "If he doesn't mind."

"He doesn't know enough to mind," the baron said with a light growl. "Drop your pants, Huvisdank." Turning to face the girl, the clone pulled a few leather strings as he complied without hesitation. Slowly, the leather slid down his legs to reveal a fabulous length of thick flesh cascading from a bed of black pubic hair. "What do you think?"

"It's a monster," Teller agreed. "But I can be flexible."

"You'd have to be flexible, if you expected to survive Huvisdank's hard-on. But that's not going to happen—fortunately for you."

"Unfortunately for me," she corrected him with a murmur, knowing her comments bordered on brazen. But she'd spent enough time around men to know what a woman could get away with. And, considering what she knew of the baron from the Gossip-Cs, it would take a lot to shock the man. "Have you had him long?"

"I got the man when I was sixteen."

"Man? He's...older than you?"

"By five years."

Teller studied the servant more closely. "But his face is so smooth. There's not a wrinkle on it."

"That's what an emotion-free life will bring you. Huvisdank neither smiles nor frowns. The man has no sense of humor whatsoever."

"Really?" she said, a shade of emotion in her voice.

The baron laughed. "If that's sympathy I see on your face, you should know it's wasted. The clone hasn't a care in the world. No troubles or concerns. And I'd guess it's a lucky man who's never experienced a moment of guilt. Huvisdank's completely honest. He has no reason to lie."

Teller gave this some thought. "Sounds like the perfect man," she decided.

"You might think so. Actually, owning a completely honest manservant can result in some awkward moments." The baron began to laugh. "One time I had—" but the man checked himself. "Well, you can imagine," he finished lamely.

Suspiciously, with an air of accusation, she arched an eyebrow at him. "I guess I'll have to, won't I? Or...I could ask Huvisdank."

The baron gave her a knowing smile. "The clone takes orders only from me," he told her again. He turned to his clone.

"Huvisdank, while you're to assist the young lady in every way she requires, you're to answer none of her questions about my...sex life."

"Yes, My Lord."

The baron's eyes returned to find Teller's interest fixed on the clone's long penis. "And you may pull your pants up now," he laughed. He dismissed the man with a wave, turned to follow him then stopped abruptly. "I should warn you about...my brother."

Teller cocked her head, scanning her memory. She'd never heard anything of the Baron Jay Kel's siblings before. Cousins, yes. But never a brother or sister. "You have a brother? Is that...common knowledge?"

"No. The family's not particularly proud of him," he stated. "His name is Hyde. He's...a few thrusters short of a liftoff. Spent most of his life in gene clinics." He shrugged the wide line of his shoulders, setting the brilliance of the wine jacket into a prisming display of color. "There's only so much modern medicine can do. He's here for a short visit. If you see him, I want you to be careful of him. He's a dangerous cre...cretin," he finished stiffly.

She nodded. "What does he look like?"

"Unfortunately, he looks a lot like me," the baron said. "We're twins. Almost identical."

Her eyes cast about the room. "Should I have a weapon?"

"No," he said swiftly. "No. I'm...sure you'll be all right. Just avoid him if you can."

Teller nodded. "I'll watch for him. If he gives me any trouble I can always use the C to call on Huvisdank—or you."

"You can try," the baron muttered to himself as he continued out through the bedroom doorshield.

Chapter Three

Teller saw the baron only occasionally during the next two days. In that time, Huvisdank visited routinely, like clockwork in fact, bringing her meals, tending to her wounds, carrying her to the washroom. Both mornings, when he first appeared, his costume took her by surprise. Today he wore an unusual period piece from some distant romantic world. Full, loose pantaloons put together in layers of filmy stuff were secured at the waist by a wrap of colorful silk. On his upper body, a short beaded vest revealed most of his wide chest. "Huvisdank," she commented. "You have the most unusual wardrobe."

"Yes, My Lady."

"I'm not a lady," she pointed out politely.

"How would you have me address you?" the clone asked with smooth disinterest.

"My name is Teller. Why don't you use that?" She paused. "Why did you choose to wear that particular outfit today?"

"The baron schedules my clothing, Teller."

"The baron! But…what do you do when he's not around to tell you what to wear?"

"If there is nothing scheduled, I wear what I wish."

Quickly, she glanced at his face, expecting to find some spark of discontent to accompany the statement. The clone's features were blank.

"What would you prefer to wear?"

The clone looked her straight in the eye. "Something more comfortable, Teller."

* * * * *

Most of the time she slept—the narcodot probably aided in that respect. When awake, she was fuzzily alert and, though she experienced little pain, she was hesitant to try out her legs and test the efficacy of the regenafix. On the evening of the second day, she accessed the baron's C-Bank for something to read. The baron's C was a great deal more sophisticated than anything she was accustomed to and it took her a few moments to find her way out of his library of recently read articles in which she had little interest—he'd evidently been studying dragons.

Upon reaching the main library, she navigated her way through the authors' list to Byrd, selecting a familiar old classic she'd read several times. Comfortably situated on the bed, she lay back to read the erotica projected on the ceiling overhead.

She'd been born horny, as far as she could estimate. Just as other youths were born with overactive imaginations, she'd been burdened with an overactive sex drive. Thank God and the Ruling Class the adult age had been lowered to fifteen the year before her birth, otherwise she'd never have made it through high school without several visits to reform hospice. Due to its size and the friction that accompanied almost every single step she took, her prominent clit was in an almost constant state of arousal. The last year had been particularly difficult for her—her current employment caused her to be surrounded by men, while her situation dictated she keep her hands to herself.

Realizing she'd read the last paragraph three times, she let her mind drift and wasn't surprised when it sailed into the baron's dock, threw out a line and tied itself off. He was a nice piece of work, one that her overactive appetite would like to work on. Despite the dampening effect of the narcodot, her sex responded sleepily to the idea and a familiar dull ache moved beneath her belly, set up camp and started a small fire.

Of course she knew of the baron, it would be hard not to. She'd read about him and seen his images in the Gossip-Cs where it was generally agreed that he was an attractive man and the planet's most desirable catch. But she wasn't one to waste time or thought on a prospect so far beyond her reach. She should have recognized him, but the highborn baron was even more beautiful in the flesh than his images had indicated.

Again, she read the paragraph, it was her favorite. Closing her eyes, she moved her hand down into the hair that feathered the apex of her legs where her clit nestled between the lips of her labia. Carefully, she moved her legs apart and stroked the familiar nub into a hard point. With her hand covering the length of her sex, and her mind covering every aspect of the baron's perfect form, she efficiently rubbed herself into the necessary and required release.

* * * * *

When she opened her eyes on the third morning, they focused on a man across the room.

It was Jay, she thought at first—then changed her mind.

"You're Hyde."

He gave her a slow smile. "How did you know?"

She continued staring at him, uncertain how she'd known. Uncertain why she felt no apprehension in the presence of the man Jay had cautioned her against.

"We're identical, Jay and I."

"Except for your eyes. Yours are more gold."

He inclined his head. "Except for our eyes."

An unwilling smile crept into her mouth. "No," she said impulsively. "You're different. You're very much different."

Hyde leaned back against the table across the room, his hands gripping the table's edge. Although his pose was casual, there was a tense edge to the man that belied his easy slouch. For some reason, he struck her as an explosion waiting to happen. His blond hair was a wild tangle, his eyes lit with a strange gold fire. He carried himself differently than his brother, she recognized. The man was like a dangerous threat powerfully contained in human form.

"It isn't only your eyes," she told him. "Your voice is deeper."

"Is it?" One of his eyebrows crept upward. "Or is it only that I speak more plainly?"

In the silence that followed, Teller experienced an unfamiliar shifting in her heart as Hyde returned her gaze. With one simple sentence, Teller was hooked—the barb caught and set, despite Jay's warning. Everything about this man was deeper than the baron—she suspected—despite their very obvious similarities. Along with a deeper voice, he appeared to possess a depth of character his brother couldn't match, as though something substantially undefined was concealed just below the surface. Something that pulled her into a far deeper attraction than she'd felt for the baron or his clone. She looked down in her lap, wanting to connect with the man. Wishing to impress him with barely a dozen words, as he had her. She wanted his warm gaze and more. She wanted to get near to him and feel the heat of the power he kept contained within.

Sliding to turn in the bed, Teller rearranged the shift she wore and eased her legs around to put her feet on the floor. "You could help me get some fresh air," she suggested.

His eyes moved to the clear windowshield leading into the sunlit yard. "Is that what you want? Fresh air?"

She pushed herself onto unsteady feet. "No," she told him, skirting the easy response and choosing instead to be bold. "I want you to help me."

A few long steps and he was beside her.

But instead of taking her elbow, he swept her into his hold and carried her outside. His body, his arms were hard, without a millimeter of give. He caged her within the stark limits of his confining hold, without an ounce of gentleness, yet with all the reassuring strength and harboring protection that could be found in a man's arms. Lowering her into a stretch chair, his body lingered close to hers.

His was an exotic scent, reminding her of stiff leather stretched and barely kept hammered in place with thick copper studs. His face brushed her cheek. His lips swept close to her ear. "Be careful what you tell the baron," he told her. "He needn't know everything about you."

As he drew away, she grasped for something to say. Anything that would keep him beside her. "Thanks for the warning. He so much as cautioned me against you."

"I know."

She forced a light laugh. "Who am I to believe?"

"You'll have to decide," he delivered simply.

"And in the meantime?"

"In the meantime, I'll make certain you're not harmed," he told her as he moved away from her with a long, smooth gait.

"Harmed? What could possibly happen to me here at the baron's villa?"

Stopping in front of the windowshield, he turned back to look at her. There was a serious, dangerous glint in his gold eyes. "Nothing...so long as I live," he said with determined quiet. "Get better soon. I'll be back when you're feeling better."

With two fingers poised against her lips, Teller stared thoughtfully at the tiled patio floor, almost certain that a part of her had left with Hyde. It was the strangest sensation and one she'd never experienced before. As though a huge part of her had gone missing. As though she was suddenly incomplete.

But the man's cryptic comments were unsettling. What possible harm could come to her at the baron's villa? Jay Kel was cousin to the Imperion Lord and, as such, a member of the very highest nobility.

Startled out of these musings, her eyes fixed on Jay as he came around the side of the house toward her, moving purposefully across the tightly trimmed lawn. The baron appeared tense as he glanced at the time projected on his left palm. "Hyde was here." His tone was accusatory as he continued without waiting for her response. "What did he...did he... Are you all right?" he asked in a strangled voice, strangely devoid of concern.

She nodded her head, slowly, measuring the baron anew. Although, like his brother, the baron wore a fine white shirt above black leather shortpants tucked into embroidered boots, the man's clothing seemed to sit him differently. While the baron's clothing appeared to fit him well—was smooth and orderly—his brother's leathers appeared both rumpled and filled to capacity at the same time.

While the baron's blond hair was smoothed into a small neat knot, Hyde's hair was an untamed tangle. She couldn't help but compare the baron's cool detachment alongside Hyde's strong, warm calm, or Jay's polished, haughty mannerisms compared to Hyde's masculine economy of motion—the aristocrat's superfluous intellectual expression as opposed to Hyde's plain, direct speech.

While she'd found herself attracted to the baron from the moment she'd set eyes on him, she had recognized it for what it was...plain old healthy lust for an attractive man with, what was surely, a nice package. What she wanted from his brother, she didn't recognize at all. But she was certain it was something more than sex and that it was fueled by something stronger than either attraction or lust. And as she stared up at the baron, Teller wondered if, perhaps, for the first time in her life, she was in love.

With the Baron Jay Kel's brother.

Hyde.

Chapter Four

Teller sighed as she watched the lights across the courtyard. One by one, they dimmed and winked out. The night sky was a black velvet tapestry stitched with silver stars. Pale blue taffeta rustled in the darkness.

Huvisdank had delivered her gown as the baron had promised. Her leg had healed and Jay had invited her to dress for the ball. Huvisdank would return for her and bring her to join in the last hour of dancing. But the summons to join the ball had never come. She'd watched a dozen hovercoaches lift away and head north for the city. That was an hour ago.

The gown was the first of the baron's promised designs. Reminiscent of sixteenth-century Pre-Expansion Earth, the incredibly tight, unnaturally long bodice dove into a V that started at her waist and descended almost to her crotch. A line of tiny, silver-like clasps marched down the center front of the dress, straining to keep it closed around her. Below the bodice, a full skirt billowed out to whisper against the floor.

"All dressed up with no place to go."

Teller nodded into the night. She didn't turn toward the voice behind her.

"That's a beautiful dress."

She shrugged. "It's not mine."

"No? Why don't we get it off you, then?"

She turned to Hyde slowly, smiled slowly. "That's the best offer I've gotten all night."

His blond hair and golden tan were warm against the formal black longcoat he wore over a soft white T-shirt. His tousled hair tumbled around eyes lit with a fierce gold heat that made his smile a wicked challenge. "It's the only offer you've gotten all night."

"You needn't point that out." Her chin came up proudly. "If you were a gentleman, you'd...at least offer me a dance, before—"

"But I'm not a gentleman. And I don't have time to dance."

"No?" Her voice was a cool challenge. "Then what are you here for, Hyde?"

Between his forefinger and thumb, he held up a shining stick of music. There was a light crack as the stick snapped between his fingers. Dropping the pieces on the patio table, he approached her slowly. The starlit night filled with a rare, romantic melody.

"I'll show you."

With a hand on her waist, he reeled her into his heat, captured her hand and took it to his chest.

Teller's eyes widened. "That song is four hundred years old. It must have cost...a fortune."

"Jay can afford it," he said without breathing.

A few herding steps and Hyde had her backed into the shadows of the styromass wall. She felt his thick, hard thigh tight against her mons as his knee pushed between her legs. Strong hands gripped her arms as Hyde bent his head and put his lips against her neck to growl. His mouth traveled down the tendon that angled from her neck to her shoulder, his teeth scoring into the back of the stretching muscle while his tongue slipped along the front. Teller shivered and found herself tilting her head and stretching her neck to give the man clear access and complete authorization to continue.

"Get rid of the dress," he rasped.

She hesitated only an instant. Then her fingers were working the tiny, vintage clasps that stretched the taffeta tight across her chest. Following her hands downward, Hyde's hands pushed into the space as she created it, peeling the dress away from her body. When she arrived at the bottom of the bodice and ran out of clasps, she started an attempt to push the skirt of the dress down over her hips.

Hyde's hand rushed to help and she heard the fabric tear.

With a curse, Hyde's hands fisted at the waist of the dress and the skirt parted down the front in a long shredding of cloth and sound.

Shivering a little in the cool night, Teller leaned back against the wall while Hyde pulled the dress open. Self-conscious about her boyish figure, she started a shy, self-deprecatory remark, but caught it back when she saw the look on the man's face. She watched his eyes as he regarded her body, showcased on a background of shimmering blue, while the tattered remnants of the long dress hung from her shoulders.

Hyde's eyes followed his left hand as it traveled up her thigh, over the blue silk shorts on her hips, up her waist, across one sleek breast to finally thumb her collarbone. His other hand slipped behind her and his long fingers spread in the small of her back as he pulled her to him. With her body tight against his, both his hands moved down to hook beneath her bottom and his fingers slid beneath her silk shorts to caress the crease where her bottom met her legs.

"You're so smooth," he rumbled, his gold eyes settling on hers with enough fire to melt an outer-ring planet. "So perfectly, beautifully smooth. You're the most fabulous creature I've ever seen."

Her eyes widened to search his deeply. The idea that he found her slim, boyish form attractive was a warming one and she lifted a finger to catch at an unexpected and embarrassingly indiscreet tear before it betrayed her. Hers was not a body every man could love. She might have thought he was mocking her except for the incendiary heat in his gaze. She wanted to immerse herself in that heat to the roots of her soul. Wanted to wade into his fire and let it lick up her thighs and kindle a flame in the small, pale snatch on her mound, bathe her pussy in every warm touch he might send her way, wallowing in his every heated action as he stoked the fire between her legs and let it blaze to engulf her sex.

"Help me with this shirt," he growled in a breath like rasping sandpaper. "I want to feel you—all of you—up against me."

Almost desperate to comply, her hands scrunched the soft white fabric up to his armpits and, immediately, he put his chest against hers. Fine gold hair met her naked breast and she thought she felt each and every one of them graze her just before contact with hot, hard muscles caused her to suck in a breath that surprised even her. Each breath he took crushed her into the wall at her back.

Hyde's left hand came around her bottom and underneath her thigh, lifting her leg, his big hand casing her long, slender thigh as he reached her knee and pushed it up beside his chest. Taking her ankle, he tucked her foot behind his back.

With one hand knotted in the gray fabric at his hip, Teller used her other hand to slide over the front of his fine woolen pants. Accommodatingly, his hips moved back to allow her hand's caress and his breath rasped abrasively against her ear as her fingers slid along either side of his erection, outlining, defining his length that stiffened in an angled stretch across his stomach. His tongue went into her ear along with his roughened breath, and Teller's body stiffened as her back arched to push into the body that captured hers against the wall. Reaching low and dragging her hand up over his erection, Teller crested the top of his pants and started to work her hand back down between wool and taut, stretched skin. Her fingertips touched hot flesh just before he jerked her hand out of his pants and to his lips.

Like an iron manacle, his hand wrapped around her wrist, lifting her hand to his lips as he sucked her fingers into his mouth. The tip of his tongue separated each of her four fingers before his mouth closed on them and started pulling on them rhythmically, the tempo of the suction matching the canting movement of his groin into her rise.

His gold gaze held hers, brimming with heated sex, full of warning promise. Her nipples fizzed and tingled as the muscles of her stomach tightened and a demanding ache settled beneath her belly and boiled to spill into her groin.

As his angled erection slid over her mons, she burned to straighten him, align him with the divot of her cleft. When she reached for him with her free hand, again he brushed her advance away. For a moment, his hand was between their bodies, adjusting his cock, putting his thick ridge straight and firm beneath her belly. Rising on her toes, she strained to capture some of him between the canted lips of her sex. As she caught him on her clit, the soft wool slid over the silk of her shorts creating a warm, heady friction that speared from the outer lips of her sex to strike deep into her womb.

A moan spilled from between her own thickened lips as she recognized the more he gave her, the more she would want. And, at this point, she was disinclined to stop until she had all of him. All of his long, thick cock stretching her wide in a long, slow fuck, forcing her open, the brutal length of his rod stretching into her pussy and hammering her into orgasm. He pulled away a fraction and Teller jumped as the air crackled between their bodies. Lowering her eyes, she jerked several times in series as she watched a flock of tiny blue sparks crawl over her silk-covered mound. The small bursts of static energy, propagated between their bodies where wool met silk, teased a desperate response out of her sex as each little spark attacked her sensitive pussy.

Apparently fascinated by the minute display of blue fireworks, Hyde pulled her leg wider and pushed into her again, rubbing his wool-covered shaft to furrow the narrow divot between her labia. When he pulled away again, the air cracked and a tiny shower of sparks played into Teller's parted pussy. A blue line arced between their bodies to smack the tip of her clit and her neck arched backward as she spiraled into a very unexpected orgasm.

Her body jerked against his and he contained it within his arms as he caught her lips on his and pressed her tossing head back against the wall. As her body convulsed in jerking spasms, he nailed her to the wall, twisting her mouth beneath his, the hard edge of his teeth catching at her lips, trapping them against her own. One of his hands pushed his loose pants out of the way and a hard smile stretched his mouth as he bent his knees and fed his cock inside the leg of her shorts, into her streaming slit. His hips thrust upward several times as he fought his way into her clenching opening. Then his cock head was stretching inside her, his inward progress forcing her open at the instant of closure, adding a full measure of satisfaction to her orgasm as he forced his cock into the tight, narrow channel.

As she came out of coitus and opened her eyes, she found him watching her face. Pushing her chest into his, she strangled a sob. "Hyde," she said in a long, low breath that felt like it was torn from the depths of her soul. "I want more," she told him.

His eyes lit as he nodded and he thrust into her once, giving her a taste of his full, blunt cock head against her cervix.

Inside her, he filled her more fabulously than she had ever experienced. Complete in a way that transcended mere physical volume filling a void. Complete in the sense that she felt entirely taken, body and soul as well as cock-filled pussy, the steel of his thick shaft seated at the back of her cunt, stretching her to the limits of her capacity.

Outside, his fingers pulled her cheeks apart from behind then slid down to skid close to her vulva. Her earlier orgasm had been just about enough to whet her appetite for the carnal creature that had her pinned against the wall and she'd known right away she'd want a full, thick, hard follow-up. The curling nest of hair at his groin scraped across the clit that now protruded well beyond her outer lips. The hammerhead of his cock nudged against her core like a blasting cap set at the head of a ruddy stick of dynamite, ready to explode and fill her at the first spark of action.

"Don't play with me, Hyde," she moaned in a keening breath of unrest. "I want it all this time."

"You're going to get it all," he warned her, his voice rough with lust. Withdrawing the thick wedge of his cock head all the way to the mouth of her slit, he thrust back into her and picked up a smooth, even, penetrating rhythm that battered her waiting cervix and carried her, inexorably, toward stunning orgasm. As she was grinding her hips to meet his, he brought it to her with a fierce delivery, rammed her full of cock as he lodged himself deep inside her.

Behind him, there was the sound of a voice being cleared and Hyde's hips jumped to make a savage drive into the searing heat wrapping his dick. Teller screamed in his ear at the same time he heard Huvisdank's voice at his back.

He covered her mouth with his hand as she entered orgasm beneath him, her body thrashing against the wall, her long, warm cunt tightening on him in an unrelenting, grasping stranglehold that milked at the length of his shaft and begged for his surging release.

He gasped and blinked, tightly reining in his own orgasm until he'd dealt with the unwelcome clone. "Fuck," he whispered, in an agony of restraint. "You...you should announce yourself before entering, Huvisdank," he rasped out, uncovering Teller's mouth and staring at the reddened, swollen lips beneath his hand.

"My Lord has given me access to all rooms," the clone reminded him politely. "I wouldn't have troubled My Lord but the Lady Aleena woke to an empty bed and—"

Hyde's body stiffened momentarily and his eyes widened in horrified realization before his forehead hit the wall. "Thank you, Huvisdank."

"Might I tell the lady when to expect you back?"

Looking into Teller's eyes, he returned her expression of shock with his own wince of regret. "*Leave* us, Huvisdank."

There were a few steps that accompanied the clone's departure.

"Teller."

Her hands came away from him as though she'd been burned alive.

"Teller. It's not what it looks like."

She shook her head as his hips resumed their driving upward motion, but by the time she thought to push him away, he had entered into his own rending orgasm. His hands locked on her waist as his body shuddered. Inside her, his cock stretched and thickened then jerked a final time before he poured into her. "I'm sorry," he gasped out as he finished inside her.

Outside in the hall, she could hear a woman's voice.

"I have to go," he whispered against her ear.

Chapter Five

Teller didn't sleep. After a long, dry shower, she straightened her room and waited in a chair for morning.

It was a long time coming.

That was an error, she kept telling herself. A tactical error. But errors could be corrected and she was a practical woman. She nodded to herself and brushed away a very impractical tear that had somehow managed to sneak halfway down her cheek. Sniffing, she caught the next tear at the source.

Damn. Jay had warned her about the man. Gene therapy hadn't been able to help the mad, delusional bastard who whispered and warned her against his high-placed brother. Why hadn't she listened to the baron?

Or better yet, why hadn't she laid the baron?

Because she'd made an error, that's why. An error of the heart. Damn. Wasn't it a bit late in life for schoolgirl crushes? Her cheeks warmed with humiliation as she considered how her heart had made her a fool. "Part of her gone missing!" She would have laughed if she didn't feel so damn miserable. What a load of shit!

There was a light rap outside the doorshield just before the baron sauntered into the room. "I'm sorry I didn't make it last night," he said lightly. A visitray followed him into the room carrying a fabulous breakfast elegantly presented on delicate Pre-Expansion china from Old Earth. Gloomily, Teller gazed at the artful pieces, each one of which would have bought a small hovercoach. She took a steadying breath. "I'd like to get out of here," she announced.

Instantly, the baron was wary. He glanced into his hand as though some sort of answer lay in the time projected there.

"Teller," he started carefully, his eyes taking in hers. "Is there something wrong?"

She shook her head.

Briefly, he searched the room before his eyes stopped at the small patio table just outside the windowshield. On its surface lay the broken music stick. "Was Hyde here? Last night?" he asked sharply.

Teller looked away.

"Did he hurt you?" The baron's voice was angry and taut. "He hurt you!"

"No."

The baron was suddenly beside her, pulling her face into his chest. "This is my fault. I'm sorry," he grated. "I should have been here. I *would* have been here, except I couldn't get free of the *damned* Imperion Lord. What did he do? The bastard! I swear if he's harmed you in any way, I'll kill him."

"No," she told him quickly.

"I'm sorry. I tried to tell you, to warn you."

"I just want to leave, My Lord."

"Tell me he didn't…attack you. Please, tell me."

"It wasn't like that."

"He didn't force you…"

"No. It was…at the time, it was mutual."

The baron cursed, holding the girl's face against his chest. *Points to Hyde for the first strike*, he thought, damn him for the animal he was. Hopefully it wasn't too late to put a little damage control into effect.

"Afterward…almost immediately afterward," she muttered. "There was a woman looking for him." The timbre of her voice rose and cracked. "*He'd only just left her bed.*"

Jay sucked in a breath. "He left The Lady Aleena to come here?"

Teller gave him a broken nod. "All the time telling me he didn't have much time. I didn't realize he was just…fitting me in between—"

"*Fucking* bastard!" The baron's hands fisted as he strode toward the doorshield. "I'll *fucking* kill him."

"No! Please, My Lord." Teller took a few, halting steps toward the angry man. "I just want to…get away from here."

"That's not true! You want to get away from *him*!"

She nodded in answer.

"Fucking bastard!" The baron spun on his heel. Lashing out with his hand, he swept a fortune in ancient china from the floating tray. Teller jumped as the porcelain slashed across the room to smash and splinter on the floor. Turning, the baron hurled his right fist at the styromass wall. With his fist bunched on the wall's surface, the baron sagged to lean his forehead against the wall.

Silence filled the room as Teller stared at the man, a little stunned.

"I'm sorry," he said again, his voice scraping dramatically low. "I should have known he'd try to get to me through you." He nodded into the wall. "He knows how I feel about you."

Teller's eyes narrowed as she shook her head.

"He knows how I feel about you. He wanted to take you from me." Jay turned a solemn face toward her. "Please don't leave. Give me a chance to make up for…what my brother has done to you. Don't let him do this. Don't let him win, Teller."

* * * * *

Jay decided to play the girl carefully, knowing her reluctant assent to stay for a few more days was a tenuous one that could collapse under the least provocation. At the same time, he had every intention of getting wet with her by the end of the day— his cock buried deep between her legs or at the back of throat. He didn't mind which—hopefully both.

It was a shame he hadn't been able to get to her last night, he ruminated, then shrugged. A man couldn't do...everything, he decided, and there were some things that just couldn't be refused.

Uncertain exactly what sort of romance would draw her toward the result he had in mind, he chose to start out conservatively. An afternoon walk in his huge park seemed like a safe place to begin.

Standing before his image projected in the middle of the room, the baron circled it with exacting consideration then ordered the C to adjust his long pants a little more snugly around the hips. As the pants tightened on him, he stepped behind the image to check out his rear then moved around to eye his groin with a critical eye. "Add faint vertical stripes in the pants' groin," he commanded, frowning at the result. Finally shrugging, he tugged at his cock through the fabric of his pants, straightened it out with a few rubs and smiled at the effect on his image.

His image smiled back.

Pulling on a tight, formal T-shirt of shimmering maroon silk, he decided to forgo the jacket as he glanced at the time in his palm and headed through the doorshield.

* * * * *

"You're not afraid of grolnigs, are you?"

Thin spears of light shafted through the leaves overhead to pattern on the stone path they followed through the forest.

Teller shook her head. "I was raised in Monmoth, next to the reserve. It wasn't unusual to find several large males sunbathing on our hoverpad in the middle of the day." She shook her head again. "They don't eat anything that doesn't run."

He smiled. "I'm glad they don't worry you. There are several on the property. I purchased them along with a dozen lions and a set of white tigers."

He grinned at her look of surprise.

"What do you feed them?"

"I don't feed them. I import antelope regularly. There are some elk and telechi on the property as well. The animals are tagged for remote surveillance—I enjoy watching them hunt. Last week one of the grolnigs killed a lion. It was just a female that died but it was…quite a show."

When she slowed to stare at him, he took her arm. "You look nice."

"You've only yourself to thank," she answered slowly, as though her mind was elsewhere.

He nodded, tucking her hand into his arm. "I like dressing you. When I first saw you, I didn't think…but you look good in everything." His eyes lingered on the fabric that hugged her bottom scandalously, leaving nothing to the imagination. Beneath the black tights that stretched all the way up to wrap around her midriff, he knew she wore a silver thong. He'd sent it to her along with the tights and the short, loose jacket that didn't reach her waist. The stiff cotton of the pink jacket rasped at her nipples and they poked at the thin fabric like little tent posts.

"When you first saw me, I looked pretty rough," she reminded him.

"You were a mess," he admitted. "I almost kicked you out of—" Realizing himself, the baron came to an abrupt halt. "I almost kicked you out of my hovercoach," he finished.

A stiff breeze rustled in the trees and riffed at her thick brush of blonde hair.

"I noticed you haven't flashed anyone via my C," he mentioned quietly, but somehow the baron's soft words sounded like an accusation as he once again resumed his steps beside her. At a distance, bright light spilled onto the path ahead, indicating an end to the forest. "Do you have a private communicator?" His eyes flicked over her ear.

Quickly, Teller shook her head. "My family...friends don't hear from me every day. They won't notice a few days' silence."

"What about your employer?" Although the question was casual, there was a prying note that troubled Teller. "What do you do for a living?"

"I'm in communications," she told him.

"Universal Horizon?"

"Yes," she lied, not really understanding the reason for her caution. "But, I'm on leave—vacation."

There was a small silence. "I couldn't find you in my C-Bank."

"You looked me up?"

"I was curious," he said mildly. "Interested, actually." Slanting a look at her, he added a smile to flirt at the end of the statement.

"My stats are often misfiled. The letter 'O' is often entered as a zero. What is your interest in dragons?" she asked to change the subject.

The baron stumbled and she glanced at him to see his jaw turn hard.

"I noticed the recently read articles in your C-Bank," she told him, suddenly feeling that an explanation was in order.

"I was on the planet Scree recently, hoping to sight one. It's commonly held that dragons have been hunted to extinction, but I thought I might get lucky. I thought a dragon would make a nice addition to my park. What do you know about them?"

"Not much. Only that they were in great demand last century. I recall something about their bodies being dried and ground into dust to be passed off as the world's strongest aphrodisiac." Disgustedly, she shook her head. "Some people will believe anything. Did you get lucky?"

A muscle twitched in the baron's jaw. "No," he said, "decidedly not. Did you know they were parasites?"

"Parasites?!" She thought about that. "Parasites are typically small creatures that can attach themselves to another animal without interfering with the host's day-to-day existence. Sometimes they even perform some service for the host that makes their presence tolerable." She frowned as she shook her head. "But dragons were huge, weren't they? I can't imagine how that would work."

"Neither can I," the baron offered in a growl.

Light washed onto the stone path, shading the slate flagstone to pale gray, and the trees thinned as the forest opened into a sunlit meadow. Together, they strolled out of the trees into the sloping meadow that rolled down to the villa. Trailing the couple by twenty feet, Huvisdank followed, a lazgun slung over his shoulder.

Upon reaching the villa, Jay left Teller to change for dinner, pleased with his performance. He'd played the perfect gentlemen with the girl. After dinner and a little wine, the right clothing and a few compliments, the girl would be charmed into his bed and onto his cock. He had too much confidence to think otherwise. And, over time, there'd been a great number of women to reinforce that confidence.

* * * * *

Sighing, Teller considered her image in the middle of the room. She wasn't sure she wanted to join the baron at dinner. Something about his attitude toward animals bothered her, especially his remark that indicated he'd enjoyed watching the lioness' death. More than anything, she was troubled by the fact that he was comfortable with his chilling conduct and hadn't thought there was any reason to hide it from her or even gloss it over a bit on her behalf.

The haltertop he'd formulated for her was simple and elegant and very modern. Made of silvered pink paper, it wrapped around her neck in a wide band and draped down over her chest just far enough to cover her nipples. The rest of her midriff, belly and on down was bared above low-rise hip huggers that only just covered her mound of fair pubic hair. In the back, the haltertop exposed the long line of her naked back.

She jumped when she saw the man's reflection in the patio's windowshield. Angrily, she spun to face him.

"*What* are you doing here?" she put to him, her voice a cold hiss.

Hyde leaned against the wall. The pose was casual but, inside his dark vest and short jacket, his muscles rippled beneath the thin silk that hugged his upper body, revealing a tightly held tension. "I had to…be with you."

His deep, hard voice was rich, and warm and enticingly sincere. Not charming. Sincere. Plain and direct and simply sincere.

Teller shook her head, realizing that's what she wanted to believe. The man had fucked her up against a wall while another woman — a stationed woman — lay waiting for him in his comfortable bed.

"The feeling isn't mutual." She measured out each word like corrosive acid and let the words drop burning from her mouth. "The next time you have a few spare minutes, *don't* bring them here."

He nodded, pushing himself away from the wall to saunter toward her. Taking each of his steps as a threat, she backed up against the resilient surface of the windowshield.

With one hand bracing himself on the wall at the windowshield's edge, he put his breath in the hair at her temple. "I have time now," he murmured, his words a seductive syrup that trickled down her spine and pooled at the small of her back, overflowing to warm her womb with liquid heat. She was certain she should have been outraged. She knew for a fact she should have brought her fist around and flattened him. Instead, she gulped in a breath and fisted her hand to stop herself from taking hold of some part — any part — of him.

"You'd only just left Aleena when you came to my room last night, your cock only just pulled from between another woman's legs."

"You don't understand," he whispered against her ear, as though the fact was her fault. And the words, the touch, the warm, humid breath against her skin sent a spike of longing that started below her belly and flashed through her weakened knees as it shot all the way down to curl her toes.

"What's not to understand?" she croaked out, almost breathless in his very near, overpoweringly warm presence.

He shook his head and his lips touched her face as he did so. She bit her lips together to hold back the grating moan that fought to voice itself. "I'm afraid you'd like the truth less than the lie."

She swallowed hard. "Try me."

He pushed his body to seal against hers. "I'd never do anything to hurt you, Teller."

She swallowed hard. "You already have, Hyde." Her voice shook on the last word. "Leave me alone."

"Teller."

"*Please*," she reiterated.

"I can't do that." His lips brushed against hers and her eyes fixed on his mouth as her lips parted to suck in a shaking breath.

"Why?"

He opened his mouth and, for two seconds, stared at her hungrily.

"Why, Hyde? Give me a reason."

His eyes fixed on the windowshield, unfocused. "You *are* the reason," he said finally, bringing his eyes back to hers. "The only reason I have to—"

"What?"

"The only reason I have."

She stared at him. "You really are mad, aren't you?"

For one stunned instant, he looked as though she'd slapped him.

"I suppose I should feel sorry for you, but I don't have time just now, I'm having dinner with your brother—" she drawled, letting her tongue linger on that last word, rubbing the point in, grinding the fact home "—and I don't want to keep him waiting."

A dangerous gold fire leapt in his eyes as, pushing away from the wall with a hard thrust, he turned and strode from the room.

Staring at the doorshield, Teller took a few moments to gather herself before she followed him out into the empty hall and down the corridor to Jay's room.

That could have gone either way, she berated herself on the way down the wide, carpeted corridor. She would have let him in, she realized with frustration. If he hadn't started with that "reason" bullshit, she would have let him in again. Into her heart—as well as her body. She would have opened herself to him, his hard, hot cock and all the hurt that would come with his intrusion into her life. She would have let him pump himself off between her legs and fill her with his unique brand of heartache.

Almost choking in disgust, Teller realized she could almost hate herself for this weakness where Hyde was concerned—for her inability to *stop* wanting him. She needed to purge him from her system. Needed to scrape the memory of his touch from her skin, replacing it with another's. Needed to do this at the soonest possible moment, before she found herself giving into temptation.

And the baron represented the perfect opportunity.

The baron's doorshield was transparent so she pushed into the well-appointed room. When the aristocrat started out of his chair, she wondered if she'd woken him. She noticed that, as he stood, he threw a tense glance into his open hand.

Chapter Six

Relieved the meal was finally over, Teller let go a breath as Jay's clone picked up the plate and whisked it away. "I sent him away," she told the baron.

They were seated at a small ornate table in the baron's bedroom. The setting was cozy, warm and intimate Teller had to conclude, as the holoflix simulated candlelight. Tiny leaves of light hovered and flickered in the air around them, glinting along crystal goblets and silver flatware.

On the table lay enough broken music sticks to pay off the planet's entire public debt. But Teller's eyes followed the clone. Huvisdank's costume belonged to an ancient era, the black-tailed coat and stiff white collar punctuating the comfortable ambiance of old-world opulence.

"I'm glad of that," the baron told her gently. "You did the right thing, Teller. Huvisdank, fill the lady's wineglass."

"Thank you, Huvisdank," Teller told the manservant in the middle of his task. "That's enough." Curiously, she stared at the clone as he continued to pour.

"The clone takes orders only from me," Jay reminded her.

"And Hyde," she said absently.

The baron raised startled eyes to connect with hers.

Teller shrugged. "I've seen him take orders from Hyde."

Jay's nostrils flared and he gave her a grim nod as his eyes swung around to burn at his clone. "Stupid bastard can't tell us apart." For an instant, there was venom in his eyes—then it was gone.

"Where's the rest of your staff?" she inquired to change the subject, no more inclined to pursue this topic of conversation than the baron was. "It must take a lot of people to run a place this large."

"The villa is fully automated, everything linked to the C. I'm a private man," he explained, "and I prefer not to be surrounded by those I can't…trust."

She gazed at the hard, uncompromising face and wondered if trust wasn't the issue, so much as control.

"You look good in pink," he murmured with an assessing gleam in his warm gaze.

"Thank you. It's…a color I wouldn't normally choose for myself."

"No? C-Access. Scan room. Identify color FF75FF. Change to 00BE00."

She glanced down at the newly green haltertop. "That's nice, too," she told him with a smile. "Do you…and your brother always dress alike?"

She watched Jay suck his cheeks into his mouth as his calculating lips thrust forward. "Hyde insists on mimicking me. It's only the least of his strange perversions." Tipping some wine into his mouth, his cheeks hollowed again as he ran the wine over his tongue. "What did you think of the wine?"

His ability to shift gears was disconcerting. She could have sworn he was angry, only moments ago—furious—to learn Hyde could command the clone. But if he'd been angry, there was no indication of it now. He had put it away, completely. She marked it up to a life invested in politics and assumed he was a man adept at hiding his true feelings. It was a concept she'd had no little experience with herself.

She shrugged. "I'm not much of a connoisseur."

"I am," he returned with a warm smile, making it clear that, for the moment, he wasn't talking about wine. "What year were you born?"

"3030."

"Good year," he observed as he pushed back his chair and stood. "Finish your wine," he directed. "I hope you'll spend the night here?" he both asked and told her at the same time, turning away before she could answer. "C-Access. Case table. Remove subject."

Reaching for her wineglass, Teller pushed away from the table as it lifted an inch from the floor and glided through the room's doorshield. Before she could consider the baron's proposal, he was addressing his manservant. "Huvisdank, you can give me a hand with my clothing."

Teller's hand halted in mid-action, the crystal rim of the wineglass balanced against her lips as she frowned, wondering if she'd understood right. Was the baron actually asking his manservant to undress him? Now? In her presence?

With an arched eyebrow, the baron caught her reaction and smiled at it. "Huvisdank is my bodyguard as well as my manservant. There isn't much I do without him."

Teller's eyes traveled to the doorshield and back as she quickly reviewed escape options. Hyde might be out there and she didn't want to run into him any more than she wanted him to know she'd left his brother so soon after dinner. Assuming he'd care, she'd like to give him a bitter taste of the humiliation and disappointment she'd experienced courtesy of his wayward appetite. Reminding herself that this was probably the opportunity she needed to eradicate the clinging memory of Hyde's warm touch, she pulled her bottom lip through her teeth. In addition to all of these emotions, curiosity warred with modesty then took the field to win a small victory as she decided to stay long enough to see how the baron's planned exposé would play out.

"Remove my clothing, Huvisdank," he ordered casually.

Immediately, the clone stepped behind his master, reaching to pull the short jacket away from the baron's shoulders—and Teller had the sure impression that it wasn't the first time the manservant had undressed his master.

"Don't rush," the baron said softly, raising his arms.

Reaching under the baron's arms, Huvisdank's finger slid down the front of Jay's satin vest, releasing the static clasp that held it closed. With the jacket and vest resting on the clone's wide shoulder, he caught the bottom edge of the white silk T-shirt and pulled it up over the stretched muscles of Jay's chest, over his head and up his raised arms, allowing Teller a glimpse of the golden, tufted hair that collected in the hollows beneath the baron's arms.

Although the clone's actions were purposeful, there was something arousing about watching the giant's large, masculine hands on his master. Teller stopped breathing when the clone reached around with both hands to struggle with the buttons leading down the front of Jay's pelvis and into his crotch. The long pants were tight across the groin and the clone fumbled at them with thick fingers.

In this modern age, most clothing was closed with static clasps. Buttons were entirely unnecessary, but just as equally fashionable—the current rage in fact—and broadly considered the sexiest damn thing ever invented.

Teller licked her lips as her breath thickened, watching the manservant work at the buttons, watching the longpants peel open from the top down. Her eyes followed a line of dark gold hair into Jay's pants, watched it join a mass of curls that collected just above an impressive length of flesh exposed just inside his parted pants. As Huvisdank worked the clinging fabric down the baron's naked flanks, Jay's erection stretched and lifted. When he stepped out of the pants, the clone got down on one knee before his master as Jay lifted a foot to the clone's thigh and Teller watched the baron's cock sway inches from the clone's sensuous mouth as the manservant removed his master's boots.

Casually, with a hand stroking the underside of his cock, Jay approached her. "Huvisdank, help the lady with her clothes."

"No," she said quickly. "I'd rather…"

"You'd rather I did it." The baron shrugged. "I'm sorry, I assumed...but most of the people I know have servants. I'm flattered." One step and he was behind her. "Let's see if I can remember how to do this." Before she could react, she felt his fingers at her neck then a yank and the paper halter came apart in two pieces. The baron grunted. "Apparently, I'm a bit rusty."

Handing the remnants to the manservant at his elbow, he traced a thumb down her spine to her quick intake of breath.

"Hyde was a bastard to ever hurt you," he said at exactly the right instant, at exactly the moment when Teller's decision to stay or leave hung in the balance. "How could a creature like Hyde appreciate a woman like you?"

As Teller's back arched in response to his thumb's teasing impetus, Jay slid his hands forward, over her pelvic wings and pulled her lower body against his. His fingers reached into her groin as he rubbed the ridge of his erection into her crease. In a needy bid for attention, her nipples tautened and her head fell back on Jay's shoulder as she surrendered herself to Hyde's double, longing for a man's rough touch on her hungry nipples.

But, by now, the baron was easing the tight leggings down her hips, rubbing against her at the same time, the naked flesh of his cock now in contact with the smooth skin exposed on her small, tight bottom. The warm, moist skin of his erection dragged the length of her crease as his hands swooped to cup her bottom and clamped on the muscles of her ass, opening her cheeks for his further ingress.

"Get rid of the pants," he rasped, all uneven breath.

As she leaned forward to accomplish this task, she heard his rough sigh of gratification and he forged more deeply between her cheeks. She felt his thumb slide beneath the slim silver ribbon of the thong that divided her cheeks. There was a rough jerk and, as though the silver thong had been designed for this purpose, the ribbon gave way, giving Jay full access to her sex. Hurrying the pants to her feet, she stepped out of them as the baron thrust against the tight crimp of her ass.

When she straightened, Teller tried to turn to him, nipples ready for the rough, grazing touch of a man's body, mons aching for pressing contact, lips alive with sparking need to be crushed. But he held her in place. As his easy access was reduced, he ran his hands into her waist and over her hips. She felt the back of his fingers between their bodies as one of his hands returned to swipe upward along the full length of his cock. "Lift her onto me, Huvisdank."

Chapter Seven

Teller's body stiffened. "Jay," she began uneasily.

The baron let go an impatient sigh. "Hold on, Huvisdank," he said as his hands traveled to her shoulders and he turned her to face him. "Don't be naïve, Teller. The clone feels nothing. He doesn't react to you in anyway. When he picks you up or stands at your back, you might as well be sitting in a chair or leaning against a wall. And let me tell you, sweetheart, he's a damn sight more comfortable than that wall I'm going to bang you up against—if you don't let him help.

"I could send him away but then I'd be without a bodyguard. I could send him across the room but, to be honest, it always seems a bit awkward when he's watching from over there."

"Always?"

There was a smile of confidence on the baron's face and in his voice just before he leaned forward to settle his lips at her ear. "Hyde knows I'm with you," he whispered, with uncanny timing.

Teller's eyes widened. "Now?"

"He *knows* I'm with you. You don't want to leave now. My brother deserves this and you know it. He deserves to wonder what we're doing in here." His knees flexed as he grasped the root of his cock and fed its head between her legs. "This will be a lot more comfortable with Huvisdank's help," he coaxed. "For both of us.

"Huvisdank," he commanded. "Take the lady gently by the waist. Lift her onto my cock."

The manservant was behind her as firm, strong hands on her waist raised her several inches. Teller felt Jay's hands on the insides of her thighs then under her upper legs, easing her legs up and out, followed by his hot, hard cock head at the mouth of her sex. Halting there, he whispered a comfortable obscenity before pulling his hips back and thrusting up into her. Behind her, the clone's hands smoothed down to cup her bottom. A fluid weakness gathered at the base of her spine and poured from there into her womb to pool at the top of her vagina in scathing, aching demand.

"Pull her open a bit, Huvisdank." The baron's voice was a muted rasp, warmed with lust, as his shaft rasped within her.

As the clone pulled her cheeks apart, the baron forged into her anew, murmuring his appreciation. The rough texture of Huvisdank's heavy jacket rasped at her back and she gasped as the baron took her deeply, hitting her solidly at the back of her cervix in that hard-to-reach spot so seldom intruded upon. With bruising intrusion, he crammed into her, slamming against the sensitive point with demanding insistence.

"A little more pressure, Huvisdank. Push her down on me. Oh, God, yes. That's it. Rub her onto my cock." Teller raised her eyes to the baron's face but his glazed eyes were on his manservant. "A little harder," he ordered the clone between erratic breaths.

The iron chest of the clone pressed into her back as Huvisdank gripped her cheeks in his large, rough hands. Using his whole body to rock her downward, the clone forced her onto the baron, forced her cunt down to sheathe Jay's cock in a steady rhythm—forced her down to receive the baron's full, hard impact. Teller's head was tucked beneath the giant's chin as the two men manipulated her between their bodies, Jay's thick cock head stretching into her vagina, slamming into her cervix.

"God," Jay grunted. "I've never been in such a tight place before. I didn't know a woman could feel this good. You were made for this, Teller. Made for a man. Made to fuck." His eyes glinted with hot, hard pleasure. "Put your lips on her neck," he growled at the clone.

Lightly, the manservant's collar scraped against her ear and Teller jumped at the sudden, damp contact of the clone's lips, intimate in their action while at the same time cool, objective in their delivery.

The baron smiled at her wide-eyed expression. "Feels good, doesn't it? Even if it is just a clone. Wait until you feel his fingers in your pussy.

"Massage the side of your finger into her crease," he ordered his manservant in a hoarse voice. "How does she feel?"

"She's wet, My Lord."

"Get her legs higher," he ordered his clone. Teller felt her muscles pull as Jay slid his cock halfway out and rammed up into her several times, his flush root sawing between her legs. "Pull them and spread them, Huvisdank. I want to fuck her all the way." He grunted, watching the root of his cock as his hips jacked into the tender pink flesh between her spread legs.

The punishing end of his cock slammed into her center one more time than she could bear and, on the edge of climax, her body fought to capture and maintain the full contact of his cock head as she struggled in the iron hold of Huvisdank.

"That's it," the baron rasped in command. "Hold her, Huvisdank."

Sliding out of her, the baron watched her face as he cupped his balls, shifting them in his right hand. "Just a minute. I've got to see this."

Teller opened frenzied eyes on the baron, squirming in the clone's implacable grasp. The clone's hands gripped the back of her thighs, just above her knees, spreading her fragile sex open for the intrusion of his master's heated gaze.

Jay's avaricious eyes salivated at the sight of her open pussy, her extraordinary clitoris displayed at the top of her wet, rosy-hued sex. Cocking his head, he smiled at her as he drew closer. "Wonder what it would take to make you come at this point," he mused, his voice rasping and thick with lust. His eyes slid down to her clit, poking through the lips of her labia—hot pink, wet pink, swollen to the point of bursting. Cupping his hand, he covered her pussy and ran his fingers through every ridge and valley set between her open legs. "You're an easy come, aren't you?"

She stared at him through a haze of consuming need, poised on the edge of orgasm.

"I'd suck on your tits if you had any," he said roughly. "That would work at this point. Wouldn't it, Teller? That would make you orgasm, make you spill into my hand." Moving in closer, he placed a thumb on one of her nipples and rasped at it as his eyes remained lowered on the hand in her wet sex. "That would make you come. You're that close, aren't you, baby?"

As his finger rode over her clit she gasped, a mangled cry of sexual distress.

Ruthlessly, he flicked her clit. "Oh, yeah. You're close and you want it, don't you? Tell me you want it, Teller. Tell me you want what your body is begging for."

Teller cried out and struggled in Huvisdank's arms.

"Touch her, Huvisdank."

"My Lord?"

"Touch her. I want to watch her slit quake." Dropping to his knees, he pulled her lips open with his thumbs and blew on her clit as he watched her opening contract in several shuddering gulps. Lightly, he ran his finger around the tiny, tight slit of her opening. "I'm going to enjoy filling this little cunt," he said softly, thoughtfully. "Stretching it wide, packing it full of cock. But first, I'm going to watch it come…all on its own. I'm going to watch it cry—beg—for a cock riding it hard and when it's streaming…only when it's streaming…then I'm going to fuck you, Teller.

"Touch her, Huvisdank. I'll take her leg. Bring your hand down here."

Teller felt the baron's hand pressing her thigh back onto her chest.

"Just a finger. Here, I'll guide you."

As Huvisdank's large, rough finger connected with her clit, Teller felt her body leap that much further forward toward climax. Clumsily, the clone rasped a rough finger over her clitoris but at this point, she didn't care that he was rough. Any movement, any friction at all was going to push her over the edge and toward the release she was approaching at dimensional speed. "Jay, please," she begged in a rushing intake of breath.

"Hold up, Huvisdank."

When he blew on her clit again, she wrenched in the clone's arms.

"What do you think, Huvisdank?"

"I think the young woman is asking for it, My Lord."

Teller strangled a moan of frustration, her parted sex almost burning her alive with a deep smoldering need for release. "Jay!"

The baron rose to his feet and cocked an eyebrow at his manservant. "What do you think, Huvisdank?"

"I think My Lord should fuck the girl, sir."

"Then put her on me," he grated roughly and without further warning drove up into her as Huvisdank held her on the baron's dick. Three hard, powerful, spine-splintering thrusts and Teller leapt into orgasm, screaming to all the gods—and all at once—as her cunt spasmed through a long series of shattering contractions and the baron delivered satisfaction at the end of his reaming cock. At the same time, the baron grunted his approval, watching her face with keen interest. His fingernails were biting at her waist when he eventually thickened to ungodly proportions and shot forth inside her.

Afterward he grinned up at his manservant, the girl still pressed damp and limp between their two bodies. "Thank you, Huvisdank," he told his manservant. "That will be all for now."

"My Lord." The clone disengaged himself and moved away as Teller's feet slipped to the ground. "Shall I return in fifty minutes, My Lord?"

"Twenty ought to do it. This girl has the tightest little slit I've ever had wrapped around my dick. I'm expecting a quick comeback. After a cold, dry shower, I'll be ready to take her again.

"And, Huvisdank."

"My Lord?"

"Get rid of that suit," he said casually, pushing the girl toward the shower case. "You're wearing too many clothes. Plan to spend the night here."

* * * * *

After the dry shower, Teller fell asleep on the baron's bed. When she woke, she was on her side. Warm arms were wrapped around her waist like steel bands—iron hands gripped her— possessive in their grasp, reverent in their caress. She looked down to find a golden head nestled against her belly. Stretching inside the warm embrace, she felt rough, dry lips track their way up her body as she was rolled onto her back. Smiling into the bed-wrecked hair on her chest, she was gasping a moment later when a wet mouth sucked up both nipple and areola.

Her back arched in pleasure and the man murmured his approval as his arms banded around her more tightly.

"Teller," he whispered in a voice filled with warmth.

Abruptly, she came up on her elbows, scrambling away from the man.

His arms clamped her tighter still as his head tilted upward and gold eyes caught at hers.

"Where! Where did you come from? Where's the baron?"

"Teller—"

"Let me go, Hyde. Get your hands *off* me."

173

Rolling on top of her, he pinned her beneath him as he worked his way up her body. Grasping the wrists of the hands that fought him, he manacled them beside her head and covered her mouth with a hot, wet, carnal kiss—his tongue thrusting to take the interior of her mouth, rubbing between her teeth and forcing her mouth to open for his tongue's invasion. Immediately, she was aware of every naked inch of his body where it touched hers and she trembled, still and accepting beneath the heavy male weight trapping her against the bed. At the same time, her soul sucked up the raw carnality being forced upon her, her mind wondering how much he'd force on her, her traitorous body hoping it was everything.

Abruptly, he broke from her, and she opened her eyes to find him panting down at her. "You need to get out of here," he said between short, harsh breaths.

She caught her breath. "No, *you* need to get out of here."

Releasing her, he followed her onto his knees as her eyes went round her, looking for Jay, looking for something that would explain Hyde's presence. "Where's Jay?" she repeated, searching the room.

"Don't let him do this to you, Teller. Don't let him seduce you. Don't let him use you like he uses Huvisdank. Like a toy."

She stared at Hyde's naked body, trying to understand how he'd gotten into the baron's room and into the baron's bed without any clothing. "It's not like that! The baron is a man who's…comfortable with his sexuality."

"The baron's comfortable with everybody's sexuality!"

"Who are you to criticize?! Stealing away from the Lady Aleena for a quick fuck with me!"

His eyebrows came together and his eyes filled with gold fire. "He promised to send for you! I couldn't bear to think of you waiting alone."

"He was busy! With the Imperion Lord! The Leader of the planet!"

"He was busy," Hyde agreed with scorn.

"Not half as busy as you!"

Hyde's eyes narrowed to thin slits.

"The baron isn't using me."

Gold eyes challenged hers.

"No more than I'm using him," she muttered defensively. "He's getting what he wants. I'm getting what I want."

The gold eyes narrowed some more as if to screen out some truth. "Don't tell me you're using him to punish me." His voice was an anvil dropping.

"Of course not," she forced the lie out of her mouth. "Although that would be poetic justice."

"Actually," he told her. "That would be the ultimate irony."

Struggling to try and understand what he might mean, her eyes flickered on him.

"Is this enough for you, Teller? To be the baron's current sex toy? Is this all you want?"

Her chin came up with a defiant tilt. "A man who isn't doing two women at once? Yeah, Hyde," she said quietly. "That's what I want."

Hyde shook his golden head. A fine twisting strand of gold fell across his eye and he brushed it away impatiently. "And yet, *you're* willing to do two men at once," he pointed out coldly.

The idea took her unawares.

"Because Huvsidank will be here in a minute and, if the baron has his way, the clone will have his head buried between your legs while the baron watches you together."

"No, he won't," she said in a small, breathless voice. "I won't let him."

"You're wrong," he stated. "You won't be able to stop that stupid, meaningless pile of DNA." His gaze turned hard and mean. "But I won't let him. I'll kill the little bastard before I let him."

"Little!" Her head jerked back in disbelief. "Are you talking about Huvisdank?" she sputtered. "You'd try to kill that asteroid-hauler who has no interest in me yet it doesn't bother you that..." Staring at his rigid cock, she stopped suddenly. "You really are identical, aren't you?"

"I'm nothing like Jay," he lashed out. "I'd never let another man touch you!"

"Except for your brother!"

He stopped his tirade. He didn't argue. "Leave now, Teller," he said in a low, menacing voice.

"The only reason I'd leave, Hyde, is because you're here."

"I don't care why you do it. Just do it!"

Scooting away from him on the bed, she threw her legs to the floor and stood proudly. "I'll leave, Hyde," she informed him. "On one condition. That you stay the hell away from me."

Hyde glared up at her from the bed.

"Do we have a deal?"

"I won't stand by and let him hurt you," he countered.

She gave him a look of scorn. "That's terribly noble of you, Hyde. To protect me from a man who's done me no harm. Don't put yourself out, man!"

"Just promise me you'll call me if you need help."

"And in return you'll leave me alone?"

He nodded.

"Done!" Turning smartly, she strode through the doorshield and out of the baron's bedroom.

Chapter Eight

Teller lay on her back, staring at the ceiling of her room, thinking about Hyde. Waking to find him wrapped around her like a warm gift, his hair tousled, his gold eyes charged with a ready fire, his naked body forcing hers deep into the resilient surface of the bed as he sprawled over her, naked and masterfully carnal as his knee pushed between her legs and his thick, moist cock dragged over the smooth skin of her belly. It was unsettling, the way those few, simple touches of his flesh against her own had eclipsed any pleasure she'd found at the hands of the baron...and his clone.

So unsettling, she hardly noticed when Jay entered the room and joined her on the small, rectangular sofa. Very bare and simple, without arms, the slick black piece of furniture was new Art Deco in style. Automatically, without thinking, she slid her feet back and raised her knees to make room for him. Without preamble, he took one of her feet and moved it up onto the sofa's short back, pushing her other foot to the floor. Her robe slid apart to expose her naked lower body.

Inwardly, Teller shook her head. Hyde was right. The two brothers were nothing alike. The baron lacked his brother's animal vitality, his raw, elemental attraction. Jay was merely a wan, shadowy facsimile of his excessively male brother.

God, Hyde was a sexy beast! Too bad he was such a fucking bastard.

"What happened to you last night?" Jay asked, as he moved his right hand into the opening of the rust-colored satin robe. Lazily, he fingered the curling hair at the top of her cleft. "We missed you, Huvisdank and I."

The words shook her out of her reverie. Husvidank wouldn't miss the sun if it fell out of the sky! "Hyde," she answered and felt Jay's fingers tighten to tug at her pubic hair. "When I woke, he was in your room—in your bed! Where did you go?" she asked him, suddenly curious.

"I…went to see what was taking Huvisdank so long," the words came out of his mouth like train cars grinding. "Did you…did he…"

"No. Of course not," she replied swiftly.

"I'm sorry. I might have guessed he'd be there the minute I turned my back. You left him in my room?"

"He wasn't there when you returned?"

The baron shook his head. "I don't want to talk about Hyde," he said suddenly as his fingers loosened.

"Tell me about the last man you fucked," Jay said in a forced drawl.

She regarded him with surprise.

"Other than me…and my bastard brother."

"It wasn't like that."

Jay rolled his eyes. "Tell me about the last man you made love to then."

Wryly, she smiled. "It wasn't like that, either."

"Then tell me what it was like," the baron insisted lazily, his finger dragging open first one side of her labia then the other.

"Most of the men I…associate with…aren't interested in me."

Staring at her flat chest, the baron nodded without argument.

"It was just sex."

"Just a quick missionary fix?"

"It was quick," she admitted.

The baron laughed. "Now I'm interested." Reaching for one of her hands, he pulled it down to the curling thatch of her hair and arranged her fingers to drape over her gold mound. Cocking his head, he surveyed his work with a critical eye of appreciation. With his fingers lacing hers, he played his hand into her pussy and casually brushed her clit. "With you on top?"

"Not exactly."

"Don't tease. It's not fair." Returning his attention to her sex, he opened her a bit with his fingers. "Touch your clit for me. Show me how you like to be fingered."

Touching herself lightly, she did as she was commanded.

The baron nodded as he watched. "Keep going. Did he spread your legs and get his mouth on this?" He circled her clit with his index finger, tangling with her finger as he did so. "No. Don't stop."

"We were too hot to fool around. We just wanted to hurry up and get there."

The baron fingered his way down to her wet vulva while he watched her finger petting her stiff clit. "You're not giving me much to go on, Teller. I want to hear about the last man that fucked you."

"It was just sex," she repeated.

Nudging his middle finger into her vagina, he smiled when she twitched. Swirling the top of his finger into the tight little space, he slid the digit all the way in and started a steady reciprocal motion. "Just sex? Sounds boring. Tell me about the best fuck you've ever had, then."

Teller was silent, her hand still, her eyes distant as her mind slipped back to a starlit night and rustling blue taffeta.

The baron's face grew cold as he watched her. "Is that how you like it?" His voice was a steel, metallic warning. His finger came out of her vagina and his hands were grasping at her hips as he flipped her over and pulled her up onto her knees. "Is that how you like it?" he said softly, coldly, shoving her robe up over her ass as he got on his knees behind her. "Mounted from

179

behind and fucked like an animal?" She heard the rough rustle of buttons undone too quickly and felt his thick cock head pressed against her tender notch. "Fucked into the ground?"

She gasped as he drove into her. "Jay!" she cried as his shaft forged, and filled and struck her hard at her limit. "Jay," she choked out, "what are you talking about?"

"Hyde," he grated in one word as his hips retracted in slow warning, only to slam forward to fill her again. With his knee, he shoved her outside leg off the sofa. She crumpled a bit before she got her foot on the ground to support her. Then his foot was inside hers, widening her stance as he continued to hammer into her. "Hyde," he snarled. "It was Hyde who raped you. Raped you, and left you broken and bleeding for me to find."

With these words, Teller felt the baron's cock thicken inside her, stretch her until she thought she would rip wide open.

"Is that the way you want it, Teller? Is that the way you want to be fucked?"

"No," she said softly, automatically. It took her no more than half a heartbeat to dismiss the baron's accusation. For all of Hyde's mad lies and wayward behavior, she couldn't be that far wrong about him. She'd felt his warmth. *Felt it!* He wasn't capable of cold, violent rape. "No."

But if the baron heard, there was no indication of it as he continued to pump his shaft into her cunt, pushing her leg wider.

"No," she whispered. "I don't believe you."

With his cock buried to his balls, the baron stilled just before a roar filled the room. A roar of harsh, male triumph. And Teller assumed he would be coming in the next instant. But there was no lessening of the hard, insistent pressure that stretched her vagina from vulva to cervix.

There were a few seconds of still silence before she felt a hand slide over the left cheek of her bottom, the thumb dragging along behind the palm, meticulous in its attention and care. The hand continued slowly down her leg and his leg shifted inward an inch as the big hand gently coaxed her to follow.

Emotions strained to breaking by this simple act of kindness, Teller fought to contain the hot, wet tears that filled her eyes. Dropping to her forearms, she freed her hands to wipe at her eyes.

Now hard, male hands dragged slowly up her thighs to caress the curves of her bottom and—all at once—Teller found herself wanting the filling, aching presence pressuring her toward fulfillment. The same action that her body had fought to reject only moments ago. Wanted the man's movement inside of her. Any kind of movement.

Instead, the man at her back leaned over to drag a kiss over her skin, his smooth, hard lips scraping from shoulder blade to shoulder blade as she trembled beneath him, her excitement building in anticipation. Involuntarily, her back arched and she pushed her bottom into the damp groin that pressed to possess her sex. Pushing backward, she stretched into him, capturing a little more of him to prod against her point of acceptance, her point of ultimate need.

She heard a rumble behind her, a rumble of rough male gratification and thought he stretched into her even more thickly. Then his hands were pulling her cheeks open, easing them wider as a thumb slid through her crease, loitering to stroke over the crimp of her ass as he slowly pulled his shaft a few inches. Leveraging herself back on her forearms, she tried to follow his retraction, tried to push back onto him and heard his breathy groan of pleasure. One hand moved to grip her right cheek while his left slid between their bodies.

With a hand beneath his moistened shaft, he reached his fingers into her folds and found the stark shape of her clit. As his hips rocked slowly, an inch given, an inch retracted, his hand followed his movement to tease across her clit and Teller gritted her teeth as he swept her nearer to the edge of orgasm—not wanting to come before he was seated deep inside her, filling her thickly, striking that point of no return. She held on, willing herself to remain open to receive his sex, refusing to allow herself to close in gut-wrenching, clamping release.

Wiping her damp upper lip, she felt a trickle of moisture tickle the inside of her thigh as her body prepared itself to receive and welcome the man at her back. She felt her vagina quaking for him as his finger left her clitoris and stroked at the wet stream on either side of the inside of her thighs. She felt him retract all the way and wanted to cry as her cunt shuddered.

"Yes," she moaned, praying that her words would bring her the hard action she waited to release on. "This is the way I want it. Now."

He gave it to her. Fully, thickly and all the way. He thrust into her and she shot into orgasm so complete she had to strangle a scream. A sound of pure, gut-wrenching pleasure caught in her throat as she drove herself back on the thick stake of his cock buried between the cheeks of her ass, her cunt sucking and squeezing and wrenching at the length that captured and captivated her body.

When the long series of quaking contractions drew to a final shuddering close, he started to move on her and she realized he hadn't yet released. Slowly at first, he came into her then picked up speed but still holding off as though waiting for something. All at once, there was a second rushing buildup inside her and she knew what he was waiting for. Pushing back on her forearms, she forced her body back into his groin as she hurried to meet him, to be ready for him. With a sudden snapping inside her soul, she sparked into orgasm again, jacking her body back violently to suck him up. Hard hands, hard fingernails dug into the flesh of her hips as he held her tight against his groin, held her on the full shafting length of his cock, held her into the fuck then released inside the hot grip of her cunt to fill her with a jetted wash of blasting cum.

This time the erotic scream of fulfillment fought its way out of her mouth.

Light kisses patterned over the cheeks of her bottom and she mewed her contentment as the man slid out of her to sit behind her, his arms wrapped around her legs as he hugged her bottom into the warm, rough stubble of his cheek. Replete and content, she sighed. The baron had just challenged his brother for the position of best-ever lover with the most perfect twin pair of orgasms she'd ever experienced. The most mind-shattering, bone-bending, soul-bonding combination of gentle and demanding, kind and punishing, soft and hard, that had all started with the word "no". What he had begun in cold anger, he had finished with as much passion and heated warmth as she had ever known in her lifetime.

When he collected her up into his arms, she let him carry her across the room to the bed. Stretched out beside him, she looked for his eyes but found them closed. The man was an enigma, she decided wonderingly. Cool and disinterested, she had thought—hard at times—but evidently capable of warmth and tenderness as well.

She watched the sleeping man, still fully dressed, buttons undone, longpants open enough to allow a glimpse of the damp, ruddy cock tucked within. With her head resting on his chest, she fell asleep thinking she was wrong again—the baron wasn't so terribly unlike his brother.

Chapter Nine

"C-Broadcast. Huvisdank, come to the large guest room on the main floor."

The baron's command intruded into Teller's sunny, golden dreams. Stretching languorously, she turned to him just in time to see his eyes slitted on the time in his palm.

His voice was warped with anger when he spoke. "Did you enjoy yourself?" With a yank that was almost vicious, he removed his jacket and slung it on the bed.

Confused, Teller eyed him without answering. Why should he be angry again?

His arms stretched as he ripped his T-shirt over his head. "*Did you?*"

Tightening the satin robe around herself, she pushed herself up to sit on the bed, nodding at him uncertainly. Why should he be angry?

"I'm glad you enjoyed yourself," he said in a voice like scraping ice. "Now I'll show you how I like it."

A noise behind her startled her, and she turned her head to stare at the manservant as he entered the room. His sequined costume was an extravagant rendition of an ancient cowboy's costume. Gold chaps covered the front of his legs, but that was all they covered. A thin belt secured the chaps at his waist while narrow strings traveled behind his legs where they were tied off beneath his naked buttocks. On his head was a black, wide-brimmed hat with a gold band. In his crotch was a thick mass of sparkling sequins, where the thong he wore covered his sex. The outfit, which might have been sexy on a more animated man, looked awkward on the giant clone.

"What do you think?" Jay asked her, watching her expression, his voice a tight challenge.

"It…doesn't suit him," she told him a little bluntly.

The baron twisted his lips appraisingly as he considered his clone. "You're right," he said abruptly. "C-Access. Locate Huvisdank. Case Subject."

Teller's head shot around to the baron.

"Apply Program 55."

"You can't do that!" From the corner of her eye, she watched the handsome clone's hands move upward and lock behind his neck as his hips, influenced by the baron's program, performed a series of sexy undulations. She pushed herself off the bed and onto her feet. "You can't case a human! It's…it's…not legal!"

The baron gave her a look of patronizing patience. "He's a clone!"

"That doesn't make it right!"

"He's *my* clone!" The baron's eyes flickered a warning that Teller chose to ignore.

"It isn't right to force a man to…to…it's not right to case a human!"

"C-Access," the baron paused, a scrape of metal in his voice. "Locate female in room. Case subject."

Teller gasped as she felt the case applied to every inch of her body from the top of her scalp down to the soles of her feet. Outraged, she attempted a protest but the casing program reduced her words to useless grunts. The baron's fist lingered beneath her jaw to taunt her as angry words piled up behind the roadblock inside her throat. "C-Access. Move Female to Huvisdank. Turn."

Teller slid across the room as the casing program put her body against the clone's.

"Apply Program 60 to both subjects." The casing program forced her bottom into the clone's groin as he grasped her hips and his lower body ground against her buttocks.

Unable to voice her dissent, she held the baron's eyes within her stunned and angry gaze.

Slowly, the baron smiled. "C-Access. Release casing."

In four steps, she was across the room. Her hand flashed to smack against his cheek. Once. Twice. He caught her wrist before she could land the third one.

On his face was the splayed mark of her hand along with his arrogant amusement. His expression was full of haughty tolerance while his hand manacled her wrist in an unforgiving grip. When she winced, he tightened his hold slightly.

And for the first time, it occurred to Teller she was at the mercy of this strange, volatile man, whether he chose to subjugate her to his whim through the application of his casing program or with nothing more than the superior male strength of his body. Alone with Jay and his servant—and his mad brother—in his remote villa, far from the city, she was his to manipulate and exploit.

"I was just teasing," he explained in mollifying tones. "I'm sorry if I offended you." His eyes dared her to believe him.

"That program—"

"I just put it together this morning. I thought it would be amusing. Again, I apologize."

Slowly, certainly, without any great loss of confidence, he nudged her across the room, his long, hard thighs moving her backward with each short, determined step. He stopped when her back came up against the wall. His warm, moist lips were against her throat as he murmured his contrition. Damp, heated breath hung against her skin as he drew his lips up under her jawline to her ear. Despite her fury, Teller felt a tingle of anticipation that accompanied the memory of their earlier, perfect lovemaking.

Despite that memory and the associated tingle, she pushed him away, or tried to.

He gazed down on her as though she were a very small problem that could easily be eradicated. "C-Access," he announced. "Case small box on dresser in my room. Bring subject."

When the box arrived to hover behind him, his hand swept back for it. Giving Teller an inch, he held it between their bodies and paused a dramatic moment. "I had this express transmitted this morning." With those words, he pulled back the box's lid.

She gasped in a breath and held it. Held her breath in disbelief as she stared into the soft glass box at the warm, translucent plates of thick plastic strung on a wide choker. Stunned, she lifted her eyes to the baron's.

The necklace was worth a fortune.

The hairs at her nape lifted and a new apprehension shivered her body like a frost wind. His brother Hyde might be mad but at least he wasn't like this—cold, calculating and manipulative. Did the man truly think he could illegally case her then buy her off with…a fortune in plastic? Automatically, her eyes went to the doorshield where Huvisdank stood, immobile, blocking the exit.

"May I?" Dropping the box, he lifted the necklace to her neck. "Turn around," he said softly. His warm breath on the back of her neck was more chilling than erotic. "You should have seen Hyde's face when he saw it. I think he was angry he hadn't thought of it.

"It matches my earpiece," he pointed out as he touched the clasp together. Turning her around to face him, he tipped his head to survey the costly jewelry against her skin. "But the color's utterly fabulous on you. Sets off your green eyes." His eyes traveled down to her mouth as his head lowered and she drew back an inch, thinking he'd kiss her. Instead, he thumbed her bottom lip with a sigh. "You're a handsome woman," he murmured. "With the widest, warmest, most beautiful, most incredible mouth I've ever seen. These luscious lips—" he caught her eyes with his "—I've fantasized about these lips. Your head in my lap and these lips wrapped around my cock." Lightly, he ran each of his fingers across her parted mouth.

Taking her hand, he led her back across the room. "Huvisdank, lose the hat. And the chaps," he ordered casually as he pushed her down to sit on the bed before him.

"Open your mouth," he rumbled, his tone cloyingly intimate. "And I'll show you how I like it." Standing before her, he straddled her legs and stroked his cock out of his pants to nudge at her lips.

Stunned, and almost too afraid to refuse him, Teller opened her mouth to take him in, glancing up at him at the same time. But the baron's eyes were across the room, fixed on his nearly naked servant. "Give me your hand," he told her, and curved her fingers in his to cup the weight of his balls.

Jay rumbled his pleasure as Teller sucked at him with hollowed cheeks, tightening her lips to pull on the rim of his helmeted cock head. "Let me tell you about the last woman I fucked," he said with a satisfied drawl. "She was on her knees while Huvisdank stood behind her, supporting her back. Holding her head while I fucked her mouth all the way to my root, my balls nudged up into her chin."

"The Lady…the lady liked Huvisdank," he continued. "She liked to undress him and play with him, smooth her hands over his chest, into his groin, jerk his pants down over his hips and play with his dick." Jay laughed, his voice rough as he panted lightly. "I think she thought she could make him hard, make him come. She couldn't. He could make her come though— couldn't you, Huvisdank?"

"Yes, My Lord."

"With his tongue." Jay grunted as his hand curved around to lock on the back of Teller's head and he thrust himself into her more deeply, almost gagging her. "Fucked her with his tongue for me. I watched them together. Huvisdank's head buried in her greedy pussy. Sat in that chair beside the bed and watched the clone take her to within an inch of orgasm, then pulled Huvisdank off her and fucked her until she screamed.

"God, she was wet. Wet by the time I got to her. Spilling onto the sheets as I slid into her life a knife through butter."

With a groan, Jay pulled his cock from between her lips. "Let's see what you can do with your tongue," he suggested in a slick voice, watching as her tongue licked out to swirl around the blunt head of his cock. Carefully, Teller continued to knead his tightening balls while she coaxed a few silvery drops from the slit of his weeping head. Moments later, his hips were moving as he shoved at her, holding the back of her skull and rubbing his penis to drag alongside her cheek. "Now my balls," he said.

"Jay?" There was a tremor in her voice and in the word.

Pushing her back onto the bed, he shoved his pants down his legs and stepped out of them. Following her onto the bed on his knees, he straddled her face.

"I want your tongue on my balls." For a moment, he was still. "That's right. Just like that...but with more feeling. Huvisdank! Do me a favor. Get her ankles and push her feet up onto the bed. Get her knees up and open her legs for me."

It was just as Hyde had predicted.

Teller struggled beneath the baron, trying to disengage herself—just before she felt the clone's rough grasp on her ankles, pushing them up and apart on the bed.

Her robe fell open beneath her on the bed and the cool air on her exposed sex was like an erotic wash of fear that swept between her legs and surged into her open sex, pulsing in small waves against the back of her vagina. Above her, the baron moved down her body to hold her wrists.

"Rub your beard into the lady's pussy."

Cutting short her cry of surprise, Teller jumped at the rough, abrasive touch of the clone's harsh stubble inside her pussy, scraping at the sensitive folds.

"D'you like that?"

"I'm...I'm not sure," she said warily, a damp film of fear forming on her upper lip and warming her body. Pinned at wrists and ankles she writhed in an attempt to wriggle free of the two men that held her.

The baron sighed. "Forget it, Huvisdank. Just suck her clit for me."

"Yes, My Lord. Just as I did for the Lady Aleena, My Lord?"

Chapter Ten

Kicking and twisting, Teller fought away from the two men. Aleena? She shook her head in denial as she scrambled to the other side of the bed, stumbled to stand, wrapping the robe around her as she backed away until the cold wall brought her to a halt. *Aleena!*

"You were with the Lady Aleena?" she rasped, her throat suddenly dry.

The baron had turned to sit on the bed and she stared at his face. Casually, with cool indifference, he smiled back, stroking his cock at the same time.

Her eyes narrowed to slits as she turned her face to the clone. "Huvisdank," she said haltingly. "Huvisdank…he can't tell you apart. From Hyde. The night he walked into my room, Huvisdank was…looking for you, not Hyde."

Jay seemed to consider his answer for a while, his eyes screened and on the girl's face.

"He was! He thought Hyde was you. He followed Hyde's command when Hyde ordered him to leave the room. That means…he thought he was talking to you when he said the Lady Aleena was looking for…you! It was you who had only just left Aleena, not Hyde."

Horror and revulsion made her knees weak. She'd reviled the man who'd done nothing worse than introduce her heart to love. She'd used Jay and their blatantly sexual relationship to punish his brother who'd never merited the abuse. She'd let Jay use her as she'd employed him in a planned campaign to hurt his brother. His brother who'd done nothing to deserve her savage contempt.

"I told you an honest manservant was a liability." Jay turned his eyes on his manservant and, for an instant, they flared. "Stupid bastard."

"You bastard," she whispered. "You've been lying all along. Lying about Hyde."

"Not exactly," Jay said finally, standing and sauntering toward her.

She shrank back into the wall.

"You see, Teller. Hyde was there, too, with Huvisdank and me. And the Lady Aleena."

She shook her head as he reached her. His hand shot out for her shoulder and she jerked away. "I don't believe you. Call him here." Her voice was a strong command.

"Hyde?"

Determined, she lifted her chin. "Call him here, *now*. I owe him an apology."

Jay sighed with false pathos. "I can't. I guess I should have told you, Teller. I have a little bit of a...personality disorder. Hyde is here now."

He grabbed for her and she fought away, screaming Hyde's name.

Leaving a long red scratch on the baron's face, she twisted out of his grasp, careened off the disinterested clone and tore through the doorshield. She continued to scream for Hyde as she headed down the hall, halting at almost every doorshield, uncertain which room was his. Running out of options on this level of the villa, she raced into her own room, chest heaving as she tried to collect herself and formulate some semblance of a plan.

A noise behind her spun her around to find a man in the door's arch, his forehead against the doorjamb. His disorganized clothing was only partially buttoned and marginally closed. From where she stood, she could see only his profile. The rest of his face was lost in the opaque shield. His hair was a jumble of loose ends and one fierce gold eye was fixed on the ground.

Her shoulders sagged. "Hyde," she whispered. "I'm sorry."

"I'm sorry, too," he rasped.

As he turned his head, his gold eyes met hers and she saw the long red streak on his cheek.

With a yelp, she took a quick step backward. "No!" she screamed.

His eyes were full of regret as he took a step toward her.

Teller continued backing away from him until her back came up against the flexible, shimmering surface of the windowshield. With a shove, she was through the windowshield and running.

Hot tears streamed from the corners of her eyes and raced into her hair as she fled the villa. There was no Hyde. There was no love. There was only a twisted man bent on toying with her soul as perversely as he'd toyed with her body. Behind her, she heard pursuing footsteps and she burst forward with furious energy. She wouldn't let the bastard catch her.

The grolnig came out of nowhere, its stunning weight slamming into her upper back like a hammer blow as her body buckled to crash into the ground. Like a bundle of rags, she saw the baron go flying and roll several feet before she watched him struggle to hands and knees, shaking his head. By then, the grolnig was dragging her away. Ignoring the chisel-edged teeth that bruised her shoulder, she kicked and twisted ineffectually as her heels scraped two uneven lines into the soft forest floor. When the monster reset its teeth in her neck for a more secure hold, she screamed in pain. Then screamed again as the bright day above her suddenly darkened.

A huge shadow hovered over her just before the grolnig released her. As her head hit the ground, spikes of grasping black pain filled her skull. There was a terrible snapping and snarling followed by a screech of scorching agony. A flurry of leathery blue. Then the baron stood above her, the clone beside him with a lazgun out and pointed toward the commotion. The edges of her vision faded just before she lost consciousness.

Chapter Eleven

When Teller came to, she was in a stone structure. Evidently, a grand mansion at one time, the building had been gutted to house the baron's collection of vehicles, both modern and antique. Somewhere far overhead, lofty ceilings disappeared into distant shadows. The only vehicle tall enough to nudge into those shadows was the baron's huge, ostentatious space cruiser.

Her fingers moved slowly to the back of her skull where she found the large lump that was the source of the dull ache filling her head. A leathery rustle followed by a metallic clank transferred her attention to the large, hulking mass that hovered to cast its shadow over her—*like a grolnig protecting its kill*, she thought, vaguely.

The creature's skin was thick and leathery, patterned blue. If the monster could be termed humanoid, it was only barely so. Rising a good eight feet above the floor, its thick neck was almost swallowed by its massive shoulders slanting out from the base of its skull.

Swiftly losing interest in her headache, Teller scrambled away from the monster chained to the wall. She kept backing away until a vintage jet bike at her back brought her to an uncomfortable halt. Teller stared at the all-but-mythical beast.

It was a fabulous animal, with a prominent brow ridge overhanging its shadowed eyes. Between its brows, a serrated line rose on its forehead to ride over its skull and disappear behind its head. A long, high ridge of a nose flared out into wide nostrils, and beneath the nose a sharp wedge of a chin was tipped with a hard spur about the size of a small square beard.

As she stared, the creature's lips parted to reveal impressively sharp canines in a mouth full of unruly teeth.

The huge, hairless creature was naked, knotted all over with giant musculature. Between its legs hung some appallingly huge apparatus, while from its back sprang two wings as big as tents.

"What…what *are* you?" she queried in an unsteady voice then answered her own question. "A dragon," she stated.

The monster's chin came up to fix gold eyes on hers.

Her back slid down the uneven surface of the bike, the satin robe easing her descent on her way to the floor. She thought she would faint. "Hyde."

There was a snort in the darkness beside her and she turned her head to find the baron slouched against a hovercoach. "Hyde," he confirmed with a sneer. "*This* is the monster you prefer to me. *This* is the animal that's been fucking you—every time I turned my back. Every time I let my guard down. *Every time I closed my eyes!*" Jay flung his arm in an arc toward the creature chained to the wall and Teller recognized his casual slouch was part of his polished act of disconcern. She suspected the man hid his full hatred—seethed with a loathing hatred he kept constantly in check. His image shimmered slightly and she realized she was as much a captive as Hyde, trapped with the dragon behind a transparent guardshield.

"I…I don't understand."

"He's a *parasite*. A *fucking* parasite. He attached himself to me when I visited the planet Scree. I didn't know there were any of his kind left or I would have taken the *fucking* antidote." The baron kicked at a visitray that hovered just above the floor and it skittered across the room, glancing off the floor, barging into antique coaches and sloping off of vintage jet bikes.

Teller shook her head, bringing her reluctant eyes slowly across the room to Hyde.

The proud creature regarded his tormentor with undisguised contempt.

"This is his true form. He's been sharing my body! He was finally forced to leave me when the grolnig attacked. He had to revert to his dragon form in order to defend himself. For the last nine months, he's been living—inside me! And when he's inside me, he knows every action I take, every thought I have, even enjoys every woman I fuck! As if that isn't bad enough, he can possess me—almost at will—take over my body whenever my defenses are down, when I'm asleep or distracted, and during that time I know *nothing* he's done!

"He's the one that injured you, raped you—almost killed you—and left you in my bed to find!

"You're fortunate he was in my body when he last raped you." With a final gesture of disgust, the baron turned and left by an ancient wooden door. "This time you won't be so lucky," he muttered just before the door slammed behind him.

Teller stared at the door for several moments before she returned her eyes to the dragon. As he glowered at the door, his eyes blazed in a fire of gold—an angry fire burning in an intelligent face. It was a gaze full of passion, one she'd come to covet, one that warmed her soul.

On the outside, the dragon was—obviously—mostly pure animal. A huge, dangerous creature with a very *male* edge. But his humanizing gold gaze clearly exposed the passion of the complex soul that lived within. "Was he lying?"

The creature snorted. "Are you asking if I raped you?" he muttered in a voice that was deeply musical.

She stared into his groin, at his massive equipment. "No," she said slowly. "I think I'd remember that…if I were to actually survive it."

The creature almost smiled. "You weren't raped."

"No? What happened to me, then?"

"You were the victim of a lazer attack."

"Then…why haven't you…why have you let Jay continue to believe…?"

"Because he still doesn't know about you. He thinks I was responsible for your injuries. He doesn't know how you were wounded. If he did, he'd have to kill you."

"Why...would he do that?" she put to him cautiously.

"Because it was the baron who almost killed you in the first place."

Teller began to understand and her expression showed it. "We were on our way to ambush a traitor."

"Only the traitor ambushed you first." The creature's voice was the rumbling sound of a rockslide heard from a distance. "Your entire unit, except for you, was killed in the first blast. You would have died in the second blast, had there been one. You had tripped just before he fired on your unit. As you got to your hands and knees, the edge of the blast caught you and scraped you across the ground. I stepped in and took over the baron's body before he could check for any survivors that might need picking off. I might have been a bit rough as I snatched you up.

"But Jay doesn't know any of that. The last thing he remembers is firing at a unit of Imperion soldiers. He thinks you're just some woman I happened across on the way home." Hyde paused. "I carried you here to the villa."

"Why?" she asked, standing and dusting herself off at the same time.

"Most of your uniform was sublimated in the blast. I could see you had a secret you hid from your companions—that you were a woman. I tore off what remained of your uniform so the baron wouldn't know you were an Imperion soldier. When he would have thrown you out, I stopped him and forced him to treat your wounds."

"That still doesn't explain why...you stepped in to save me—in the first place."

"No. It doesn't." Hyde jerked his head an irritated inch. "I can't explain. I'm not sure I understand it myself. I only know...I'd have done anything to save you. I'd do anything now." As though puzzled by this admission, the dragon stopped, his features twisted by an idea too difficult to grapple with. "For some reason, you've become...the only reason left for my existence. If I didn't know better, I'd say I was in love with you." For several moments, he considered this statement then laughed cynically. "That seems unlikely when there's no word in my language for that particular emotion."

"No? What word comes close—to describing what you feel for me?"

"Hunger. Need. Lust."

She watched him struggle with the idea.

"And something more," he admitted finally.

She frowned. "How would you describe the feelings a dragon would have for its young?"

The dragon thought about this for a while. "Protection," he said finally. He nodded to himself. "Protective." His eyes moved slowly to meet hers. "As though I'd kill the man who tried to harm you."

"Like a devoted guard dog." She nodded. "That's why you left Jay's body, to protect me from the grolnig."

"—and crush the man who tried to mate you."

Her mouth curled into a smile. "Now that's something altogether different."

Slowly, he returned her smile. "How did you manage to get into the Guard—and keep your secret in an all-male army?"

"It wasn't easy," she admitted, scrubbing her hand through her shorn locks. "Boot camp was hell, although I'm tall for a woman and pretty fit. I developed a broadcast program and installed it in my C-Link. Every time they run a test on me, my I.D. emitter overrides their scan and broadcasts my 'male' data."

The dragon appeared to be impressed. "What happens if they scan you without your knowledge?"

Teller tapped the shell of her ear. "I built the program with sensory capabilities."

"Can you do that?"

She nodded, a little proudly. Staring at the door again, she frowned, shaking her head. "I don't understand. Why did Jay accuse me of...fucking you every time his back was turned?" She returned her gaze to the dragon. "We were only together once."

With a diffident jerk of his shoulders, the dragon lowered guilty eyes.

It took her a moment to catch on. "It was you," she told him with slow dawning revelation. "It was you behind me on the sofa. It was you making love to me...wasn't it?"

He seemed reluctant to admit it. "I was afraid he was going to hurt you. I stepped in, took over his body, though he put up one hell of a struggle."

"But...you promised me you wouldn't interfere unless I called on you."

There wasn't a trace of remorse in the dragon's hard gaze. "I also told you I wouldn't let him harm you.

"Initially, it was easy to possess the baron's body, when he didn't know of my presence. But after he learned of it, possession grew increasingly difficult. And after I brought you to the villa, he decided to draw the battle lines and make a point of reclaiming his body from me—so he could use it on you."

"I'm sorry," she told him with a reluctant shake of her head. "I was wrong about him. I let him use me." She looked disgusted before she brightened a bit. "But you were there at the same time?"

He appeared startled. "That doesn't bother you?"

She shrugged. "Should it?"

He looked a little ashamed. "I don't think we're the same species—or in the same genus for that matter. The baron was right, Teller. You've been a fucking an animal."

She looked in the direction the baron had left, smiled wryly and nodded her agreement.

Hyde sighed. "I'm not proud of myself for deceiving you. I'm…the last of my kind—as far as I know." He gave her a look of significant warning. "There are no others—there are no female…dragons—left."

Glancing behind her, she made herself comfortable against the jet bike.

"Do you understand what that means?"

She gave him a slow nod. "Dragons are about to become extinct?"

"Do you know what that means for *me*?" The creature was suddenly impatient. "Don't you get it, Teller? The only way I can experience sexual coupling is either by dominating another man's body—actually taking over his body—or by sharing his experience.

"When I took over Jay's body and made love to you as Hyde, I experienced the act fully and completely, as any man does—and Jay doesn't recall a minute of it. But that's not all." His head came down a notch, protecting his pride. "I can enjoy a woman when I *share* his experience." His voice lowered. "When he was fucking you, I was fucking you and it felt—almost as good."

"Almost as good," she stated flatly. "So, if you could have, you'd have taken him over completely—the baron—and never let him back in?"

He shook is head. "Heaven knows I'd have liked to. I'd have liked to for no other reason than you. But Jay has dug himself so deep into trouble—is living so many lies—I wasn't sure I could keep them all going. Keep them all going without landing in shit up to my elbows and placing him in danger. Putting myself in danger. Bringing danger to you," he finished. "I can't write in your language," he confessed, "or read. I'm sure I could have picked it up in time, by looking over the baron's shoulder, so-to-speak. But until then, how could I be the baron?

"Besides," Hyde sighed. "That would be like taking a man's life—not much better than murder. I'm not a monster."

Thoughtfully, she nodded her agreement. "Why...did you let me believe it was you with the Lady Aleena?"

He didn't answer right away. "Why didn't I tell you the truth? Because one truth would have led to another. To who I was. *What* I was. How would you feel about fucking a dragon—an animal—like me?"

Chapter Twelve

He didn't dare look at her — until he heard her response.

"Oh, I don't know." Teller smiled slowly. "I can be flexible."

His head came up and he stared at her in wonder, uncertain he'd understood her correctly. She smiled back at him, her eyes interested, her smile sultry. His eyes descended into his crotch and he shook his head. "You'd have to be a lot more than flexible," he said ruefully.

He was huge. He was hung like a bull with a massive pair of testicles that swung below the thick hank of his penis. With arms folded, Teller eyed him with open fascination. As though contemplating how to best approach a difficult task, she frowned at his huge cock clad in thick, leathery armor, mottled in shades of blue.

The dragon's eyes softened as he watched her, knowing what she was thinking, knowing it was impossible but loving her for the thought.

His thick hide was mottled blue and gray, without hair on his crotch. In its quiet state, the wide shaft of his penis stood upright, covered in rough blue hide. A line of small, dark blue knots tracked their way down either side of his cock.

"You look horny," Teller stated.

He shook his head. "Actually, it will come down more...when I'm more aroused. More...perpendicular to my body." He shrugged. "Dragons are put together differently than humans."

"Understatement of the year," she muttered to herself. "May I?" She gestured to his groin.

He closed his eyes and opened them again. "Please," he whispered in a rough voice.

She took a step toward him and ran the fingers of one hand up the length of his leather-bound shaft. She seemed most interested in the knobs running up either side, which was all right with him. He grunted as she fingered the knobs separately and gasped when she got a finger on each of them and circled them cautiously.

"You needn't be so gentle," he groaned.

She looked up at his face with interest. Experimentally, she covered each knob with a fingertip then tightened her hand around…half of his mighty circumference.

His head jerked back on his massive shoulders. His eyes closed as his breathing roughened.

"Does that feel good?" she asked him.

He groaned again. "You have no idea."

Teller's other hand joined her first as she placed her fingers on the knobs studding the opposite side of his shaft. She played with him a while, trying to decide what he most enjoyed while Hyde was propelled slowly out of his mind. He'd never been touched before in his life, in his dragon form. Her every light touch was a longing prayer answered. Opening his eyes, he watched her hands as she experimented on his sex.

Leaning against the wall, his knees bent slightly, his hardening cock straightened to point between her breasts. She had only to stoop to put her mouth on him. Of course, he was too big to fit in even her wide mouth, but…

"Teller," he rasped. "Your tongue."

Looking into his golden eyes, she nodded her understanding just before her hands slid down to weigh his heavy balls. At the same time her tongue rasped around his knotted sex and—with his breath held and his mind blank—he tried to decide which he liked better, her hands caressing his hanging scrotum or her tongue doing figure eights up and down the knots that lined his massive dick.

The girl was inspired, he decided in the next instant when her fingers slid between the knots. Locking both hands around the cock that strained toward her, she squeezed her fingers together and pulled on him with both hands. The sensation of her pulling on his dick, while at the same time pinching the sensitive knots between her fingers, drove him rapidly to the edge of orgasm.

A line of warmth tickled down his chin and he realized he'd bitten into his lower lip. A trickle of blood teased a path down his chin as he wrapped his wrists in his chains, fighting the instinct to mount, fuck and reproduce.

"Quickly, now," he warned her. "Quickly, Teller. Or I'll have you on your knees, trying to take you like a dragon in heat. God, love. Do it quickly."

She yanked on him hard, several times, her face anxious as she watched his eyes. His straining body was ripped with wild animal lust as he fought to free himself from the chained bonds he'd only recently imposed on himself. Fought to free himself in a desperate, urgent drive to grasp and penetrate and pump his seed into the nearest warm receptacle. Fought to mount and fuck the female who had brought his animal form to this state of arousal.

Opening her mouth wide, she at least got his tip inside her mouth and sucked hard.

With a roar, he started coming. There was a rushing pressure in her mouth then a blast in her face and she was blown off his cock as it detonated into orgasm.

Moments later she found herself sprawled on the floor, laughing as shimmering sparkles fell and settled around her. Hyde's huge cannon was still emitting spurts of dry, silver sparks and his eyes were still closed, his head still back.

She watched him shudder, watched his eyes open and settle on her with pure golden adoration. She smiled back at him as a feeling of sensual warmth swept her from head to toe.

"I'm sorry," he said with a smile not the least apologetic. "I've rained all over you."

She shrugged slowly, surprised that the simple act felt impossibly sexy. "It feels good," she told him.

"It should," he said.

She cocked a sultry eyebrow at him.

"It's the most powerful aphrodisiac in the galaxy."

She cocked her head as she considered this information.

He nodded. "That's why there are no more dragons. We've been hunted to extinction by every known species in the universe. All for this," he said, gesturing toward the glittering mess on the smooth stone floor.

Stretching, Teller lay back in the silver dust that littered to pool on the floor. She chuckled breathlessly, filled with sensual pleasure. "Oh — my — God," she said in slow, sultry revelation. "You must be worth a fortune, Hyde."

"Dead *or* alive," he stated.

Rolling to cloak herself in his silvery seed, she got onto her knees and ran her glimmering fingers into her hair as she threw back her head.

"More…more alive, I should think," she panted. "Why were all the dragons killed? Why weren't they carefully bred to assure a never-ending supply of this stuff?"

"Dragons don't breed in captivity," he told her. "Like most intelligent animals, we prefer not to mate in front of an audience."

Her knees slid apart as she was suddenly desperate to get entirely naked. Hyde watched her pull the satin robe open then dip her hands into the sparkling dust on the ground beside her, watched her hands as she rubbed the silver into the smooth golden skin of her chest and face. "Oh, God," she moaned. Dipping a finger, she traced the outline of her lips on her mouth and afterward made circles around her nipples with her fingertips. Together they watched her nipples grow absurdly tall, poking expectantly, hopefully, from the small mounds of her chest.

Her eyes fixed on his, dark and full of lust. "I've never felt so sinfully sensual," she breathed at him. Her eyes wandered over his massive body to rest on his cock and he had to smile at her ambition.

"Slip out of your robe," he suggested in a deep animal rumble. "It only gets better."

Her eyes widened as she realized exactly what he was alluding to. Her robe was slung across the room in an instant as Hyde tightened his hold on the chains that anchored his wrists. The girl moaned as she rolled her long, nude body through the pool of silver again. She was losing control, he realized—and ground his teeth, knowing he couldn't allow himself to do the same.

She came to an uneasy rest on her back, before him. As her legs parted, she swept up a fistful of silver to rub into the curling hair at the top of her cleft. A few specks found their way between the lips of her labia, and he rumbled a growl as her back arced in a writhing curve, the tiny crystals like salt on her sexual appetite, her pussy's mouth watering in anticipation. With her weight on her shoulders and her legs spread wide, her knees rose as she took a whole finger full of silver dust and stroked it into the lips of her pouting sex. Hyde watched her finger start low in her pussy and slowly ascend almost to the top. There her finger hesitated in its progress, playing between her lips at that location. Straining in his chains, he leaned forward for a glimpse of the clitoris that was the subject of her finger's erotic attention, but the tip of her finger was buried between her soft, thick lips and her hand blocked his line of sight. Groaning, he let his eyes drop to the watering, pink slit of her opening.

Grasping the chains in his knuckled fists, he watched her come on her own, on the floor, with her legs open and her cunt streaming. It took her forever, her bottom unstill as her hips quested upward off the floor, hungry for a male presence to fill her—her back arching, her small breasts straining helplessly, needily, her body desperate for a male and a male's dominance bearing her to the ground. By the time she finally got through the long series of body-racking convulsions, he was erect again. She climbed to her knees, gasping, the fire in her eyes only partially subdued as she eyed his cock greedily, her intent obvious.

He shook his head in warning. "No," he croaked. "No, Teller. I'd fucking kill you."

"Or kill me, fucking me," she rasped as she threw herself at him, plastering her long slim body against his, her arms reaching for his sloping shoulders. "What a way to go," she breathed, pulling his lips down to hers as she thrust her tongue between his rough blue lips, backing his careful resolve into a dangerous corner.

At some point, his cornered resolve broke loose and he went over the edge. With a roar of animal anguish, he shook himself free of the chains he'd locked around his forearms, turned her body swiftly and fell on her. Even kneeling with his legs spread wide, his cock rode over the top of her back, so he pulled her ass up as she braced herself with feet and hands on the ground, legs spread wide to take him in. Sweeping his hand through the silver dust on the floor, he wrapped his cock in his fist, coating it with his glittering release. He watched her spread cheeks, her glistening cunt while he pumped himself hard and straight. All the time, she begged for him in anxious whispers, pushing her bottom at him, trying to bring her quavering cunt to his monstrous head.

Groaning, he pushed his tip along her hot, wet sex and heard her gasp at the raw, abrasive contact. The silver dust coating his cock mixed with her juices as he rode through the bumps and ridges of her sex, sharpening her arousal into a hard edge of need. With shaking hands casing her thighs, he let her rub her wet, rose-flushed sex into his massively blunt tip.

Still she begged him for it. Begged him to enter her.

He gazed at the tiny slit, wanting it more than she did. "I'd kill you," he panted.

"Just the tip, Hyde," she moaned. "Please."

He stared down at the heart-shaped bottom in his hands then at his knobbed fingers, realizing they were perfect for her. Slipping the longest one between her cheeks and into her slavering vagina, he fucked her with his finger into clenching orgasm. With his finger shafted at the back of her cunt, his palm was splayed out over her crease, the rest of his fingers scraping into the thick wet folds that lapped around her clitoris. As her sheath gripped his finger in a series of choking strangleholds, he prodded her as deeply as he could with his long middle finger, at the same time rasping his thick digits into her salivating pussy. As she came, he pushed his lower body up to hers and, with his hand between both their bodies, let her buck against him like a wild, new filly.

By the time she was done thrusting her sex into his hand, he was long past ready to spill. Losing control, he tried to enter her—and she tried to accommodate him—as he pounded and slid through the soft, swollen tissue layered in her pussy. She cried out at his attack and he groaned, knowing his rough hide wouldn't be very welcome on her delicate flesh—tender and sensitive following orgasm. With his massive hand shaking, he realigned his cock downward between her thighs, but couldn't stop his hip-thrusting action.

When he scraped between her legs, she closed them quickly to squeeze the rod of roughened flesh between the strong muscles of her upper thighs. The slick, damp skin of her inner thighs clamped to put an amazing amount of pressure on the sensitive blue knots either side of his cock. Rapidly, the knots transmitted a jumble of signals to his brain, all of which spelled out extreme pleasure arriving at many points all at the same time, along with the warning of imminent ejaculation. Her straining flesh bound him in a cruel, tight grip while he dragged his dick between her thighs a few more times then thrashed into orgasm, washing them both in a spurting rain of silver.

Afterward he collected her up as his lungs bellowed, his back against the wall. Resting back on his haunches, he smiled softly at the woman curled in his lap. Replete and as content as he'd ever been in his lifetime, he watched her trail a finger through the shimmering dust on the floor.

Lazily, Teller dragged a winding pattern into the silver sparkles. "We should bottle this stuff," she said, "blow this place and make our fortune."

He smiled as his eyes closed. "I wouldn't mind getting out of here," he drawled, his voice rich and fully sated. "Although I consider my fortune made—in you."

She laughed.

"Look at me," he murmured. "A captive—in chains—and the happiest creature in the universe."

Chapter Thirteen

Teller stretched then snuggled deeper into Hyde's arms. He smiled as his arms curled around her.

"How…did he know your name?" she asked, fingering her only article of clothing — the fabulous plastic choker at her neck.

"The baron? The baron gave me my name."

Curiously, she frowned at him and shook her head.

The dragon shrugged. "I'm named for some famous character in some ancient Earth myth."

Again, she shook her head unable to place the name into any myth she'd studied. "What's your real name?"

"You wouldn't be able to pronounce it," he told her evasively. But as she waited expectantly, he took a deep breath. The sound that rumbled from his chest sounded like several timpani drums sounding in rapid succession.

"That's your name?!"

He nodded.

"Sounds more like indigestion than a name."

The dragon smiled. "Call me Hyde. It sounds good in your mouth."

"How did you…attach yourself to the baron?"

"Scree doesn't get much traffic. He'd gone there to hide…an escape package, I guess you'd call it. A man who's involved in politics, especially treacherous politics, needs several getaway plans. This one included hovercars, bikes, food, water, a small space cruiser and the equivalent of a great deal of money. The western hemisphere of the planet is riddled with small, scattered iron deposits, making it an ideal place to conceal a spaceship. Any scan of the planet's surface couldn't differentiate between a small ore body and a space cruiser.

"I hadn't seen a human in forever. When I found him in my valley, I helped myself to him."

"How do you do that?"

"So long as I'm within arm's reach of a man I can enter him."

"Didn't he know…you were there? Inside him?"

"Not at first. He saw me, drew his weapon then saw me disappear. It wasn't until he was back here, several months later, that he realized—occasionally—he lost track of a few hours at a time. Eventually getting suspicious, he accessed the C-Bank and studied everything he could find about dragons…and learned I was with him."

"But you're so huge! How does all of you get into the baron's body?"

"When I enter another, I'm transformed to nothing more than loosely held energy."

She jolted to sit upright. "Why can't you do the same to get free of the chains? Why can't you transform?"

He nodded. "I'd need a host to accomplish that. If I could get the baron or his man close enough, I'd do just that."

"What about me?!"

"What about you?"

Her face was excited. "Why don't you enter me? Long enough to get out of the chains?"

He tipped her chin up with a thick, hard finger. "That wouldn't work."

"Why not?"

"You're a female."

"So?"

"So all of me wouldn't come across." He smiled into her lap. "I'd lose my…male attributes. Personality-wise, I'd be a…eunuch."

She looked appalled at the prospect. Then resigned. "Well, we can't have that," she grumbled then followed it up with a shrug. "I guess we'll just have to wait for the Imperion Forces."

He frowned uncertainly. "Imperion Forces?"

"The Imperion Army lost five soldiers the night you picked me up. Their bodies must have been discovered by now. After waiting a week or so for me to turn up, they'll order a satellite scan…and find me here."

She shook her head. "The Imperion Lord, Var Kel, is a wonderful man and the best leader we've had in centuries. Jay had it made. Why would he risk all he has? Why would he betray his cousin?"

Hyde shrugged. "Men are never content," he said with short, curt wisdom. "And Jay likes to be in control. Will you know when they get here?" He pointed at her ear. "Will your C-Link inform you of their scan?"

She nodded. "I'll get a vibrational signal when my C-Link picks up the scan—although—I think about two seconds after they've located me, we'll know it. Because, as the only surviving member of the party that went to ambush a traitor, my presence here is going to look damningly suspicious for the baron."

* * * * *

Hyde stretched a wing to shield her head and shoulders. There was another blast and Teller hunched into the dragon's broad, leathery chest as small rubble bounced and scraped along his wing on its way to the floor.

"Good one," she squeaked with a shaky voice.

His wing pulled her closer to him as his head swiveled to rake the weakening stone walls. Balling one fist into a mallet, he heaved on the chain that secured him to the wall. The anchored bolt might have rattled a bit in its setting but it didn't budge. In the meantime, the building was literally falling down around their heads. The upside was the guardshield had gone down in almost the first blast.

Hyde had pushed her toward the exit as soon as it dissipated but she'd clung to the spines of his wing. "The Army will have my exact coordinates," she screamed at him, "from the scan of my C-Link. They'll avoid killing me if they can!"

Now he had to wonder just how hard they were trying. Teller was only a very junior communications officer and probably not particularly indispensable from the Army's point of view. "You have to get out of here!" he shouted.

"I'm staying with you!"

The narrow, wooden door slammed open and the baron hurried across the garage, cursing as he did so. Yanking at the door of a sleek hovercoach, he spared a narrow, suspicious glance at his captives, just before he ducked inside. Seconds later Huvisdank backed into the building, a degen gun held at waist level. His eyes swept the pair without interest as he made his way to join Jay.

Several bursts shook the walls as stone and plaster exploded from a ragged hole near the roof.

Hyde bunched his muscles and strained against his chains. "Jay!" he roared. "Don't leave us here! Free us and give us a chance to run at least."

Huvsidank disappeared inside the hovercoach.

"Jay! Take the girl with you." With a wing, he pushed Teller toward the coach.

The doors closed and the coach lifted, hovering before old iron-clad garage doors that didn't open. Rotating slowly, the coach stopped. There was an explosion as a lazbeam shot from the hovercoach nose and cut a messy hole in the mansion's wall. The door to the coach opened and the baron leapt out to curse violently at the huge pile of stone now blocking his escape. "C-Access," he tried once or twice, tapping the C-Link on his ear. Angrily, he turned his eyes on Hyde.

Drawing a small handlaz from its pocket beneath his arm, he leveled the weapon at the dragon's head. Hyde had only time to duck before the beam sheared the chain at the wall.

"Get this fucking rock out of my way," he screamed, centering the lazgun sights on Teller's forehead. "This is your doing, isn't it?" he yelled at her. "What are you, a fucking Imperion spy?"

Hyde's wing came around her like a shield and the sighting beam glowed orange on his leathery blue hide.

"Nothing so grand as that," she shot back, bravely, pulling her robe tightly around her body. "I'm nothing more than a junior officer you tried to kill — and failed."

"Junior officer! That's impossible! You're a..." The baron halted himself with a curse, recalling his uncertainty about her sex when he'd first found her. "My mistake," he said, changing tack.

"I can tear off half your wing and kill her at the same time," the baron pointed out to Hyde, coldly. "Move the fucking rock!"

Another burst hit nearby. Instinctively, Teller crouched at the edge of Hyde's wing. Like a sail snapping under a gale wind, Hyde's wings stretched wide to protect her as he lunged toward her at the same time.

The tip of one wing touched the distracted baron at the door to his hovercoach.

And the dragon disappeared.

* * * * *

There was a lull in the barrage being flung at the old stone building. In that time, the man who had been Jay Kel raised golden eyes to Teller, across the room. But it was the manservant he addressed. "Huvsidank!"

The huge clone slipped out of the coach to face the man he thought was his master.

"How many Imperion fighters are in the sky?"

"I told My Lord earlier. Nine are hovering in our space. Five more on the way."

Teller watched the golden head nod as Hyde turned grim eyes to hers—then swiftly turned and, drawing the handlaz, shot out an ancient glass window.

"Huvisdank, take Teller on the jet bike—it will fit through that window—to the city. Buy a used hovercoach and ship out to the Satelland circling Scree. Follow all of Teller's commands with one exception. Don't return here."

Teller danced backward in an attempt to evade the approaching clone then fought Huvisdank's iron grasp. "Hyde! What are you going to do?"

Hyde flashed a hard smile her way. "You're getting out of here."

"But why Huvisdank? Why not you? The Imperion Forces will know it's me on the jetbike."

Hyde shook his head. "But they won't know who's with you. They'll see two vehicles trying to escape and they'll target both, just to be safe."

"You could order Huvisdank to stay here and let him continue the fight!"

"I may be an animal, but I'm not a monster," he reminded her. "I won't condemn a man to death, not even a clone. The baron's going to put up a good fight that will distract the army long enough for you to escape then he'll surrender."

"No," she screamed as Huvisdank grappled with her. "They'll never accept your surrender. They'll kill you. They'll kill you both."

"We'll make it. I'll come to you, Teller. Give me a week before you leave the Satelland."

"No!" she screamed as Huvisdank slung her in front of him on the jet bike and gave the start command.

Chapter Fourteen

"Unlock doorshield," Teller muttered just before she pushed through the opaque surface and into the small Satelland room she shared with Huvisdank. The clone was where she'd left him two hours earlier, floating in the room's only bed. She frowned at the huge man who took up more than his share of space in the room, and in the bed for that matter.

She'd declined his polite offers of oral sex, and not very politely. But if her refusal was less than courteous, the fact was lost on the big man. Despite her efforts to turn up some sort of personality hidden within his huge frame, she'd come up empty-handed. The huge, beautiful clone was a virtual walking automaton, a relatively useless assemblage of DNA on the emotional front. Turning away from him, she massaged the back of her neck with one hand.

It had been too long. Months. He should have been here by now...if he was coming at all. She'd sold the fabulous plastic necklace to finance their stay in the Satelland, but money was getting scarce after the prolonged length of their visit. It was unfortunate Hyde hadn't given her the coordinates of the baron's getaway package.

"Where have you been?"

Teller continued to rub her neck as she answered the clone. "Out looking for news."

"The baron is dead."

That didn't mean Hyde was dead, she thought stubbornly, realizing at the same time it was, in fact, the most likely scenario. It had been more than two months since Huvisdank had dragged her from the baron's garage. The baron's treachery and subsequent death were, by now, old news on the Gossip-Cs.

According to news, he'd died in the ruins of the old stone mansion. If he'd attempted a surrender, the Imperion had chosen not to report it.

"A message was delivered while you were gone."

Teller spun around to stare at the clone, now standing at the bed's edge, his eyes on a small minimon on his open palm. His black leather clothing, bed-rumpled, stretched to enclose his huge, muscular frame.

"Who...who—"

"The young man who brought it didn't identify himself."

"Is the message signotated?"

The clone shook his head.

Hesitantly, almost fearfully, Teller considered the message resting in the clone's large hand. "What does it say?" she finally asked.

"It's addressed to you."

Teller felt a tremble go through her.

"Shall I read it?"

Teller fell into the chair behind her. The chair was gray. The same bleak gray as the walls of the tiny room.

"The message contains news of how the baron died. It says he never had a chance to surrender. He was pinned beneath a falling beam and died before...before he could be freed. The old mansion collapsed to bury him."

"Is there...does it mention the dragon—at all?"

"No, My Lady."

"Teller," she corrected him, fixing on the unimportant detail while she shook her head, filled with sick dread and the beginnings of heavy tears held back for far too long. "Perhaps you've...missed something. Let me see the message."

A few long strides brought the clone to her side as he placed the minimon in her hand.

She stared at the message in her hand, turned it over. "Expand," she said in a weak voice and watched the image double in size. Her voice shook. "There's nothing on this." Fearfully, she searched out his eyes. "It's someone's shopping list."

"Yes, My Lady."

Huvisdank's normally clear eyes were gold. Warm, glowing, fierce gold. The manservant dropped to his knees before her. His hand fastened around her knee and moved up her thigh.

"But. You can't lie, Huvisdank."

The beautiful giant shook his head and a few long, black strands of hair escaped his braid to slash across one eye. "Actually, I can't read," he told her.

"Is there…" Her voice caught and she swallowed. "What else has changed?"

The clone cupped his balls, weighing his scrotum in his large hand before he ran his palm up the front of his groin. The tip of one finger slid down the front of his leather longpants and the static clasp spread open in a V to release the thick shaft that hardened to force its way out. His mouth kicked up at the edges and creases appeared at the corners of the clone's mouth as he smiled for the first time in his life. "I think you're going to like Huvisdank's equipment," he said warmly.

"Do you suppose he'll mind…being used?" she asked in a breathless rush, hating to ask the question and hoping the answer was no.

"Not after I push him to the edge of his first orgasm and leave him there for his first taste of sex."

Her lips trembled upward into a smile as Huvisdank's handsome features rippled behind tears. "What took you so long, Hyde?"

Pulling the snaplock from the end of his plaited hair, Hyde flipped the loose, black braid behind his back and shrugged. "You'd be amazed how hard it is to get around when you can't read." He smiled. "It's the first thing you're going to have to show me."

He watched her hands as her fingers slipped down the static clasp and her jacket opened. "Well. Maybe the second thing."

* * * * *

"C-BedOn," Hyde commanded, as he stood to pull his finger down the static clasp on his leather shirt. Slowly, he drew the shirt open and shrugged it down his arms as he watched Teller hurry to get out of her clothing. With his attention on the girl's slim form, he toed off his short boots while Teller got her pants down her legs. As he reached for the top of his long pants, she stopped him.

"That's mine," she told him and he watched her long nude body as she went to her knees before him, reaching for the edge of his pants and pulling them down past his sex to expose the long, thick shaft of his erection. Neglecting his clothing at that point, she pressed her lips against his veined flesh, leaving him to step out of the forgotten pants puddled at his feet.

With a warm sigh and a hand at the back of her head, he pulled her face into his groin, flexing his knees as he rubbed his crotch into her kiss at the same time he felt the sharp bite of her nails on his backside. Pulling her head away with a clamping grip on her skull, he used his other hand to grasp his root as he smeared the length of his ruddy shaft over her open mouth. Her tongue came out to rasp along his length and she tried hard to swallow him but he controlled her access, allowing only her tongue's caress at the crown of his bulging head.

Smiling as he teased her, he was forced to tighten his grip on her skull as the girl made small hungry sounds at the back of her throat and her tongue strained for his tip. One of her hands left his ass and he watched with a held breath of pleasure as her legs slid apart and her fingers dipped into her delta to caress her own sex. He allowed her a scant, few strokes before he lifted her suddenly and threw her at the bed.

"Not without me," he growled at the wide-eyed girl floating in the bed. "You don't come without me. Never again. Never without my tongue on your clit, my fingers in your pussy, my cock buried to the root and fucking the hot, sweet length of your cunt."

Chapter Fifteen

Stepping up onto the bed, he joined her. "C-Access. Case my feet and fix to bed's surface." Immediately the casing program fixed his spread feet to the bed while he reeled the floating girl toward him. Pulling her legs apart, he drew her pussy toward his face. "C-Access," he whispered in a rough rasp. "Maintain my fingertip temperature at forty degrees Fahrenheit." With a lightly teasing touch, he pulled his cold fingertips down the inside of her legs then moved them slowly to the top of her thighs, where he played them at the edges of her sex, just at the crease of her legs. Teller made a little sigh of pleasure as her body stretched and her arms folded behind her neck. "Do you like that?" he asked her and she murmured her approval in answer.

"Do you trust me, Teller?" he put to her carefully. "Because I want to use the casing program on you. I won't use it on your whole body," he added swiftly, "and I won't use it to manipulate you. Let me show you what I mean." His cold fingers pulled her sex open a little and he watched her nipples harden in response. "C-Access. Case Teller's outer labia and spread to her body's limit." Hyde felt her body stiffen as the girl gasped and his fingers slipped into her spread lips. "Is that all right?" he asked in a lust-roughened voice, pulling his chilled fingers through her sex. He let out a held breath when her chin came down in a small nod.

With his head between her legs and one hand supporting her body in midair, he swiftly formulated his next command. "C-Access. Case my penis," he said. "Create duplicate image and reduce by twenty percent. Insert into Teller's vagina." His breath was coming hard and shallow as he watched the invisible case push and hold her vagina open. "Rename penis to cock.

Effect gentle reciprocal motion to cock. Rename motion to fuck," he said hoarsely. "Continue to fuck Teller."

Teller moaned and twisted slightly as he watched her open pussy create a bath of moisture around the transparent cock he'd created. She moaned again, and he realized both his hands were clutched on the globes of her ass, holding her sex firmly before his face. Making a mental effort to relax his grip, her suspended body began to wave in the air like a loose golden flame.

"Fuck," he cursed gently, his eyes glued on her open pink sex and the high peak of her clitoris as dewy beads of moisture gathered at the base of her stretched vulva to collect in the valley of her ass. "C-Access," he almost whispered. "Apply slight static charge to my lips." With the lips of her sex spread wide and the transparent cock gently fucking her, he pulled her pussy into his mouth.

She screamed at that first electric vibration of touch and he felt her hands in his hair as he continued the long, hungry kiss inside her open sex, his tongue rasping her clit with a male passion he couldn't rein in as his fingers locked tighter on her ass, greedily forcing her tender sex into his mouth.

With a vicious yank, she managed to break his lips from her pussy and he panted as he stared up at the girl now bent into a sitting position. "*What!*" he demanded impatiently, tearing his angry eyes out of her pussy to burn up at her.

"Harder," she gasped. "I want it all! Hard and fast! Now!"

Hyde groaned into her cunt. "Lay back down," he commanded, and she jumped beneath his lips at the renewed application of static electricity. "C-Access. Increase speed of fucking motion by thirty percent. Expand cock to its full size. Fuck Teller." With these words, he resumed his static kiss, sucking her clit hard into his mouth as he used his tongue to push it against the rough edge of his teeth. His mouth flooded with her cum and he swallowed her taste as he crushed her twisting body in his grip and continued the long, passionate kiss into her orgasming cunt.

She was still sobbing when he gave the command to release the cased cock. Pulling her down to his hips, he shoved the real thing into her clutching, streaming vagina. Her delicious cunt closed around his virgin flesh and he squeezed his eyes shut as he groaned, the sound a hoarse admission of sinfully raw bliss as he grappled with his body's stunned reaction to sex for the first time. Pure racking pleasure exploded over his senses as he piloted Huvisdank's untried body in its first sexual experience — as he thrust Huvidank's un-jaded cock toward orgasm. The clone's body had never undergone anything of this sort during its mint-in-box existence and his shocked nerve endings fairly screamed in pleasure at the exquisitely novel sensations being introduced to his sex — being forced onto the hypersensitive head of his steel-hard shaft.

His dick jerked a few times inside her — his cock's desperate plea for release, but he fought back his body's demand to loose as he held her still on his spurting shaft. For several moments he held her, fighting to regain control of the body that hurtled toward imminent completion. Clenching his jaw, Hyde flicked black hair out of his eyes as he took a deep, determined breath — that almost cost him his sanity.

When Teller opened her eyes, he watched her gaze go into his dark groin before his eyes joined hers. Carefully, he moved his hips as he watched the root of his cock drag in the tight fit of her cunt. Slowly, he fucked her into a second short, hard orgasm that hit her suddenly, surprising them both. As she came, his pulsing flesh was caught in the tight, throttling grip of her clenching channel and he saw stars as his release exploded to burn through his bursting cock like an interplanetary train flashing through a wormhole.

Coming out of orgasm, he stared down at the woman who'd given him this — the sweetest fuck he'd ever experienced — recognizing that the deep level of satisfaction he had shared with Teller could be largely credited to Jay's iniquitous know-how, along with Huvisdank's perfectly engineered body.

"Where did you learn to do that?" she asked a few moments later, as they floated in the bed, looped together in a loose love knot.

"Where do you think?" Hyde murmured, his voice thick with contentment and near-sleep.

Teller nodded against his chest as she let out a sigh. "Jay wasn't all bad," she said, softly.

"You're a generous soul," Hyde stated sardonically. "The man would have killed you without a second thought." His chest expanded in a short admission of regret. "He was killed almost instantly when a piece of the roof came down. I had only enough time to get out of his body and take my dragon form before he died. The first soldier that came to investigate became my first host. You won't believe how many hosts I went through before I got here."

Again, he felt her nod. "*You* came through. That's the main thing. And Huvisdank makes the perfect host," she told him, reaching down to play with his long, wet cock. "Perfect," she repeated in a warm voice.

"You like me in the clone's body, then?"

"Oh, yesss," she replied.

"And you don't think...it's wrong? For me to commandeer his body?"

Teller stretched in his arms as she shook her head and smiled. "Trust me on this, Hyde. Huvsidank will never miss himself."

About the author

I slung the heavy battery pack around my hips and cinched it tight — or tried to.

"Damn." Brian grabbed an awl. Leaning over me, he forged a new hole in the too-big belt.

"Any advice?" I asked him as I pulled the belt tight.

"Yeah. Don't reach for the ore cart until it starts moving, then jump on the back and immediately duck your head. The voltage in the overhead cable won't just kill you. It'll blow you apart."

That was my first day on my first job. Employed as an engineer, I've worked in an underground mine that went up — inside a mountain. I've swung over the Ohio River in a tiny cage suspended from a crane in the middle of an electrical storm. I've hung over the Hudson River at midnight in an aluminum boat — 30 foot in the air — suspended from a floating barge at the height of a blizzard, while snowplows on the bridge overhead rained slush and salt down on my shoulders. You can't do this sort of work without developing a sense of humor, and a sense of adventure.

New to publishing, I read my first romance two years ago and started writing. Both my reading and writing habits are subject to mood and I usually have several stories going at once. When I need a really good idea for a story, I clean toilets. Now there's an activity that engenders escapism.

I was surveying when I met my husband. He was my 'rod man'. While I was trying to get my crosshairs on his stadia rod, he dropped his pants and mooned me. Next thing I know, I've got the backside of paradise in my viewfinder. So I grabbed the walkie-talkie. "That's real nice," I told him, "but would you please turn around? I'd rather see the other side."

…it was love at first sight.

Madison welcomes mail from readers. You can write to her c/o Ellora's Cave Publishing at 1056 Home Ave. Akron, Oh. 44310-3502.

Also by Madison Hayes

Tale of the Dragon

Chapter One

"Roar!"

"Rrrrraaaawwwwrrrrrr!"

"Hush, Maldovaar. I am moving as quickly as I can. You didn't have to move into my cave, even though it was the farthest from the lake. I saw one that was perfect for you and within a few feet of a nice sandy beach." Lyra moved deeper into the dark cave, carrying the water buckets two at a time. The steep and rocky path from the pond, which was around one hundred and fifty yards from the opening, added to the inaccessibility of her rocky hideaway. It didn't matter the valley was virtually cut off on three sides by mountains and the other by the ocean. This cave had always been the perfect place for her to escape to.

Water sloshed onto her ankle, reminding her of the task at hand. Sure, she had cheated getting the water up here. But Maldovaar didn't need to know that... after all, she rationalized silently... a little guilt keeps a dragon humble. If her mother knew she was using magick again, there would be hell to pay. Still, what her parents didn't know wouldn't hurt them either. The fact her father was the King did bother her at times, but still she was determined this time. After all, this would most likely be her last chance at a brief moment of independence, and rebellion.

"Here you go, Mal." Lyra filled the huge pot she'd stolen from Castle Wyston's kitchen with the water. "Drink up!"

"Wine!"

Lyra stopped as she bent to pick up the second bucket. "No, Mal, you can't have wine. You keep forgetting that you are here to work, not play."

"Dragons are not meant to work, little princess. We are mighty fierce beasts whose sole purpose is to strike fear in the hearts of brave knights, the king's soldiers and human peasants."

Lyra set down the bucket. She moved across the large cave to sit on a large rock. After shifting for a few seconds and still not finding a comfortable spot, she settled for being cold and having her butt hurt. "Yes, well, that is your cousin's responsibility. For now, Mal, I need you to sit tight and not move."

"If news of this ever gets out, I will be ruined, you know."

Lyra shook her head in denial. "No one will ever know. Besides, I don't see what the big deal is."

The huge dragon stood gingerly, and using his shorter arms, pulled up his overweight belly. Lyra saw precisely what she knew was there… a nest with a single egg in it. It was an unusual shell, having a multitude of colored spots all over it.

"I'm sitting on an egg, darling!" Maldovaar drawled in a deeply gruff and masculine voice. "Fire-breathing, village-destroying male dragons don't sit on eggs!" He ended his statement by crossing his arms across his chest.

Lyra nodded, but said nothing as the overweight dragon settled back down on the nest. "First of all, Mal, I haven't seen a puff of hot air leave your mouth for a year, other than when you burp after eating too much garlic. Second, the only village you came close to pillaging was because you ate the entire vegetable garden. Now, you agreed to be mommy—"

Maldovaar shook his finger angrily. "I am not this thing's mother."

"Yeah, yeah, yeah. I get it. All you have to do is sit, eat and keep it warm until it hatches." Lyra stood and went over to the large sack of food she'd brought to the cave. "It shouldn't be too much longer, and then I will take over the mothering duties."

"Toss me that big tomato, Princess," Maldovaar requested as she began setting out the different foodstuffs. He caught it easily and bit into it eagerly. "Yum! Where are you getting such delicious veggies, darling?"

"I'm not telling you. The last time I did that you went on a midnight feeding frenzy. You aren't pregnant and, therefore, you are not allowed to have food cravings."

"Hmm, a nesting dragon's gotta eat, sweet pea. Now, I don't suppose you care to chop that up and make me a salad?"

Lyra shook her head. For a fleeting moment, she considered pointing out that a supposedly fierce dragon would be eating raw meat not salads, but she held her tongue. "I don't have time today. My parents told me to be back in time for dinner. They have guests coming. I'm going to duck out early—"

"Duck? You are bringing me a duck, you say?" Maldovaar's big pink tongue darted out and licked all the way from one side of his long, narrow mouth to the other. "I love duck." He paused to lick a couple of fingers. "Don't forget the orange sauce!"

"Ducks are your half-cousins. Isn't there a rule about eating relatives?" Lyra asked in disgust, folding up the sacks she'd used to carry the food. She'd been careful to use her magick out of Maldovaar's sight, just in case. Besides, it did him good to think he was making her work even harder to keep him happy. Hiding her smile, she bent to the task of emptying the buckets.

"My dear Princess Lyra, dragons are in a class all by themselves. We share some similar traits—"

"You lay eggs and have scales, just like reptiles," Lyra reminded him.

Maldovaar picked up another tomato, biting into it gently, as if savoring the whole experience, letting his eyes roll back a little. "Unlike reptiles, we are much more active and warm-blooded, not to mention more popular. Humans write epic poems and songs about us."

"Present company excused on the active part," Lyra mumbled under her breath, but nodded in agreement. "You should be a mammal since you have the typical four-chambered heart and the fact that your teeth are specialized."

"Your grandmother should never have given you that science book," Maldovaar added with a superior look cast down upon her. "True." He paused to chomp his teeth together a few times. "But mammals produce milk." Maldovaar lowered his arms so his hands could press flat to his upper chest. "See, missy, no tits, unlike you." A second later, one of his hands moved towards her with assured intent.

Lost in her thoughts for a moment, his big claw-topped hand almost touched her. "Hey! Watch it you dirty old dragon!" She slapped away the dragon. "Now that leaves the bird family, and since you have hollow bones and lay eggs and fly... Isn't that what you should be classified?" Lyra questioned him further.

"Now, there is an idea... not! Birds don't have six members," Maldovaar told her quickly.

The smirk on the dragon's face, followed by the wicked upward movement of his bright red, overgrown eyebrows, made her cut off his reply. "Don't say it, Maldovaar. I'm not in the mood. This is all interesting and we can discuss it another day."

"My dear girl, I would never be as crass as to intimate I was blessed in my 'dragon-parts'. Needless to say, though, my bird-cousins have hollow legs and lay eggs, as well. I concede I have three kinds of kissing cousins."

"Yes, well, be that as it may, there *still* will not be a duck for your dinner. Now, I really do have to get going. I will be back tomorrow."

"What? You aren't coming back this evening? I thought we could chat, maybe play some cards and eat the dessert you are going to bring me."

Lyra saw the smile curving Maldovaar's mouth upwards. "So long as you promise not to cheat—"

"Of course, and I have no need to cheat. Now scat, little girl, and off to your ball. Oh, and cheesecake sounds ideal for dessert." Maldovaar picked up one of the books Lyra had pilfered from her father's vast library. "I'll choose a story for you to read when you come back with my treat."

Lyra paused at the exit of the cave, looking back at the very unusual dragon inside. For a chartreuse-colored being, he was impressive. What detracted from his formidability was the shock of bright red hair at the top of his head and the newly cultivated beard on his chin, growing long and thin to mid-chest. Still, among a rapidly diminishing breed, Maldovaar was something of a legend. It was for his knowledge that Lyra had blackmailed him into nest-sitting for the stray egg she stumbled across in one of the caves. Now, she just hoped she'd been in time.

* * * * *

"Derek, the bold."

The small, blond-haired boy shook his short wooden sword in the air. He slashed right and then left. Jumping from one stone to another near the edge of the pond, he continued his imaginary fight.

"Derek, the dragon-slayer!"

Lyra stepped out from behind the bushes and walked the short distance to where the boy played. "Why do you want to slay a dragon?" she asked him without preamble or forethought.

"Aay!" The small child cried out.

Lyra raced over, reaching down to grab hold of his clothing. She helped to pull him up onto the stone precipice, which still felt warm from the afternoon sun.

"Are you lost?" she asked, lifting one hand to push the lock of hair from his forehead.

"No! Who are you?" Derek demanded fiercely.

Lyra knew this child was used to being answered, and undoubtedly, catered to as well. "I live near here, and my name is Lyra. This land belongs to my father, and it shall one day be mine."

Derek shifted around on the stone, staring at Lyra. "My father says all of this belongs to me. As his firstborn son, I get it."

Lyra scooted away and off the rock. A sense of foreboding moved through her. Her father had deeded this to her... suddenly she felt the deep need for reassurance. Pointing at the child, she admonished him even as she backed away. "You should go home and play with other babies your age. And you will not kill any dragons on my land!"

Lyra turned and hurried all the way back to the castle. Today she did not pause to enjoy the beautiful appearance of the white stone edifice. The stone had been quarried centuries earlier, and yet it still retained the sparkle of newly quarried rocks. Lyra had often believed it resembled the castles in fairy tales her beloved grandmother read to her as she grew up.

After her meeting with the boy, she was in a rush to speak to her father, and didn't dally like she usually did, greeting people, many of whom she'd known for most of her life. Upon entering the castle, she rushed to the rooms where her father conducted the region's business each day.

Surprised to find the doors closed, she reached for the handle. The guards stepped forward, effectively blocking her. Shocked, she looked from one tall soldier to the other. Smiling deliberately, she batted her long eyelashes. In the past, this technique had always worked well. "Hello! I need to speak to my father for a moment."

The black-haired soldier shook his head. "I'm sorry, Princess. We are under orders to admit no one."

Lyra nodded in agreement. "I can understand that, but those edicts never apply to me."

The taller and older soldier cleared his throat before he spoke. "Yes, well, Lord Elroyd, Master of the Court, specified that even you were not to be allowed in today."

Lyra crossed her arms, tapping her foot against the soft carpet beneath it. "Who is in there with him?"

"We are not at liberty to discuss that either, Princess."

"What difference does it make whether I know or not? It is just a name after all, and it isn't like I can tell anyone, right?" Lyra smiled up at the soldiers, even going so far as to blatantly bat her long eyelashes.

Neither soldier replied.

Disgusted, Lyra turned and walked away. She was on her way to the kitchen, planning on stealing more food for Maldovaar when her mother stopped her.

"Why are you not upstairs and getting ready, darling? You must hurry or you will be late." Queen Taala spoke quickly to her daughter, pausing to check several sheets of papers she held. "Don't argue, dear. I'm rushed off my feet. Now hurry along!"

Sighing heavily, Lyra watched her mother rush off in the opposite direction. Slowly, she walked upstairs to her third floor room. She'd chosen this tower room several years earlier because it was separated from the rest of the regular rooms. When they had guests, she wouldn't be alone. Undoubtedly, her parents' visitors would be staying in the rooms in this wing of the castle.

Walking up the stairs at the end of the hall, Lyra entered her room. On her bed was the gown her mother had specially made for the ball tonight. Since she had at least four other gowns, from other such parties, Lyra thought a new dress was silly. Taking off her clothes, she walked into the bathroom. Adding bath oil and soap, she started the water in the large tub. Less than five minutes later, she slid into the warm water. Ducking her head, she shampooed her hair first, rinsed it and then applied a thick, special conditioner, the herbal recipe she'd been given by her grandmother.

The heat from the water relaxed her and released the scents of the conditioner. It was sweet and permeated her senses.

Leaning back, she let her mind roam back to the incident this morning that had been niggling her conscience ever since.

Leaving this morning, she had seen the arrival of guests to the castle. Pausing to stare along with other people in the courtyard, she noted at the front of the group was a slender, very finely dressed man with blond hair. From the moment his boot touched the ground, his nose lifted as if he were constantly sniffing the air. Something about him just rubbed her the wrong way.

Then a rearing horse, neighing loudly, caught her attention. Turning, she'd seen a tall, broad-shouldered man, dressed like a soldier, tugging on the reins. Across the distance, she could hear him talking softly to the skittish animal, obviously trying to soothe the beast amidst the confusion of the arrival.

She should have left right then. Instead she stood, staring.

He turned abruptly, his gaze seemingly shooting straight across the yard and locking onto her.

Freezing, Lyra felt like she shouldn't move, or he would see her. She told herself that was silly, yet she didn't move. Slowly, she realized the way he watched her... looked her over... was completely different from the way any man had in the past. This man's gaze seemed to linger on her fuller curves. Finally, his gaze met hers and he smiled. Gasping in disbelief, Lyra had spun on her heel and run from the yard.

The warm water wrapped her in a restful cocoon. Allowing herself the time to mull over the incident, she let it go and returned to the present time.

Later, she heard a noise in her bedroom. Looking through the open doorway, she didn't see anything at first. "Is someone out there?" she called out.

A few seconds later, she saw a small blond-haired child step out from behind a chair. He stood up tall and straight, staring at her. His wooden sword was tucked into his belt.

"What are you doing here?" Lyra asked, amazed at who her intruder was.

"I saw the stairs and I wanted to see where they went." Derek glared, his lower lip pouting defiantly.

"And now that you have, a true knight and gentleman would leave," Lyra pointed out. She didn't want to admit she was starting to like this rather audacious young stranger. With the right kind of attention, and discipline, he might be enjoyable. Abruptly, she realized one other thing. "Did you follow me?"

"I thought you might want to play with me. I'm stuck in my room and I can't find any other children here." Derek kicked his feet at the carpet, but slowly walked towards Lyra's bathroom.

Lyra smiled. "Yes, well, there are a few children. The trick is that you have to know where to look."

"So, you wanna play with me?" The little boy prodded her again

"You don't appear to be stuck in your room now." Lyra pointed out the flaw in his argument.

"Only because I snuck out. So, you got any games?" Derek crossed the remaining distance and sat on the floor near her tub.

Lyra paused, gazing at the small boy. She had to wonder if this was a sign of her luck in the future. Perhaps it would be better if she said "bad luck", because that seemed to be the only kind she was getting lately! Shaking her head, she hoped things would look up, and soon. Looking at her visitor, she spoke again. "I do, but nothing a person can play in the bathtub. Also, I think you should step outside while I finish my ablutions." When she saw the stubborn tilt to his chin, she hastened to add, "A proper knight would not accost a lady in her chambers."

Derek stood slowly.

Lyra could see him thinking about what she'd said. It was like watching the wheels turning in his head.

He finally nodded. "Just outside the door?"

"The hallway would be the proper place for a king's knight."

"You might lock the door," the pint-sized dragon-slayer added from the doorway into her bath.

Lyra had to fight to hide her smile. Obviously, that trick had been played on the lad at least once before. Quickly, she shook her head. "I would not. That would not be fair."

"My papa says women don't play fair. He told me you can't trust what a woman says," Derek told her from the other room.

Gritting her teeth, Lyra angrily sped through her bath. Can't trust women? What kind of idiot was raising this child? How could this child ever expect to have an honest relationship with any woman? He'd never have a friendship with a little girl, to develop his softer side. Wrapping in a small bath sheet, which covered her important parts, she came around the corner into her main bedroom, still combing her hair.

* * * * *

Thomas shook his head as he hurried up the stairs. He had worked for his lordship for so long that he still had trouble accepting the small boy into their lives. It had come as quite a shock to learn his master had a son, let alone the wild ragamuffin that was presented by a disgruntled grandfather nearly two years ago. At that time, the child was only a few years old, but already he'd been running free like an animal.

Obviously, his Master, the Duke of Krytan, had sown a few oats into a fertile womb before the "war to end all wars". The child's mother had died in childbirth, and only the old man had been left to raise the boy. It appeared he was a survivor, in spite of the odds against him to date. But ever since Derek had come to live with his father, his Master had decided the only person he trusted to look after his heir was his own manservant, Thomas.

Thomas cursed as his knees objected loudly to going up still another set of stone steps. The king's soldier standing guard on the floor below said he spotted the boy going into his room, but Thomas had spent too many hours with Derek to believe that he was still there. A quick check in the large room proved his theory correct once again. Only after he'd walked to the far end of the hall, discovering there was nowhere else to hide, had Thomas turned quickly to come back. He would question the guard once more. The last thing he wanted was to let the duke know he had misplaced his son once again.

There was little doubt in his mind His Grace would point out this fact. It seemed to be a regular thing of late and while he would enjoy being relieved of this onerous duty, he also wanted to return to his previous duty—that of being the duke's much-respected and privileged manservant. As caretaker to the whelp, he was the butt of jokes amongst not only the knights who rode with his lordship, but also the servants of the soldiers. At the duke's castle, he had lost all semblances of admiration and proper decorum that he had grown used to. Damn it all! He wanted it back.

His anger had increased his speed, and this created airflow as he raced back down the hall. This time, though, he noticed large tapestry hanging on the wall moved. Immediately, he thought it appeared to dip into the wall. Using the flat of his hands, he pressed against the elaborate and heavily embroidered cloth and realized it concealed an opening in the stone. The moment he pulled it back and saw a staircase that curved as it went up, Thomas knew where the future duke had to have wandered in the child's never-ending quest to make his own life miserable.

"Derek!" he muttered. More steps to walk up!

"Thomas!"

His Master's voice stopped him on the first step. Relief and fear raced through him simultaneously. Glad he could possibly avoid another set of stairs won out, though. He turned to the duke with a smile. "Yes, Your Grace?"

"Where is my son?"

"I believe he is up in this tower. It might be an old nursery."

The duke put his hands on his hips as he stared up the narrow, twisting stone staircase. "Hmm. Seems an odd place for loving parents to put a nursery."

"No indeed, Master. It is away from the other rooms, secluded, and would therefore be quiet," Thomas pointed out, proud of his ability to see things so clearly.

The duke slowly turned to look at him. "Thomas, I get the impression sometimes you are not enjoying your current position in my entourage."

Thomas swallowed hard, wanting to agree with his Master. Caution stopped his rash rush to agree. "Uhm, well, perhaps I am too old—"

"Not at all, Thomas. It is your wisdom I wish you to use in your dealings with Derek's youthful and occasional headstrong impulsiveness."

"Thank you, sir."

"Well, I'll go up and find him. You can wait in his room. Maybe put your feet up for a while?"

Thomas watched as the Duke of Krytan turned to start up the narrow stairs. The big man's shoulders nearly stretched the width of the narrow opening. The duke was an impressive figure, both physically and verbally, and yet Thomas had never seen the child cower in fear. Of course, he'd never seen the duke raise a hand to the child, even though there had been several times he would have thought it might have helped. Turning, with relief, he decided the opportunity to put up his feet was too good to pass up.

At the top of the curving staircase, Krytan found a hallway. Walking the short distance, he came to a room where the door stood open, and sunlight from within the room poured into the dark passageway. Just inside the room, he discovered his missing son. Standing in the open doorway, Krytan caught the tail end of what the young boy was saying.

"You can't trust what a woman says."

The duke shook his head as he wondered whom the boy had discovered up here. Perhaps the King was hiding some crazy member of the royal family up here, safe from prying eyes and harmful gossip? More than likely a servant was up here cleaning…

Also, he realized that once again the child had listened to him. Somehow, the words came out with a totally different connotation than what they had been meant in the first place. With regret, he remembered when he had said those very words, but he had been recounting a war story and it had involved the use of women as spies. Luckily, whomever the boy was speaking to would be unable to recount the words to His Majesty, who might see the duke in a new light.

This marriage was important for his people, and Derek's future. The last thing they needed was for loose little lips to ruin everything by talking to servants, or daft people.

"Psst! Derek! Come here! You need to get cleaned up before dinner," Krytan hissed at the youngster, gesturing with his finger for him to cross the room to the doorway.

Derek turned to look at him and brandished his sword in response to his finger. "I've been telling the lady how I've come here to slay dragons."

Krytan looked towards where Derek had gestured with his sword and saw naked feet, followed by long legs, ending in a wrapped bath sheet, concealing the body. When he finally met the clear green-eyed gaze of the woman in front of him, he quickly looked away. With great regret, Krytan wished he had taken the time to change from his dusty, travel-stained clothing. Undoubtedly, he looked like one of his knights, or even a servant.

Damn!

"Derek! Come with me, now!" he spoke roughly, and the surprise on Derek's face revealed that he rarely heard that tone.

It must have gotten through because the child took a few tentative steps in his direction. Krytan took hold of the boy's shirt collar, pulling him closer.

The woman spoke to him. "I invited him up here. Please do not tell your Master of the child's presence. He has caused no damage."

As the woman paused, Krytan let his gaze move slowly over her curves. Her skin glowed and he assumed she was a servant girl, since she was here alone. In his experience, ladies, and most certainly royal princesses, would never be attending to their toiletry alone, and never would an unknown child have been allowed to enter. In fact, from his experience at the King's court, most ladies rarely had any contact with their own children!

Lyra felt like she couldn't look away from the big servant's intent gaze. This was not good, she knew. Her father would have a fit if he ever learned she'd been entertaining not only small boys in her bedchamber, but now an unknown servant, or even a knight, who obviously was in someone's employ. She should be glad, reminding herself quickly, that at least it was a servant and not one of her father's supercilious guests!

Lately, since the war ended, there seemed to be a never-ending line of visiting dignitaries. She hated pomp and pageantry, and had a whole list of excuses to avoid attending official functions and parties. Her father had started to lose his patience with her, but her mother was able to mollify the situation, most of the time. Yet, something in her father's tone had indicated to him the visitors he was expecting today were very important to him.

Shaking her head, she shoved her hair back behind her shoulders, ignoring the dripping locks. She hated the way her body reacted to this man. No, he was just a servant, right? Whatever she was experiencing was due to tiredness and the stress she was feeling lately. Something made her pause to wonder if this could possibly the man she'd seen in the courtyard earlier. While it had been some distance, certain things in his figure and demeanor made her question if it was him. Tilting her chin in a way she knew looked slightly imperious, she spoke to the man. "You may escort this young knight back to his father. I suggest you take better care of your charge next time. He wandered quite far today."

Abruptly, she shut her mouth. She'd had no intention of betraying the young boy and hoped the servant wouldn't have caught her slip. Looking at the man, she was immediately aware of the blatant way he looked at her! Never before had any man dared to look so boldly… not since this morning anyway.

Her breath caught in her chest as her heart raced. She was dimly aware her fingers trembled slightly as she lifted one hand to run it through her wild locks. Suddenly, her mouth seemed dry and she licked her lower lip.

This was very strange indeed!

Krytan tamped down his bristles at the wench's highhanded gestures and tone. He wasn't used to being confused with a servant, yet he didn't rush to set her straight. In the back of his mind was the thought that perhaps this wench might be interested in providing him one last tumble before his nuptials.

Deciding discretion would be best, he tugged on Derek's collar. "Come along, young man. We should leave this wench alone so she can get her chores done." Hiding his grin, he turned and left quickly.

* * * * *

Lyra turned from the open doorway. She now knew the child's father was obviously a noble and most likely more than a knight who'd fought for her father. Only someone titled and well off would have a caretaker dressed so finely for such a young child. Undoubtedly, this "nanny" had no patience with the child, and that was a shame. No child deserved being treated like that. Derek didn't ask to be born into this world, nor to people who obviously didn't want him.

Sitting on her bed, she decided to take a nap. At this point, she didn't care if she overslept. She'd made it quite plain to her father that he could toady up to whoever he chose, but that didn't mean she would do the same. Since the end of the war, he'd spoken to her several times about her future. But each time she'd pointed out she was quite happy and so there was quite simply no need to worry about her life. When the time came, she'd make her own plans.

Her mother's reply was always the same. "You can't spend the rest of your life chasing after things that are better off left alone."

They all knew to what the beautiful Queen Taala was referring. Still, no one ever said it out loud. And as far as her parents knew, she never ventured into the old valley anymore. Closing her eyes, Lyra reminded herself that what her parents didn't know couldn't hurt them. She would hate to be forced to make a decision, or choose...

* * * * *

King Aldous seemed to be able to talk, eat and drink at the same time. Or that is how it appeared to His Grace, the Duke of Krytan, as he sat beside the King during the royal presentation dinner. So far, his son was behaving without mishap, seated beside him at the long dining table. He thought everything was going quite well until the King received a message shortly after the meal began. After reading the small piece of paper, the King betrayed his true reaction by crumbling the note in his fist. If he'd not been watching so closely, Krytan would have missed it. Immediately, King Aldous began laughing and chatting to him once again.

Schooled quite well in his courtly manners, Krytan waited ten more minutes before he asked about the presence of the missing dinner companion he'd been promised. Actually, she was a great deal more than just someone to share the meal with… against his own misgivings, he'd given into his own advisors and agreed to marry the King's only daughter.

On the one hand, he knew it looked like a pretty good deal for himself. One day, he would have rule over the entire kingdom, not just his own lands. He was also receiving several new tracts of land, including one new title, which he'd be able to pass onto his son, or even divide up should this marriage bring additional progeny. Of course, that was what the King hoped for—continuing his bloodline upon the throne, which had already held reign for nearly two centuries. That alone was unheard of, but to have followed upon the recent war it became incredibly important for the King to have remained in power.

Still, Aldous did not do it alone and his forces had been joined in the fight by loyal houses from the surrounding areas. The duke's knights formed the largest contingent. Surprising all of the loyal followers had been the King's compassion to his rival, Sir Ranal, for the throne. Instead of having him brought up on charges of disloyalty to the King, casting him out of the region entirely or even killing him, he offered him and all of his soldiers' reprieves.

Krytan admitted he doubted the old man's senses, but then he assumed perhaps the King was planning to wed his only daughter to the losing rival knight, Sir Ranal, Earl of Hodynaar. In his mind, that would have been the best way to keep the future peace. He was willing to accept the offer. All he needed to do was marry a woman he'd never met. That should be simple enough, he reminded himself once again. And then, just as he had many times before, he wondered if he could ever care about her.

Unbidden came the mental picture of the half-naked woman he'd seen that afternoon. While the serving wench was a little highhanded, which undoubtedly came from working in the king's palace, he had no doubt he could seduce that out of her. Very easily, he could imagine the woman in his bed, and he between her thighs. That long red hair spread across the pillow looked like liquid flames. What he'd seen of her pale flesh, he'd liked. In fact, he was quite eager to see more. Perhaps he could find her to share some pre-connubial bliss…

Unpleasantly, he recalled he had responsibilities, though, to his son, his own knights and people. The alliance would benefit everyone in his region. How could he say no? Krytan cleared his throat. "Is the princess delayed, Your Majesty?" He wasn't sure, but he hoped he wasn't betraying his own growing sense of uneasiness.

Aldous flushed red as he obviously fumbled about trying to come up with an answer. The fact the old King couldn't answer immediately was all the answer Krytan really needed. Still, he waited for the king's reply.

"Yes, well, uhm… it appears my daughter went out this afternoon and spent too much time in the sun. She was forced to take to her bed in order to recover fully. By morning, she will be fine and we'll be able to move forward with our plans."

"Ah, I see. That should be fine, Your Majesty."

* * * * *

Lyra knew she was no longer alone several moments before the bed moved beneath her. Turning her head towards the movement, she knew who the intruder was. Yes, she found herself looking into blue eyes, surrounded by brown gold-tipped lashes and brows, and shaggy blond hair falling forward onto his brow.

"Derek, what are you doing up here?" She sighed heavily as she spoke.

The boy grinned. "I came up to see if you wanted to play. I'm not sleepy."

Lyra shifted her covers to maintain her decency, struggling to sit up in her bed. "I was asleep." She crossed her arms and waited for his brain to process the discrepancy.

"Now you're awake!"

Barely biting back her smile, she acknowledged his cleverness. Obviously, logic was not going to work. Perhaps if she took him back to bed, and read him a story. *Damn*! That reminded her about sneaking back to visit Maldovaar. She'd slept so long that if she left now, it would be morning before she was back.

"If you'll bring me my robe." Lyra pointed to the blue one lying across a chair. "I'll read you a story so you can go to sleep."

Downstairs, Derek led her into one of the more elaborate guest rooms. She wondered just who was this little urchin to be staying in one of her father's best bedrooms. The little boy went straight to the perfectly made large bed, using the wood stepping stool to climb up. He slipped under the covers, lying back and resting his head on a pillow, and then patted the mattress beside him. "Come here and read to me, please."

Lyra felt something inside her being tugged in a way she'd never felt before, not even with the orphaned animals she was always rescuing and befriending over the years. She couldn't say what the feeling was, or why. She just knew it didn't feel comfortable. For a moment, she recalled the few times she'd been allowed to sneak into her parents' bed. With a suppressed sigh, she asked, "Where are your books?"

"I don't have any."

She made a few disparaging remarks silently to herself for a moment. What kind of parents drag a boy from his home and don't bring even the most basic of toys for him? Shaking her head in disgust, she joined the little guy on the bed. Without a book, she was at a loss about what to tell him. Then she remembered his earlier fascination with the dragon and decided to weave a tale.

"Very well," she told him as she eased down onto the bed. "It was during the Great War—"

"The one to end all wars, right?"

Lyra looked down into his eager eyes and had to smile. "By the way, my name is Lyra."

"I'm Derek."

Lyra held out her hand to the child and he shook it quite solemnly, which struck her as odd, considering their current circumstances. Nonetheless, she settled down on the bed to recount her tale. "There was a dragon that lived in a valley not too far from here. He was quite happy living alone."

"Was he mean and fire-breathing?" Derek interrupted with excitement in his voice, his eyes sparkling.

"Who is telling this story, you or me?" she countered quickly, hiding her smile.

Derek grinned as he replied, "You."

"Very well, I'll continue." Without comment she noted that he appeared to be totally unrepentant. "No, he could blow fire, he just chose not to. Or rather, he only used his flame to start the occasional camping fire and so on. Now, he was not in the least bit mean, but he did have a strong propensity to cheapness."

"What's propens… what is that?" Derek interrupted her again.

She needed to remember this was a story for a young child, not one for her diary. "It's like a tendency… uhm, let's say you have two choices between white cake or chocolate. For the last ten times you had this choice, you went for the chocolate." She paused as Derek nodded his head vigorously. "You chose the chocolate nine out of ten times. That means that you pretty much always pick the same thing. Do you understand?"

"Chocolate is what I would pick!"

"Me, too, unfortunately."

"Huh?" Derek frowned.

Lyra looked down into the innocent face looking up at her. Children at this age were usually so pure and untouched by adult prejudices, she realized in surprise. Derek, with his little boy eyes, had not cared she wasn't a svelte, slender beauty. During the war, she'd become painfully aware of her shortcomings in the looks department. In spite of handsome knights, lords and soldiers coming in and out of Castle Wyston, not one had been struck breathless, or anything else, by her looks to propose marriage.

She wasn't surprised, really. There were lots of mirrors throughout the castle and each one had reflected back a pudgy little girl who developed into a plump teen and was now what her father called a "solid woman". Luckily, she didn't cry anymore when she heard him refer to her like that. He didn't mean it in a hateful way. For a man in his sixties, her father was very handsome. Her mother was still beautiful in her early forties. She knew her parents looked at her and wondered what had gone wrong.

Her father's family all had raven-black hair and striking blue eyes. Her mother's family was all pale blondes, usually with blue eyes as well. Somehow, she'd popped out with a mop of unruly red curls and eyes that couldn't decide on being blue or green most of the time. Granted, her eyes were like her father's. But when she looked in the mirror, she wasn't sure what was wrong. Her eyebrows didn't meet in the center, nor was her nose tilted up like a pig. Her teeth were white and straight, and when she smiled, she thought it made her look quite nice.

Still, she knew that most men wanted a slender woman for a wife. An elbow nudged her.

"Go on!" Derek added to reinforce his action.

Lyra looked down at the child curled up much closer against her now. Funny feelings were going inside her, she realized in surprise. A warm and fuzzy sense, along with a desire to hug him washed over her. Sighing heavily in confusion, she continued her story. "His name was Maldovaar and he had once been the leader of a large clan of dragons. Others envied his life because he was chosen to lead the attack contingent for the humans. Mal was brave and led his dragons into the battle fray boldly and decisively. But it soon became clear a truly incompetent ruler was leading the soldiers who rode the dragons, and therefore directed their flight and the battles.

"As the war raged on, Mal saw more and more of his family, friends and fellow dragon-soldiers die because of this bad leadership. It saddened him to see what was happening to the last of his kind. You see, over the last several thousand years dragons were dying off as more people moved into their lands. They were running out of places where they could safely play and live."

Lyra stopped as she heard a sniffle come from Derek's bent head. She didn't say a word, but lifted her arm to pull him closer, his head resting upon her breast. Gently, she stroked his hair, hoping to soothe him. Whispering, she continued the story.

"So, Mal gathered the remaining members of his family, and those he could convince to follow him, and late one night they flew away from the camp. It took some time, since they were a tired, hungry and injured ragtag bunch, but eventually they reached a new place to call home. Quickly, they saw how beautiful this place was. There was water everywhere, including a magnificent waterfall.

"Time passed, and they healed and recovered their full strength. And then one day, Mal was exploring a new cave for himself, deciding privacy and solitude sounded like a good idea."

"Was there a bear inside the cave?" Derek asked from his comfortable position.

Lyra saw his thumb crept suspiciously near his mouth and he tucked it quickly into his hand. Observing the gesture of vulnerability affected her deeply. Her throat tightened and tears welled in her eyes. Quickly, she blinked and swallowed to force back the emotions.

"No, the cave was empty. But Mal did discover lots of cut leaves and fronds to make the hard floor a soft place to lie down. He took advantage of this and settled down for a nap. When he woke, he would go looking for food around the nearby pond. Closing his eyes, he slept more deeply than he had in years. He was warm and cozy and felt safe."

Lyra softened her voice and slowed her words as she felt the boy drifting to sleep against her. Soon, she would be able to slide out of the bed and return to her room.

"Mal awoke hours later and made his way down to the small pond, where the waterfalls drained into the far end. The sheer beauty of this little corner of the new valley that was the dragon's home once again astounded him. This is where he would live."

A soft snore interrupted her and she smiled. Relaxing beside him, Lyra decided to stay put until she was sure he was soundly asleep. That way, she would be less likely to awaken him. It wasn't long before their shared warmth coaxed her back to sleep, as well.

Her father had always been well known for having the most comfortable beds for visitors anywhere in the land.

Chapter Two

Krytan dismissed his personal guards at the end of the long hall, walking the remainder of the way alone. He passed the closed doorway of his son's room, expecting the boy to have been asleep for hours. It would be best if he didn't disturb him. Thomas would not like having to settle him down once more.

The door to his room was partially opened, which surprised him since he remembered having closed it when he left for dinner hours earlier. Walking into the room, he spotted a small light beside the large bed, as well as the tamped-down fire still burning. A moment passed before his eyes adjusted and then he realized there was a lump on his bed. Immediately, he assumed it was Derek. But as he neared, he realized it was too big for his little boy. As he crossed the room quickly, his attention was attracted as a flicker from the damped fire highlighted a riot of red curls across his pillow.

Immediately Krytan felt a kick to his gut. Desire shot through him and his cock hardened in need. Taking a deep breath, he leaned over the bed. He saw Derek was cuddled against the sleeping woman. His gaze slipped down to where the woman's robe had fallen open. He was treated to an entrancing sight. She was lying partially on her back with one arm resting beneath Derek and the other thrown above her head. Her lower body twisted slightly to the side, so with the open robe, he saw the inner curves of deliciously full white breasts and a rounded belly before the cloth concealed what lay below.

Damn!

His gaze moved back to her soft belly and he was struck by how sweet it would feel to bury himself inside her and cushion his hips with each downward thrust. A very long time had passed since he'd been with a woman, choosing to be circumspect around his son. Suddenly, he wondered if this comely serving wench was a present from the King. It was a common practice for the host to offer one of his servants, and in some houses, even a titled lady, to warm the guest's bed. Since nothing had been said, and his purpose for being here was marriage, he was quite surprised to find such a delightful gift.

Carefully, he moved to the far side of the bed. As gently as possible, he lifted Derek off his bed. It took him less than a minute to return the child to his bed, closing the door between the two bedrooms. Standing once more next to the bed, this time he had a better view of the charms now only partially concealed. Looking at her face, he saw dark reddish-brown lashes lying against pale cheeks. Her lips were full and he couldn't help but wonder how sweet they would feel against his, or even wrapped around his manhood. That thought almost had him growling out loud as his cock stirred to full attention, demanding some female care, and soon. If it were possible, he decided the woman had more than fulfilled the promise he'd seen in her earlier in the day.

On this side of the bed, he could see her breasts were exactly like he preferred—big, soft and womanly. With her body covered by the loose bath sheet, he had only been able to guess at what her body might truly look like.

Her waist wasn't narrow as many ladies he had met at the King's castle so far, but he liked a woman who was built to handle a large man such as him. As a knight, and a dragon-rider, he was tall and strong, with arms and legs like tree trunks of muscles. No doubt, a lot of that would change now the war was over and he would spend most of his time in meetings to rule his properties.

Quickly, he shucked his clothes and eased down onto the bed. It appeared that this visit was going to turn out much better than he had anticipated. Gently, he pressed his palm flat to the middle of the sleeping woman's chest. He paused for several long moments, letting the heat from her body seep into him.

From beneath her warm flesh came the strong steady beating of her heart. The reaction that shot through him at that second surprised him. Pushing away the strange feelings, he moved his hand sideways, cupping her uppermost breast.

"God!" he whispered as he felt the large, soft globe fill his hand. Actually, she nearly overflowed it, which wasn't easy since he was such a large man. He groaned as he realized that he wanted to suck her teat. Shifting carefully downwards, he moved over and began licking at the pink nipple he found topping the white mountain of woman flesh.

Using his hand, he pushed her breast up from underneath, allowing him to take the pink bud inside his mouth.

A soft, yet completely audible whimper escaped the woman's throat. Unconsciously her body shifted towards him.

What started as a taste quickly turned into suckling deeply as if he could actually gain his necessary sustenance from her. A growl echoed from his throat and a few seconds later, he lowered his hand to stroke its way down over her stomach, her soft belly to her loins.

His fingers inched the way slowly, searching for soft curls to delve into. Later, he would make love to her with the lights on so he could enjoy the beauty of her pussy fur. For now, his need was to be inside of her. Abruptly, he stopped as he touched her cleft. For several seconds his fingers didn't move. But the silky smooth flesh was too inviting to ignore.

Releasing her nipple, he eased back, rolling her fully into a supine position. By the dim light, her pale flesh was clearly visible. Any regret he might have felt about the lack of her pussy fur quickly dispersed as his gaze moved over her soft belly. Her nether region was as bald as a baby's butt. Like a knife thrust to his gut, the eroticism was overwhelming. He dipped one finger down between the plump lips he hungered to get between. As he felt the wetness, he growled like a wild male animal, scenting his mate in heat. Without a moment's pause, he zeroed in on her clit, and began an erotic seduction of the flesh.

* * * * *

Lyra shifted in the warm, big bed. She was having the same erotic dream. In fact, this was the second… no, third time she'd had this same dream tonight. And it was so amazingly erotic that she did not want to awaken.

In all of her life, she'd never felt so alive. This had to be a dream for her to feel like this. Nothing in her life came near —

"Ahh!" she sighed.

What was happening? She was too sleepy to consider the ramifications. Instead, she focused on the sensual sweetness she was experiencing between her thighs. It felt so wonderful… almost like a warm, wet rag was playing an enticing game of hide and seek all around her body.

The way her nipples felt alternated between was maddening and exotic. First one was hot and wildly tingling, and then the other would start. She wished the hands would return to her breasts. "Touch my breasts," she whispered.

A moment later her hands were pulled up to cover each mound. Pressure squeezed around her hands. Before she could make sense of it, the warm, big hands were busily holding her thighs up… yes… and against the inside of her legs, she felt the hard warmth rub insistently. That made her more conscious, and she zeroed in on the central core of her body.

Yes. She knew that pleasure, but only at her touch. Dimly the inconsistency seeped in. She felt empty and yet the sweet rapture of the orgasm was fading. Then she realized the hard, hot heat was pressed against her wet pussy. Her lips were spreading against the insistent, driving —

There it was… the source of her pleasure… hard, searing hot and it thrust inside her with her next breath.

"What?" Lyra opened her eyes and was shocked to see a great hunk of a man in that exact position as her dream. The reality was fierce, though. This was not her fantasy, protected by sleep. Uh-uh. He was hard, hot and most assuredly ramming something —

"Oh my God!" Lyra cried out. "You!"

"It's much too late for protestations now, my sweet dove. The deed has been done." He leaned down and kissed her parted lips. "And may I say how sweet and unexpected the gift of your virginity truly was. I shall reward you richly for saving yourself. I know it is unusual for serving staff… "

His words were sinking in slowly.

She was having trouble connecting her thoughts because her body was behaving unlike anything she'd ever experienced before. Gasping, she felt her hips move and jerk against him, drawing him more deeply inside her wet, tender flesh. "I'm not—"

"I rather thought you'd awaken that time," he cut off her explanation. His hips flexed, and he drew out, and then slid back inside her body several more times. "But, alas, all you did was moan and groan and bite my neck as you came beneath me."

Lyra gasped at the man's words. The last thing she remembered was the wine she'd drank that came with her dinner tray. She'd fallen asleep… no, wait. The boy had awakened her—

"Derek!"

The man laughed, but he still didn't pause in his pursuit towards completion. "I'll forgive you this time, darling, for saying another man's name in my bed, especially since it is my son's name. But no other man's name shall ever be spoken in my bed by you. Once we reach my home, I'm going to keep you in bed for the first few weeks."

Lyra shook her head instinctively. Not only was she being used for sex, she had not fought, nor had she protested… Of course, she had not been conscious to say yes. Then she realized that this man was talking about taking her to his home.

It all connected! This was the Duke of Krytan, not some servant. And Derek was his son! And in spite of her attempts to escape vows, there would be no getting out of the marriage now.

Her father would demand it once he learned they had spent the night together. And this Duke was considering it a "done deal" already.

"Oh yes, my sweet. We'll spend hours in bed. I could easily spend days on end sucking these pretty lush boobs of yours. I've been imagining all the wildly erotic ways we can make love. I want to have you on all fours, bouncing off your sexy, round butt, holding onto your fat hips."

Lyra stiffened at his words. "Fat!" she spat out the word at the insult.

Obviously, he had no illusions about her size.

It surprised her that he actually sounded attracted and not repelled.

Before she could think further, Krytan spoke again. "You have the right kind of hips for a woman. You aren't scrawny or skinny like so many ladies of the court. It won't be long until your soft belly is swelling from the seed I'll plant from all this plowing. Very soon my babe will have your belly fatter and your pretty tits growing bigger each day."

Lyra wanted to deny his words, but a moment later she felt her body responding. Oh God! The tension was building, growing. Just like in her dreams… seconds later, she cried out. "Yes! Oh, my God!"

Lyra's hips jerked forward, hard, spasmodically and out of control as her orgasm crashed through her body. Over and over, she came in his arms. She was still completely aware of the hard male member deep inside her body. Then she felt him begin to respond—

Like a flood, the duke's seed shot into her ripe womb. Again and again, his hips jerked forward and shot still another potent load of baby-making seed into her fertile body. Focusing on her body, she felt her womanly organs, her flesh, sucking, nibbling and actually pulling his cock as deep as humanly possible within. It was as if her subconscious was striving to subvert her desires of escape and get her pregnant with the duke's child.

Before she could even think of what to say next, Krytan was pulling out of her body. There was a loud wet sucking sound, followed by a plop as his rod left her cunt. If she'd thought she was embarrassed before, it was nothing compared to now. Lying beside him in the silence, she was intently aware of the wetness leaking from her body. All of these were things she knew were related to the sex act, and only in her marriage bed, with her husband, should she experience them.

The fact it would happen like this... with her a little drunk, asleep and with a stranger seemed too much to bear! How could she tell her parents what had happened? They would be ashamed of her —

Now what was she supposed to do?

For at least a minute or two, she just laid there, quietly and unmoving, scarcely breathing. Perhaps he would fall asleep and she could slip away.

Krytan's hand landed heavily atop her left breast, cupping it almost familiarly in its casualness. Almost idly, he began molding it, lightly squeezing and then rolling the nipple between his fingers. His fingers tugged and pulled on her hardening flesh.

Lyra moaned a little, partly from sensitivity due to overuse and also because she was becoming aroused under his clever touch.

It was almost as if he knew what pleasured it her because he repeated it almost immediately.

She felt him move closer.

Then his breath brushed the side of her face as he spoke. "I can't remember the last time I've had such a busy night, my sweet. At this rate, I won't be able to perform for my new bride. But you need not worry. As my concubine, you will live in comfort and never have to work another day. Your children will be cared for and educated."

Lyra found it hard to speak. Her future husband was talking about keeping a whore and treating her on a par with his duchess. At this point, she was too tired to logically rationalize that it was all rather moot since she was both women. One thing did stand out, though. She had acted like a whore, a slut. Her body craved him once more and she didn't really know this man.

Of course, the fact that arranged marriages were common and she would have been expected to sleep with him tomorrow evening, after their wedding, didn't hold any weight right now. What did matter was that she'd made love... although she wasn't sure if it counted that she'd been asleep during the better part of it? Suddenly, she felt the overwhelming need to run away. She needed time and space to think and build a wall to protect her emotions. Her movement was stopped even as it started.

"Relax, darling," Krytan told her quietly, kissing the side of her face. "We still have hours until dawn. There is plenty of time to creep away before the servants awaken. We should maintain the illusion of propriety until we return home." He paused to squeeze her breast firmly and then deserted it.

Seconds later, she felt his hand circling and caressing its way down over her soft belly. When his hand cupped her mound, she gasped, both in surprise and immediate reaction. Her hips lifted to meet and welcome his clever fingers. Shamefully she realized that her thighs were already parting to allow him greater access. Beside her, she heard his deep chuckle at her response.

"Don't fret, sweetheart. Just because I'm worn-out doesn't mean you can't enjoy pleasure again. Never let it be said that I've left a woman wanting more."

Lyra told herself to push away his hand. Speak out and deny the need. She didn't, though. His fingers were very dexterous it seemed, and they were quite skilled. Within seconds, he knew the perfect place to touch her, the rhythm to use and the perfect pressure. When his head lowered to suck on her breast, she curled one hand to the back of his head, pushing her breast more fully into his mouth.

"Yes," she murmured softly. Her hips lifted and thighs fell apart wantonly, welcoming his possession. As his fingers slid inside her body, she felt his seed seeping out even as it aided his movements. Instead of feeling slimy, she felt even hotter, thrusting her body upwards.

"That's it, my sweet. Hump my fingers like my prize birding bitch in heat! Keep going. That's it, little one. Move your hips and shake that pretty round ass for me. Come on, darling! Come for me! Come for me! Come!"

Lyra followed his words like a puppet. When he demanded her response, her orgasm hit like a wild animal. She groaned loudly, opening her mouth to cry out. Only Krytan's fast action in covering her lips with his other hand prevented her from awakening anyone else. Moments later, he was kissing her while his fingers coaxed every last drop of response from her body. Only when she lay completely spent and exhausted did he finally pull his hand from her body.

Dimly, she was aware of Krytan covering their bodies with the covers once more, but only after dragging his wet hand up over her flesh, wiping off the dampness. She knew he settled down to sleep beside her, but she was too tired to force herself to leave his bed just yet. In a few minutes, she'd go.

Light was filling the room when Lyra awoke. Instead of being confused, immediately she knew where she was. Her second realization was that Krytan was once again inside her body.

She was lying on her side and he had entered her from behind. His hand was on her belly, holding her firmly as he thrust in and out of her juicy cunt. The sheer eroticism of the intimate act overwhelmed her. This was just how she'd envisioned lovemaking might be... with a man she loved that is, slow, gentle some times and wildly hot at others. But marriage to this man was not what she wanted, in spite of what her father believed to be best.

"That's it, darling," his husky voice whispered in her ear. "There is nothing as sweet as a tender joining in the morning. Slow, easy and taking our time to build to climax. I actually wasn't sure you were going to wake up at all. I'll bring you off first, but you must cover your mouth. I can't afford Derek waking up and finding you in here."

Lyra told herself to deny her needs, but instead she heard herself reply, "All right."

Immediately, his hand slid down and without pause he found her clit. As if he'd done it countless times before, he coaxed and teased her flesh into a speedy, but fulfilling, climax. She covered her mouth to stop her cry and it shocked her, the intensity of her reaction. This wasn't her. She didn't act like this. Things like this never happened to her… so it really had to be a dream after all, right?

Behind her, Krytan thrust forward quickly and surely. She told herself that she didn't like the feeling of him inside her. And she repeated it several times, to convince the stubborn parts of her psyche. Yet, there was no stopping the way her bottom wiggled back against his body as he exploded within her once more.

He didn't pull away immediately as she expected. Instead, his hand came up and cupped her upper breast, idly holding it rather than squeezing or caressing. The simple gesture felt even more intimate and erotic than if he had attempted to pleasure her, or himself, with continued sexual movements. Soon his hand felt heavy and she knew that he'd fallen asleep. As carefully as possible, she eased away, sliding out of the bed. Her robe was lost in the bedclothes so she grabbed the long tunic Krytan had discarded and pulled it on. The bright blue material fell to her knees and quickly she skulked from the room.

Upstairs in her room, the first thing she did was remove the tunic and look at her naked body in the long mirror her mother had given her in hopes that it would encourage her to lose weight. It hadn't and just made her depressed until she stopped glaring at herself each time.

Now, she stared at her reflection. Her hair was still a long fall of untamable curls when it was humid out, as it had been the last few days. Her round face looked the same, but partway down on her neck, she could see a red mark appearing. Shifting slightly, she saw her body from the side. There was no missing the rounded belly and heavy breasts. And yet it had appeared that such things aroused Krytan. There was also the more likely reason that he'd been desperate and taken what he believed was an offer from his host, the King.

She'd been asleep in his bed, although she had not known it was his bed. Somehow, he had carried Derek back to his bed and returned to ravish her... again and again. Turning back to face the mirror, she looked at her shaven pussy. That part was new, but he couldn't know that. Her mother had come to her the other evening, accompanied by two of her maidservants, and announced it was time for Lyra to become a woman.

Anxious to please and be accepted by her mother, she had rested upon her bed. As her mother talked and explained traditions, the servants had proceeded to first trim her pubic hair and then shave it all away. Then the Queen had applied a special cream, as they waited the required time, she'd gone on to explain that this was a powerful pleasure tool, and by using the cream she'd stay smooth from now on. Eventually, use of the cream would be unnecessary.

A bright blush flooded her cheeks as she recalled how embarrassed she'd been by the forced intimacies. The two serving women had been bland and matter-of-fact about the whole process. Listening to her mother talking about such things had only made her more uncomfortable. Now, she wondered what Krytan had thought when he first discovered her smoothness. Had he thought it strange to find such treatment on a serving girl? More logically, he was too busy to care.

Finally, she turned to look at herself from the side view. Lyra cringed as she took in her heavy breasts and below her full waist and rounded belly. Her bottom was tight and muscular from her walks and riding, but it was still full. Unable to stand the self-critique a moment longer, she walked to her bathtub. Filling the tub with water, she climbed in and took a very quick bath.

Wrapped in a large bath sheet, knotted at her breasts, she sat in front of her mirrored table. Her mother had given her a lovely assortment of facial cosmetics to primp with, as well as several combs, brushes and hand mirrors over the years. Looking at the wild mop of hair, she knew it was representative of her life. Everything was corkscrewed, knotted and going in the wrong direction.

She had to leave the castle. If she did not, she was going to end up married to the duke, or be taken from here as his concubine. Since her father was the King, most likely it would be marriage.

Logically, she reminded herself sternly, it could be argued nothing had really changed. The Duke of Krytan had come to marry her, and that was still the plan as far as everyone was concerned. The duke was now thinking he'd be leaving here with a bride and concubine. Somehow, she didn't imagine he'd be so upset at her deception that he would call off the whole thing. Still, if that were to happen, she could find herself having to wed Hodynaar.

Her whole body shook as she considered that option. She'd seen the man from afar, and that was plenty close for her. He was attractive enough, and in fact, she had overheard several other young ladies in the castle talk about how good-looking he was, or that one or another of them had actually spoken to him. He did not look properly chastised for having been the one to lose the war. But that was most likely because of her father's desire to quickly restore peaceful relations between their people and lands.

His black hair reminded her of shiny coal, but the true color of his eyes was concealed by the enlarged center. His skin was tanned, and very mildly pockmarked on his cheeks. No doubt he had survived the last scourge of the pox that swept through three decades earlier. In comparison to the duke, they were similar in size—height-wise. Beyond that, Lyra had gone out of her way to avoid Hodynaar. She'd heard more than enough about him from Maldovaar.

Smiling at her reflection, she remembered the day she'd found the big, ostentatious dragon camped out in her favorite cave. She'd taken the shortcut to the valley that morning, bringing enough food to spend the day and feed some of the animals. She wanted to coax some close enough so she could sketch them. Walking into her carefully maintained home away from home, she found things had been moved around.

At first, she was upset to think someone else had moved in on her territory. After a few moments of looking around, she realized that the place was much cleaner, and several amenities had been added. Needless to say that made her even more disturbed. It showed that the intruding "someone" cared more about the place than she had to make such large and permanent adjustments.

As she moved further into the cave, she discovered that at the moment, it was empty. The burning fire was maintained inside a well-built stone enclosure, which could be easily added to, or doused, but would prevent sparks and cinders from causing havoc. A little further back, the new bed had been established and from first glance she had seen that it was much bigger, more padded and very well maintained. Stepping up, she stood on the soft area, marveling at how bouncy it felt.

"I wonder what is on the bottom here to make it so comfy," she pondered out loud, jumping up and down to test it.

"Nosy little girls who don't know better to stay out of dragons' caves!"

"Aaarrggggghhhhhh!" Lyra screamed as she saw a dark something had filled the opening to the cave, and now it spoke to her... threatening her. She scrambled for her knife, but in her haste, everything came undone and fell onto the bed and the surrounding floor. Her pouch with the food landed wrong-end down, soon fruit, vegetables and her drink rolled across the floor towards her intruder-captor.

"Oranges! I haven't had an orange in… damn! I can't remember the last time I had one. What else did you bring me, girl?"

In disbelief, Lyra watched as the big dragon bent down to pick up one of the oranges. He sniffed it a few times, and then opened his mouth wide to pop it in whole.

"It would taste much better if you took off the skin and ate it in sections. That way you can really get the juice." She stopped as the dragon stared, slowly tilting one of his bright yellowish-green, very long and almost impossibly wild eyebrows.

"If I had opposable thumbs, young lady, I would do precisely that." With that he showed her his hands, or perhaps they were called paws?

"I'll peel it for you, but you should know that this cave is mine."

"YOURS!!!!!" The dragon's voice roared through out the cave.

Lyra moved back on the bed, dropping down into a kneeling position. It had been rather stupid, she reminded herself, to cross a fire-breathing dragon. "Uhm, sorry, but I'm the one who had it set up the way it was when you came upon it. I come here when I want to get away. Obviously this place was mine," she added with a smug tilt to her chin.

The dragon crossed towards her, holding out the orange. "Peel."

Lyra accepted the fruit and began carefully pulling back the skin. She considered pointing out she was a princess and he was merely a dragon, but something about the tilt of his head told her that might not be her wisest course of action.

A few seconds later, the dragon moved closer and sat facing the bed. "I am Maldovaar. I am leader of the greatest dragon legion to ever fly in service to a lord."

"Why are you living in this cave, alone? Shouldn't you be off somewhere, with your troops?" She finished peeling, and then began separating the orange into sections. Leaning forward, she offered the small pieces to the big beast. She was surprised when Maldovaar reached out and took a single section with just two fingers, carefully popping it into his mouth. As she watched, the dragon's eyes closed and she could see his enjoyment of the juicy fruit as he chewed. "It's good, isn't it?" she pointed out eagerly. "Much better this way."

Maldovaar's eyes opened again, looking straight at her. "You are quite right. You may stay as my servant, if you wish. You can clean up after me and peel my fruit."

Lyra laughed out loud at the suggestion. "I am a princess, dragon. I will peel a piece of fruit when, and only when, *I* feel like it."

Maldovaar leaned forward, his long neck easily stretching over the bed and coming within an inch of her face.

She fell back onto her palms, twisting her legs out from beneath her at the awkwardness. It was impossible not to cringe as he breathed hotly, reminding her that he could blow some fire her way, should he so desire. Still, she didn't back down.

"Very well. Since you are a princess, you may stay here when you visit. I think you should always bring extra fruit, though." Maldovaar slowly went back into his sitting position at the foot of the bed. "We'll need to share the bed. I used your design to enlarge it to this one. It is by far the most comfortable I've ever slept in."

"The war has ended. Why are you here?" Lyra asked softly.

Maldovaar's head lowered until it was below his shoulders.

He looked so sad that Lyra was hard pressed to not rush forward and offer her sympathy, for something.

"I was the leader for my herd. When I saw how poorly we were being led, and so many of my family and friends had been slaughtered needlessly, I spoke to my herd. Those who wished could follow me and I promised to lead them to a new home, a valley of beauty and great sustenance for us all."

"And you led them here, into my valley?" Lyra prompted Maldovaar when he paused.

"Your valley? No girl, this is our land now. We have claimed it as our own. It is vastly unpopulated with humans due to its remoteness."

Lyra shrugged. "Well, it is pretty much unapproachable by three sides. You most likely came in over one of those. But the fourth side is how I come and go. And the land is mine. My father is King, and I asked him for this land several years ago. He gave me the deed for my birthday celebration when I was sixteen."

Maldovaar suddenly loomed forward, baring his teeth, glaring and snorting as he came right down into her face once more.

Lyra almost scooted back, away from the threatening stance, but she held her ground.

"Do you have the soldiers, or the dragons, to protect it?" Maldovaar questioned her with a sly smile curling one side of his mouth.

Lyra stared into the dragon's eyes. This was the turning point. She sensed its import even as her stomach quivered from the beating of a thousand butterfly wings. She relaxed her body and held out another slice of fruit.

"I have you to protect it. With you and your family living here, that should keep out any intruders we need to worry about." She bit into a piece as Maldovaar accepted the offered slice.

"Are you sure you aren't the King in disguise, girl?"

Lyra grinned and shook her head. "No, but I am glad to have made a new friend today."

From that point on, she and Maldovaar had slowly developed an interesting relationship. Slowly, as the days passed and she came at different times to visit, she found him making her cave into his home. After that was accomplished to his satisfaction, he began making changes to himself. He let his beard grow, and then his eyebrows and mane. The surprise came when he had an old wizard he knew change the color. Against the natural greenish-yellow scales, the bright reddish-orange was something of a shock.

A sound outside her window drew her attention. Quickly, she walked over to one of the windows in her tower room. Looking down, she saw the courtyard was beginning to stir. Two large horses were saddled and she wasn't surprised when she recognized Krytan come into view seconds later. Another man approached him and then the two mounted and rode out of the enclosed area.

Lyra turned away and knew she didn't have much time until someone would come looking for her.

She could stay here and accept this man's plans, and her father's, for her future. He would take her to another land, and her life would resemble that of a noblewoman. No doubt, the duke's desire would wane quickly, and he would move his attention to another female.

It was impossible to remain at the castle.

Therefore, she must flee. Of course, she would go to her valley. If she filled several large bags with food, she could sneak back in a week or so, and take additional provisions at night. There were several places where she could slip in and out of the castle. One of the old caretakers had shown her some of the secret passages her great-grandfather built when the castle was expanded.

Once the egg hatched, she would decide what to do next…

Lyra stared at her reflection in the mirror. She would have to make sure she wasn't recognized too easily, she sighed heavily. Picking up the scissors off the dressing table, she sliced off the hair. A tear escaped and slid down her cheek. Quickly she cut her hair to a hodgepodge of lengths from one to two inches. Next, she pulled on plain, simple clothing that could easily pass for any commoner she might normally encounter. Knowing she could only take her usual pouch, she crammed it full of necessities.

Pausing, she added an old leather journal and a small wooden box. The journal contained the writings of her maternal great-grandmother, whose skills as a witch had been well known. In the box were small charms and special mementos.

Without further pause, or thought, she hurried down to the vast kitchens that served the castle.

* * * * *

Inside the bustling cooking room, people busily prepared breakfast for the King and his guests. But along the back wall, there were several long tables where the servants of the castle could come and eat during the day when their duties permitted. Since she wasn't wearing any makeup, jewelry or her signet ring, it was quite easy for her to fill a plate and sit at the table without drawing attention to her presence. Twice she filled her plate, putting extra biscuits into her pockets and pouch.

Stuffed to the brim, she made her way to where the fruit and bread was stored. She grabbed a sack used to bring in food, filling it rapidly with anything that looked good and most likely wouldn't be missed, until she saw the small sweet cakes that were being made. Cursing her weakness for sweets, Lyra stole a napkin and filled it with the cakes. Hopefully, the cook wouldn't mind making a fresh batch.

It was tempting to take her horse, but that would risk drawing attention to her escape. She was hoping to make a clean getaway before she was actually missed. Hopefully, her mother wouldn't come looking for her until noon. Once she skipped that meal as well, her mother would check with the kitchen to see if her daughter was having her meals delivered to her bedroom. After learning she was not, the Queen would make the tedious journey into the guest wing, where Lyra's tower room was.

As she walked out the back of the castle wall that faced the ocean below, she could just imagine how her mother would be grumbling by now over her tedious daughter. The Queen hated having her routine upset and this was definitely going to put a crimp into the carefully planned activities and events. Of course, this wouldn't be the first time Lyra had done something that disrupted her mother's schedule. Still, this time was different.

Closing her mind to the precise differences, she walked slowly along the treacherous promontory, until she was approximately a mile from the castle. At this point, a thick forest grew in wild abundance. Rumors had always existed that the forest was home to mystery, magic and the unexplained. Maldovaar had hinted his wizard friend lived somewhere in the forest, but Lyra wasn't sure she believed any of it. She had learned her magic from her maternal grandmother, when she was a child. But pixies and fairies? Lyra wasn't too sure about that.

Still, she never lingered on the walk through the thick trees. She was half afraid the huge trunks might suddenly come to life, and reach out for her with thick limbs and gnarled fingerlike branches. With a sigh of relief, she finally left the forest and entered the beautiful valley. It wasn't far from here to the cave and she covered the ground quickly. At the mouth of the cavern, Lyra walked in and gratefully down set her pouch and food sack.

"Mal?" She called out, expecting him to be sitting exactly where she'd left him yesterday… on the nest. He wasn't, though.

Racing across the stone floor, nearly tripping on one of the rush mat rugs Maldovaar had thrown down, she slid to a stop beside the nest she'd made. Inside the sad-looking ramshackle incubator, she saw the solitary colorful egg, wrapped up in a blanket, surrounded by several kittens. The mother cat also appeared to be missing, Lyra noted, not altogether surprised. But half afraid of disturbing the sleeping brood, she backed away silently.

Turning towards the entrance, she crossed to retrieve her bags. At the food bag, she found the errant feline mother rubbing against the outside, purring softly. Smiling, Lyra picked up the bag and her satchel of clothes.

"Come along, little mother, and I will give you a treat." As if it understood her words, the cat followed her to the bed. Sitting on the soft blankets Maldovaar had added, Lyra patted for the cat to jump up. Once there, Lyra pulled one of the biscuits from the sack and began feeding small pieces to the hungry mother, as well as a few for herself.

Rubbing the cat's head, she spoke to it softly. "Where did you come from? Your babies don't look very old. What will you do when my dragon baby comes along?"

"I stayed up quite late last night, Princess, waiting for my nonexistent cheesecake."

Lyra looked up as Maldovaar spoke. He took slow lumbering steps as he came towards her. "You're walking as if you are carrying a baby in your belly. You are supposed to be sitting on it."

"I found something better, as you can see. The heat from those little fur balls should do a very nice job. What did you bring me to eat?" Maldovaar crossed to the bed, stretching out across the covers. The mother cat meowed once and then hopped off the bed. She quickly resumed her spot next to the dragon egg, arranging her sightless kits so they could all nurse.

Lyra turned to look at the lounging lizard. Lying on his side, he had his head propped on the palm of his bent arm. "That sexy look is wasted on me, Maldovaar."

"Perhaps I'm expecting company," Maldovaar drawled. His free hand lightly rubbed circles around his belly.

"You promised you wouldn't let anybody in!"

"I haven't, Princess. Relax. I had a dream about this stud muffin last night. Hubba hubba, girl child! Now that was a dragon who could solve this dragon's draggin' problem, if you get my drift!" Maldovaar poked Lyra with a finger.

"Very funny. I also thought we agreed to be especially careful and quiet. I don't want anything falling and damaging the egg. So no playmates, or play-studs, until you are a proud papa."

"All right, play hardball with me, Princess. Besides which, you are the mama, I never signed on to be a father." He reached out and flicked a finger against her short hair. "You don't look very happy. Is something wrong? Did someone attack you with a scissors?"

Lyra glared at the big lounging dragon. "Yes, damn it all, Mal! I've left home and I can never go back."

"Left home? Move in with me! I don't think so, little lady. Sharing this abode once in a while has worked out fairly well… but if I start living with you… I mean, if it gets around a girl is living with me—the ferocious, the leader of dragons… Great Maldovaar, well, it won't be good." Maldovaar shifted on the bed, lying on his back. Taking in a deep breath, he exhaled slowly. After a few moments, he started idly kicking his feet in the air, as if he didn't have a care in the world.

"I had to find you when I discovered the egg, so I know you aren't hanging out here all the time." Lyra could feel her tears threatening to spill over at any moment. The dragon's relaxed pose irritated her beyond belief. Her life was falling apart and he was worried about sharing his cave. "I'm the one who is suffering here, Maldovaar. I've gone from a life of luxury to a cold, dank cave!"

Before a tear could escape, she got up and went over to the nest she'd made. Sitting beside it, she lightly touched the kittens sleeping inside. The scruffy-looking mama-cat was settled down inside the blanket. Her head rested lightly on the eggshell and the kittens all nuzzled their way close as they continued nursing.

"What's her name, Mal?" she asked softly, rubbing the purring cat between her ears. She may be an indiscriminant gray color, but her babies were anything but that. One was longhaired and white with black patches around both eyes and its muzzle. Touching this one, she spoke softly.

"Your name shall be Mystery, and Misty for short."

Maldovaar had rolled to his side and watched her.

She saw his intent gaze when she glanced up. "What did you name their mama?"

"I didn't. She told me her name was Tramp."

Lyra gasped at the offhand way Maldovaar said the name. Perhaps it was just her increased sensitivity, lack of sleep or whatever, but she took exception to that name. Easing her fingers beneath the gray cat's chin, she rubbed gently until the yellow-eyed gaze met hers. Staring into the sad eyes, Lyra shook her head.

"No more shall you be called that horrible name. You deserve something much better. You have some beautiful babies, and we want them to grow up proud of their mother. Help me name your kits, and then you can tell me what new name you choose. Now, this pretty black kitty… " she paused to shift the kitty slightly. "This boy kitty… how about Night Hawk?"

Maldovaar shook his head. "Why are you bothering to name them? As soon as squirt pops his shell, they'll be on their way."

"No, they won't be leaving, Mal. They need a home, and I need someone friendly to be with the little dragonet. I'll enjoy playing with the kittens as they grow up."

"Who is going to feed them?"

"I will. I can catch fish. Their mama will nurse them, and she will teach them how to catch mice and other little things. But if I keep them well fed, they'll have no need to go hunting. You could fish, as well." She ignored the disgusted sound from the bed and turned her attention to the longhaired calico kitten. "What name would you like?" She moved the little animal just enough to peek. "Little boy kitty. You need a good strong name like your brother and sister. I know a good name for you… Duke. What do you think, Mama Cat? Do you like the names for your precious babies?"

She tickled the gray cat's head as she purred softly. Suddenly a shifting in the blankets drew her attention. Lyra lifted the blanket and saw that a fourth kitten had somehow gotten down between the blankets and was nestled close to the egg. She pulled it out and immediately set the mewling kit to her mother's last spare teat.

"You poor baby! How did you get under there?"

Maldovaar groaned from the bed. "Not another one!"

"Yes, Mal. A pretty orange-striped girl this time. We should let mama name this one." Lyra looked at the gray cat.

Maldovaar scoffed loudly, reaching for Lyra's food sack. "You didn't bring much food, did you? You promised to bring me lots of food every day if I agreed to do this for you, or did you forget?"

Lyra muttered under her breath. "As if you'd let me." She raised her voice as she looked at Maldovaar. "It appears to me you aren't doing the job you agreed to, having palmed it off to this lovely lady here. She is the one who deserves the food." Getting to her feet, she walked over and grabbed the bag from the dragon's hands. Pulling out several pieces of cheese, a flask of water and the small package of cakes, she tossed the sack back towards him, walking back to the nest.

"We'll need to move this nest before nightfall."

"Are you crazy? Why?" Maldovaar lifted his nose out of the food sack, his mouth trying to hold onto a biscuit as he spoke.

"So, they are warm enough tonight. We can't take any chances. They can share the bed with us." She cupped her hand and poured a small amount of water into it. The mama cat lapped at it gently. Lyra laughed as her tongue stroked her skin to capture all the moisture. "There's more, sweet kitty." She refilled her hand and offered it once more. "I think we should call you Mama Mia for now, and then Mia once the kittens are grown. How does that sound?"

Lyra ignored Maldovaar's rude scoff and grunt. Beside her the cat in question purred loudly. "Good! I'm glad you like your new name, Mama Mia. What shall we call your secret kitty? You want to name her after Maldovaar? Are you sure? I know he let you stay here, but he was only using you for his own convenience."

"Hey! I'm right here and I can *hear* you." Maldovaar protested in between bites of an apple.

Lyra grinned back. "I know. I like the name—"

"Princess!" Maldovaar interrupted, not bothering to hide his irritation and impatience with this name game of hers.

Lyra laughed out loud. "That's it! The ginger cat is Princess. That way, you'll always have me with you, Maldovaar."

The look of horror on the dragon's face was priceless and she laughed again. Seeing that she'd disturbed the kitties, she apologized and moved away. "You have a real family now, Mal. You've gone from being carefree bachelor dragon about town, to father of four, soon to be five! Quite a lifestyle change to say the least, huh?" It probably wasn't wise to tease a fire-breathing dragon, but Lyra couldn't resist.

"I see nothing in the least bit humorous about this whole situation, Princess. By the way, will there be anyone else showing up to share this humble abode?"

Lyra shook her head. "No, Mal, it will be just us—one dragon, five cats, one human and one dragon egg."

She heard the dragon mutter behind her a few moments later.

"That makes seven too many!"

* * * * *

Lyra awoke reluctantly, wishing she were back in her warm bed. She had not slept very well at all, the cave being somewhat cooler than she had anticipated. Of course, if Mal had slept in front of the entrance like she requested, he would have blocked most of the uncomfortable chill. Yawning, she pushed away memories of the argument following *that* suggestion. She was constantly amazed how anthropomorphic dragons really were. No doubt it was because of their superior intelligence. Some people questioned that dragons were the more advanced race living here… Damn!

Lyra cursed and crawled out of bed. Now, she was even beginning to sound like Maldovaar. Standing, she looked back and saw Mal was snoring loudly. The nest, complete with kittens and egg, was nestled up close against him. Now seemed like as good a time as any to go bathe in the pond below. Gathering some clean clothes and a towel, she crept from the cave as quietly as possible.

Chapter Three

Krytan moaned as he finally awoke from his deep sleep. Undoubtedly, he owed his exceedingly restful slumber to the king's expensive mulled wine. Perhaps he could just surrender for once and sleep in. Smiling, he realized this was an activity he'd not done since he was a child. Even after spending a long night of rambunctious sex with a pretty maid, he was always the first of his men to rise and face the new day.

Shifting on the bed released the scent from their passionate night. With his eyes still closed, Krytan only took a few seconds to remember he had not slept alone the previous night. He had returned to his guest chamber and discovered a very comely wench sleeping next to his young son. A grin curled his lips upwards and he rolled onto his side, opening his eyes. Making love sounded like the perfect way to start today.

"Mornin', Papa! I've been waiting forever for you to wake up."

Krytan saw his son occupied the other side of bed, and the boy watched him intently. Quickly, he adjusted the covers to conceal the instantaneous response his body produced when he'd remembered the pretty bedmate. Obviously, the wench had followed his earlier words about creeping out before daylight. That was good, he reminded himself. It wouldn't be good for his son to see him with one woman in his bed one day and marrying a different one later the same day!

"You're up early, Derek. Were you unable to sleep?" Krytan reached out to push the soft hair from his son's forehead.

"I am looking for my friend, Papa. She was in here with me when I went to sleep."

Krytan smiled at his son's innocent acceptance of things. "Don't worry, son. I'm sure you'll be seeing her quite soon. In fact, there is a good chance you'll see her frequently."

"She didn't believe me at first, but I convinced her we were dragon-slayers." Derek lifted his small wooden sword.

Krytan grimaced as he jerked sideways, avoiding the pointed tip at the last moment. "Remember that talk we had, Derek, about no swords in bed?"

Derek nodded and slid out of bed, dragging the sword. "Does that include knives too, Papa?"

Krytan sat up in bed, smiling at the beguiling boy. How smart of the young lad! He was connecting things and using his deductive reasoning. Of course, he most likely recalled the rather pointed discussion they'd had about the day Krytan had told Derek snakes and worms were not happy inside the house, and especially not in beds. Thomas' cry of alarm sounded over the frogs in his bed, and Derek quickly extrapolated toads also were not meant for beds. Feeling quite proud of his son, Krytan directed him to ring for the maid. Time to get on with the day, he decided. The sooner he had this wedding behind him, the quicker they could return home.

Immediately he imagined how nice having the luscious wench he'd enjoyed last night in his bed once more. This trip was going much better than he had ever anticipated.

* * * * *

"I'm afraid I must have misunderstood, sire. The princess is where?" Krytan had taken three slow, very deep breaths before he asked the question.

"Well, that appears to be the problem." The King stood for what had to be the third or fourth time since they'd begun this conversation.

The hour was dusk, and all day long Krytan had been given excuse after flimsy excuse as to why the princess was delayed. The wedding should have started nearly an hour earlier.

Instead, he was in the king's private chambers while the guests milled about nervously in the castle's main hall and gathering rooms.

Queen Taala was still smiling, even if King Aldous was not. Suddenly, he became aware of Derek's restless movements beside him. The boy had followed him into the room, since he'd been standing on the dais as well, awaiting the arrival of the bride-to-be. Looking down at Derek, who was quite impressive in his formal attire, complete with a real sword, he was quite proud of how well he'd behaved himself during the long day. Since he was being closely watched, Krytan had agreed that having a real weapon should be fine for the short period of the ceremonies.

"Derek, son, go out and find Thomas. We'll be out shortly," Krytan told his son quietly, his hand resting atop his head and lightly ruffled his previously neatly combed hair.

"All right, Papa," the small boy replied, reluctantly starting for the exit.

The door suddenly opened and in walked a tall, imposing figure, dressed entirely in royal purple, red and gold. Behind him came an entourage of men and women. Abruptly, Krytan realized this late arrival was none other than the Earl of Hodynaar.

"I apologize for the lateness of my arrival, Your Majesty. I was fearful we'd missed the ceremony and would only be able to enjoy the festivities. But I hear things have been delayed and I am in time after all to witness the wedding of the lovely Princess Lyra and His Grace."

Hodynaar executed a perfectly respectful bow to his sovereign before he nodded to Krytan. There was no love lost between the two men, who had often faced each other during the wars. But all that was behind them now, Krytan reminded himself. Pretending to tolerate other titled nobles and royalty was something he'd have to get used to, as well. Hopefully, King Aldous would live for at least another twenty or thirty years!

King Aldous nodded in recognition, but it was obvious to Krytan that he had not expected Hodynaar to attend the wedding. The Queen interrupted and Krytan saw the relief on the King's face.

"How good of you to join us, Sir Ranal. It's always a pleasure to welcome you, and your family, into our home."

Hodynaar smiled, but Krytan could see that it was cold and didn't reach his eyes.

"Thank you, madam. My sister would enjoy standing with the princess, on her processional. She was quite saddened when it appeared we were too late."

Even the man's voice sounded chilly when he spoke. Krytan watched as a woman moved forward. She had the same black hair and pale skin as her brother, except she had pale blue eyes. He couldn't recall her name, but she was tall and quite slender. One thing was sure. He didn't misinterpret the looks the woman kept directing in his direction.

Queen Taala nodded. "How delightful! I'm sure Lyra would like that."

"May I go and visit with the princess now, Your Majesty?"

Krytan watched as the Queen glanced quickly towards her husband and then nodded in agreement.

"Yes, Lady Deirdre. Come with me."

* * * * *

Derek had managed to elude Thomas once again, and he was feeling quite proud of himself. He overheard the Queen talk about seeing the princess as the women passed by him. Being small, and usually ignored, it was easy for him to follow the small group. But he was surprised when they didn't go where he expected.

He had been busy today, while people kept running about wildly. His first objective had been to find his new friend. To learn the woman he sought was none other than the princess his papa was to marry had made him very happy. Keeping this information to himself, he had played quietly for most of the day. Now he crept up the stairs leading to the princess' rooms. He was surprised that she wasn't there. Whenever he wanted to hide, his room was the best place.

The beautiful white dress on the bed didn't mean much to him, but the note on the floor did. Quite proud of his ability to read beyond his years, he figured out the words "run" and "away" from the note. That much he understood easily, and had no trouble guessing where he could find his friend. He would pretend they were playing hide and seek.

After he changed his clothes and packed a small knapsack, he walked right out the main doors of the castle. Several women remarked on how "sweet" and "precious" he looked, but otherwise he escaped without incident. As quick as possible, he made his way into the valley not far from the castle.

After he found the pond, it was easy to make his way up the stony path to locate the cave opening. He was surprised to find it empty. He had been so sure he would find his princess waiting for him… his disappointment was equal to his hunger. A few seconds of foraging, and he found some food. That's when he heard the tiny "meow, meow, meow" sounds from the bed. Climbing onto the mattress, Derek grinned when he saw the kittens.

"Wow! Kitties!" he murmured, reaching in to pet the babies and their mama.

Soon the excitement of the day, the long walk and finally the lack of a satisfying conclusion to his trek forced young Derek to succumb to exhaustion, and he fell asleep on the bed. One hand draped into the makeshift nest to rest on the mother cat's back.

* * * * *

Lyra guided Maldovaar easily into a light landing a short distance from the cave's entrance. She slid off the dragon's back.

In less than one second, he was already complaining. "Who taught you to steer?" Maldovaar looked back over his shoulder. "Would you please hurry and remove this saddle? Talk about dated. No one uses that old saddle-style anymore. Get it off now!"

"Shut up, Mal! I'm no happier than you are. I'll take it all down in a moment." She paused to grab her bags.

"And that's another thing, Princess. I don't like carrying so much weight when I fly nowadays." Maldovaar was stretching his neck when all of a sudden he screamed out in pain. "Yeeeeeoooooowwwwwww!"

Lyra glanced up to meet his glare with a forced look of calm. His blowups and tantrums were getting on her nerves. "Yes, Mal, is there a problem?"

"Did you just dare to slap my buttocks?"

Lyra paused, taking in the haughty expression on the dragon's face. "Dear, dear Mal, if I had wanted to slap you... there would be no doubt I had done so. Also, you do not technically, even though I know you long for one, have a booty. Thus, it is a waste of your time to stand around 'shakin' your bootay' all the time."

Maldovaar turned huffily, folding his short arms across his chest.

As she continued to observe him, he lifted his nose even higher into the air. She felt compelled to add out of spite, "The extra weight you are complaining about is coming from your big ol' under-exercised thighs! Now, take this one pack and let's get going. I want to fix something to eat." Grabbing one of the bulging backpacks, she started the final rock climb to the entrance of the cave.

Maldovaar easily flapped his wings and soared out and then up the last yards to settle right in front of the entrance. Turning, he looked down. "I am not the only one who could use a little extra exercise, you know."

Lyra glared upwards, blowing a puff of air to cool her flushed face. "I'll wake you up earlier tomorrow and we can do some calisthenics together."

As she reached the level for the entrance, she found Maldovaar seated, arms crossed, reclining back, resting on his tail and his lower legs crossed at the knee.

He shook his head side to side. "No, Princess. I don't think that would be wise. You know how I hate getting sweaty, especially for no good reason. I think I'll nap while you fix my dinner." Maldovaar rose and walked into the cave, in front of Lyra. "Aaaaiiiiiyyyyyyyyiiiiiiii! What is that? What is that wretched thing on my bed?"

Lyra raced around Maldovaar's large tail and saw the young boy who had obviously been sound asleep begin to awaken. He yawned quite loudly, his eyes not completely opened yet.

"Great gods above, what do you have against me?" she asked quietly. Not once had she considered her curious, and tenacious, new companion might decide to look for her. He knew where she might be. Now she wondered if he'd told anyone he was coming. Undoubtedly, he'd run away, just as she had, and now the castle was in a real uproar. "Damn and double damn!"

Derek was now sitting, rubbing one eye, the other still closed. "My papa says you shouldn't curse… unless you have a really, really good reason."

Lyra took a step closer. "Trust me, I have a good reason. Hello there, Derek. Trespassers often find themselves skewered, or worse, you know."

Derek's eyes were now open, and quite wide open at that. He stared in disbelief at his first-ever dragon. "Wow," he said softly as his mouth opened and stayed that way. "You didn't tell me you owned a dragon, Lyra! This is so amazing. Can I ride it? Does it play? Can it breathe fire?"

Maldovaar rose up to his full height. His head curved down so he could look down his nose as he replied. "No, you may not ride *it*, you insolent little boy!" He spat the last out as if it were a dirty word.

Lyra watched as he haughtily tilted his chin in the air and crossed his little arms over his chest. No matter whatever else one might think upon first viewing his chartreuse coloring and the reddish-orange hair for forelock, bushy, mobile eyebrows and scraggly chin hairs, Maldovaar could be impressive.

Lyra was unsympathetic to his believed plight, though. "I'll have you know, Maldovaar, this is the famous Derek, the bold dragon-slayer!" She stopped as she saw the proud tilt to Derek's blond head. The vulnerable look on his face told her much more than words what was missing in his life. "Why don't you stay here, Derek? Perhaps you could get in some good slaying practice."

"Yeah! Yeah!" Derek clapped and cheered, sitting on his knees.

"Are you insane, Lyra? I won't have this grubby little *boy*," he spat the word out as if it were a disease, "staying here in my cave!"

That's when she heard the strange noise for the first time. A fluttery warbling sound came from the bed. Lyra rushed over and saw a tiny, most unique dragon. The skin, or coat, was greenish-purple in color, and its scales looked to be iridescent as it moved across the bed to begin climbing up Derek's knee.

"Ow… ow… ow!" the little boy said as the small claws sank into his skin, but he didn't push him away. "Hey, what is this?"

Lyra climbed onto the bed beside him. She reached out and gingerly pulled the tiny dragon off Derek, bringing him to her bosom, cradling him gently as she rubbed her fingers over his shiny scales. Turning her head, she smiled at Maldovaar. "We did it, Mal! We've got a baby dragon!"

Derek looked at her and then at the big reptilian creature in wonder. "You mean you and him are this little guy's mom and dad?"

"Great jumping toads, no!" Maldovaar looked aghast, red eyebrows tilted and wiggling, while his mouth dropped open. As his gaze moved from the baby dragon to the boy, he added, "What nonsense, boy! I am not that thing's sire."

"Hush, Mal! You are scaring my baby dragon. Shh, shh," she cooed softly to the dragon who was now lying in her arms, quite happily letting her rub and stroke his, or her, belly. "What a pretty baby you are! I think you must be the prettiest dragon ever. You'll need a name."

Lyra paused. She wanted to give the dragon a name to be proud of and was dignified and noble.

"We could call him Bob," Derek offered quietly, moving closer to her side. Tentatively, he reached out to touch and pet the baby.

"First, we need to find out if this little guy is really a guy or a girl."

"How do we do that, Lyra? Is it like boys and girls?"

Lyra hid her grin, not looking forward to the speech that would entail one day for this inquisitive young man. Luckily, it was not her problem, but his father's. Her smile faded slowly as she recalled her other problems. Running away had not taken into account this young man. The tiny animal's mewling sounds were mingling with the kittens', which were beginning to nurse from their mother.

"Pretty mama cat, will you please take this little fellow and feed him, as well?" Lyra asked the mother cat, petting her softly between her ears. When she heard the deep purring sound, she lowered the dragon to an open teat, in between two kittens. He allowed Lyra to nudge him to drink and then he was gobbling it down.

"Wow! Lyra that was so cool."

"Well, there was a good likelihood she would accept him. By having lived in the nest with the kittens, he picked up their scents as he broke out of the shell. He's got a good chance of growing up thinking he's a cat."

Derek shook his head. "That's not a good thing though, is it?"

"Luckily, he'll have Maldovaar to show him what a true dragon does."

"And me, Lyra! I'll play with him, and the kittens, too."

Lyra lifted her head to find Maldovaar staring.

"What if the little critter can't drink the milk?" Maldovaar asked quickly.

"Then I'll go to my backup plan of you and me flying down to steal a milk-producing goat."

"Stealing is wrong," Derek told her seriously.

"I'd make sure payment was left, of some kind. Don't worry." While Derek turned his attention to the kittens that had finished their snack, Lyra contemplated that the old dragon was thinking about the boy and who would come looking for him. His father might be willing to let a possible wife disappear, but no doubt he'd draw the line at having his son and heir do the same. With a heavy heart, she prepared some food for them all.

* * * * *

Krytan was losing what little patience he'd been holding onto when Thomas came to him and reported Derek was also missing. After he swallowed the bile that rose from the gut-wrenching fear, he considered announcing he was leaving to find his son and he would return for his bride later. But this was the King, and he also knew Hodynaar's presence here was unexpected and suspicious. He didn't want to let his imagination run away, or listen to the conspiracy theorists busily spreading rumors, throughout the castle either.

Entering the King's chambers, he bowed to the older man. "I've had bad news, sire. My son is missing."

Queen Taala gasped and moved forward into the light. "The poor little dear! We must begin searching the castle at once."

Krytan had not realized that she was here as well. "Thank you, Your Majesty, but I've already employed my officers and a number of your staff for the last two hours. I didn't want to cause an alarm and upset the merrymakers."

Queen Taala nodded. "That is most kind of you, sir. Has he ever done anything like this before?"

Krytan fought the urge to stiffen and react negatively. "He is like most boys, pushing and testing his boundaries and exploring all the time. He's been out and about your grounds since we arrived, although I'm not completely sure where all he has gone."

The King shifted his feet, restless to get started. "The land offers many places interesting to a young chap with lots of time and imagination."

"I have no leads except that last night, one of your maid servants read him to sleep. I've not yet been able to locate her." He didn't accuse her of anything, but still his unspoken words were enough to be understood.

"I assure you, sir, all of my staff is trustworthy. Now, what did this girl look like? I'll call my house mistress and she'll be able to identify her."

"Ah, yes, of course, ma'am. Well, she's a robust girl, you know. Not a stick figure! And she had dark auburn or reddish hair. Does that sound like anyone in your household?"

Taala didn't need to ring for her head housekeeper after all. Slowly, she turned her head and looked at her husband. "Oh, my," she whispered. "Did you search her room in the turret?"

The King shook his head side to side. "No, of course not. We had her things moved from the guest wing to the main hall in preparation for the wedding. Could she have slipped back?"

"I've been so busy, that I've just been grateful she wasn't underfoot complaining." Taala twisted her hands, wringing them over and over. "I'll go and look myself."

"Wait, Taala!" King Aldous spoke quickly. "Perhaps it would cause less trouble if we sent one of the servants."

"Why don't I go?" Krytan offered. "I'm the restless bridegroom. I'm sure my movements won't attract undue attention, if that is what is worrying you."

Already her stomach was in knots. Taala nodded, eager to pass on this chore to someone else. She loved her only daughter, but at some point, they seemed to have lost the ability to communicate like when she was a small child. As long as Taala's mother, Lyra's grandmother, was still alive, Lyra had been a very happy child. Of course, that only made sense since the old woman devoted all of her time to the girl.

Taala had only caught her mother once teaching the old ways to her precious little three-year-old. Knowing how her husband felt about magick, she had requested Lyra's grandmother to stop. She had assumed her mother had done that.

Shortly after that, the two began spending even more together, and Lyra became more distant with her own mother. As Queen, Taala had been quite busy, so the arrangement had fit into both her and her husband's hectic schedules. Only after her mother's death a few years ago had she realized just how much time the two had spent together. Quickly, Lyra's penchant for finding trouble returned. Unfortunately, the war had broken out, and no one had the necessary free time to closely monitor the young sixteen-year-old budding woman-child.

Lyra had settled down the last few months, but her father had still been bent upon marrying her off to solidify the tenuous peace. Taala admitted she should have been more involved with Lyra the past month, helping her make the adjustment from unmarried princess to married woman. But the few times she'd approached her daughter, Lyra had always had some other pressing matter to attend to.

Now Lyra was missing, as was the duke's son, and she had no idea what might even be going on in her daughter's mind. Learning Lyra and the duke had met last evening showed that much more might have transpired than just her daughter disappearing for a few hours in protest of this marriage day.

"Duke Krytan, please, rest here and I'll send someone to check." Aldous turned to ring for a servant.

Krytan strove to keep his tone even as he replied. "Sire, my son is missing. The only link I know of is this serving wench. I wish to speak with her as soon as possible, please."

Taala moved forward.

He noted again the nervous movements of her hands, in fact, her whole body. He couldn't help but wonder why she seemed even more nervous, after he brought up the servant girl. Surely, she hadn't kidnapped his son. Had she done it out of anger? He'd promised to bring her with him. What else could she want?

The far door opened, and an old woman walked in.

Taala greeted her. "Hello, Marsa. This is our chief housekeeper," she paused, explaining to Krytan. "I don't believe that in our earlier efforts of cleaning and inspecting the rooms we remembered to inspect the turret room."

Marsa looked from the Queen, to the King, and then back. "You mean the pri—"

Taala immediately interrupted her. "The prison chamber, Marsa. Yes, the old prison chamber. Perhaps you would go personally to make sure it is undisturbed."

Slowly, the housekeeper nodded.

Krytan decided the woman was sure her sovereigns were crazy, if the look in her eyes was a good barometer. "I'll return to the main hall and visit with the guests. You'll find me when you have some information?"

As soon as Aldous nodded, Krytan left the King's chambers. He didn't go into the hall, but instead waited until the housekeeper left their Majesty's rooms and started on her quest. He hung back several yards, walking carefully to keep his footfalls silent as possible for a man his size. Somehow, he wasn't all that surprised when they ended up in the same wing and level as his own room.

At the bottom of the winding stairs, he waited until the woman was all the way up before he followed. He didn't want to shock her, nor did he want to allow her a chance to brain him with something in a small, confined space. The room was a shock when he saw how nicely decorated it was. The glimpse he'd gotten while retrieving Derek had revealed little of the surroundings. With a nearly naked woman to stare at, he'd found the rest of the room to hold little interest. Taking into account the finery, and if this was where the servant girl lived, perhaps she was more than just a peasant in servitude to the King?

Glancing about, he didn't realize the old woman had crouched down to pick up something. As she stood again, he saw that she held something in her hands.

"Good God!" Krytan called out when he realized the housekeeper was holding long ropes of the lovely hair he'd caressed last night in his bed. Damn it all! The wench had cut off her beautiful hair.

Marsa screamed. "AAArrrrrrgggghhhhhhhh!"

In less than a few seconds, two of his guards bounded into the room, swords drawn. If anything, the poor woman screamed even louder and then fainted. She fell to the floor in a heap.

"One of you put her on the bed and the other go fetch the Queen."

He reached over and took the strands of silky hair that he remembered quite easily from the old woman's limp hand. Rubbing the shiny, soft strands between his fingertips, he acknowledged it felt just as wonderful as it had last night in his bed. The thought of someone cutting it off angered him deeply.

"Ooooooooohhhhh."

The moan from the bed caught his attention and he turned to look at the old woman. Holding the strands of hair in front of her face, he spoke quickly. "Tell me quickly, old woman! What is the name of the woman...?" He stopped and shook the limp hair instead of finishing the question.

Marsa didn't hide her fear. "The P-p-princess Lyra, sir."

Krytan was surprised by her answer, though. Suddenly, quite a few things made sense. First and foremost was why the wedding kept being delayed today. His bride had absconded... and, unbeknownst to her parents, he was most likely the cause. Still, even though she had not revealed her identity while they were in bed together, he was fairly sure she could not have been alarmed. Their marriage was a "done deal" and all that remained had been the actual ceremony. In his opinion, the fact she surrendered her maidenhead sooner than planned was not a problem.

That meant the trouble existed inside Lyra and something she believed to be true, or had no faith in. He didn't like that she might not trust him. In all of his adult life, not once had he betrayed his word, once given. He paused as he realized that she had no way of knowing his history of honesty.

So, why she had run from him didn't make sense... to him anyway.

Compounding this was the fact his small son was missing. Somehow, he had eluded Thomas and the fact they were in strange territory made him uneasier about the boy disappearing. He knew the child's hiding places back home.

Realizing that the princess was the woman in his bed was mind-boggling. He now had a sexy bedmate and wife in the same person. Few noblemen got that lucky.

Frowning, the connection between both of them disappearing was odd, to say the least. He doubted the beautiful woman knew where his son was, but he wondered if his son had not followed her into hiding. Perhaps the capricious woman had had a favorite spot to run to when she was a child as well.

A noise at the doorway caused him to turn. He saw the King's gaze immediately drop to the hair he still held in his fist.

"Oh my goodness!" The Queen couldn't contain her cry of concern.

Marsa recovered upon appearance of the Queen. "Oh, Your Majesty! I fear the princess has been kidnapped. I'm sure someone cut her hair to disguise her."

Krytan saw the tears on Taala's cheeks for the first time. It appeared that his bride-to-be had disappeared in the past, but to have gone this far to conceal her appearance, seemed to show her parents this time was different.

"Does the princess have a favorite place to go?"

King Aldous nodded even as he put his arm around his wife's trembling shoulders. "Quite a few, I'm afraid. I sent my soldiers to check a few of the nearest ones, but so far… nothing."

Krytan dropped the hair onto the bed. He'd never been a man to waste time worrying about the past or what couldn't be changed or corrected. "Where could she go, that a small boy might have found… say within a few hours' walk."

"I'm not sure, sir. As you know, I have some very extensive lands."

"Of course, but word of the wedding would have spread. Most likely, she'd have to go somewhere she wouldn't be recognized, or she wouldn't be seen," Krytan added, hoping to jar something in the king's memory.

"Well, there is one place," Queen Taala started to explain, but then stopped. "But she knows I don't want her going there."

"Where is that, Your Majesty?" Krytan prompted quickly.

Taala shook her head. "I know our daughter is headstrong at times, but I don't think she would go against my wishes."

Even as Aldous patted his wife's shoulder, Krytan could see in his eyes the older man wasn't as sure as his wife.

"Excuse me, ma'am," Marsa spoke softly, edging off the bed. "A few weeks ago, one of the maids told me she'd cleaned black sand off the princess' shoes."

"Black sand?" Krytan repeated, looking at the king.

"Yes… uh, well… that is reachable. There is a pathway… but it is rather dangerous."

"Just tell me where the hell it is and I will go immediately."

"It's getting late, Lord Krytan, with not much light left to travel by. The path is craggy at best. Perhaps you should wait until daylight," King Aldous offered quickly.

"I agree, my lord, and I could have the kitchen prepare some foodstuffs for the searchers in the morning… " The Queen added her suggestion as well.

"No. I'll leave immediately. Marsa, have the kitchen prepare two packs for me to carry on my back. I'll go alone."

Chapter Four

The cave was finally quiet. Lyra sighed loudly, and then glanced around quickly in case she'd been too vocal and awakened someone, or anything. But alas, no, and she took a deep breath, very quietly, in relief.

On the bed, almost in stark denial of what had happened earlier was Maldovaar, lying on his side. Nestled close against the dragon's belly was Derek, sound asleep since his body hit the mattress after the dinner she'd fixed. No doubt, he'd had quite a day. Derek's arm was draped forward, across a well-padded box, which was now serving as the home for four kittens, their mama and one baby dragon. Other than Mama Cat licking one paw, her charges were well fed and asleep.

The only thing Lyra wanted was to lie down and sleep, as well. But Derek's arrival meant she must now change her plans. She'd have to return him to the castle, and get away again, before she was seen or detained. There was also the problem of convincing the boy to stay silent about what he'd seen, and especially where he'd been.

Lyra paused to light a torch and carry it to the front of the cave. Several rocks, almost perfectly aligned, made for a comfortable seating area, which also afforded a clear view of the water below. The setting sun was gone now, and soon the sky would be as black as the ocean just beyond the rocky promontory and forest protecting her secret world.

Sitting here now, Lyra acknowledged running away had been wrong. She'd betrayed her parents, who loved her, even if they didn't understand her. Possibly, even worse, she'd caused a rift between her father and this duke. It wasn't likely the duke would consider a war over such a trifling thing as being deserted by his bride-to-be—

"Few men consider it trifling, madam."

Lyra jumped in surprise at the deep voice interrupting her. She was shocked he'd heard her, only now realizing she must have spoken her thoughts out loud. She slid off the rock, landing on the hard gravelly ground below. "You!"

Krytan nodded once towards his errant bride-to-be. Once she'd appeared with the torch a few minutes earlier, he'd located her easily. He quickly extinguished his own light and climbed silently towards her perch. Pausing a few feet away, he'd listened to her speaking her thoughts while he took in her altered appearance. Her face appeared slimmer with her shorter haircut, and the way the edges curled up, reminded him of a wet puppy, partly dry.

Of course, as his errant bride-to-be looked at him, she didn't have a puppy's usual happy manner. But there was no mistaking her look of… hmm. Yes, she definitely had the look of someone who had done something that wasn't right, was fearful of getting caught, and yet determined to argue her way out of it. In a way, she reminded him of Derek, except in all the important ways, which easily helped his body recall their lusty lovemaking last night.

"Now, back to my trifling emotions," Krytan spoke in a demanding way, staring down at Lyra.

She scrambled for a moment on the gravel, refusing the hand he held out.

He waited until she finished brushing off her clothes and looked up. There was a black smudge across one cheek, and he barely restrained himself from reaching out to brush it away.

"I didn't mean to insult you, sir," Lyra replied quickly. "I did not realize that I was not alone. A gentleman usually announces himself."

"I was carrying a torch, and I did not creep up on you, as you seem inclined to imply."

"Sorry, but I was thinking and I guess I didn't hear you."

"Perhaps you were daydreaming about your upcoming wedding?" Krytan offered quietly.

Lyra stiffened.

He could see the red flush that spread quickly over her cheeks. He wasn't surprised when she shook her head.

"I was trying to decide how to return your son without being seen."

Krytan nodded, shifting his stance so his back was towards the valley, and he could clearly see Lyra, as she stood in front of the cave opening. "Yes, I assumed he had followed you here. I didn't realize until today who you really are."

Lyra placed her fisted hands on her waist. "As I recall, you had ample time to discover the truth, considering—" her voice trailed away.

"Yes, Princess Lyra, but you and I were in the same bed, as well. Yet, you never bothered to correct my false impression as to your identity either," Krytan accused her, just as loudly as she had him moments earlier.

"I didn't have time!"

Krytan smiled, narrowing his eyes as he looked at the fiery redhead in front of him. "Not enough time, madam? All night wasn't long enough? Allow me to continue your time frame."

"Shush! Are you crazy? You will wake your son, or worse."

"I guess you are right, but that doesn't mean I can't still have my wedding night, as originally planned. I'll just have to make sure you don't scream out like you did last night a few times. There are no thick walls to hide those cries of passionate release like we had in the dark in my bed. I assume… " he gestured broadly with a sweeping gesture of his arm. "You have some sort of bed up here."

His smile only aggravated her more as she stomped her foot, folding her arms across her waist.

"How dare you assume that I'll allow you to make love to me again?"

"Allow is no longer part of the issue because you are now my wife. I had your father perform an absentia ceremony. That way, he and the guests could proceed with their celebration. Also, this would save your parents the embarrassment which you obviously had no compunction about foisting upon them."

Her recoil was as if he'd struck her physically. He had not thought she cared, but apparently she did. Krytan was relieved in a way to know she'd not undertaken this foolhardy adventure without considering her parents. Still, she had gone ahead—

"You can't make love to me because Derek is asleep on the bed with Maldovaar."

"Good God! Are you insane, woman! You are letting my son sleep with a strange man?" Krytan took a step towards the entrance of the cave.

Lyra reacted instantly, putting out her hands to stop him. "No! Wait! Oh, and shh! I had an awful time getting everyone to finally settle down to sleep."

Krytan stepped back, propping one foot on a nearby rock. Consciously, he took a deep breath, relaxing his hands to lie at his sides again. "Just tell me who the hell is sleeping in that cave, madam. And I suggest you do so quickly."

"Tell this cretin the truth, darling, so you'll both shut up! I'm trying to get my beauty sleep in here!"

The stranger grabbed for his sword, but just as quickly Lyra rushed forward to stop him. Her hands grasped his forearms and her momentum was just enough to knock them both off balance. Less than a few seconds later, both the humans went tumbling back over the ledge, rolling down the grassy incline until they reached the next level shelf, about thirty feet below. Gingerly, Maldovaar picked up the unlit torch the man had carried, and then moved forward until he could lean over the side. With a soft puff of air, the used torch flamed to life again. As his eyes adjusted to the night, he could see them moving down below.

"What's up, Maldovaar? Are you going to burn somebody? Can I watch?" A young, chipper voice asked with obvious glee.

Maldovaar turned to look down at the boy who had been snuggled so trustingly up against him just moments earlier. The little tyke had gotten under his skin, even though he had done his best to keep him at wing's length. But the boy was tenacious, and they had ended the evening with a rousing "ride the dragon" game about the cave before he finally settled down to sleep. What was surprising was he was worn-out, as well, and had ended up sleeping in the scanty space left on the big bed. He'd been expecting Lyra to kick him out when she was ready to sleep and instead shouting voices just beyond the cave's entrance had awakened him.

Normally, he would have raced to defend the princess. But he thought she'd been behaving a tad bit recklessly of late, and perhaps a little dressing-down might do her some good. He'd hung about inside, listening to the tirade, until he finally decided the princess' bridegroom deserved a little "comeuppance". That was when he made his presence known.

Maldovaar lifted the torch to better light the fallen combatants. At this point, the knight was lying on his side, next to the princess. But as he moved the light, they both looked upwards.

Beside him, Derek waved his little hand side to side and a smile curved up his mobile lips. "Hi, Papa! Look what I found!"

Maldovaar looked down and saw Derek was now pointing at him. Shifting slightly, he glanced back down. No doubt, the princess was going to be ticked at being sent on a headlong tumble down the mountain at this time of night. Maldovaar enjoyed a good jest... lifting his hand, he imitated the small boy's wave for a few seconds. He was tempted to comment about stray animals and children. Against his better judgment, he added with a dragon-like smirk, "Your baby is hungry, Princess, by the way."

Maldovaar straightened as he heard the man's voice booming out from below.

"Baby? Baby!"

Maldovaar patted the boy's head, who then tilted back to look up at him. "Perhaps we should go back inside, Derek, and leave the princess alone. I don't think she's going to be in a very good mood."

"All right." Derek nodded. "Could you blow me just one flame?"

Maldovaar grinned widely. "Aawwww, why not?" Turning, he roared his flame outwards, knowing full well it would arc high over the edge, presenting an impressive and, to the unsuspecting, frightening experience. When he heard "what the friggin' hell is that", Maldovaar knew he had succeeded.

Lyra pushed against Krytan, struggling to her knees. "What the friggin' hell did you think it was? It's a dragon's flame!"

She stopped abruptly as she realized Krytan was already climbing back up the grassy incline, leaving her behind. So much for being a thoughtful and considerate husband, she thought silently for a moment. She realized how strong and muscular his thighs were, and what an amazingly taut—

"Hurry up, woman! We don't have all night!"

Lyra shook her head and saw Krytan had stopped and was now extending his hand back for her. Accepting the help, he pulled her up easily. Lyra started to scramble up and felt Krytan's hand on her bottom, pushing her along. She wished she could say it felt like a lover's touch, but it seemed perfunctory at best. Her reaction to his caress didn't make any sense, that much she knew, but knowing she was married, and to *him*, well—

Maybe the fact that she'd thought about him constantly since she'd left his bed allowed her the freedom to accept the feelings she'd wanted to deny. She'd fought the passion she experienced at his touch, but suddenly, the war she had waged was over. Nothing made sense, but then, since she'd experienced his caresses and possession, nothing had.

Ever since leaving her father's castle, she found herself daydreaming and feeling the strangest yearning in her loins... that she didn't understand. She felt on edge and very uncomfortable and quite unsure of what to do next, which only made her crazier!

As she was within the final step, Krytan's hand came down and literally dragged her up the rest of the way. She dropped to her knees, though, since he immediately released her to enter the cave. Quickly, she got up, ignoring the pain in her legs, and followed him. At the fire she'd tamped down earlier, Maldovaar was flaming it nicely with fresh logs and some short flames from himself.

Derek stood a short distance away, watching and holding two small logs in his arms. The serious look on his face told her Maldovaar had assigned him a "very important task". Glancing at Krytan, she saw he appeared to be quite absorbed in watching his son. Without saying anything, she moved over to the bed. Her smile burst forth as she watched the kittens nursing eagerly from their mother. Her baby dragon, though, was the one who was closest to the maternal cat, and he was receiving full benefit of the cat's loving care. Chuckling, she did marvel at what the poor mother must be thinking of her hairless baby.

"What the hell is that?"

Lyra jumped at Krytan's voice, surprised she'd not noticed his approach. Turning, she looked at her "husband". He looked a little more relaxed and less likely to begin slaying anyone. She reached down and lightly scratched the mother cat's head, just between her ears. The mama purred sweetly.

"I believe you made that same sound a couple of times last night, my sweet wife. Of course, I was touching your—"

"Shh!" Lyra glanced over her shoulder and breathed a sigh of relief when she saw Derek was still across the room. "You shouldn't talk like that around your son."

Krytan shrugged nonchalantly, but she remembered how concerned he'd been just minutes earlier. She had no doubt he was a good father, or at least a protective one. She'd seen proof the boy needed more time with his papa. More playtime, anyway. She wondered if that's why he really chose to marry now. Did he intend for her to be playmate and mother to his son? Where was the boy's real mother?

She glanced up and found her gaze snagged and held fast by Krytan's night-dark eyes. Fire and heat seared through her, the longer she didn't turn away. It was only when his hand lifted to cup the lower side of her face, curving gently along her jaw that she finally drew in a deep breath. But that stopped when his thumb lightly caressed her lower lip.

"Tomorrow we shall return to your father's, but just long enough to gather supplies to return home." Krytan lowered his hand from her face.

Lyra felt cold, feeling the chill from his tone and words, rather than the look in his eyes. "I can't leave now, but feel free to take Derek with you when you leave in the morning. The danger is too great."

Krytan had started to move away but he stopped abruptly upon hearing her words.

Lyra shivered as she watched his back stiffen and he slowly turned to look at her. She met his gaze.

His left eyebrow lifted as he spoke. "Madam, the three of us will be leaving in the morning."

"I'll come as soon as I can, but it's too soon... tomorrow is anyway. Maybe a couple of months when the baby is older, and then I should be able to travel."

"I'm thirsty, Lyra."

Derek's pleading voice interrupted her explanation.

Krytan gestured with a sweeping motion of his hand, as if he was giving her his permission to see to his son's needs, and that only irritated her further. She bit her tongue as she stood and walked to the fire. There was no way she'd be childish and take her fury out on an innocent child. But her narrowed gaze should have warned her husband to be wary.

* * * * *

Krytan leaned back on the makeshift bed. Not quite the way he had planned on spending his first night as a husband, to say the least. Lyra had insisted on two more beds being made before anyone could retire.

He'd been watching Lyra as she managed to maneuver one recalcitrant eight-year-old boy back to bed. Surprisingly, he enjoyed the time taken to corral the kittens and what he had since learned was a real, live baby dragon, back into their bed. Mama cat had decided to eat, so Lyra had her hands more than full trying to keep mewling kittens, one smoke-puffing baby dragon and one hand-clapping boy under her control.

Perhaps control wasn't the word he should use, he decided with a smile as Lyra ran one hand distractedly through her hair. Now, her hair looked as frazzled as she most probably felt. He could offer to help, but he'd gotten cozy… not to mention the fact he'd been forced to go rushing across the land in search of his runaway bride and his son. Admitting that he'd not taken into consideration the changes Lyra would be forced to make with this marriage felt uncomfortable. All he had seen was how it would affect him, and his son.

Granted, most husbands would not consider such things. He considered he was normal, not abnormal in his lack of concern. If he thought about his future bride and how she would adapt to her new life… he just assumed she would become his wife, and like other women, she'd be happy to be a wife and mother. He could now see that as far as being put in the position of defusing outlandish plans his son might create, Lyra probably wasn't an ideal choice.

Especially if past behavior were the true indicator of the future, he'd have to say Lyra could lead the pack as far as *over-the-top, no-way* and even *you've-got-to be-kidding* plans went. Hell, she was living in a cave. She'd disobeyed not only her father, but also her sovereign. Living with a dragon was something knights used to do. So it wasn't completely odd, putting aside the fact he'd thought any remaining dragons had all gone to distant lands. What she was doing, aside from everything else, was breaking the law.

The law was centuries old, but it had been decreed unlawful to keep a dragon as a pet. Sure, it dated back to a time when dragons had a much larger role in the world of humans. Over time, as their numbers decreased, dragons moved to more isolated areas, and it became a moot point. But he'd never heard of a woman having any relationship whatsoever with a dragon. Only men had ridden dragons into battle.

Slowly, Krytan turned his head and looked over to where Maldovaar was lying sprawled on his side, and his head rested on a pillow bearing one of Lyra's embroidered cases. His infrequent snore was just one more nuisance piled onto an amazingly aggravating and annoying day. He smiled as he recalled something the obnoxiously green dragon had done as he was settling down to sleep on the far side of the fire.

Lying on his side, with his head propped on his short arm, Maldovaar tossed his head, which had of course sent his red mane flying. The dragon had then blinked his eyes, while wiggling his long, expressive eyebrows at Krytan a few times before he'd asked him a question. "So, you come here often, big boy?"

Before he could formulate a reply, suitable or not, Lyra yelled at her dragon friend. "Stop it right now, Maldovaar! You aren't making matters any better."

Lyra shook her finger at Maldovaar. But the big dragon had not appeared convinced until the princess put her hands on hips and stomped her foot. "Let me remind you, Lord Flames-a-Lot, that if I go, so does all your nice food."

"All right, all right, Princess." Maldovaar lifted one hand to his mouth, imitated closing a key and then tossed it away. The dragon had then settled down to sleep, but not before he winked one long-lashed eyelid in Krytan's direction.

Krytan would swear the damned dragon then went to sleep, grinning.

As he looked back towards the bed once again, he saw finally Lyra had everyone settled down to sleep.

She straightened, still standing beside the bed, pressing her hands against the small of her back.

He couldn't resist offering his help. "I'd be happy to massage your back."

Lyra glanced over her shoulder. There was no confusing the rush of emotion shooting through her body at Krytan's low, husky voice. She wanted to feel again what she'd felt when he touched her. The thought of his big, warm hands on her back… and even lower, made her knees go limp. Her legs buckled and she sat abruptly on the side of the bed.

Krytan was already standing and crossing the cave towards her. The fire highlighted his craggy face, and Lyra felt her stomach turn over. Her body wanted him to repeat his tender caresses.

Was it possible that her mind was giving up the fight as well? Surely, she wasn't that wimpy, she asked herself silently. How could she give in to her weak, womanly desires?

Her eyes lowered to Krytan's bare chest. When he'd casually removed his outer garments, she'd had a hard time keeping her eyes from staring the whole time. At one point, one of her hands actually lifted, curved just enough to caress the muscular, tanned body. Now she groaned. The attraction to him was even harder to resist when he was close.

He stopped just a foot away, his husky voice sent shivers up and down her spine. "If you lie down on your stomach, I can rub your back. It will get the kinks out so you can sleep."

Lyra tried to hold his gaze, but she looked down nervously. Unfortunately, that had her looking right at his bulging manhood. She doubted he would try anything here, in the cave… not with Derek here.

"All right," she replied, twisting around to lie down. She wasn't at all sure what would happen next, but her body was tensed, awaiting his touch.

"Scoot towards the middle more. There's plenty of room."

Lyra obeyed, grateful for the comfortable bed again. A second later, the leaf-filled bed shifted and Krytan kneeled astride her thighs. Before she had time to fully adjust to this, he was pushing her shirt up to her shoulders. Quickly, she pulled her bent arms into her sides to conceal her mounded breasts. This allowed him no resistance at all when he jerked down the loose-fitting trousers low on her hips. She gasped as she realized that she was now half-naked. Less than a moment later, his hands curved to her waist, his thumbs pressing inwards.

"O-o-o-oooh!" Lyra sighed softly followed by an animal-like sound that came from deep inside her before she even knew it was going to be audible beyond her subconscious.

Krytan obviously heard it because his touch changed slightly. He massaged her upper back, slowly but surely working his way down past the flare of her bosom, her waist and then onto her hips. It wasn't much longer before she felt him easing down her pants another inch or so, and then he cupped her ass cheeks in his big, and very strong, hands. For a few seconds, he was only lightly caressing and stroking her butt.

She was surprised when she felt his warm breath across her back and realized Krytan had leaned down, towards her ear.

"I can use some very deep massage, if you'd like."

Lyra had trouble speaking around the dryness in her throat. "I-I… uhm, guess it's all right."

She no sooner finished speaking when Krytan's big, strong hands began squeezing her ass cheeks. What she didn't expect was for him to start talking, very softly.

"You have the softest skin, Lyra. It is warm and silky smooth under my rough fingers. Your ass is soft and round like a succulent peach. Last night, I wanted to take a bite."

"Oh my—"

"Of course, it is your nipples that truly excite me. It was very sexy last night, sucking on those pretty boobs."

Lyra didn't want to, or that's what she told herself, but she still groaned and felt her pussy flood with wetness. This could easily become addictive. She moved her hips against his hands… wanting more even as she knew they couldn't.

Abruptly, Krytan withdrew his hands, pulling her clothes back into place. "Lie on your side and face Derek," he told her quickly.

Lyra scooted to the center and then she felt Krytan easing down to lie behind her. His hand snaked forward across her waist. It was only when she felt his hard manhood pressed intimately against her that she understood the brusqueness in his voice and the sudden change in his actions. She couldn't stop the small smile that curved her lips in knowing he was even more aroused now, after touching her. A moment later, she wiggled her butt against his hardness, fully aware of what she did. His immediate response didn't surprise her.

His hand moved quickly to cup her upper breast, even as she felt his breath brush across her ear and cheek as he leaned close to speak. "Be fair warned, madam, that as soon as time and circumstances allow, I will show you precisely how such behavior is rewarded."

At his words, Lyra felt a warm, promising glow deep inside. She wasn't scared, which did strike her as a little strange. But for right now, she would just accept it. Exhaustion caught up with her a short time later, and she fell into a deep sleep.

Krytan groaned softly as he became aware Lyra had indeed fallen asleep. Of course, he knew it was for the best. No matter how much he might desire to make love to his wife of one day, he would never do so under these conditions. Lifting his head just a little bit, he could see his son sleeping quite soundly on the bed a few feet away, with his little arm draped forward over the basket of cat, kittens and dragonet.

The closeness and attraction his son had for Lyra was unexpected, and something he had not even taken into consideration prior to his decision to marry. Derek needed a mother — someone to care for him, and his wife would have that responsibility. That was what he had rationalized. But the fact the two might not like one another had not figured into his plans.

Like a bolt of lightning, he realized Lyra and Derek could easily dislike one another. People had such instant reactions all the time. Yet, he had assumed they would be mother and child simply because he demanded their compliance. He had been foolish to assume such things. Now he recognized how lucky he was that Derek bonded and formed such a strong feeling for Lyra.

Adding in the tender look on Lyra's face as she tucked in Derek, pausing to lightly caress his cheek with her fingertips, and lastly pressing a kiss to his forehead, he knew how lucky he truly was.

The gut-wrenching feeling he experienced as he witnessed Lyra's actions chagrined him at his shortsightedness. A cruel, or uncaring, woman could seriously hurt little Derek, and he was smart enough to admit he was an incredibly lucky man seeing how well the two were getting along so far.

Finally, he took a deep breath and let himself relax completely. Closing his eyes, he let himself listen to the sounds around him. Nearby was the barely audible sound of Lyra, which was more notable by the soft movement of her body. Derek's breathing was slightly more audible, but not by much. He hated the thought, but it appeared he would be going to sleep to the sound of Maldovaar's loud, but amazingly rhythmic, almost melodic and hypnotic snoring.

His last thought was how unbelievable this night had turned out to be, and how hard he'd be laughing if this were happening to one of his men!

Chapter Five

King Aldous looked up from his noon meal as he heard the commotion that had been in the distance, but was rapidly closing the gap. Surprise filled him when he saw Duke Krytan striding towards him, carrying his son in one arm. Leaning sideways, the King tried to see his daughter behind the man, but there was no sign of her. His heart sank because he had been hopeful Krytan would find his daughter with the boy. Beside him he heard the queen's chair being pushed away from the table.

Taala walked quickly towards their new son-in-law. "Welcome back, Krytan. I am so glad your son is safe."

Krytan nodded his head once. "Yes, Derek is fine, just not happy."

"I could have stayed, Papa. Lyra said I could."

Hearing his daughter's name, Aldous jumped from his chair. "You found Lyra? Where is she?"

Before Krytan could reply, Derek spoke. "It's a secret. We promised." As his father set him down, Taala gestured for him to take her seat at the table. Derek twisted his head to smile up at her, hearing her order a fresh plate of food. "We pricked our fingers, spit and shook on it."

"Oh, my... well, that sounds pretty serious," Taala replied, but looked at Krytan with raised eyebrows. "My daughter is safe?"

"Yes, madam, she is quite well. Our plans have changed slightly. Derek and I are going to clean up," Krytan paused to look at his son. "No more arguments," he added quickly. "Then, with your permission, sir, I would like to stock several large sacks of food, and we shall return to where Lyra is. We'll return in a few weeks, and then after you've had time to visit and reassure yourselves she is fine, I'll take her home."

Aldous looked from the placid, almost happy face of the child to the glaring and patently disgruntled face of the father. He had no doubt things had not gone as the duke had planned. It wasn't easy to hold back the smile that wanted to break free, but it was somewhat reassuring and affirming to see that his big, strong and quite proud son-in-law was having as much trouble managing Lyra as her father!

* * * * *

Lyra could hear the shouts as she added wood to the fire.

"Lyra! Lyra!"

There was a brief pause, undoubtedly his father was telling him not to shout and watch his step.

"Lyra! We're back! Maldy!"

Lyra straightened and walked to the entrance of the cave. She moved to the edge of the outcropping and saw Derek about ten yards ahead of his father. The boy used a broken branch as his walking stick. His pockets were bulging, as was the knapsack he had on his back. She couldn't help but wonder what he had brought back. Unable to stop herself, the next time Derek looked up, she waved her arm widely over her head, making sure he saw her.

Immediately, he stopped and waved, jumping up and down. "We're back! We're back! Where's Maldy? I brought him treats."

Even from the distance of hundred yards or so, she saw his mouth drooping. It had been obvious to her Derek had formed a very strong attachment for the standoffish dragon. What surprised her was the apparent acceptance and eventual liking Maldovaar had taken to the little boy. He was notorious for not liking children, or even dragonets. Undoubtedly, his self-absorption and his understanding of his own self-importance had limited his past relationships. But Derek had pretty easily gotten under the big dragon's skin.

In fact, within an hour of Krytan and Derek's departure yesterday, Maldovaar had been moping about. He griped about the kittens mewling for their mama, and he moaned and groaned the whole time she made him fly around gathering firewood while she watched their newborns. Nearly every time he came into the cave, he recounted another story involving "that boy" and something he'd done. At first, the stories were complaints, but quickly they had changed to "had she seen the pipsqueak do this" and "the little monster said that".

Without her correcting him, Maldovaar was soon calling him Derek and not "monster" anymore. Then she had noticed Maldovaar was talking about what he would show Derek once he returned. While Maldovaar chatted almost nonstop, she stitched together a makeshift pouch to enable her to carry the dragonet around, close to her body for safekeeping. The she-dragon, which they had determined this morning, was becoming more active and was going to require a closer watch than the kittens. This way, Lyra would be able to feel more secure about her "baby".

Derek yelled something else and that was when she noticed her husband. She shivered as she thought of him that way, seeing Krytan had stopped and looking towards her. With the sunlight shining down on him, he did look mighty fine indeed today, she acknowledged with a small smile of something she finally noted was pride. Not as nice as he had yesterday morning, at the pond...

* * * * *

Krytan watched the shadowed form of his wife in the distance. When she waved at Derek, he could see the way her breasts bounced freely beneath her loose-fitting clothes. He could easily recall how wonderful those soft mounds had felt against his skin, both wet, yesterday as they enjoyed a swim, and more, right before he and Derek had departed.

He grinned as he recalled how he had arranged the whole thing in the first place.

… Shortly after dawn the previous morning, he and Derek had gone down to the pond at the base of the cliff that housed their cave to bathe before breakfast and their departure for the castle. All the way down to the water, Derek had taken great pains to point out to his father the fallacy, his word not his son's, of bathing before taking the trip.

"It's a waste of water, Papa," Derek added, pausing to look over his shoulder once more. "Why spend all that time washing off the dirt when we are only going to get dirty right away? It's dumb, isn't it, Maldovaar?" Derek called up to the dragon flying just a short distance above them.

Maldovaar had grudgingly agreed to accompany them, but only after Lyra added her words of encouragement to Krytan's, along with the end of her makeshift broom.

"Being up at this time of the day boggles an intelligent dragon's mind! I have much better things to be doing than coming down here to splash about in the water."

"I should imagine getting fed ranks near the top," Krytan had muttered under his breath, and then been surprised that dragon's hearing was so remarkably sharp when Maldovaar replied.

"I do my best thinking just before I awaken in the morning! When I lose those precious minutes… well, I can't be held accountable for what happens!"

It was only natural Derek would finish his ablutions first and scrambled eagerly up the cliff towards the cave.

As Maldovaar shook himself off to follow, Krytan stopped him. "I'll bring you back something very special from the castle, Maldovaar, if you'll do me a favor this morning before Derek and I leave."

Maldovaar turned slowly, looking at the man still swimming in the pool of clear water. Acting nonchalant, as if he didn't care for such frivolous things as manmade treats, he licked one paw and then smoothed it over his bright forelock. "What is it that you want?"

"When you go back to the cave, tell Lyra I've gone for firewood and the pool is free for her to bathe now."

"Is that all?" Maldovaar asked softly, still feigning disinterest.

"And keep Derek occupied for a while," Krytan added.

"In return I receive... what?" Maldovaar held one paw out as if he were inspecting his "fingers". As Krytan watched, the dragon lifted his paw to his mouth, blew on the claws and then rubbed them back and forth against his stomach.

"Name it!" Krytan told him, treading water.

Maldovaar had almost smiled as he spoke his desire. "The cook at the castle makes the most delicious cinnamon buns each day. But you must get to them early, or they disappear."

"Done!"

Maldovaar took a few steps and then turned to lean his head down so it was quite close to Krytan's, meeting him eye to eye. "Don't hurt her, human!"

Krytan was surprised by the look in the dragon's eye. There was no misinterpreting the intelligent beast's concern for the princess. Nodding, he replied, "She is my wife, Maldovaar, and I shall protect her with my life."

"Human men are known to protect their women from everything but themselves, the one beast with the ability to hurt them the most."

Krytan was stunned by Maldovaar's insightful words. He wouldn't have thought it possible, but he was coming to respect this intractable, totally dislikable dragon! Carefully, he nodded. "I understand your meaning, Maldovaar. If she says 'no', I stop."

Maldovaar reared back. "Fair enough, human, but understand this—Lyra is my Princess and I protect her with my flame. I owe her my life and I was the leader of the last dragon brigade to ever fight in the wars. I have not forgotten how to fight."

Maldovaar flapped his great wings and rose gracefully, flying towards the cave entrance once again. Staying quiet in the water, Krytan didn't have long to wait before Lyra was at the water's edge. Quietly, he enjoyed the view as she dropped her clothes, liking the way her full breasts hung heavily, swinging slightly as she bent over. Immediately, he had erotic thoughts of taking her from behind, thrusting in and out of her tight flesh, all the while hanging onto her tits, wildly bouncing from his movements.

Only when she was in the water and near the center of the pool, did he swim out of the reeds, which had concealed him. Speaking softly, he greeted her. "A water goddess has joined me for my morning bath. And it appears she has perfect timing for I need help with my back."

Her surprise was evidenced by her startled cry and the fact that she slipped below the water for a moment. Coming back up, sputtering and spitting, she ran her hands over her face and then backwards, slicking her hair flat to her head. "Maldovaar said you'd gone for wood!"

Krytan swam closer. "Yes, I know. And don't worry about interruptions, the old dragon is going to watch out for Derek and give us some newlywed privacy."

Lyra moved back from him, closer to the edge of the water until she could stand up. "Newlywed!" she repeated in disbelief. "He never would have agreed to this!"

"Everyone has his or her weak point," Krytan pointed out, following her through the water, stopping just two feet away. When he stood, she backed up more. He knew she was completely unaware of her actions as her movements in the water now revealed all of her breasts, so that they almost floated on top of the water. Krytan barely suppressed his groan of arousal at the sight.

"Cinnamon buns!" Lyra answered a moment later. Slowly she smiled, shaking her head. "You'll have to get up very early."

"Or visit her before bedtime and offer her something equally tempting to save them for me. All good things are worth their price."

"It's a lot of work just to get me alone," Lyra pointed out.

Krytan reached out, unable to resist temptation any longer. As he spoke, his hands cupped the floating breasts, again catching her by surprise. "You are worth every bit of effort, my sweet. Last night was torture, lying in the bed with you and yet unable to follow my instinctive responses."

He moved closer, sliding one hand down her body and between her thighs. As he slipped one finger over the soft folds of womanly flesh until he found her clit, he felt all resistance leave her body.

Lyra surprised him as she jested, breathily. "I felt how 'hard' it was for you."

Krytan laughed out loud. "You little minx!" He kissed her without pause, taking her breath away. He caught her as her legs went limp and he easily moved the two of them out of the water and onto the soft, grassy edge. Just like last night, he was indeed very hard once more. But he took his time to pleasure Lyra first. As his one hand continued to conquer her nether regions, his mouth sucked her nipples, using his tongue and lips to flick, nip and tug on each tender, turgid tip.

Soon, Lyra was moaning and moving restlessly beneath him.

Easing down her wet body, he moved between her thighs. She resisted at first, but he firmly pushed them apart. As his tongue enslaved her clit, he slid two and then three fingers into her slippery cunt. Over and over, his hand matched his mouth's rhythm until Lyra finally cried her release. She squirted her juice as her body contracted its orgasmic explosion, and Krytan lapped up as much as he could.

Seconds later, he moved back into position and his cock slid into her dripping flesh. He had to push firmly as she was newly tight, his almost-virgin bride. God! It felt sweet and crazy-wild to be inside her again. As he looked down, Krytan was surprised by how good it really felt. All the while he had pleasured Lyra, he had worked hard at maintaining his control to ensure she was fully aroused. Now that he was inside her, he knew the next time it was going to be much harder, knowing how amazing it was going to be as soon as his cock was buried deep inside her hot, tight pussy once again.

"God!" he moaned loudly, looking down at his wife. Her eyes were closed and he leaned down to kiss her lips fiercely. When he released her mouth, it was bright red and swollen from his sucking and light chewing. He wanted to mark her as his woman even though he knew the response was primitive. Instead, he lowered his mouth and sucked on her tender skin, near the front of her throat. Every time she touched the tender spot, she'd remember him and this!

Groaning, he stiffened suddenly and came hard and fast inside her. His muscles all tightened hard and fast and his hips jerked forward five, six... no, seven times, pumping his seed into her body. He didn't fight the image that came to his mind of a baby growing in Lyra's belly.

He pressed firmly against her once more and then he slid from her body reluctantly. Dropping to the grass beside her, he breathed in and out harshly. Birds flew overhead and he knew it was a day just like any other, but somehow, it felt different. Something sure as hell had changed!

Looking up at Lyra now, Krytan was surprised at how much he had missed her. And of course he'd tossed and turned most of last night, hard and wanting to be with her again. But it appeared these feelings represented a much deeper need, beyond just the physical, which was something he wasn't completely comfortable with.

Krytan had always kept women in a separate area of his life that had little to do with the rest of his world. But he had not really considered what having a wife would mean, or how it might change his life. Reluctantly, he admitted that Lyra was getting under his skin. Like ivy vines growing along its support, Lyra was getting not only into his mind but his heart, as well.

* * * * *

Lyra wanted to blame the flutterings in her stomach region as entirely due to the movements of her companion. But she knew by the heated flush on her cheeks, the source was internal and most likely caused by her remembering the time at the pool yesterday morning.

After making love on the grassy edge, they had returned to the water, gently swimming about. When Krytan had taken her into his arms, she had not resisted. When his hand moved between her thighs, spending quite some time stroking back and forth over her pussy lips, his innocuous words only made her more aroused.

"Rubbing briskly helps to cleanse the skin almost as effectively as soap, you know." Krytan had told her softly, pausing to cup his hand over her mound for a moment. As he resumed his rubbing, he smiled. "I feel, as a good husband, it's important for me to help you stay clean... in lieu of proper bathing facilities."

Closing her eyes, Lyra could almost feel his hand between her thighs once more. Last night she'd gotten very little sleep, and finally she'd slid her own hand down. After a brief battle with her conscience, ignoring the teaching of the old priest from the castle, she duplicated the clever caresses she'd learned from Krytan until she finally moaned softly in release. She'd fallen asleep after that, even though the experience hadn't been as nice as when he'd done it.

Looking down, she saw Derek was nearly to the ledge where she was standing. Was it possible that he'd grown since she'd seen him? Surely not, she thought to herself, shaking her head in chagrin. Isn't that what parents were always saying?

"Lyra! We have a surprise for you!"

A few moments later, the small boy was running towards her. He surprised her by throwing his arms around her legs and hugging close. Against her stomach, the dragonet shifted away from Derek's head, making a snuffling noise in protest of having being awakened so abruptly. Placing her hand atop Derek's head, she looked down as the boy looked up. His eyes shone and he smiled brightly. His words changed her forever. "I missed you, Lyra! I'm glad to be home."

Shocked, Lyra thought she felt her innermost organs move in response to his simple words. Of course, that was silly. She wasn't his birth mother... but all of a sudden, she knew she loved him as if he were her flesh and blood child. She dropped down to a half-kneeling position and hugged him tightly.

Derek, being a typical boy, returned the gesture for a moment, and then squirmed away. "How are the kittens? Did they miss me?"

Lyra smiled, nodding as she choked back the tears that fought to escape. Swallowing hard, she replied, "Yes, I think they did. You should hurry in and say hello."

As Derek eagerly went in search of his newest best friends, she lifted her fingers to remove tears now running down her cheeks. It didn't make sense. How could she care for someone else's child, let alone so quickly? Yet, there was no denying she did care for him. Immediately upon this thought, she realized even if she had a child of her own, she would love Derek just as much as if he'd been carried inside her body for nine months. There wasn't a doubt within her just then. She was now the mother of a little boy, and she loved him with her whole heart.

"Are you all right, Lyra?" Krytan's words drew her back to the present.

Turning, she looked up at her husband. "Yes, I'm fine. Derek just caught me off-guard."

The dragonet shifted against her once more, and this time she lifted her hand to cover the pouch where she rested. It reminded her that they still needed to pick a name.

"So, what's this surprise Derek is talking about?" she asked Krytan.

"Besides a few extra cinnamon buns?"

She laughed, unable to stop the bubble of joy she was feeling. "You must have gotten up very early."

"I visited her last evening, and discovered your father's cook is amenable to bribery."

"That doesn't sound good… for my father, that is. So, what did you manage to bring?"

"One very big sweet cake for Maldovaar. He is going to take Derek for a couple of hours this afternoon."

Lyra had started to go into the cave when his words stopped her. Looking back at her husband… she saw the determined look on his face. No doubt, his plans involved getting her on her back once more! Immediately she was torn between elation at the idea and betrayal for doing so. Before she could twist back around, Krytan had grabbed her arm.

He grinned down at her. "I was thinking we could make use of that makeshift bed for a short time. I'd be happy to continue your wifely education, as a good husband, that is."

"Oh!" She jerked her arm free and walked into the cave. Against her midriff, the little dragon was fluttering her wings as she fully woke up and began moving about. Glancing around, she saw Maldovaar was already eating a cinnamon bun and Derek was on the bed, talking to the kittens.

As she neared, the little boy turned. "Where is he?"

Lyra crossed to join him on the low mattress. "He has turned out to be a *she*, and she is in here." She paused and pointed to her stomach, where the pouch rested. A second later, small movements came from under the fabric. "She's awake now, and we still need a name." Reaching into the bag, she eased the shiny dragonet back out.

"Oh! Look how big he… uh, she's gotten." Eagerly he petted the dragon's head and long neck. But the dragon was intent on mother's milk, and was scrambling towards the kittens and the mama cat. Derek watched as the dragon settled to eat, almost purring when the cat licked her in welcome. "Is she going to be as big as Maldy?"

Lyra smiled, shaking her head. "No, she's female and they are much smaller."

Krytan sat on the far side of the bed. "She'll still be too big to keep indoors."

Lyra didn't reply.

But Derek expressed his thoughts quick enough. "Aaaawwwww, Papa! Sure she can. We could make her a place in the stables with the horses."

Lyra hated to be the one to tell him, but she knew quite well what the future of this sweet little creature would be. "How would you feel if you had to stay in the stables all day, Derek, with no one else who is like you? It wouldn't be any fun, would it?"

Derek slowly shook his head. "No, but I'd visit her."

"She would feel the same… cut off from her own kind."

"All right," Derek murmured quietly, but there was no hiding his sadness as his shoulders hunched over and the corners of his mouth turned down.

Lyra reached out and gently pushed back a lock of hair from his face. "She still needs a name. Why don't you choose her name?"

"I only picked out boy names," he replied, still stroking the little dragon.

Krytan leaned forward, propping himself up on his bent arm, his head resting on his hand. "Perhaps one of those names will work just as well for a girl."

Lyra slid off the bed to her feet and dusted her hands together before turning to face the bed again. "Derek, you and your father can pick out a name while I go sort out all the supplies you two brought back."

Krytan spoke quickly. "What was the first name you were thinking of, son?"

"Joey."

Lyra glanced up and met her husband's gaze and she grinned for just a moment. She'd leave him to iron out that problem. Walking away, she moved to the far corner of the cave and separated all the goods in the sacks and backpacks.

Easily her mind wandered back to yesterday morning down at the pool and how wonderful being with her husband had felt. She was embarrassed to admit she was actually looking forward to his touch once more. Just imagining it and she felt the wetness seeping out between her pussy lips, oozing down to her upper thighs.

"Bye, Lyra!"

Suddenly she looked up and was surprised to see Derek waving from the cave's entrance. Krytan was walking towards her a few seconds later, alone. She didn't miss the slow smile curving his sexy mouth. She felt delicious chills chasing up and down her spine at that look from his eyes. Before she could ask him anything about Derek's departure, he was reaching his hand down to her.

"Come with me down to the pond while I wash off this travel dust."

Lyra stood, accepting his hand. "I'll sit and watch."

"Fine. I enjoy an appreciative audience," he told her with a grin, pulling her behind him out of the cave. Once they reached the edge of the water, Krytan was already stripping off his clothes before she even stopped walking. Nude, he looked back at her over his shoulder, telling her with a wide grin, showing off his white teeth, "Feel free to applaud."

Lyra gasped in surprise at his audacity while Krytan walked into the water and then dove beneath the surface. After a minute or so, she sat down on the edge, watching him swim through the water. She loved the water and it was hard to resist diving in.

"Join me!" he spoke loudly, from the center of the pond.

"You'll want to do more than swim," she accused him quickly. She stopped as she realized that she wanted to do precisely that… more than just play in the water.

"I am your husband, madam!"

Lyra stood, getting ready to give in. "Promise you'll behave like a knight of the realm."

"I am insulted, wife."

"All right, I'm sorry."

She turned away from the pool and slowly began removing her clothes. She was always self-conscious of her size, and she was still unsure about all this nakedness with a man she hardly knew, even if he was her husband, technically. She released the string tie on her trousers and let them fall to the ground. Stepping out of them, she dragged her shirt up and over her head. Letting the top fall to the ground, she ran one hand over her cropped hair. Now, she regretted cutting her hair. Her hair had been her prettiest asset, according to her mother anyway. Of course, parents had to love you so she always took what they said with a grain of salt. Quickly, she turned and ran into the water.

* * * * *

Krytan treaded water as he watched Lyra remove her clothes. For a few seconds, if that long, he had considered turning away, but then decided under normal circumstances, he would be very well versed with his wife's naked body. If anything, he had a lot to make up for!

Her thighs were revealed first, and he appreciated their plump roundness as he then saw her well-curved calves. Yes indeed, his wife was quite pleasantly built. Before he could think further, he saw her pulling her shirt up and over her head. His breath caught in his chest as he saw her naked back, which ended with her lush, heart-shaped buttocks. He could easily imagine caressing those full globes as he thrust into her tight...

She was walking towards the water and he had seen the way she ran her hand over her hair. But he was quickly distracted by the way her large, pendulous breasts swung with every step. God! He was hard already... this was going to be harder—hell! He shook his head as he swam towards her.

Lyra didn't hear Krytan come behind her until one arm was sliding across her body, covering the tops of her breasts. She was immediately pressed backwards and felt his hard manhood against her bottom. Squirming only heightened her awareness.

"Sir!" she spoke quickly, hoping to feign outrage, or at the least, indifference.

"It dawned on me, my Princess, I was remiss as a knight in not seeing to your every need."

Lyra shook her head. "There is nothing I nee—" Her voice drifted away on the lie.

Krytan took the opportunity to shift his arm below her breasts, and they now floated and bounced against his forearm.

Her nipples were already taut and elongated. Her gasp was lost as his other hand cupped her womanly mound. Against her ear, she heard Krytan whisper, even as his fingers began moving.

"I provided no soap, and the only other good method for cleansing is... well, I'm sure you remember. I deem it my duty, madam, to provide you with all the necessary rubbing you need."

Lyra couldn't reply as his fingers were already teasing and exciting her clit. It shocked her how quickly her body shook and shivered in response. The next thing she knew, Krytan held her against him, his strong legs moving in the water and keeping them both floating.

His voice was husky as he spoke a short time later. "Let's go back to the cave, sweetheart."

Lyra barely managed to keep up with her husband on the trek back up the hillside. Inside the cave, he moved them over to the bed. When he placed her on her back, she didn't fight him.

He came down next to her, cupping her nearest breast. "Such pretty round boobs," he told her quietly. His hand moved back and forth, and then he shifted in the bed to kneel astride her hips. Now both hands cupped her breasts from below, and he pushed them together and up. "So big and soft, my sweet. Nice fat pillows for my head to rest upon."

Lyra heard his words on one level, but her body was overwhelming most of her brain with wild, previously unknown and amazing messages. The way his hands touched and held her breasts was almost unbelievably erotic. His words just made her hotter with each passing second. She squirmed beneath him.

Krytan chuckled softly, but still caressed and played with her breasts. His fingers rubbed back and forth over the taut nipples poking up hard and long. He paused to roll them back and forth, and plucked and tugged at each one until he finally released one at a time.

Her eyes were closed, savoring the wonderful, wild feelings when Krytan's voice caught her attention.

"I think it's time for some exploration, my sweet. Hold on!"

Lyra wasn't sure what she was supposed to grab hold of, but she felt him sliding down her body. Lifting her head from the mattress, she looked down over her body. Seeing her husband between her widely splayed thighs, smiling up at her, she recalled all the luscious and delightful ways he made her feel yesterday.

"Lay back, my sweet!"

Lyra barely touched her head to the mattress when she was forced to cry out. "Oh... aaaayy!"

Krytan's fingers stroked and caressed her pussy lips and his tongue delved with impunity between her folds. As he found her clit, she cried out again. Quickly, she crammed one hand into her mouth. The rest of her cries were muffled as Krytan teased and flicked her body to release again.

Dimly, Lyra was aware of Krytan moving her body so she was on her elbows and knees. She felt his hard manhood pressed between her thighs and his hands grabbed her rounded hips. A moment later, he thrust forward and his cock entered her tight pussy.

She gasped, and then realized he was pulling away. Her body seemed to tighten to prevent him. Still, it didn't change anything and he thrust forward again seconds later. This time she felt him bounce against her bottom, followed by the sound of his balls slapping against her wet flesh. She blushed hotly at the audible proof of their lovemaking.

One of Krytan's hands moved down to squeeze one heavily hanging breast, caressing and then rubbing across the taut nipple. She shivered as she felt him speed up his movements. His strokes shortened. Without warning he thrust hard and jerkily forward, bouncing against her butt.

"Oh God! Yes!" Krytan groaned as his cock moved like a piston, pumping his seed into her body. She could feel it leaking out and down her inner thighs.

Her head spun as he turned them, still joined, to lie in the bed, spoon fashion. His top hand came forward to cup her uppermost breast. She listened as his breathing slowly calmed and returned to normal. She had no idea how long it was before his fingers toyed with her nipple, coaxing it again to a taut, tender elongated state. The tips of his fingers rubbed over the flat surface, and then flicked quickly, back and forth. He alternated that heavenly torture to the eager bud between rolling it between his fingers and then tugging and pulling it out to finally release it and let her breast bounce back to rest.

She was still acutely aware of his cock, soft and still just inside her pussy.

"I can't decide whether I want to nap like this," he spoke softly, his breath gently rustling the strands of hair over her ear.

"Nestled between these pretty plump cheeks, or sleep on your lovely big pillows and be free to suck a nipple like a suckling babe. Which do you prefer?"

Lyra was caught off-guard. She opened her mouth to reply.

Immediately moving his hand, Krytan shifted their positions again, rolling her onto her back. A second later, his hand cupped her pussy, curling his fingers in and up.

"Oh my!" she murmured in a curious mix of arousal, satiation and wonder.

"Yeah, I rather like this option, too. I can sleep beside you and suck your nipples when I want. Plus I get to keep my hand in a really nice place."

Lyra felt her lips curving upwards. He certainly made her feel good about herself, and this. She squirmed a little, getting more comfortable. When Krytan groaned, she looked up at him. "What's wrong?"

"When you wiggle like that, sweetheart, your body does this delightful jiggle."

"And you don't like that?"

Krytan leaned down and kissed her quickly. "I like it very much. You have a very luscious body, Lyra."

"I'm too plump. I always wanted to be skinny like my mother, or the other girls I grew up with." Lyra froze the second she realized she'd spoken the words out loud. She didn't want to hear him lie and deny the truth. Then again, she didn't want to hear him agree with her!

"Shh! You are the right size for me. Full, soft and round." He paused, and his hand shifted upwards to cover her belly. "Soon, I hope you will be even rounder."

Lyra knew exactly what he meant. "Is that why you married? To have more children?"

Krytan's hand rubbed small circles over her soft tummy. "No, that is not why I married. I think Derek would enjoy a little brother or sister. He's had a rough time of it, coming into the world as he did."

Lyra slowly admitted that she liked the feel of his hand on her lower stomach. It felt warm, heavy and possessive.

Oh, yes!

She more than liked this lovemaking with her husband. It was sweet, warm, comforting and made her feel accepted. More importantly, she felt wildly passionate, desirable and wanton whenever his hands caressed her.

Oh, God, yes!

Being with Krytan, like this, in the glowing aftermath, and the incredibly volcanic orgasms, were her destiny. She was meant to be with him—

Abruptly she stopped as a thought popped into her brain. "You weren't married to his mother?" she asked softly, not sure if he would reply.

"No. I regret to say she was a camp follower, during the war. I didn't even know I had a son, until one day her father showed up, with Derek in tow. She had died—" He paused, taking a deep breath. "I love him now, but at first being a father, a parent, turned out to be pretty tough, for both of us. Hell! I still feel like a novice and I have no idea what to do. I know nothing of children, and neither did any of my men."

"I met Thomas."

Krytan laughed. "Poor old soldier deserves better than chasing after that scamp all day."

"Children need discipline, guidelines and love. I think there is an unwritten rule stating a child's duty is to test the boundaries we set. That is how they learn and grow. Adults must keep them safe, and pull them back from the edge, reminding them of the rules."

"You make it sound simple," Krytan whispered softly, pressing his lips against her temple.

"I had a very wise granny." She stopped and yawned.

Krytan pulled the covers over them. "Let's sleep while we can. I'm sure Maldovaar will be back before too much longer."

Lyra was sure a spirit took over her body because a moment later she heard herself making a very saucy suggestion. "There will always be tonight!"

Chapter Six

Krytan returned to the cave the next afternoon, leaving Derek and Maldovaar to entertain one another at the pool below. He was glad to discover the crusty dragon was so easy to bribe. Today he had achieved his goal by offering the flame-haired curmudgeon a glass of the King's prized bourbon tonight before bed. He was just glad he'd thought to ask for a bottle for his journey.

His new father-in-law had nodded his graying head. The older man's eyes had twinkled when he gave him the bottle, wrapped carefully for travel. "Only one thing better than this, my son, for cold nights."

Krytan smiled, feeling quite pleased that so far his nights had been pretty warm. Walking into the cave, he stopped cold. He had not told Lyra he was coming back early, just in case he had read Maldovaar wrong. Nothing, though, could explain what he saw as he looked across the cave's expanse to where his new bride was supposedly doing the chores which kept their quarters so spick and span. Nothing except his drinking the bottle of bourbon… which, of course, he had not!

Lyra stood with her back to him. Behind her, a broom busily swept the floor and a small cloth danced like a butterfly through the air, dusting any surface that was free of clutter. The small reed rug she had woven lifted itself up as the broom passed beneath it.

"What the he—" Krytan shouted in surprise as the broom reached him, paused until he stepped aside and then it proceeded to sweep the dust out of the cave.

His words caught Lyra's attention because she turned suddenly.

The dust rag dropped to the floor, but landed on the edge of a small table.

The rug fell flat on the floor, making a whooshing sound in its wake.

A clattering sound told him the broom must have fallen against the cave wall just outside the entrance.

Lyra dried her hands quickly, starting towards him.

Krytan held up his hand, palm facing her. "Hold it right there! What's going on here?"

Lyra shrugged.

Maybe he was imagining it, but he thought he saw guilt on her face.

"Maybe you should sit," she told him softly.

Krytan moved across the room and sat on the edge of the bed. Immediately, the kittens left their box to start over towards him. He looked up when he saw Lyra had stopped right in front of him. The look on her face was priceless. He saw everything from guilt, fear and even the naughty expression of a child caught with its hand in the wrong place. Slowly, he folded his arms across his chest.

Lyra had been lost in her thoughts, knowing she was alone in the cave. She assumed she had an hour until everyone returned, so she took advantage and used her magic to speed her cleaning activities along.

Until today, no one except her grandmother had ever seen her practicing magic spells. She'd been very careful, as warned by her beloved relative. Only behind a locked door or alone in the woods, did she freely practice her spells and powers. She'd felt quite safe, though—

"Uhm… " She bit her lower lip as she pondered what to say. She should have considered this happening, but never had she thought about what she might say.

Lie!

The thought popped into her head like a ray of hope.

Just as quickly, she knew she could not lie to her husband. Nothing good would ever come of that, not to mention that it set a bad example. Nervously, she folded her arms, imitating her bridegroom's pose. Rubbing her right foot on the ball, in a small arcing movement, she wondered what to say.

"Do your friends have names?"

Krytan's voice drew her out of her blue fugue. "What? Names. Who?" Lyra asked in confusion.

"The broom and dust rag, darling. I assumed they must be friends of yours because I've never met them before."

The silliness of his words struck her and she giggled. "Oh, them. Old friends of the family. They only stopped by. I don't see them often, really."

Silence followed and she waited nervously to see how he would react. Most people didn't believe in magic because they had never experienced it. When they did, many simply put it down to "seeing things" or "being too tired" and, most commonly, "too much wine consumption". Krytan had complained of none of these and instead asked her outright what was going on. She wondered which he would choose?

"And just how often might I expect to see them in the future?" he questioned in a calm tone a few seconds later.

Lyra smiled. "Not very often?" she offered quietly.

Krytan shook his head. "You practice witchcraft, wife?"

"No, I learned magic spells from my grandmother. Sometimes my lazy nature gets the better of me. I give in to the need to make things a tad bit easier." Lyra clasped her hands in front of her, meeting her husband's gaze. "I am very careful no one is around, usually."

Krytan nodded his head. "Granted. I had told you we wouldn't be back for an hour or so, and then I sneak back to surprise you—"

"And instead you are greeted with a dancing broom and swinging dust rag. It's a good thing I hadn't started to wash the dishes, huh?" She smiled at him hopefully.

Her husband reached out and dragged her down onto the bed, twisting their bodies so he loomed above her. "Let's not go down that road just now. Does Derek know?" Krytan stopped her answer by covering her lips with his. As he lifted his head, he spoke again. "Never mind. If he knew you could make things dance then I would have known."

Lyra wiggled against him.

He responded by moving his hand up past her waist, beneath her shirt. A second later his hand covered her breast.

Lyra sighed loudly as she felt the sweet capture of his grasp. Even though she knew it was impossible, it always seemed as if her flesh swelled as he held it tenderly. When he began squeezing and fondling, she groaned loudly.

"Do you like that, wife?" Krytan asked softly, pressing his mouth to the side of her neck. "What about this?" he added, lightly rubbing his fingertips back and forth across the rubbery nipple.

"Yes!" Lyra whispered, arching her back.

He busied himself with treating the nipples of both breasts the same way. Soon each bud was taut and distended to its maximum length. Pushing her shirt to her armpits, he moved one hand to cup her nearest globe. As his head lowered, he blew puffs of air across her flesh.

Lyra shivered. "Oh God!"

Her husband's mouth enclosed her nipple a moment later. Threading her fingers through his hair, she cradled his head.

"I could suck here for a long time," he told her a short time later. Instead, he moved over to the other one.

Lyra didn't resist his hands tugging her pants down to her ankles. She kicked them off, wanting to feel him inside her again. Her need for her husband seemed to be growing, instead of waning.

"Ooh!" Her head spun as he moved them in the bed. Suddenly, she was lying atop him.

"That's it, sweet one. Just sit up." Krytan encouraged her into the position he wanted.

Lyra gasped as she straddled his hips. He had already freed his cock and it pressed hotly against her wet flesh. She didn't wait. Reaching down, she guided his flesh, raising up to position him perfectly…

"Aah," she sighed loudly as she relaxed her thigh muscles and his hard manhood pushed inside her.

Krytan's hands moved to her hips and seated her fully, completing their joining. He groaned loudly. Without pause though, he began pushing up her top over her head.

Lyra pressed her hands over her breasts, half-concealing them. Suddenly, she was shy about him seeing her naked in the bright light of day.

He was not having it, though, and tugged down her hands. "Why do you feel the need to cover yourself? I am your husband."

Lyra nodded, but wasn't able to meet his gaze. Biting her lower lip, she mumbled her reply, "I'm too big."

Krytan grinned and covered each breast with a hand. "This looks like a good fit to me," he told her assuredly. He massaged them for a few seconds and then slid his hands to her hips. Curving his fingers into her soft flesh, he told her, "You have good wide hips, the kind perfect for carrying a babe, especially the offspring of such a big knight."

Lyra couldn't resist wiggling her hips in response to the feelings inside her. She smiled when Krytan groaned in response. This wasn't just arousing, it was sweet, and fun and—

"I don't like women who are skin and bone, Lyra," Krytan told her decisively.

Lyra met his gaze and she believed his words. Her body reacted intensely and she curled towards him responsively. All she could do was moan in reply because no words would form in the confusion in her head.

Krytan watched the face of his wife. She was so beautiful, even with her hair cut off so that she looked like a street urchin. Her spirit was so loving and lighthearted that he had felt himself falling more and more under her spell with each passing hour in her presence. The fact she knew real magic wasn't all that much of a surprise. Everything about this unusual woman had seemed to be more than just what one might expect in a princess.

As he felt her flesh reacting around his cock, he gave way to the physical sensations. Sliding his hands from her tempting breasts to her hips, he held her tight as he thrust his hips upwards. With quick, short jerks, he shot his seed into her hot flesh.

As Lyra fell to lie upon his chest, Krytan savored the heated little after-spasms he could feel deep inside her body. As far as wedding nights and honeymoons went, he knew this one went beyond atypical!

* * * * *

Krytan watched as Lyra pulled on her clothes while standing several feet from the bed a short time later. "That would be a lot easier, darling, if you'd sit on the bed."

Lyra shook her head, shooting him one quick glance before bending her head again to concentrate on her balance while trying to slip one foot into her pants. "I tried that a few minutes ago, remember?"

He grinned and lazily rubbed his chest. Beneath the covers of the makeshift bed, he moved his legs restlessly. Indeed, he did recall quite easily how difficult he'd made it for Lyra to redress after their lovemaking. "I'll let you change the subject since you seem so intent on leaving this bed. What I do want to know, though, is why you and Maldovaar? I never would have figured the two of you together."

Lyra tied the string on her waist. She ran her fingers through her disheveled hair.

Glancing up, Krytan met her gaze.

"I made a mess of my hair, didn't I?" she asked him softly.

He paused, unsure whether she was doing this to distract him or whether she meant it. When he saw a tear trailing down her cheek, he knew she was genuine in her distress. "It has a certain charm, cut short. Also, I don't have to keep pushing it out of my way to play with your treasures."

Slowly Lyra grinned in response. She shrugged once. "As to Maldovaar—" She walked over to where they kept a pitcher of water. Pouring herself a glass, she drank it quickly. "Maldovaar brought the dragons here, to the valley. They had lived here a long time ago, according to my grandmother. Or at least they were here when she was a child, and then they went away. This land belonged to my mother's people for generations, until only my grandmother was left."

"The land became your father's upon his marriage to your mother?" Krytan asked her a moment later.

"Not exactly. After my grandmother's death, the land was sort of just there. Technically, it was my mother's and—"

"According to the law, it was therefore your father's."

Lyra glanced up quickly from where she had moved to their small table. She had taken a loaf of bread, but stopped before picking up the knife to cut it. "Yes, well, he deeded the property to me when I requested it a short time back. Some time later, he learned the dragons had returned. Essentially, the land is impenetrable unless you can fly, or come by the pathway you followed."

Krytan sat up in the bed, watching Lyra as she began slicing the bread. "What are your intentions?"

"What do you mean? I have no ulterior motives, if that's what you mean," Lyra replied shortly, her irritation evident in her tone.

Krytan slid from beneath the covers, grabbing his trousers and pulling them up easily. Bare-chested, he walked across the cave. Upon reaching the table, he sat on one of the makeshift chairs, which were just large rocks. In his opinion, they couldn't return to civilization, and padded chairs, soon enough. "I meant, what is your plan for the dragons' future? I'm sure you don't supply them all with food."

Lyra laughed softly. "Oh, the food? That is just temporary. I was bribing Maldie to watch over the dinosaur egg. I wanted to see if it would hatch, and I knew I couldn't take it to the castle."

"And otherwise, the dragons will be able to survive here without outside help?" Krytan asked.

"Yes, or at least they did so once before. There were many more of them in my grandmother's time. I'd hate to see such noble creatures disappear from our world. They served during the war and they deserve repayment," Lyra spoke vehemently, gesturing with the knife.

Krytan carefully removed the knife from her hand when she stopped moving it. "I agree, sweetheart, except they fought for the other side."

"And they stopped when they saw what an awful leader Hodynaar truly was. All I'm doing is restoring what they once had. I know it is what my grandmother would have wanted."

Outside the cave, Krytan could hear the approach of his son. "Promise you won't set up any more habitats without discussing it with me first, all right? I don't relish losing my lands to lost herds of unicorns. Although I could see the advantage to maintaining a herd of Pegasus mounts and my knights would enjoy a pond full of sea sirens."

Lyra opened her mouth to reply but was stopped as Derek burst into the cave.

"I'm hungry! Is it time to eat?"

Krytan grinned as he met his wife's gaze. He had no doubt Derek wouldn't be the only one bringing strays into his home in the future. There would be no complaints so long as she didn't come home with the frog that could talk!

* * * * *

The next two weeks passed much too quickly for Lyra. Almost before she knew it, she was the one planning trips to the pool and arranging for Maldy to watch over Derek. She flushed each time Krytan would catch her eye as she set the plan in motion. Ignoring the grin, which would usually curve his lips upward, she would busy herself with something else, and it was usually unimportant.

The grin got her goat each time. The last several nights, alone on the mattress Krytan had made just for the two of them, she had been the one who turned to him first. Reaching her hand to lightly touch his waist or his chest, she would just let it rest there, for a minute or so, before she moved it about, caressing his skin lightly.

Then last night, she had awakened several hours after being made passionate, but very quiet, love to by her husband. To her surprise, and chagrin, her hand was resting not at Krytan's waist, but much lower. In fact, her hand curled around and cupped his manhood quite familiarly. Shocked, she started to withdraw.

Krytan's hand covered her hand with his own. "I don't mind, my sweet. I rather like it, to be completely truthful."

The tone in his voice told her he was more than just "liking it". For a moment, she considered pulling away, but something stopped her. A few seconds passed before she realized she wanted to make love to her husband. The desire rose from deep within that she needed to pleasure her mate, lover... master? Perhaps she wouldn't go that far, but she did admit she wanted to be with him. There was a growing need inside her to make him happy, and not just in their bed.

"We need to think about leaving here soon, my love." Krytan's voice drew her back to the present.

Slowly, she turned her head to glance at Krytan's outstretched form, naked, lying beside her on the grass embankment at the pool's edge. Seated with her knees pulled up, she'd been completely lost in her thoughts. He had every right to be perturbed with her. After the way he'd just made love to her, she owed him a bit more of her attention.

"Joey is barely two weeks old."

Krytan sat up beside her. "Yes, and she is nearly as big as Derek. I think Maldy is right about his taking her to the large dragon escarpment just over the ridge. We'll set up times to visit and have Maldovaar bring her to you in between times. I know he'll be agreeable to that. After all, without you, none of them would have such a nice and safe home."

"I know, but I hate leaving her."

Krytan wrapped his arm around Lyra's shoulders, pulling her close. "Darling, she has much to learn from her own kind. If she grows up in the human world, she'll never fit in completely in either one. This must be her home, and we can be the people who care for her when she comes to visit."

Lyra sniffed loudly. "You are right. I know you are... it just—" Her voice broke.

Krytan chuckled softly and kissed Lyra's temple. "But it still hurts, doesn't it? Trust me, my love, I do understand. Most of my childhood was spent bringing home all kinds of animals to share my bed. My mother had a fit when she came in to kiss me goodnight and found a snake on my pillow."

Lyra laughed. It was almost too easy to imagine Derek doing the same thing. In just the time they'd been here, he'd been bringing back all kinds of critters he found on his exploratory walks. They had many a wild chase once Joey figured out something new had been added to their small entourage. She got most irritated when Maldovaar and Krytan just sat back and watched the madhouse unfold in front of them.

Turning slightly, she looked into her husband's eyes. "Please talk to Derek and make sure he understands there will be no snakes, spiders, rats or mice in his bedroom either."

Krytan's bark of laughter burst forth. "I was just thinking the exact same thing. Derek seems a tad bolder than even I was at that age."

Before she could agree or disagree, they heard the commotion coming from the top of their trail.

A few seconds later, Derek's voice called out. "We're home!"

Krytan grabbed his trousers, pulling them on quickly. "I'll head him off"

"All right. Could you have Maldy bring Joey down here? I'll give her a quick bath."

A few minutes later, a soft scuffling behind warned her of Maldovaar's arrival. His long neck extended over towards the pool, and carefully he released the small dragon from his mouth. The shiny little dragon came towards her quickly, lowering its head for her to rub between its ears. As soon as Lyra did so, Joey began purring and snuffling rhythmically. Slowly, the baby animal relaxed and lowered itself to lie beside her, its head on her thigh.

"Why so sad, Princess? I thought you were enjoying married life."

Lyra didn't bother to turn at Maldovaar's question. "We need to leave in a day or so."

"Aah, yes. 'Parting is such sweet sorrow—' Alas, I shall of course miss you all."

"I need you to return to the herd for a while, Maldy. Joey needs some family with her, until she is fully grown. I think she is destined for some kind of dragon greatness, you know."

Maldovaar's head appeared over her shoulder a moment later. "I thought you were going to raise her, Princess. Wasn't that the great plan? I only signed on for the nesting job, remember?"

"I know, Maldovaar. But Joey deserves to live with her kind, regardless of what I want. She could live in either world, yet never feel as if she belonged. I wouldn't want that for her. I want her to be happy." Lyra sniffed loudly, surprised at how much this hurt. She wasn't completely sure if she was crying for her lost dreams, or because this was the right thing to do. Did it matter, in the end? She argued with herself silently. What was different was that she was no longer considering her wants and desires first.

"Will you do this for me, Maldovaar? I'll deed you this land—"

"Nice gesture, Princess, but dragons can't own land."

"I'll deed it to Derek, and he'll protect it as I will. I give you my permission to close all the entrances into the valleys. That should make it impossible for any humans to intrude on your solitude. The land is large enough to completely support the whole tribe, even if it should more than double in size."

"Tempting offer, Princess Lyra. Uhm, you had better get busy with the bathing because I am sure young Derek will be making his way down here quite soon."

Lyra stood slowly, gently coaxing the little dragon into the edge of the water. She was still leery of going too deeply, and Lyra splashed her quickly, washing off most of the dust. When she was finished, she left the pool, and began pulling her clothes back on. She turned as she heard a loud splash. Surprised, she saw Maldovaar was now in the water, standing in the center, and his neck extended easily quite high above the water.

Once she was dressed, she sat and began tying her shoes. The rocks sliding behind her told her that she had just made it.

"Hey, Lyra! I'm back!"

"Yes, I can see that, Derek. Did you have fun with Maldovaar?"

Derek sat quite close beside her, his eyes watching Joey, who appeared to be captivated by the way Maldovaar dipped his long neck and lowered his head under the water. Almost as if he now knew he had an audience, Maldovaar blew the water out of his mouth in a wide arc. It splashed back down, some of it landing on Joey's head. She looked around, startled, not sure where the spray had come from.

"Do it again, Maldy, I think she likes it!" This delighted Derek, who clapped his hands.

Perhaps it was luck, or the fact Lyra had spent a lot of time around the feisty dragon, but she jumped to her feet and stepped back up the bank. She moved just in time because the next arc of water managed to splash Derek.

He squealed in surprise and ran to the water's edge. "Hey!" he challenged the big dragon.

Maldovaar looked quite innocent as he slowly lowered his head until it was level with Derek, and just a few feet away. "You spoke, boy?"

"Yeah! What's the big idea? You got me wet!" Derek shouted at him, but without any rancor in his tone. Joey had come close to Derek and was nudging him with her nose. He was already reaching out to wrap his arm around her neck.

"I heard you say that you would like it," Maldovaar replied with a smirk, straightening once more to his full intimidating height.

Derek shook his head, scattering water droplets everywhere. "I meant Joey!"

"If you come in further, I bet she will also," Maldovaar suggested quietly. And then he filled his mouth with more water and shot it skyward at least twenty feet. As the water came down, Maldovaar bore the brunt of the intended shower, but Derek and the baby dragon suffered some, as well.

Derek twisted around to look at Lyra.

She nodded her head, smiling. "Sure, go on in and swim for a while. Maldovaar will watch out for you." She looked up at the dragon. "Don't let him stay in until he looks like a prune!"

Lyra turned and started up the path towards the cave mouth. She was sure she heard Maldovaar muttering something disparaging, but when she turned back to look, the big, yellow-green dragon was smiling and waved one of his short paws, wiggling the long claw-like fingers. His problem was his hearing was so astute she could never catch him off-guard. Accepting it as a lost cause, she returned to the cave.

* * * * *

Krytan lounged on the big bed, letting the kittens climb all over him when Lyra came walking in. Even dressed as a lad, she was sexy. When she bent over to add another log to the fire, he enjoyed the rounded ass cheeks pointed towards him. Silently, he admitted he longed to be home, in his own bed, with a good, sturdy lock on the door. Now that was the kind of place where a man could really make love to his wife.

Not on a skinny pallet in a cave with dragons, kittens and a small boy. Some honeymoon this was turning into. If this were happening to one of his men, it would make a wonderful story to tell, and something handy to needle the man with over the years. But since it was happening to him… well, he wasn't so sure he would ever share the details with anyone.

Lyra moved and he watched as she began doing things around the cave. He reminded himself there would always be one person who remembered exactly how things had been. No doubt over the years, something funny would be said and they would both turn to look at the other. The moment their gazes meet, they would know precisely what the other was thinking… as well as the shared memory. Suddenly, he liked the warm feeling he got when he considered such a thing, the like of which was certainly not common.

"Tsk, tsk, tsk," Lyra called out softly, tapping the side of a tin plate. "Here kitty, kitty! I have your din-din for you, little mama."

Krytan rolled onto his side to better watch his wife. "Why do you treat her like that?"

Meanwhile, the cat had hopped from the foot of the mattress and was walking towards Lyra. When it reached her, the cat rubbed up against the side of her legs, walking partway around her and then back. The purring she was doing was quite loud.

Lyra laughed. "Yes, pretty mama, I have your special food. Just for you!" She bent to rub the cat's head, between her ears, and then lowered the plate to the cave floor. The cat paused for a few more seconds, enjoying the rubbing, and then settled down to enjoy her food.

"She deserves to be spoiled after giving birth to four beautiful babies. Not to mention she is nursing them and must keep up her strength." Lyra walked over to the mattress, putting her hands on her hips. "Do you mean to tell me you think a new mother should be out in the field, working all day?"

Krytan pushed all the kittens out of the way and then pulled Lyra down beside him on the bed. "Where did you get that idea? I never said that?"

"You didn't have to! I read it in your eyes! I'm sure you are the type who never mollycoddles anything, not even a skinned knee."

Krytan held her still with one leg over hers and his hand pressing firmly against her stomach. Since her shirt had slid up, his hand rested on her warm skin. Only a few seconds passed before he held her gaze with his, and without saying a word, his hand moved upwards slowly, until he cupped her farthest breast. Like it was the most delicate of china, he held her fleshy globe in his hand. Slowly, he began caressing it, barely rubbing his fingers back and forth across the taut nipple. With each pass, he struggled harder to control his responses. And his desire to control and hold back was lessening, as well.

"I believe I could handle a skinned knee with a loving hand." Krytan heard the hoarseness in his voice and hoped it didn't betray just how close he truly was to losing control. Being this close to Lyra was easily driving him crazy with desire. Deliberately, he increased the attention he was paying to her nipple, working it with the tips of his fingers.

"Aah," Lyra groaned in response, her body shifting restlessly, finally pushing upwards, into his hand.

"Tell me what you are thinking, my sweet," he whispered into her ear a moment later.

"How you can make me feel like this and yet we hardly know each other!"

Krytan smiled as he prodded her for more. "What else?"

"I'm weak," she murmured quietly.

"Never!"

"Oh, yes… I am so spineless."

Krytan kissed her mouth and then he asked, "Why do you say that?"

"Because I don't want you to stop!" Lyra cried out a moment later as Krytan's hand moved between her thighs. "Yes!"

"This is too sweet to want to stop it, my love. Why should we stop?" Krytan slid his fingers along her wet pussy lips, slipping within to find her clit.

"Oh God!"

"No, it's just me, my sweet. Tell me what you want!" Krytan told her quickly.

Lyra thrashed her arms and legs restlessly, lifting to uselessly push against Krytan's arms and legs.

"Should I stop, my sweet love?" he asked her softly.

"Yes… no… wait," she gasped, drawing air into her lungs fast and deep. "No, don't stop!" she demanded.

"I'll never stop, not ever, darling!"

Krytan covered Lyra's mouth just as her body climaxed against his, catching her cry of release before it could echo around the empty cave. He lightly sucked on her lips as she panted in the aftermath of her passion. A shout from below alerted them both to the fact that soon they would have company.

Lyra scrambled to pull down her shirt.

Krytan reluctantly pulled his hand from her soft flesh. He did grab a fistful of her top to stop her as she tried to scoot away. Holding her in place, Krytan kissed her mouth lightly, almost tamely. But he took long enough for Derek to see them.

The boy's giggle told of his presence. "Yuck!" Derek called out as he walked towards them. "How come you gotta do that?"

Krytan picked up his son and put him on his knee. He smiled at the boy and then watched as Lyra moved across the cave to add more wood to their fire. "That is something mothers and fathers do, son."

"Is Lyra my mama?"

Even Maldovaar froze at the innocent question.

Krytan looked at Lyra, seeing the startled look in her eyes. They had not discussed this subject, but he assumed Derek would call her that. Of course, he was already used to calling her Lyra, and he wasn't sure if he remembered any tales his grandfather had told regarding his natural mother.

Lyra felt her heart leap into her throat. She hadn't thought that to Derek she would be considered by most to be his new mother. Did he resent the fact his real mother was gone? Before she could drive herself any crazier with questions and worry, she heard Krytan reply.

"I think you should ask her, son."

Lyra met his gaze. God! She couldn't believe he was dumping this on her! He had married her and that made these his problems, right! Or was it her problem, she considered silently a moment later. A mother was so much more than the woman who gave birth. Sure, there was the nine months she carried the baby and then the delivery, but it was really after that where things mattered the most. How you loved a child, cared for them, provided a safe and secure environment and let them know their boundaries as they grew was what really determined a child's ultimate destiny.

Poor little guy sure had been given a raw deal so far. He needed so much… but was she the one to give him the love and support—

The nagging question was if she didn't, then who would? Slowly, she walked across the cave floor. Sitting on the mattress next to Krytan, she smiled at Derek. She didn't wait for him to ask her though.

"I know I'm not your real mother, Derek. I can't take her place. But we're friends, and I love you—" Her voice broke, surprising her at the depth of her sudden emotions. "A mother sometimes makes you do things you don't like for your own good."

Derek nodded his head, still looking quite solemn. "I know."

"A mother makes you clean your room, take a bath and do your studies," she added quickly, straining her brain to recall all of the negative things a parent has to do. Perhaps, if she pointed out the bad parts first…

"Thomas does those things already," Derek told her quietly.

"Oh, uhm, all right. Well, I would be doing them as well."

"Will you tell me stories at night and tuck me into bed? Would you kiss me goodnight?"

Lyra nodded quickly. "Of course, we'll do stories, and I don't have to kiss you if you'd rather not."

Derek paused before answering.

Lyra wondered if he was thinking kissing was for sissies and babies. She didn't have to wait too long.

"If you want to kiss me, well, I guess it would be all right. I've seen other boys' mothers and they kiss them."

Lyra put her hand towards him to shake as she spoke. "Well, I think this sounds like a good deal. Shall we shake on this mother and son thing then?"

Derek stuck his little hand into hers, and shook it twice.

He was so sweet and serious she knew he now had the power to break her heart. Quickly, she sniffed as she felt tears welling up.

"Don't cry, Lyra!" Derek spoke quickly. "Come on, let's make lunch."

Derek hopped down from his father's knee, and then put his hand out for Lyra to take.

She accepted it a second later knowing from this point on, her life would never be the same. As they started across the cave floor, she glanced back at Krytan. The smile on his face and the look in his eyes told her all she needed to know about his feelings for her. He might not be completely aware of them, just as she had not been totally in tuned with hers either, at first. But now she knew for sure, she loved them both!

Facing forward, she walked with Derek towards the food supplies. From this point on, her life had new purpose and meaning. Not only did she now have a husband, she most definitely had a son. Now, it just remained to be seen which male would give her the most trouble!

Epilogue

Maldovaar leisurely batted his wings, flying easily, catching the winds and gliding at times. Life was good, he decided. Much better than he had ever anticipated. He had been living with the dragon tribe for more than a year now and even though he rarely had wine anymore, there wasn't much to complain about.

It turned out Joey bore the birthmark of royalty in the color of her scales. Therefore she was instantly made the new leader of the tribe and Maldovaar reaped all the benefits of being her guardian. Word had spread, and many smaller factions of dragons, including splinter groups from the war, had come and joined the group. They were quickly reaching sustainable numbers and extinction didn't appear to be looming on their horizon any longer.

Today, though, they were returning from a visit with Princess Lyra. After this, he and Joey wouldn't be able to return as often to the duke's castle. Joey was assuming her full role as tribal leader upon their return. Watching her fly, she was beautiful. Her scales gleamed like a rainbow of colors and her forelock was silky and black. She had dark eyes and long black lashes. Maldovaar had little doubt that before long she would be fighting off eager suitors' right and left.

But this visit had been purely for pleasure. Lyra had been in good health and the baby, a cute little girl… or at least the humans all called her "cute" and he accepted that he'd grow to like her, just as he had with Derek. Once she was older and didn't smell, then he could take her for rides…

Joey and Lyra had both shed tears when it was time to say goodbye. Derek had sniffled a little, but he had bravely smiled and waved as they flew away. The duke had held Josie, who had been named by her brother, and she apparently worshipped him. Maldovaar had noted that the pink bundle was always reaching towards the boy.

"I'm limiting your wine to just one cup a night, you know."

Maldovaar turned as Joey flew close to him once more.

"I am quite capable of setting my own parameters of behavior, little missy."

"Perhaps, but you only have two cups of wine in your flask. Lyra was careful to give me the rest of it to carry."

"Of all the nerve!" Maldovaar glared at the young female dragon at his side.

"No, she just knows you well, as do I. Your liver will do much better with a limit. I promised Derek we'll return in the spring."

"You'll have your duties to attend to," Maldovaar added quickly.

Joey did a somersault in the air and then flew backwards so she could face Maldovaar. "But families always come first."

"They are humans."

"True and we are dragons, dear old Maldovaar. Family comes from many places and not just blood. I've had one of the most unique families, thanks to the princess, Mama Mia, and you, of course."

Joey turned gracefully, flying straight once again.

Maldovaar glared for a second. "Well, *I at least*, will certainly go in the spring."

Joey hid her smile by turning her head. "Then it is settled. We will go together."

About the author

Mlyn lives in Indiana, USA. She worked as a Registered Nurse for 23 years in Pediatrics. Reading Barbara Cartland and Harlequin romance novels in high school spurred her to start writing. She did technical writing for her employers until she started writing erotica four years ago. She began her own website for people to view her stories. Mlyn is single and lives with her cranky cat Georgia, whom she named after her favorite artist for inspiration, Georgia O'Keeffe.

Mlyn welcomes mail from readers. You can write to her c/o Ellora's Cave Publishing at 1056 Home Ave. Akron, Oh. 44310-3502.

Also by Mlyn Hurn

Enjoy this excerpt from

Close Quarters

© Copyright Tielle St. Clare, 2004

Brenna shivered as she clung to the last tendrils of sleep. She wasn't ready to wake up and she was cold. Eyes closed, she reached behind her, trying to find the blankets and drag them back over her. Her hand came back empty. Groaning and a little disgruntled, she stretched farther. Still nothing.

"Where the heck are my bla—" She opened her eyes and yelped.

Not my blankets. Alastair's blankets. She was in Alastair's room. *Naked* in Alastair's room.

She sat up in the huge bed and searched for the missing blankets, or a sheet—anything. They had to be somewhere. She could *not* be lying here, naked, when he came back.

The thought propelled her out of the bed. She couldn't be there at all. Her midnight escape had been foiled but now, he was gone. She would get dressed, slip downstairs and get the hell home before her mind truly realized what her body had done.

Damn. Too late.

Her groans and pleas came back to her as an auditory hallucination. She pressed her hand against her stomach, trying to quell the hollow arousal that returned at the simplest memory.

As if to remind her just exactly what she'd done and how many times she'd done it, her nipples tightened. She glared down at the hardened points. *Now is not the time, girls.*

She had to get dressed and go home. *Her clothes.* The physical memory of them being stripped from her body the first time and pulled from her hands the second slowed her down, but she took comfort in knowing they would be where she'd dropped them. She looked toward the door expecting to see her suit in a heap on the floor. There was nothing on the floor or on the chair behind the door. She spun around. Except for the furniture—a chair, desk, lounger and the huge bed—the room was empty.

Maybe Alastair hung them up. She opened the closet.

Empty.

Suspicion mixed with dread and made the acid in her stomach burble. She hurried to the master bath. Maybe he put them there. Or towels would work.

She stepped into the room and her heart plummeted to her roiling stomach. Empty. No towels, no shower curtain. Nothing.

That bastard had left her naked. With nothing to put on.

She walked back into the bedroom. There weren't even curtains on the windows. He'd stripped the room of absolutely everything made of cloth.

She stared at the bed dominating the room. There was still the fitted sheet. But that was a last resort and she hadn't given up hope. Not yet.

The shadow under the bed drew her forward. People stuffed items under beds all the time and forgot them. Maybe, just maybe, there had been something left behind that Alastair had missed.

She dropped to the floor onto her hands and knees, and peered underneath the bed.

And gasped. It had to be the cleanest, emptiest under-bed she'd ever seen. Whoever cleaned his house vacuumed under here on a regular basis.

Brenna released a frustrated sigh and stuck her head farther underneath. She slapped her hand into the shadows, blindly searching. There had to be something.

The quick snap of the door opening froze her in position— on her knees, ass in the air, presented to Alastair as he walked in.

"Damn it, Alastair, what were you—" She stood up, whipped around and yelped.

Three people stood in the doorway. Two she knew. One was a stranger. None of them were Alastair.

"Mitchell, Genevieve." Brenna skimmed her hands down her body, laying one arm across her breasts and sliding the other hand to her pussy, trying to casually mask the fact that she was naked—in Alastair Reynard's bedroom—with two of the most notorious gossips standing before her.

"Brenna?" Mitchell said. His mouth dropped open. Then his eyes dropped—not politely to the floor—but to her breasts, partially covered by her arm. "I didn't know you and…Alastair Reynard?" His question was laden with reprimand. His wife, Genevieve, didn't say anything. Her eyes widened as she looked at Brenna. Then the woman winked, as if commending Brenna.

"Oh my," the third party gasped. "Mr. Reynard must have forgotten to mention that we were showing *the house* this morning." The way she said "the house" was as if Brenna was a tacky decoration that the owner surely should have hidden in a closet before company came over.

Brenna felt a blush creep up her breasts and her neck.

"Yes, he must have," she replied, lifting her chin and staring them down. They stared back. And stared. "Uh, do you mind?"

Her sarcastic prompt jolted all three out of their stupor.

"We'll, uh, just wait downstairs until you finish…dressing."

"Yes, and could you send Mister Reynard up here?" Brenna asked, though how the words were able to escape through her tightly clenched teeth, she didn't know. She was going to kill him. How dare he embarrass her like this?

She sank down on the edge of the bed. Had he actually planned this? It seemed impossible. He couldn't have. But why else would he have taken her clothes and every scrap of material from the room?

Mr. Reynard forgot to mention that they were showing the house. I'll bet.

The door swung open. Brenna was on her feet and stalking that direction before Alastair made it across the threshold. She slapped her hand against his bare chest—he was at least wearing shorts—and stopped him.

"Just give me my clothes."

"Brenna—"

She ignored the hint of apology in his voice. "Don't speak to me." She shifted her hand until it was in front of his face. "Just give me my clothes," she repeated. He handed her a rumpled pile of material that used to be her suit. "You really are a bastard, you know that? I've never been so embarrassed in all my life," she snapped as she snatched the clothes from his arms. "Mitchell and Genni will tell the world."

He raised his eyebrows arrogantly. "Well now, maybe you'll understand how it feels to have your private actions talked about around the water cooler." He backed out the door. "Have a good day, Ms. Hennessy."

His words hit her like a fist in her stomach. It couldn't be. It had all been about revenge? *I shouldn't be doing this. I hadn't planned it this way.* His words as they'd made love the first time came to haunt her. She slapped the memory away. She couldn't think about it now. She had to get dressed and get the hell home and then she would decipher what Alastair meant.

Why an electronic book?

We live in the Information Age—an exciting time in the history of human civilization in which technology rules supreme and continues to progress in leaps and bounds every minute of every hour of every day. For a multitude of reasons, more and more avid literary fans are opting to purchase e-books instead of paperbacks. The question to those not yet initiated to the world of electronic reading is simply: *why?*

1. *Price.* An electronic title at Ellora's Cave Publishing and Cerridwen Press runs anywhere from 40-75% less than the cover price of the <u>exact same title</u> in paperback format. Why? Cold mathematics. It is less expensive to publish an e-book than it is to publish a paperback, so the savings are passed along to the consumer.

2. *Space.* Running out of room to house your paperback books? That is one worry you will never have with electronic novels. For a low one-time cost, you can purchase a handheld computer designed specifically for e-reading purposes. Many e-readers are larger than the average handheld, giving you plenty of screen room. Better yet, hundreds of titles can be stored within your new library—a single microchip. (Please note that Ellora's Cave and Cerridwen Press does not endorse any specific brands. You can check our website at www.ellorascave.com or

www.cerridwenpress.com for customer recommendations we make available to new consumers.)

3. *Mobility.* Because your new library now consists of only a microchip, your entire cache of books can be taken with you wherever you go.

4. *Personal preferences are accounted for.* Are the words you are currently reading too small? Too large? Too...**ANNOYING**? Paperback books cannot be modified according to personal preferences, but e-books can.

5. *Instant gratification.* Is it the middle of the night and all the bookstores are closed? Are you tired of waiting days—sometimes weeks—for online and offline bookstores to ship the novels you bought? Ellora's Cave Publishing sells instantaneous downloads 24 hours a day, 7 days a week, 365 days a year. Our e-book delivery system is 100% automated, meaning your order is filled as soon as you pay for it.

Those are a few of the top reasons why electronic novels are displacing paperbacks for many an avid reader. As always, Ellora's Cave and Cerridwen Press welcomes your questions and comments. We invite you to email us at service@ellorascave.com, service@cerridwenpress.com or write to us directly at: 1056 Home Ave. Akron OH 44310-3502.

Need a more EXCITING
Way to Plan your Day?

Ellora's
Cavemen
2006 Calendar

Coming This Fall

THE
ELLORA'S CAVE
LIBRARY

Stay up to date with Ellora's Cave Titles
in Print with our Quarterly Catalog.

Lady *Jaided* Regular Features

Jaid's Tirade

Jaid Black's erotic romance novels sell throughout the world, and her publishing company Ellora's Cave is one of the largest and most successful e-book publishers in the world. What is less well known about Jaid Black, a.k.a. Tina Engler is her long record as a political activist. Whether she's discussing sex or politics (or both), expect to see her get up on her soapbox and do what she does best: offend the greedy, the holier-than-thous, and the apathetic! Don't miss out on her monthly column.

Devilish Dot's G-Spot

Married to the same man for 20 years, Dorothy Araiza still basks in a sex life to be envied. What Dot loves just as much as achieving the Big O is helping other women realize their full sexual potential. Dot gives talks and advice on everything from which sex toys to buy (or not to buy) to which positions give you the best climax.

On the Road with Lady K

Publisher, author, world traveler and Lady of Barrow, Kathryn Falk shares insider information on the most romantic places in the world.

Kandidly Kay

This Lois Lane cum Dave Barry is a domestic goddess by day and a hard-hitting sexual deviancy reporter by night. Adored for her stunning wit and knack for delivering one-liners, this Rodney Dangerfield of reporting will leave no stone unturned in her search for the bizarre truth.

A Model World

CJ Hollenbach returns to his roots. The blond heartthrob from Ohio has twice been seen in Playgirl magazine and countless other publications. He has appeared on several national TV shows including The Jerry Springer Show (God help him!) and has been interviewed for Entertainment Tonight, CNN and The Today Show. He has been involved in the romance industry for the past 12 years, appearing on dozens of romance novel covers and calendars. CJ's specialty is personal interviews, in which people have a tendency to tell him everything.

Hot Mama Cooks

Sex is her food, and food is her sex. Hot Mama gives aphrodisiac a whole new meaning. Join her every month for her latest sensual adventure -- with bonus recipe!

Empress on the Mount

Brash, outrageous, and undeniably irreverent, this advice columnist from down under will either leave you in stitches or recovering from hang-jaw as you gawk at her answers to reader questions on relationships and life.

Erotic Fiction from Ellora's Cave

The debut issue will feature part one of "Ferocious," a three-part erotic serial written especially for Lady Jaided by the popular Sherri L. King.

COMING TO A BOOKSTORE NEAR YOU!

ELLORA'S CAVE
2005
BEST SELLING AUTHORS TOUR

Discover for yourself why readers can't get enough of the multiple award-winning publisher Ellora's Cave. Whether you prefer e-books or paperbacks, be sure to visit EC on the web at www.ellorascave.com for an erotic reading experience that will leave you breathless.

www.ellorascave.com